xXxYOUNGxNUNSxXx

Joey Molinaro

To Ben S. Jacob and Basilica.

Preface

I think one could read this book as a wacky spoof where the author whimsically combines disparate elements to create a zany romp of a story. But that's not how *Young Nuns* was concieved or written. I don't feel inclined to justify its existence here within the text, but I will tell you that this narrative started to form almost two decades ago and came to maturity in my mind as a follow-up to my first novel, *Heart of Gold*.

In the exposition, I portray the boys of the Young Nuns in a historically accurate, politically incorrect fashion. I encourage readers to see how I develop these characters.

1.

The NEOH Raid

"Woah, hold up." Cody held the flip phone up and gazed at it slack-jawed, with one big brown eye bulging at the display and his round chin beard dangling below his expressive face. "What does the 'T' mean?"

Darren lowered his hood-swaddled head from outside the hatch into the van and stumbled down from the crate, pulling his rifle in behind him with one thin lanky arm and then closing the metal portal with the other. "You saw a 'T'?" His heart was racing and his palms started to sweat.

Will cranked the rattling starter, stomped on the accelerator, cursed, "Damn— mother— come on!" and then the old Dodge van rumbled to life, belching ripe gasoline and charred oil.

"Huh?" Cody asked, his big bushy eyebrows pushing up to his short frizzy brown hairdo.

Will flipped up his drab Castro hat, adjusted his small tortoiseshell glasses, checked his mirrors, pulled his pistol from his shoulder holster, and chambered a round. Then, as he put the van in gear and crept down the country road at a jogging speed, he jammed the pistol back into his black Levi's denim jacket pocket. He barked, "We're going to work our way due East. We're losing daylight, we don't have time to run the flank. Tell us when you get two bars."

Cody picked at the flaky boogers hanging around his big nose. "Oh, no, I didn't see the 'T.' I just don't remember what it means," he said, adjusting the stained, light blue Under Armor athletic shirt that hung over his wide shoulders and stringy, neglected muscles.

Darren pulled back his hoodie to reveal long, scraggly red hair that hung above his small eyes and long face, "Dude, for real?"

Will shrugged his round, broad shoulders, "So much for your idea. I'm working the grid now, and that's final." He scowled and violently scratched his patchy beard, then punched the gas before Darren was seated.

"Woah, hey, hold on!" Darren clambered up to the passenger seat with his rifle in one hand, only to fall face-first into the floor pan when Will cornered onto a perpendicular country road.

Cody laughed mockingly as Darren tried to right himself, lowering his legs onto Will's armrest causing his scrawny white ass to halfway emerge from his black skinny jeans. Cody chuckled at this with unbridled glee and Will began angrily swatting at his bandmate's legs which not only tramped on the sleeve of his Levi's but swung dangerously close to the gear shift.

Darren worked his way into the seat properly, his face now beet red and pissed off. He huffed, "If it's a new tower, it's only going to work intermittently. We can't scout it out by driving around the grid."

Cody leaned forward on the back passenger-side seat and dangled the phone in Darren's face until he snatched it. "This job sucks man, I'm'a peep the binos, dog." and he pulled out a pair of binoculars.

Darren sighed, gazing at the flip phone. He mumbled, "The little 'T' thing means it's roaming. It's the same as having one bar."

Cody squawked cartoonishly, "Binos, nigga'!"

The ginger closed his eyelids gently and leaned his head back until it bounced off the headrest. He didn't see the point of rehashing the 'n-word' argument with his drummer so he once again glued his gaze to the flip-phone, looking for any indication of cell network activity.

Will slammed the clutch and dropped the shorty Ram van into third. Darren flexed his brow, turned his head to the driver, and inhaled disapprovingly, but Will kept his eyes on the road, responding in kind with an indignant sigh.

Young Nuns started playing regional gigs in 2007 and would

borrow Darren's mom's Honda Odyssey minivan. However, they were planning a full US tour and needed a proper van. Will got the 1973 B200 from a biker for $500, and it barely made it back to Will's parents' house.

Everyone else in the band loved it but Darren thought it was stupid. The driveshaft seemed to hang much lower than it should, the giant knobby tires lifted the van three feet off the ground, the sliding door never worked right, none of the gauges and electronics worked, and it reeked of cigarettes. Furthermore, it was painted two different colors of greenish-grey, each being used haphazardly to touch up the other.

The only feature he liked was the cross-hatch treaded steel plate welded along the fenders where the frame met the body to reinforce and prevent rust. Although it looked campy, it matched the face plate of his Mesa Boogie amplifier.

Cody, Will, and Tyler spent months in the garage doing stuff that Darren never cared to understand. During practice breaks, they would banter on and on about divorced transfer cases, valve jobs, three-on-the-tree, and side pipes but the only improvements that Darren could identify were that the stinky interior was ripped out, the sound system was embarrassingly good, and the van stopped breaking down so often.

They never went on their US tour, and the van had only been modified a few times since then, but Will had become obsessed with its maintenance to the point that Darren was surprised he drove it at all.

Darren's one contribution was his discovery of a pallet of Kevlar fabric at a burned-out marina which they used to make Van Hellsing's bulletproofing.

He turned toward the door and prodded at the yellow packing tape-wrapped ceramic tile and kevlar panels that lined the interior.

Darren was the point person on this raid, a task that the three bandmates and their entire enclave encouraged. Will typically bossed the jobs and ran them at a deficit of fuel and time, but also complained constantly about having to be in charge.

The skinny kid in the passenger seat looked out the opposite window to observe the gray Northeast Ohio countryside speeding past his scowling bassist behind the wheel. He faced front and looked out the windshield where the scenery moved slower and took in the slightest ruddy vibrance of evening tinting the otherwise monochrome landscape of overgrown farmland, unplowed snowy roads, and dilapidated agricultural buildings.

There was a grove of trees between properties, and he instinctively looked down at his rifle. The hordes always preferred buildings, even a smoldering one without a roof, but he had seen them living in groves before, and it rattled him.

He rocked the twenty-five round .22lr magazine free from his Ruger and poked it with his finger to be sure it wasn't jammed. Then, sliding forward and shimmying his hips, he pushed two fingers into his pants pocket and pulled out a single round. He pulled back the bolt, which was literally a bolt ever since the original catch had snapped off, and plugged the round into the chamber.

Suddenly, he remembered the phone and flipped it open to see that it had a full bar of service. He shouted out, "Put it in second!"

Will scoffed and pushed his small, plastic, epoxy-spangled glasses further up his nose.

"Put it in second, I got a fucking bar."

Will rolled his eyes and complied.

Behind him, Darren could hear the mechanical sound of Cody racking his AK-47.

His eyes oscillated between the road and the phone, but suddenly he called out, "Hey, stop here, I lost it. Wait, no. Just wait."

Will gestured rudely to the pale sun approaching the horizon.

Darren commanded, albeit shyly, "Yeah, I get it. I'm telling you though, we have to be sure it isn't a dropout. Just back us up a hundred feet and we'll park."

Cody whined, "For how long?"

Darren sputtered, "*Pfft*, a few minutes. Soon, though."

Will gestured toward the sun with an even more pedantic expression.

Cody croaked, "Five minutes?"

Darren shouted resolutely, "We listen to Jane Doe, and then either the signal returns or we turn around."

Cody growled comically and then said in a sing-song intonation, "O-kay." He continued. "Dude I miss the early days of the collapse, when we were just starting out. We'd go out and clear hundreds of these fucks."

Will offered somberly, "How about we go back to Super Tuesday and finish booking that tour."

They sat silently for a moment as Darren loaded in the tape adapter, flipped through the CD wallet, reached into the glove compartment, and pressed 'play' on the CD player.

Darren had a moment to brood while the Discman got situated on track one. He had scarcely met anyone new in years, and the best he could hope for was mere survival with his childhood best friends, assholes though they were.

The guitar intro started and he hoped that by the time they rolled back to the enclave at sundown, they would be able to say they'd earned their keep. He felt like he was living on his knees— but then the riff dropped with the full band and he had no pain.

The trio bobbed their heads to the beat, then gestured with outstretched palms, lipsyncing the iconic noise-saturated verse. The chorus came in with driving rock before turning the beat around into a 2-step breakdown reminiscent of NuMetal and Darren signaled its entrance with victory arms held high. The song grinded out a coda and Will and Darren looked back at Cody who was air-drumming the whole thing. And one-hundred-twenty seconds after it started, *Concubine* ended and the next song began.

Darren clapped a furious improvised descant to the vaguely Latin intro rhythm, and all three of them conducted the choke and entrance of the d-beat verse. Will clutched the steering wheel and bounced violently in his seat as if he were riding a galloping horse. Cody laughed out loud, rocking back and clutching his belly until his feet came off the floor. When the breakdown dropped he tensed his fists and grunted, "Hell yeah," then flung open the sliding door and stomped in the snow around the van.

Will rolled down his window, "Find any pennies out there?" to which Cody started flinging hands full of snow with each floor punch before popping back in the van.

"It's fucking cold out there."

The instrumental section came up and Darren held his rifle like his old Schecter guitar. He laid down the melody cooly and correctly, without any chicanery through the final section until the blastbeats at the end, at which point he couldn't resist banging his head so that his wild red hair became a halo.

Distance and Meaning came up but rather than continue to play air guitar Darren checked the phone. Still no signal. Will beat his chest to a steady beat while the crooked guitar riff worked around him for nearly a minute. Then when the bass came in he sang the part, fingering the air slowly in time. Soon all three of them were playing through their parts with invisible instruments.

The next song started with a sparse bass line, and for some reason, Cody announced, "Ladies and Gentlemen. Can I testify about the goodness of the iPhone? I wanna wanna testify about the iPhone. I'm gonna testify about the iPhone."

Darren laughed, "What the fuck?"

The hardcore beat came in slow, subdued and rock steady and Cody articulated with his hands as he busted a freestyle flow.

I love the iPhone, puts me in the right zone.

Will rubbed the tears from his eyes as he squealed with laughter.

> *It's like a nitro, it might go right home.*
> *Shove it in my tight hole, it's — um —*
> *It's like a motherfuckin' —uh—*
> *do you remember Gack Floam?*
> *That little shitty toy that you had?*
> *I put it in your sister's hair and she was mad?*
> *Kind of sad?*
> *And we had to take her and her friends to the mall,*
> *So said your dad?*

The metal riff dropped in and he quit his freestyle. Darren and Will reached back to slap his palm, and then Darren faced front again, reclining his seat a few clicks and staring once again at the flip phone.

Homewrecker landed and Will started pumping his fist. Darren hated looking at the phone. Everyone did. There were still people who would kill him just for even touching a phone in 2013, but the obsolete technology of the flip phone was so much safer than the smartphones that led to the whole collapse. Suddenly the top right corner blinked to show one bar of service.

"We're up. Let's go."

In a single motion, Will paused the album, started the car, put it in first, and peeled out so aggressively that they almost slid off the road.

"Shit, two bars."

Will shoved it directly into third and sped down the two-lane road. The adrenaline was palpable in the van as they neared a crumbled highway overpass. He dropped it back into second and looked around, then dropped it into four-wheel drive and the van bounced and groaned as it devoured ditches and curbs.

"There dude, it's got to be there." Cody spit, tapping on the sliding door window toward a large industrial building.

Will nodded as he pulled the rust-patinaed Mossberg Maverick from where it hung above the windshield and pumped a 12 gauge shell into the chamber.

"Hold up," Darren muttered.

Cody hesitated, popped open the massive sliding door just a crack, and then froze, save for his right leg violently bouncing then added, "Come on, let's go!"

Darren didn't respond and he tried to appear calm but his seat was still reclined so he sat up tall uncomfortably.

Cody cursed under his breath, "This is gay."

"No, this can't be it. There are just two bars."

Will played with his door handle, then unfolded the Mossberg's shoulder stock. "We'll just run the flank to be sure."

Darren shook his head, "No, we… shit." The phone was back to displaying an 'X' for 'no service.'

Cody asked, "Lose it, dude?"

"Come on," and Will swung his door open.

"Stop." Then he raised his voice, which made an embarrassing crack: "Fucking STOP!"

Will folded his shotgun back up with a violent snap and then slammed his door with brutal force. Cody kept his hand on the sliding door handle, his big eyes darting around and his leg bouncing.

Will punctuated his words with stiff punches on the steering wheel, "We've been everywhere on this highway from Parma to Westfield. They've got to be here, it's the only exit we haven't cleared."

"They're not always at the exits."

Cody and Will responded almost in unison, "What the fuck are you talking about?"

Darren's voice was low and calm, "We got them at exits a lot, but we got them all sorts of places. We just always happen to look at the exits."

Cody swung his door open wide and took one step outside, "They're fucking in there, I guarantee."

"Maybe, but the tower isn't. If we don't get the tower there's no point. Close the door."

"I'm just—"

"Close the door NOW."

Cody slammed the door and then crossed his arms and looked out the window. The door was mostly closed but not fully latched, and that was a situation they had all come to accept with this van.

Will removed his glasses and rubbed his face, "OK, then where do we go, huh?"

Darren stated plainly, "Just drive, keep going East."

"Can we at least follow the highway?"

"East."

Will drove the van back through a series of overgrown fields until he once again was on a country road. Then he put it back in two-wheel drive and accelerated like a rocket until they were in third gear at 45 MPH.

"Woah, woah! Stop!"

Will didn't even slow down. "Do you have three bars?"

"Yeah. Stop."

"OK, what's your plan?"

"I need to go up on top and scope it out."

Cody moaned, "Just let him check dude."

Will spun his head around, offended that Cody was taking Darren's side. He slowed down and stopped the van.

Darren considered crawling over the center console to the back seat but was still embarrassed from falling on his face so he opened the door, hopped out, closed the front door with all his weight, and then executed the familiar trick of putting two fingers into the partially-closed sliding door while jiggling the handle and finally thrusting it open. He used the inertia of the door bouncing backward to slam it shut properly.

He pushed open the re-purposed school bus emergency exit, stood on the seat, popped his head and shoulders out, and then pulled his Ruger 10/22 rifle through to look through the magnified scope. The front lens had a crack in the corner but it still worked alright. "There's trees over there. Tall trees. Three streets down turn left, I think maybe two miles or so."

Will snorted, "Trees? What is this, Planet of the Apes?"

Darren climbed down and sat in the rear seat next to Cody but left the hatch open. He pointed his finger, "That's where we're going."

Cody protested, "Yo, I know where we are. There's nothing there."

Will put it back into gear and started rambling. He went two streets over and turned left, drove for about a mile, and then made an extreme evasive maneuver to pull the van very far into the ditch.

Darren jumped back up onto the hatch, rested his rifle on the roof, and took in the perimeter. Will had an incredibly intuitive sense of danger. The whole country was full of busted cars, skeletons, shell casings, and garbage but certain signatures communicated different kinds of threats and Will could read them like tablature.

Will shouted, "Run it!" then tumbled out of the van and took cover behind the door, pointing the shotgun downrange while Cody ran flat out to a nearby trailer dwelling. Darren turned his scope to observe the trailer as Cody kicked in the flimsy door and quickly re-emerged to post behind the truck parked outside with an open hood and flat tires.

Darren turned his scope back down range and hissed to Will, "We got you."

Will jogged down the street past an abandoned multi-vehicle collision. He crouched behind a wide brick pillar that supported a dangling lamp at the end of a paved driveway and then peered around it.

Cody sprinted through a few hundred feet of backyards to take cover behind an ornamental wishing well.

Will pantomimed 'Drive up here,' with a steering wheel motion and a sternly pointed finger. Darren lowered himself back down into the van, set his rifle on the passenger seat, and started the Dodge.

With great effort, he strained his shoulder to engage the four-wheel drive and pull around the wrecked cars. He coasted up to where Will had gestured but advanced another fifty feet so he could park just past the lazy hill where the road had a slight bend.

From his new vantage point, he could see his comrades working their way forward but also down the road to where it dead-ended at an overgrown grove of very tall oak trees lining a vast gated driveway that led to a big brick building.

Up in the trees, he saw something unusual and immediately identified it as a crude, makeshift microwave antenna for cellular service. He scanned the ground with his rifle and saw a quick flash of movement.

An unkempt figure in a filthy shirt and tattered sweatpants was puttering around, wearing shoes wrapped in duct tape. Its back was hunched and its arms were contorted, its face locked in an aimlessly wide-eyed sneer, its greasy hair matted with leaves and filth.

He put the crosshairs right between its eyes and dropped it with a single shot, and the earthy, feline smell of gunpowder wafted over him.

He found another target, this one similar but wearing only a white trash bag like a sumo wrestler's diaper that scarcely covered its crotch. He dropped that one as well and started to line up a very fat man wearing nothing but flip-flops and American flag boxer shorts but a burst of automatic gunfire grabbed his attention.

He dropped the Ruger into the van and clambered to the driver's seat. He ducked down and waited until he heard the next burst and then cranked the engine, banged the shifter, and stuck the clutch. As he launched into the intersection he noticed that the brick building was much bigger than he realized and after making a quick sharp right turn he parked the van on the street and dove into the back seat to recover his rifle.

Most cell towers were defended by yuppies, their only foes with the capacity to operate weapons. They used to have different kinds of guns but now they almost exclusively run AR-15s converted to fully automatic fire. It was always nerve-racking when the rounds started flying but they had terrible aim and their guns jammed regularly so it was always best to rush them.

Darren pulled open the sliding door and rolled out onto the wet grass, crawling to hide behind the front passenger side wheel. He called out, "Cody!"

A voice shouted something back but was interrupted by another burst of gunfire, then another that was directed at Darren and their van. He heard three "whacks" from bullets passing through the sheet metal of the quarter panel and then Cody slid like a baseball player to join him. "He's up in the tree, with the antenna." Then he sprinted away wide right and shouted back, "Shoot him!"

The dirt and snow sprayed into the air from murderous bullets around Cody's pounding feet, and he found refuge behind a tree barely a foot wide. Darren took a breath and rose to rest his gun on the steep, short hood of the Dodge. He located the tower and then peered into his scope to identify the gunman.

She was lying prone on a branch wearing a maroon pantsuit with no blouse, her long, loose, noodley breasts dangling down from the open blazer. She dropped an empty magazine and reached back to load another but instead pulled out an iPhone and gazed into it for a moment, and in that instant, Darren sent a bullet toward the lady.

It went over her head, and she scrambled to put the phone back in her pocket, then loaded a mag and racked the slide. He was too eager and put up two more shots off the mark, and just as she seemed to point her rifle right at him, he hit her with a fatal shot to the forehead.

His voice cracked as he hollered, "I got her, Cody!"

He scrambled back into the Dodge, revved it up, and rammed it through the front gate, knocking it down flat. He jumped out of the van and turned back to the tree where he last saw his bandmate, "Hey, where's Will? Cody? Code?"

Just then, the front doors of the brick building opened up and a whole horde flooded out. All of them were twisted and loathsome, horrid creatures seeking to consume his flesh just for the violence and satisfaction of it and they rushed toward him with murderous indulgence.

Darren fired the .22 rapidly into the center of the mob while backpedaling out of the gate. The mass of creatures thinned but did not relent, and as soon as he heard the first 'click' he loaded it with another full clip of 25 rounds and did the same.

The assailants were now reduced to ten or fifteen but they were almost upon him. He dropped his empty rifle and drew his Hi-Point pistol but he had no time to chamber a round so he swung his flimsy arm around and swatted at their heads and arms with the gun.

They dropped like flies even after he stopped swinging, and he gazed in astonishment at their silent demise until he realized that Will's shotgun and Cody's short-barreled AK had temporarily deafened him as they roared on either side.

Another group of attackers ran out of the front door and this time Darren was able to cock the pistol and pop off shots along with his bandmates, leaving the assailants in a heap on the porch.

One of them had an AR-15 and Darren walked up to toss an extra bullet in its head just in case. A different downed body, a thin man with black hair who may have been young despite his haggard appearance muttered despite his liver which spilled out onto the pavement, "Just like, I want to mooove. I don't really like, like, *grass* and shit. My girlfriend is in Brooklyn—" and Darren dispatched him in kind.

A middle-aged lady in a tennis dress curled her upper lip as she stared into her iPhone and scrolled furiously, her ruptured jugular covering the screen with smeared blood. A shirtless boy in board shorts and a tank top under a puffy Mighty Ducks winter coat slithered urgently toward the glowing rectangle with the lower-left quarter of his body hanging on by a couple of veins and a tendon and Darren immobilized each of them with a loud *bang.*

A lone skeletal silhouette shuffled out the door with one hand busily thrust down the hairy, crusty crotch of her ultra-low-rise jeans and her other hand angrily scratching her mean, nasty face. Darren sighed, rolled his eyes back to his bandmates and with a cluster of 9mm rounds she crumpled into a heap on the front steps.

Darren took a few deep breaths and the ringing faded slightly. He walked up to the front door and shouted, "Should we clear it or just burn it?"

Cody threw up his hands, "We got to clear it, got to bring down that tower and maybe claim some ammo."

Darren knew they wouldn't just burn it but it smelled so foul that he didn't want to enter, but Cody strode forward to clear the front entryway and a defunct electronic security door and Darren followed him into a vast oaken foyer with blood-stained marble accents.

Cody looked around in awe, "What the fuck is this place, man? It looks like some Illuminati sex party house. How did nobody know this was here?"

The front reception area had hip, designer furniture, and art, all of which were stained and shredded under a giant stylized cursive logo that said *Pranayama Luxury Wellness Center*. There was a restaurant and cafe off to one side, a conservatory filled with dead tropical plants, and a toppled Steinway concert grand piano.

There was a hallway with a dramatic curve that appeared to lead to the bulk of the building. Darren gestured with his pistol and called out, "That way. On me."

Darren led the party from room to room down the hallway, checking each room for fiends or supplies but only found empty dormitories, lounges, yoga gyms, and meditation temples. He turned to his group, "It's empty. Let's just go back."

But a figure with long black hair lurched out of the next room and he turned with a snap, leveling his pistol to catch her in his sights.

She yammered, "BWA-WHY-YOU-DID-WHY-YOU-NO-I-WANT-MY-WANT"

"Shoot her, Darren!" Cody had his own rifle pointed toward her but Darren was in the way. "Fucking shoot her, dude!"

Darren couldn't squeeze the trigger. Something didn't feel right. "She's just a girl, man."

Cody stomped his foot and yelled, "Shoot her! She's a muttering hipster, man."

Darren shook his head, "No I mean it, she's one of us."

Will bellowed, in between gasps, "She ain't a human anymore. She'll kill us. Don't test me."

Cody looked back at Will and then stepped to the side to set his sight on the girl, but Darren knocked his barrel away.

The girl shrieked and put her hands up to the sky, "YOU ASSHOLES, LEAVE ME ALONE YOU ASSES! HOLES!"

Darren patted his hand on her shoulder, "What are you doing here?" She stayed put for a moment, then batted his hand away, and crossed her arms stiffly over her chest in defiance. A moment later she started bawling and buried her face in his blood-streaked hoodie with both hands.

Darren holstered his weapon and stroked her nappy hair. "Dude, she's a normal person. And I'm pretty sure it's Britney Spears."

2.

The Suburban Compound

Will woke up at dawn before the others, but he heard Cody turn over and stretch so he whispered, "You up, Cody?"

The frizzy-haired drummer inhaled lazily and replied with a yawn, "yeeeah." Then he smacked his chops and sat upright in the bottom bunk across from Will's cot. "Do you think he'll really shoot her for being a zombie?"

Will didn't answer the question, assuming it was rhetorical since it was well known that Rick never changed his mind. He responded, "Britney. She's got Stockholm Syndrome."

Cody rubbed his eyes, "That's like, the thing… In love with your kidnappers? That kept her from turning?"

Will sat up and stretched, "I don't know. But I think that's why she's so mad."

A soft, startled, high-pitched female voice in the next room said, "Oh! Hi. This is my room. Do you need something?"

Will threw off his blanket and stepped to the door, alarmed that someone was intruding in his girlfriend Maddy's space. But when he got to the door he hesitated upon hearing Britney's warbling, congested voice.

"I just wanted to say… *sniff*… I think you and your dad are nice. And the guys who like, I guess, '*saved*' me, maybe they're nice too… *sniff*…" There was a touch of sarcasm in the last part of her acknowledgment.

Cody stood and stepped to the door to eavesdrop alongside his bassist.

Maddy said in a patronizingly maternal voice, "Do you want a shower?"

"Yeah, I haven't…" Then she broke down and started to cry. They could hear Maddy take a few heavy footsteps and Will assumed she was hugging the pop star.

Britney squeaked in a voice that ascended higher and higher in pitch until it disappeared, "I just need… a shower… can you… do you… think…"

Maddy cooed, "I have a clean towel, some really good shea butter, and an argan oil shampoo. And an oatmeal lavender soap. And you're first, so there's still hot water. Come on, let's get you cleaned up!" And they walked downstairs together. When the footsteps faded the boys crouched low, grabbed each other's shoulders, and jumped for joy.

Will whisper-screamed, "She's going to be OK!"

Cody responded enthusiastically, "I knew it, yo!"

"You wanted to shoot her!"

"Well not after we knew."

Will patted his shoulder and then pointed his finger, "Alright. Go down and ask Rick for some lard."

"That's a good idea. I bet I can get an apple too."

The two boys got cleaned up and dressed while Darren slept in like a corpse.

Cody asked, "What will she do if she stays?"

Will shrugged, "I'm sure Rick will come up with chores."

Cody held up his palms, "But like, you know, his daughter—"

Will interrupted, "Maddy gets those migraines, you know that. Come on." and he punctuated his statement by whipping on his Castro hat.

They stepped out into the upstairs hallway which passed across the great room and its giant windows which overlooked the North fence and the sprawling corn fields which used to be a golf course. They shuffled down the polished wooden stairs in their stocking feet and Cody stopped to sit on the bench and pull his boots on without lacing them up. Will continued to the kitchen and offered, "Good luck. Don't tell him about Britney. And bring a gallon of water."

Cody cleared his throat, "OK, see you in a bit."

Will put an apron around his strong but sloppy waist and plunked a couple of spoons in the pocket, then picked up a knife with his thick, stumpy fingers and ran it along a whetstone a few times. He rinsed the cutting board, went to the pantry, and took out six potatoes, a clove of garlic, and two yellowed paper packets of salt and pepper. He double-checked the valves from the big blue torpedo-shaped gas tank to the stove, grabbed the Zippo from the counter, and lit the range.

There wasn't much water in the bucket but he scooped a few cups in the pot and put it on the fire, plus a little bit that he poured into a glass. Then he put the potatoes in the bucket, cleaned off the dirt, and rinsed them from the water in the glass.

He stood at the counter and sliced potatoes on the cutting board with disciplined bravado. He smiled and fantasized about being back at *Fa-Heat-O's* restaurant, where he was expected to be the youngest head chef they ever had at age nineteen. He used to chew out people twice his age for overcooking steak, could cook for two ten-tops at one time, and even got his signature fajita listed on the menu.

Maddy stalked past, a wraithlike presence despite her super wide hips and thick thighs. She sighed without stopping or making eye contact and then returned to her room upstairs and closed the door.

Will hesitated mid-potato, but then snapped out of it and finished chopping, albeit with less enthusiasm.

There was a rustle at the front door and Cody entered, kicking off his boots and shouting, "Got that *lard,* AND some pork jerky, AND a mothafuckin' APPLE, son!"

"Water?"

"Yeah, dog."

"Did you tell him about Britney?"

"He knew she was out and about as soon as I asked about the lard."

Will filled up the pot with the water and then started chopping up the apple. "We have to talk to her first."

"No doubt. Maybe Maddy should talk to her."

It was a reasonable request, but Cody and Darren never really grasped how difficult it was to get his girlfriend to have genuine interactions with anyone at all. He changed the subject, "How about you set the table? Dole out some vitamins and get a fire going?"

Will boiled the potatoes, simmered the garlic and lard in a cast iron, and then scooped the potatoes into the pot. Maddy skulked by to deliver a makeup kit to Britney in the downstairs bathroom. This time as she jogged past she uttered breathily, "I'm going to eat in my room." and then groaned as she trod up the stairs.

Will added the pork to the pan and was about to chop the apple to add it to the potatoes but decided to slice it and serve it on the side.

The bathroom door cracked open and Will halted, then looked up and saw Cody too was frozen in front of a burgeoning fire. She seemed to be waiting them out like a thief, so they went back about their business. Britney tiptoed down the hall and looked into the kitchen. Will sensed her gaze but didn't look up. She continued tiptoeing and instinctively sat at the properly-laid table.

Cody sauntered from the great room across the dining room to the kitchen and offered a civil "Good morning." in a vaguely British intonation.

She patted the towel wrapped around her wet black hair and responded mechanically, "Good morning."

Cody went to the pantry and pulled out various dried leaves and stems, dropped them into the potato water, and stirred gently. "We drink this tea here, it's not very tasty but it's got a lot of nutrients. Nettle, dandelion, burdock, sassafras. There's a vitamin on your plate, they're expired but we got a whole pallet of them a couple of years ago…"

Will elbowed his loquacious friend and left Brittany to sit in silence while he finished preparing the tea. An upstairs door swung open and creaked ever so slightly, and Britney jumped and tensed her shoulders in panic.

Cody consoled her from the kitchen, "It's OK, it's Darren. The first guy you found. Hey Darren, Britney's here."

Darren walked to the railing and waved from the second floor. Britney relaxed her arms but didn't wave back. Darren remarked, "Pork. Alright." yawned crudely and bumped into the wall on his way to the stairs.

Will fixed a plate and left it in the kitchen, then brought the cast iron to the table as well as the cutting board with the sliced apple as Cody strained the tea into a teapot and mentioned to the other guys, "Rick says we're on biomass today. He wants us all out there ASAP."

She muttered, "How do you guys know Rick?"

Will pulled out a chair and served himself and Britney each a scoop of potatoes, signaling everyone else to dig in. "His daughter Maddy's my girlfriend. And Cody has been working for him forever. Bottled gas. Fuel, clean water, whatever. Darren's in our band, he helps out too."

There was a long pause.

"Why did you kill everyone at Pranayama?"

Everyone started talking at once, "They're not people—" "They were going to kill us—" "Why didn't they kill you—"

Darren held up his palms toward his bandmates. "Guys, guys." The silence persisted for a moment and then he turned to Britney and said "We would love to hear your story. Starting with Super Tuesday."

"What is Super Tuesday?"

The boys looked at each other and then Darren continued, "February 5, 2008. You don't remember?"

Britney put her face in her hands as if she was about to sob, but then peeked through her fingers at the scoop of potatoes on her plate. She sat up, speared a single narrow slice of potato with a single tine of her fork, and nibbled it slowly.

"I was sick, I had a disease. I just wanted to see my kids and they wouldn't let me."

Cody took a breath to respond but Darren raised a finger to stay him. She continued grazing, slouched in the chair staring at her plate. There was a rustle in the kitchen as Maddy took her plate of food and returned to her room.

Will passed the cutting board and everyone took an apple slice. After she ate a bite she continued, "My medication was out of balance. They said they just wanted me to stay there until they got my meds right. I had a tour and I was just really stressed, and so they gave me too much Klonopin, I think. I don't know."

Darren nodded and then prodded gently, "So that place, what did you call it, *Pranayama*? It's like a medical place?"

She nodded.

Darren clarified, "Like a rehab? Or like a… mental… place?"

She growled, "They were going to help me see my kids and YOU TOOK THAT AWAY FROM ME!"

Cody tried to interject but again, Darren shook his head. Instead, he poured himself a tea and filled everyone else's cups as well.

She picked up the fork and resumed tediously pecking at her potatoes. "They took my phone and my computer. And my meds and everything. At first, we did a lot of classes and exercises but then I just sat around and waited. I did everything they asked for, but I couldn't see my kids. The others, they didn't do things right and they'll never see anyone." In an instant, her face turned red and veiny and she blubbered out "They're all dead!" punctuated with a sob that launched an unchewed chunk of potato out of her nose and across her chin.

The boys sat and wordlessly sipped their tea with bowed heads until her crying slowed down. Cody broke the silence, "Just wondering— I mean— I think I get it— I think we all get it— but I'm just wondering, did

you notice that they were acting differently? Like, all hunched up and…
murder-y?"

She wiped away her tears, picked up her tea, and smelled it, but
immediately put it back on the table. "They stopped talking to me. They talk
with each other though. They were testing me. I wanted to pass the test so I
could just get my kids back." She closed her eyes then rocked back and
forth and her lip quivered but she took a breath and pushed back her tears.
"Please, let me call someone. Let me call my dad. Or let me call the police. I
won't say anything about this. I promise."

A chuckle escaped Will's mouth before he could slap his hand over
it. The guys looked at each other in disbelief.

"You really have no idea what's going on in the world?"

"They took my phone and they don't have any TVs. And they took
my phone!"

Cody crossed his arms and leaned back, saying to his bandmates,
"Yo, how do we even describe this."

Darren started, "So you know the dopamine crisis, right? When
iPhones came out?"

Britney rolled her eyes, "Ew, yeah ok, whatever, so some people
have iPhones. Deal with it. My assistants are the best, and they couldn't do
their job without them."

Will asked point blank, "Did you use an iPhone?"

Britney shrugged, "I had one but I never got to use it. My PA kept
it, I only got to have it sometimes."

There was a collective sigh of relief, then Darren continued. "It
turns out it was a big deal. It was a really big deal. The Trogs were 100%
right. You know who I mean? The anti-smartphone people."

Britney blinked confusedly with a repugnant sneer as Darren
continued. "Think about the pyramids, or terrorists, or crusaders, or
whatever. When people interact with religious texts just once a week they
can be blind and dangerous. As soon as the iPhone came out people were

engaged 24/7, and not with any god, but with just this technological void that makes you more and more impulsive, and alone, and… well not human!"

Britney scoffed, "Well if you don't like it then just don't use it."

Will laughed with disdain, "A lot of people thought that, and they're all dead."

Britney looked back at Darren, mouth agape.

Darren explained, "It's true. On Super Tuesday the Democrats confirmed Hilary Clinton as the nominee, meaning that both parties took the same position to eliminate smartphones with military force. Overnight the zombies raged, it was the first time they were coordinated in their violence. It was civil war and a week later the USA was pretty much over.

"You could still talk to them back then. They weren't all hunched animals. It was like a combination of politics, self-expression, vanity, impulsive violence, and addiction. It was really hard, we all lost family and friends but anyone who used an iPhone was a lost cause. That was when Rick fortified this place, and it was a good thing.

"Then just a few years ago there was a thing called the Trog Ultimatum. Word got around that surviving Trogs who support the ban wanted to wipe out the iPhone users all at once. A lot of good people who talked like you talk — we called them Toolies — stepped up to support them and both sides nearly obliterated each other. Then the zombies finished off the Toolies and now it's mostly them and just a few of us. We haven't seen anyone outside our enclave in almost a year.

"Around the Ultimatum is when they got into these really specific classes. Everyone calls them something different but we call them yuppies, hipsters, and posh."

Cody jumped in, "So most of the zombies are posh. They're dumb rich iPhone users who got turned and now they're total dopamine junkies. Most of them don't even have phones anymore, they just sometimes get to use the yuppie or hipster phones. They're thirsty for blood and sometimes meth, and also they like to…"

Cody brought his hand to his lap and made a fist but Will grabbed his wrist and pulled it away, barking "Dude. Not now."

"OK yeah, my bad, well you'll see. Then there's the hipsters."

Darren interjected, "Those are the ones you heard talking."

"Yeah, they mutter a lot. It's really hard to kill them because they seem like real people, but they're not actually saying anything."

Will took over to spare their guest the discourtesy of their brash drummer. "They were students or went to college. Now they work on the cell towers and factories. Used to be smart, now they're useful but dumb."

Darren added, "I was in college when this went down. At Baldwin-Wallace. English Literature."

Will rolled his eyes, as this was not relevant but Darren never missed an opportunity to mention that he was once a college student."

Cody jumped back in, "Oh yeah, they have factories and stuff. Pretty sure they just make 5.56, .22lr, 12 gauge, and 9mm—"

Darren clarified, "That's ammo…"

"Yeah, they make a little bit of fuel and speed…."

Britney shouted, "And you kill them? These are people!"

The boys shrugged, then Darren looked around and whispered, "Listen, we've all had those feelings. Early on we all felt like you do. But you can't say that. That's Toolie talk and it will get you in trouble."

"Maybe it's better that way."

The boys shushed her as one, and Will pointed a finger to address her directly with a soft, stern voice. "Do not say that on this property. Some people didn't want you here in the first place and they don't trust you yet."

Darren chimed in soothingly, "I'm really sorry, but he's right. Please, please just listen and whatever you do don't say that out loud."

Cody offered a distraction, "Oh yeah, and then there are the Yuppies."

Darren added, "We don't see a lot of them."

"They're kind of like the managers. There are always a few at a tower. They're the only ones that can shoot guns."

The front door swung open and closed and a stocky man with salt-and-pepper hair and tanned skin walked in, kicked off his Crocs, and hollered, "When you're finished *dining,* some of us have work to do. Miguel is all by himself at the mixing tank and nobody's running the centrifuge. Crystal, Doug, and the Parkers are out with the truck picking up those corn husks from the pigpen, and the Eichenouers are in the greenhouse where *you guys* were supposed to be. We need more god-darn biomass, or we won't have any F-T gas to run the machines. Darren! Nice to see you in the morning. No beauty rest today?" He stuck his hands in his belt loops to appear nonchalant but the gesture only seemed to exaggerate his massive gut that jutted out like a pregnant lady.

He nodded at the new girl, "You ready to put in a day's work? Got any work clothes?"

Will looked down to see that Britney was wearing an Ohio State windbreaker over an oversized men's t-shirt with the belly ripped out to make a crop top, and extra large men's dress pants tied up with a string and cut off at the ankles. She had nothing on her feet except crusty grip socks.

"Maybe Tiffany has something. OK, well go on then. Git! Come on everybody, hup to!" He gave Britney a hearty slap on the shoulder, and she nodded and rose to her feet. Then, everyone scrambled to clean and suit up for the day.

3.

Britney Gets Bit

Britney sat curled in a ball in the passenger seat of the Dodge watching Will bang on a plow through the open van door. The other guys were out working in the field but Will had to get the plow fixed so they could plant the neighboring one.

Her hair was now blonde, having been fixed and bleached with Maddy's products. She kept it up in a messy bun, and the fragrance of the purple shampoo helped her feel at home in the otherwise stinky barn.

Will knelt down and groaned as he violently shimmied one of the parts off of the frame. He grunted and threw it to the side. First he looked at her with a condescending sneer, then he smirked and beckoned her over. She was wore small men's cargo shorts and a frumpy floral-pattern ladies' button-down blouse. The shirt was dirty but her pants were clean.

She slid down out of the van and tiptoed over to him. The red Vans slip-ons were a size too big and she had never worn such tacky shoes but she ventured a guess that they wouldn't be much more comfortable even if they were the right size.

He looked up and demonstrated, "So… problem is… this blade is bent. The tractor will stall out if we try to pull it. You remember how I told you about stalling?"

Her eyes darted around as the thought, then she responded, "Yeah, like the engine doesn't have enough power and shuts off."

He smiled broadly, "Yes, exactly! Okay, so… I have to take *this* blade off to get to *that* blade…"

She beamed with pride, feeling smart and capable after feeling incompetent all week. She straightened her hair with her fingers and balanced her weight on one foot like she was about to execute a pirouette. She felt smart, beautiful, and brave but suddenly Will snapped her back into the present.

"Brit? I'm asking which wrench I should use."

She lilted, "Whichever one you want," then smiled and popped the pirouette.

Will looked disappointed and huffed, "Brit, we need you to be a part of the team. If you can't take any responsibility, I don't know what we can do."

She felt a bitter shame, but her emotional floor gave way and she broke into tears, "You're upset with me and that makes *me* upset but I shouldn't be upset because I disappointed you, I should be upset because *I lost my kids*," and then she started to wail, "*waaaah, wha-wha-whaaah*."

Will ignored her and continued with the task despite her fortissimo bawling. There was a rustle and he reached for the pistol on his hip but it was just Cody and Darren.

Darren was a great listener, Cody could usually distract her, and Will tried to teach her things. But between the three of them and Will's girlfriend, she felt as lonely as ever.

She retreated back into the van, wept lightly, and kicked around shell casings. After a few minutes, Will walked to her and said, "Hipsters coming this way. There are a lot of them but we aren't in any danger. Can you get in the back?"

She climbed over the middle seat to the cargo space, which had a twin bed mattress, a crate of ammo, and a small pile of cornstalks. She sat on the ammo crate but when the Dodge started up and lurched forward she tipped over and slid to the back with a thud. Cody turned around, "You alright there?"

She nodded and opted to recline on the mattress instead. The van bounced down the country road for almost a mile. Cody filled her in, "In order for them to spread, they have to set up cell towers. We know they control a lot of them near Cleveland but out here they have to make new ones or they get bored and aimless. They're dangerous without cell phones too, but if they get a tower up they start moving in in droves. That happened two years ago, and we barely survived."

Will parked the van next to an abandoned pickup truck and took the shotgun from above the windshield, then jogged away. Darren popped out of the hatch, and Cody slid open the van door and ran. Darren spoke out loud, "So this is the flanking maneuver. It works pretty much all the time. I pick them off from up here and then the boys—"

Britney interrupted him with a deafening shriek. A thin woman with hair like a rat's nest and a face like a coral reef crawled in through the sliding door and started to tear up his leg like an angry cat. He kicked wildly and she bit his thigh again and again. He squealed and pulled himself through the hatch and out of harm's way, then shouted "Britney, get out!"

Britney peeked above the seat and screamed as the lady caught sight of the top of her head and dove after her. Britney laid back on the mattress and attempted to cover herself with the corn stalks but the lady started biting her legs. Britney threw the corn stalks at her, sat up, and shouted "Go away!" The figure hesitated and seemed to understand her.

Darren was jerking at the back door but the latch was stuck. Britney shouted again, "Go the fuck away!" and the lady turned and staggered backward. Britney sat forward to see the lady shambling away from the van until her head was splattered off her body with a shotgun blast.

Britney screamed, "NOOO!" and plopped back on the mattress but was overcome by pain. "Ow, ow, ow…"

Darren crawled in through the sliding door and peeked over at her, "Where did they get you?"

Brittney grit her teeth and inhaled, "On my legs."

Darren answered, "You'll be OK."

She laid on her back, closed her eyes, and tried to cover her wounds as she heard gunshots in the distance.

Darren started the van and drove to where Cody was waiting. The back door flung open and Will tapped her shoulder, saying "Come on, we have to dress your wounds."

Darren sat on the edge of the sliding door in his plaid boxer shorts, "Dude, don't make her see this." but Will was unwavering.

He said, "Sit over here next to Darren, We have to clean you up."

She instinctively submitted to his request, and even though she felt like she had witnessed a multiple murder she felt safe around them.

Cody pulled the first aid kit from above the passenger side windshield, set it on the bumper, and unzipped it. He poured some peroxide on a wad of gauze, wrapped it around his wounds, and then taped it up. He said, "She must have been hiding in the truck."

Britney asked "They're not, like… I mean the bite… It's not like —"

Darren chuckled, "You're not going to turn into one of them. Wait…" Then he rolled back his eyes and shook violently, chanting in a guttural, demonic voice "*Solvet saeclum in favilla…*"

She grinned and reeled back, punching his tricep with all her might like she used to do to Kevin Federline when he was cheeky, but she immediately realized she had dealt Darren a blow he was not in shape to handle. He made a single whiny groan, then closed his eyes and rocked back and forth as he rubbed it.

She patted his shoulder and put her other hand on his chest, "Oh my god, I'm so sorry."

He shrugged and said in an artificially deep voice, "It doesn't hurt."

Cody finished Darren's bandage and then used the scissors from the first aid kit to cut Britney's cargo pants into shorts. "Here we go, it's gonna hurt a little," but the peroxide barely stung.

She looked around and saw the bodies on the ground, wearing stained mismatched clothes repaired with duct tape and plastic bags. They were somewhere between her age and the boys' age. They were twenty-five or twenty-six, and she was thirty-one.

She had seen zombies tear apart and consume the other patients at the clinic but they kept bringing her expired junk food and allowed her to do whatever she wanted.

Now she was around people who bathed, cooked, sang, and argued and she could see that zombies were ex-humans who had no authority over her or her children. But she still believed that killing was wrong.

Her new companions were decent people, to say the least. Before going inpatient at Pranayama, everyone in her life was duplicitous and manipulative. Her captivity by the zombies seemed like just another manipulative exercise that her father, baby-daddy, or record label would impose on her.

She watched Cody as he carefully taped up her leg, and Will helped Darren stand up to take a few practice steps. Then she blurted out, "I want you guys to take me to California."

Everyone froze.

She reiterated, "I want to go to LA and see my kids." She steadied her gaze and measured her breathing to stay strong and keep her raging emotions in check.

Darren held his breath, then exhaled noisily, looking at his bandmates.

Will spoke first, "I can't leave Maddy."

Then Darren followed, "Nothing is safe out there, nobody comes back."

Cody continued "Yo, we've got it made out here, yo."

Britney sighed, laid on her back, and watched the clouds through the hatch "I'm going to find a way." She noticed the boys staring at her from the corner of her eye. It wasn't a lecherous gaze; she could feel when she was being ogled a mile away. They seemed inspired.

She sat up and cocked her head to the side, "So what was your band like? Young Nuns?" and she flicked the tip of her tongue through her teeth and raised her eyebrows.

They laughed and backpedaled. Darren shrugged "Oh man, I don't know what kind of stuff you know. Do you know any metal?"

She was indignant, "Uh, yeah, come on! I know Korn and Limp Bizkit. And Metallica. And MCR." She flipped her hair behind her shoulder when she mentioned the last band by nickname.

Cody nodded approvingly, "Metallica, nice. You know *Ride the Lightning*?"

Britney shrugged, nonchalantly.

"The Metallica album?"

She shrugged again.

"Well, which Metallica albums do you know?"

"Uh, well I guess I don't *actually* know them, but I know *of* them!"

Will jumped in, "Metalcore is fast and jagged but it builds up to heavy, slow parts. It's angry but not hateful. It's the kind of anger that makes you drive fast or look for a better job."

Cody packed up the first aid kit, opened the glove compartment, and pulled out a CD wallet. "Norma Jean?"

Will said, "Hatebreed."

Coday asked, "Botch? No…"

Darren moaned, "Killswitch."

Cody echoed, "Killswitch!" loaded a CD into the Discman, and played the first track. She bobbed her head sportingly but couldn't make sense of the emotional spoken words in the background of the sparse distorted guitar.

Darren called out, "Next track."

A blistering guitar riff attacked with accented hits from the band. There was a rest and then the singer brought in the full band with a galloping groove that made her sit up tall and start shaking her hair around. The guys loosened up as well, and when the verse closed out she put her arms high over her head and bopped from side to side.

The chorus had a melody, and she fixated on every aspect of it. It had screaming behind singing, which she had never heard before, and it caused her to wrinkle her nose and purse her lips with curiosity.

There was a classic-rock-sounding interlude and she looked up to see Cody and Darren doing funny spastic dances to it. She hopped up and started mimicking some of the moves but the chorus dropped back in and she sang along in a creaking sultry voice:

Breaking the foundation…

As she sang, she swayed her hips wide and gyrated her torso. She stepped very far in front and swiveled from hip to hip, and at the end popped her thighs in unison with her palms. As the chorus switched to screaming she screamed in turn,

Building a revolution…

She parted her feet wide and bent over, arching her back so her chest was knee-high and parallel to the ground, and then whipped her hair behind her head to reveal her come-hither eyes, twisting her fingers as she slowly spun around weightlessly.

The chorus ended in a broad melodic breakdown, and Cody rushed over to genuflect on one knee, take her hand, and lip-sync in a melodramatic operatic style. Britney pretended to be swooning, clutching her chest and fanning her face with her flattened hand. The music crescendoed and Britney looked over to see Will cranking the volume. The boys were building up for something big, and the breakdown dropped in a broad 3/4. Darren started throwing windmill punches, cartwheeled, and then leaned on the van to balance on his elbows and kick behind him.

Cody threw scissor kicks in the air with the flair of a martial artist, with just a little bit of rhythmic bobbing and weaving at the end. Out of nowhere, Will grabbed him in a bear hug and tossed him onto the van, and Cody bounced off and knocked Britney to the floor. Will came over to offer her a hand but she somersaulted, pounced, and bodychecked Cody back into the van.

She hopped over to Darren, faced him head-on, pulled her knees akimbo, rested her hands on them, and banged her head like a heavy metal goddess before squaring her shoulders and gently ramming his chest with her shoulder.

Now even Will was dancing, pumping his fist, lifting his knees high, and jerking his heavy frame unpredictably. Darren scampered up the hood and stood on the roof of the van. Britney followed him, waving her arms and swaying dramatically to the beat. Cody stood on the back seat and pulled himself through the hatch, and Will climbed the ladder from the rear. From where they stood they could see the broad post-pastoral chaos of the landscape, from the dead bodies at their feet to the horizon.

Britney put her arms around Darren and Cody, and Will rested his hand on her shoulder. She realized she hadn't heard music of any kind in years and this style suited her. She asked, "Do you guys need a singer?" and the next song came in with a steady count-off on the hi-hat.

4.

The Departure

"Dude, wake up. Wake up, we have to go." Will shone a flashlight around the room while he jammed his possessions into a gym bag. Cody rubbed his eyes in protest but then lurched to grab his rifle and ammo pouch.

Will treaded toward him and patted his elbow, "Relax, it's not an attack, but we have to go. Rick is going to equip us for our tour, but we have to go now."

Cody groaned, "Yo, you're being crazy. Let's talk about it tomorrow."

"No man, he's pissed off. I asked Maddy to marry me yesterday."

Cody slapped his forehead, "What?"

"Yeah, and she told him, and he's pissed."

"So? He's always pissed."

"So he's going to kick us out, man."

"He's always talking about kicking us out."

"Yeah, but if we go now, he'll give us fifteen gallons of gas, a thousand rounds, ten gallons of water, pork jerky, and canned soup. I already have it in the van. Plus, we can keep Van Hellsing and our guns."

Cody grunted, "Oh, that's nice. He'll let you keep your own van. What a dick."

Will barked, "Come on. Now. Hurry!"

"Fuck Rick!"

"We don't have a choice anymore. He's going to come and kick the shit out of us. You thought it was bad when you blew the transmission in the tractor?"

This grabbed Cody's attention, as it reminded him just how intense Rick could be when he was angry, and it started to sink in that they could be in serious trouble.

They had talked about a tour nonstop for nearly a month, and they resumed band practice at a clandestine farmhouse with Britney as their singer. Her style wasn't what they were used to, and she didn't know the songs yet, but the music gave them meaning, and the prospect of touring gave them hope. But nobody thought it would happen.

Cody felt like the rest of his life was going to be spent in this purgatory, where he had to keep playing at being the same person he was as a teenager, where he had no closure with people from his past, where they knew a disastrous attack would come but had to pretend it wouldn't, where his desires were neglected to the point of withering away. They accepted the drudgery in the spirit of survival until they met Britney.

He dictated, "If everyone else is in, I'm in. That includes Britney."

Will pulled off his glasses and rubbed his eyes, "Okay, I have to go over to Crystal's and get her."

"I'll go. I can climb up to her bedroom. You have to wake up dickbag there," and he pointed to Darren, still sound asleep.

Cody grabbed his duffle bag and guns along with *A Wizard of Earthsea* in paperback, and clambered down the stairs. He stopped short, thinking of things he'd like to take with him: the herbs for tea, extra clothes, a spoon, and fork. But Rick surely had taken stock of all that, and if anything was missing they wouldn't be welcomed back. Nevertheless, he grabbed a handful of salt and pepper packets and tossed them in his bag.

He slipped out the front door and jogged across the cul-de-sac to the opposite five-bedroom house with a three-car garage. He stood on the porch railing and climbed to Britney's window, aided by his strong, thick wrists.

He tapped, "Brit, you up? It's Cody."

She came to the window and pulled it up high.

Her eyes were narrow, puffy slits but she tried to be cheerful, "Hey, monkey man."

He whispered, "Hey, we have to go. We're going to California."

Her red-rimmed eyes widened like saucers. "Oh my god, when?"

"Now. Like, right now."

"Do I need anything?"

"A bedroll, extra socks, uh, a jacket. I don't think you can take anything from the house, everything belongs to Rick even if it doesn't."

"OK. I'll meet you downstairs, *mwah*!" She blew a kiss and closed the window.

Cody swung back down, walked across the street, and tossed his gear in Van Hellsing, loaded with their music equipment for the first time since 2008.

He heard her skipping out of the house, holding a garbage bag full of clothes.

The door to Rick's house popped open, and Will pushed Darren out to the sidewalk, holding the skinny boy's rifle and backpack over his shoulder. "You tell her."

Darren held his hand up in surrender and turned around to scowl at the bearded bassist.

"Look, I just don't think we should go. We need to practice more."

Cody made an 'X' with his hands and bounced it off his crotch, "Suck it."

The guitarist whined, "Why are we taking fucking instruments with us? We need more guns and ammo, gas, ethanol, corn oil—"

Will protested, "We have more supplies than ever. We'll never get this much gas."

"Okay, well, farm equipment then, or stuff to trade. Biomass, even. We need to plan the route, and we need to check our guns. What if the fuel pump goes? We should have an extra."

Will and Brittany started jawing at Darren,

"I have two fucking kids—"

"I'm going to marry Maddy—"

"I spent two years in a cell—"

"Like we're going to get signed?"

A soft voice from the front porch intoned, "Here he comes." Maddy stood with her arms crossed in a purple camisole and Pink brand shorts. Her flawless makeup had been removed, but her face was shiny with moisturizer.

Everyone stopped bickering as they saw the headlights approaching. Rick's turbo diesel duelly F250 pickup with an extended lift kit made an unmistakable whistling sound.

Cody walked up to Darren and put his hand on his shoulder. "Listen, you're going to die alone here. Both of us — All four of us are going to die alone here. There's literally nobody here for us."

He gestured back to Brittany. "There are people out there. People like her, people like us, who feel stuck. Could you imagine if *August Burns Red* rolled up to the enclave? No, no wait. Remember that shitty Kentucky band, *Buttchugger*? If they played a gig here tomorrow, that would be the best day of our lives since 2008.

At first, Darren rolled his eyes, but the thought seared in Darren's mind. He looked at his shoes, then jerked his head up and nodded, "Okay, okay, alright. Let's just go."

Will punched the air, "Yes! Everybody in Van Hellsing. Darren, start it up." He went over to Maddy, who shied away as he planted a few pecks, and then returned to the house.

Will slammed the door and drove a hundred feet until he crossed paths with Rick, who turned on his deer spotter and shone it into the van. "Okay, you're really doing it, huh? I guess I won't have to beat your ass after all. You took the orange water barrel, right?"

"Yeah, the one that smells funny."

"Okay, okay. You're going to get me my ethylene and ammonia?"

"Yeah, and as much crude oil as I can find."

Rick hesitated, then nodded and said, "Alright, well... Maybe see you around, Will," and he drove away as Will reached out for a handshake.

Will pulled out onto the country road and continued snaking left, then right, generally heading westward through the night.

Brittany inquired, "So we're going to Columbus?"

Darren responded, "I think we're going to try to head to a different town first, maybe like Marion."

She asked, "Because the cities are bad?"

"We don't know for sure. Back when we used to get travelers, we heard that some cities were even safer than the countryside. Cleveland and Detroit are really messed up, but we heard different things about Pittsburgh, Cincinnati, and Columbus."

"Nice. Mmm, I've been to some of those places, but I honestly can't remember anything about them. It was all hotel rooms and airplanes."

Cody pursed his lips and shook his frizzy head, "Yo, what's that like, performing for all those screaming fans?"

Brittany crossed her arms and pouted, "I fucking hated it. I wish I could take it all back. It's constant stress and judgement. You have to be a boss but you can't be a bitch, you have to be beautiful but also spend hours at the gym getting pumped up. You have to be sexy but never a slut, you have to be a mom but can't give up your job. And if you slip up at all, thousands of your fans will be let down. And you're making millions of dollars for all kinds of people, but they won't let you see your kids, or eat french fries, or have your phone. IT SUCKED."

The van sat in awkward silence for a moment as she turned to look out the window into the pre-dawn darkness, bit her lip and grinned, then croaked out "I fucking loved it." and everyone laughed along.

Cody took advantage of the candid moment, "So do you think that the zombies at the clinic— or the lady at the barn— were they your fans? Is that why they didn't attack?"

Darren tried to change the subject, "Sun will be up in ninety minutes. Let's do an ammo check and maybe strap down the—"

Britney waved her hands, "No, it's OK. I'm over it. They killed all of those other patients, and I was able to protect a few of them for a couple of days, but as soon as I left them alone… Anyway, no. They're not fans. But listen, not to sound all uppity, but Brittany Spears is a big deal, you know what I mean? Those guys were glued to their phones all the time, so they would know me. They would know my face even if they weren't fans."

Darren replied, "Well, we need to get you a gun anyway."

She clapped, "I liked yours! I didn't like the machine gun."

Cody winced, "It's not technically a machine gun. We had a full auto AK-47 at the enclave but that ammo is hard to come by." He flipped on the dome light and showed off his piece." This one is crazy rare. It's chambered in 5.56, which is all over the place. But we couldn't swap the machine gun parts into it. Technically, it used to be an AK-74, but now it's something else entirely. It doesn't have a stock, and has a shorter barrel, so it's really good for short or long range."

She tapped on the recoil spring, "I like how you can see inside."

Cody laughed. "The dust cover is broken, so I use it without one. It's never been a problem. It's supposed to have a piece of wood to hold on to here, but the handguard broke off, so I just wrapped it in this old waffle shirt sleeve."

Cody could tell that her interest was feined, but she pressed on, "What's it say on the ammo clip? It looks like you have two of them taped together."

Darren and Will started laughing maniacally, taking on different accents vaguely reminiscent of Russian, Arabic, or Chinese, barking out:

"Kick Bitch!"

"Why you kick fuck? You no kick fuck, ass bitches!"

"Ass bitches kick my fuck!"

"You kick bitch, I ass fuck!"

"I will ass your bitch!"

"Fucky kicky fuck fuck!"

Cody slumped back in his seat, and it was too dark for anyone to see, but he was blushing with embarrassment. He muttered, "It's called a suicide mag. When you're empty, you can flip it instead of pulling out another." He took a deep breath and swallowed, "One side has '*Kick*' at the top and '*Ass*' on the bottom, and the other one says '*Fuck*' and '*Bitches*' at the bottom, but it's upside down and when you look from the side, it's hard to tell what it's supposed to say.

She nodded, "Ah, '*Kick ass, fuck bitches.*' That's fun. Well, I didn't like the kick back when I tried it before. I felt like my shoulder was going to fall off."

He gritted his teeth, thinking about how insignificant the kick on his semi-auto rifle was, but held his tongue to be polite.

Darren jumped in, "Yeah, my .22 is nice, but I can't give it up. I have this Hi-Point pistol as a sidearm, but I need that since my rifle only has a scope. Will has two pistols, but he says he needs one to draw from the left and one from the right, and he's not going to change his mind. We've tried. A lot. And you certainly don't want his Mossberg."

She moaned, "Rick showed me his gun room; I should have asked him for one."

Cody chuckled, "It's a good thing he didn't take you shooting. He always gives girls the biggest, meanest guns and then laughs when they can't handle them. And most of his collection is left-handed, like mine. The guy who used to live in Miguel's bunker had a hundred guns but a lot of them suck to shoot if you're right handed. Left-handed guns are pretty specific, so I'm pretty lucky to have this lefty. Rick was smart and traded a lot of the odd calibers after Super Tuesday. But I have something you can use."

Will interjected with a stern hand gesture, "Not the Heizer."

"I know, man! Whenever we take a break, I'll show you."

They rambled on, and then Will turned and suggested, "We should sleep in shifts anyhow."

Cody bounced up and down, "Are you kidding? I'm way too stoked!"

Britney asked, "Can we listen to the demo? I want to write my part."

Darren opened the glove compartment, situated the CD player, then checked his ammo, loaded magazines, and arranged the hastily packed area around the front seats. The overloaded demo played soft but abrasively, having been recorded first on cassette via a boom box with an internal mic, then recorded from the cassette to a PC via a headset microphone plugged into the computer.

Cody woke up still sitting in the back seat, parked in an overgrown field with the blue light of dawn all around. He was embarrassed and disappointed that he drifted off, but he looked around to see Will checking fluids under the hood while Darren gave Britney a tutorial on a pistol.

He stepped out of the van and stretched. Will slammed the hood and rubbed his hands on his jeans, then stroked his brown beard and told Cody, "We're ten miles east of Marion. There were a couple fields, definitely farmed."

Cody yawned, "Do you want to find the farmers?"

"I don't think so. It was a hack job, probably a half-ton pickup pulled a plow, and then some guys with shovels finished it off. I don't think they live out here. Probably find them in the town." Then he walked back to the van.

Cody walked over toward Britney, who was listening diligently to Darren's firearms instruction. He didn't want to interrupt, so he squatted on a grassy patch and took a moment to shave some of the hair off his lip and cheeks with his knife, but as always, he left the little ball of hair on the end of his chin. He was too lazy to shave it all, but if he had a fuller beard, people teased him and said he looked like Al Qaida.

Brittany aimed at the "No Trespassing" sign, then fired with a wince and a whimper. She shook her hand and recoiled in horror, "Oh my god, that's so scary! Did I hit it?"

Darren responded, "No, you jerked the trigger. Pull it slowly; let it surprise you."

She obliged, gritted her teeth, and shot another round.

Darren coaxed, "Keep trying."

She tightened her shoulders, leaned back, and loosed another five rounds before it jammed.

He encouraged her, "You have to hold it tight. Wait, are you closing your eyes?"

"Yeah, it's scary!"

Cody popped up, "Here, use this one," and passed his Smith and Wesson 351 revolver to her.

"Ooh, a six-shooter!"

"Seven, actually. Here's the safety, ok go ahead and shoot. Eyes open though."

She cringed as before, but the report from the .22 magnum was not as intimidating. She knit her brow and fired until the gun clicked.

"Did I hit it?"

Clearly, she hadn't. But Cody skirted the question, "We're going to keep this under the back seat. I might grab it if I need it. You can use it, but for emergencies only."

Brittany held up her fingers like guns and went "*Pew, pew, pew, that was fun!*" and skipped back to the van. Cody turned to Darren, turned his head slowly, and mouthed, *"No way."*

Will was raring to go, so they packed up and cruised down a few miles of country road until they reached a dilapidated town.

Brittany gasped, "This place, it's in ruins! There's nothing left."

Darren turned his head and said soberly, "In fairness, it's been like this for decades."

Cody thought about how a successful pop star would have never seen a town full of vacant storefronts, shoddy houses collapsing into rubble, and forests reclaiming concrete parking lots, with less than half the population sticking around to wallow in the despair. Except for the abundance of bullet holes and the burned-out automobiles piled in the streets, the place appeared the same as ever.

He called out, "I say we go over to where Roland used to live. It's in the Southeast.

Will nodded, "Yeah, I remember."

They rambled along the streets, and once they got out of the town center, they could see more of a shift. The normally well-groomed suburban houses were now gutted and overgrown. There wasn't much hope that they'd find Roland at his mom's house, and now Cody doubted that they would even find the place.

Will crisscrossed a few blocks and parked in the street, then turned to face the group, wordlessly asking for an idea.

Darren spoke first, "This isn't going anywhere. But I don't want to leave quite yet. This is further out than we've ever been. Let's take a break? Bust open a can of tuna, play through the set? How about right there?"

There was a small park with a playground and a gazebo. Will drove through the tall grass and parked the van so close it almost touched the structure. They got out their instruments, and Darren pulled a can of tuna from the small food tub in the back of the van. Will pulled a small PA speaker, amplifier, and bundle of cords out from a gym bag and put them in the gazebo, and then they plugged the power strip into the van's inverter. Will and Darren ran the guitar and bass through the PA to get an adequate level for a quick practice session.

Cody didn't want to take the time to unload and set up the drums, which would have overpowered the others anyway. So he stood and ripped paradiddles on the wooden railing as everyone else got situated.

Darren started playing the opening riff to *"Dying Wish,"* Will joined, and once Cody joined, tapping the beat on the railing, none of the boys could resist playing it straight through.

Britney clapped lightly, holding the mic in one hand. "That song sounds hard. Like, hard hard and also difficult hard. Which part is the chorus? Is it the like, *da-na-na* part or the *chung-chung-chung?*"

The guys looked at each other blankly, and Will answered, "It just kind of goes. We never really thought about it."

Darren added, "Tyler used to sing this one part during the thrash section, and then in the blast he had a kind of spoken word thing that built up to the hardcore vocals in the breakdown."

Britney put her finger aside her lips, "I kind of remember him singing and also screaming, but I think it would be better if I came up with my own part."

The guys looked around and nodded in agreement.

She requested, "Can we go section by section?"

At first, Cody played along on the wooden railing as Britney tried different things, but his diddling didn't help anyone with their part, nor was it scratching his musical itch. He called out, "Hey guys, I'm going to go on patrol."

Will and Darren snapped to attention, realized they weren't paying attention to their surroundings, and swiveled their heads around to scan for zombies.

"Oh shit,"

"Good call."

Cody retrieved his Kalashnikov, hung the sling around his neck, tucked his sticks in his belt, then walked down the boulevard and checked the houses along the way. He walked into the first, and it showed many of the telltale signs of looting: cabinets stripped bare, trash everywhere, flipped furniture, and broken dishes. But he couldn't resist poking around, and in the mildewed bathroom cabinet he found a small tube of antibiotic ointment.

He mumbled, "Score."

He continued checking the houses on the boulevard and was about to swing back to the gazebo when he saw a largely intact police car around the corner. Police were largely disbanded after Super Tuesday, as it became impossible to enforce the law within the schism of a civil war, so they mostly worked as private security for the few remaining rich people who abstained from the iPhone.

Cody looked inside to see that the shotgun was missing, but he was able to reach in through the broken window to open the door and let himself in. He rooted around the glove box and found a few loose 12-gauge shells and a multitool. As he pulled himself out of the car, his sticks fell out of his belt and bounced on the ground.

The sticks felt different in his hands. They were 2Bs, the same heavy sticks he always used, but they felt extra heavy, probably because he wasn't as strong as he was as a teenager. He twirled the sticks between his fingers and started hammering out rudiments on the hood of the police car, eventually breaking into the cadence of his high school marching band.

In the middle of a nine-stroke roll, a car zoomed by so fast that he played on for a few more beats before realizing what he saw. A white Volvo station wagon with no doors and loaded with armed men breezed past and shouted something. By the time he turned around, the car was gone. He sprinted back to the gazebo to tell the others, and as quickly as they could chuck the gear in the van, they were rolling.

Cody hollered, "Follow them! That way!"

Darren screamed, "What the fuck? Don't follow them, run away!"

Britney asked, "Did they seem nice?"

Will grunted, "Let's see what's up with them."

They continued in the general direction of the car and pursued several different routes, but it was a lost cause. In ten minutes, they were well out of town near a development at the base of a highway overpass.

Darren shook his head. "This is zombie land here. Right by the exit? There should be some around." He pulled the phone from the glove compartment and reported, "Negative, no signal."

Will pulled his hat off and scratched his head. "They probably passed this way, though. They were speeding out of town, for sure."

He turned onto the main drag and gestured to Darren, "Roof."

Cody switched spots, the lankier one pulling his entire body out of the hatch so he could take a position behind the barrels and cargo strapped to the roof rack.

Will said, "Roll the windows down and open the door. Listen."

He got up to third gear, slipped into neutral, and killed the engine. They rolled down in that fashion for a quarter mile until Van Hellsing slowed to a crawl.

Darren shouted down, "There, that blue building. Go that way. I hear something."

Will hit the ignition and drove them in that direction at a quick but conservative speed.

Brittany asked, "Is this bad? Do they want to hurt us?"

There was no answer, so she tried again. "Is this usually bad?"

Cody turned and answered, "We don't know what's going on."

Darren called down, "That car, it's running. The brown one."

It looked like an insignificant wrecked car, but the engine was running, belching tufts of black smoke from a pipe jammed into the hood.

Cody and Will exited the vehicle and checked each corner of the building, then they returned to the van to talk strategy.

Darren asked, "Are they charging the battery?"

Will responded, "No, it's a diesel. It doesn't need a battery. They're probably using it as a generator for this building. We spotted the Volvo right outside. It's empty."

Cody proposed, "Let's wait here. We don't want to spook them since we don't know their deal."

Dozens of gunshots rang out from inside the building. Cody started jogging and shouted to his comrades, "Let's help them!"

Darren shouted back, "We don't know them!" But Cody followed his instinct, rounded the corner, and found himself between the building and the Volvo.

Suddenly, the front doors burst open, and the men he had glimpsed in the car charged toward him full bore with fear and combat in their eyes while they clutched their weapons tightly. Cody held his gun limply, like a child holds a lunchbox, as the front door blossomed with a thick plume of zombies.

Three men made it back to the Volvo while two others were encircled, engaging in mortal hand-to-hand combat with bloodstained poshes. The men at the car were white or Indian, and the men overtaken by the horde were black. They all had long, full beards.

Cody took cover behind a large concrete planter and rapidly fired into the mob, but the assailants clung too closely to the downed men for him to risk a shot.

A couple of the man's fellows ran in to re-enter the fray, one with a knife and another with a claw hammer, but the horde was dense with the inhuman ghouls, despite Cody loosing thirty bullets into their midst.

As he spun his mag around for a fresh volley, he heard "*BOOM, chk-chk, BOOM, chk-chk, BOOM, chk-chk, BOOM, chk-chk, BOOM, chk-chk, BOOM, chk-chk, BOOM, chk-chk, BOOM!*" The entrance of Will and his barking shotgun allowed the entire Volvo crew to rescue their companions and make a full retreat amidst the flying debris of ears, skull shards, rib splinters, and clumps of lung.

Cody now swung to the middle of the building to take cover behind a busted pickup truck and send a hail of death through the patio and foyer.

He scanned the area to make sure Britney and Darren were alright and found that they were right beside him, crouched behind the truck.

He dropped his suicide mag but looked up to see that three flabby ladies had gotten a hold of Will's shotgun, and one of them inadvertently knocked him to the ground when her pants fell to her ankles. Cody snatched Darren's Hi-Point from his hip and ran forward to his friend, sending a burst of nine millimeter rounds echoed by seventeen shots from Will as he rose to a seated position with his pistol.

A rail-thin old man leaned against a nearby car, drooling and staring downward as he hunched his back and smacked his misshapen crotch like a fiend. Cody shook his head, then sighed and clobbered him to the ground with a pistol whip.

A few pops sounded from inside the building, and the bursting concrete and whizzing bullets around them meant they were dealing with armed yuppies firing from within.

Cody sprayed the rest of his 9mm ammo in the direction of the front door, then ran back and took Brittany to safety behind the Volvo, where the five men were jamming loose ammo into magazines. He shouted at them, "No time, move! Move!" but as soon as he turned back toward the fray, he was tackled by a big, bald oaf.

The man wore woefully sagging Dockers khakis and numerous filthy t-shirts. The zombie bit him twice on the arm and raked at his eyes with his brown fingernails, but he was able to jab it in the eye with the barrel of his rifle. The oaf was beating Cody's head like an ape as he struggled to wrest his Heizer from his pocket, but a barrage of bullets from the South Asian guy turned the attacker's chest into liquid.

He freed himself and found cover behind the Volvo, then watched Darren move to a prone position under the abandoned truck and release two quick double-taps from below the undercarriage, followed two more pairs from a standing position.

He gestured to Will, who advanced to a post just outside the front doors and was about to make entry when he was joined on the opposite side by the two bearded white men. The first one pointed to himself, his partner, and then Will, and on his signal, they stormed the building in that order.

Britany was putting pressure on a wounded man's chest, one of the guys who had been overwhelmed by the horde. The man who had saved Cody opened a small glass jar, drank some, and drizzled more on his wounds.

She asked him, "Are you OK?"

His voice was deep and smoky. "Yeah, it's OK." He pulled a can of 5.56 from his pack and started loading his magazine.

She asked Cody, "Where is Will? Where is Darren?"

Cody caught his breath. "They're OK. Will is clearing the building, and Darren is on overwatch."

She cooed to the man she was caring for, "You're going to be OK! You're going to be just fine." Then she turned to Cody, wrinkled her nose, and tensed her neck, "Were some of the zombies... masturbating?"

The building erupted in gunfire like the fourth of July, and Brittany turned and screamed, "NO! NO! NOOO!"

5.

Columbus, OH Distillery School

Van Hellsing was parked inside an aircraft hangar, and Darren sat on the back looking out into the daylight. Next to him was Fakhar, one of the Volvo men who engaged the zombies. They shared a pungent apple cider and looked around at nearly a hundred real live humans outside. Darren had his hood up and wore the same skinny black jeans as ever despite the festive party atmosphere.

Fakhar wore a sparkling white t-shirt, tucked into relaxed-fit blue jeans rolled up at the right leg to reveal a muscular calf and a clean white sock. He asked politely in his low, raspy voice, "This van is crazy. What's with the axle hanging out beneath the frame?"

Darren stretched his fingers and answered, "I don't know much about van stuff. I think it's because it's lifted so high. Do you do a lot of work on your Volvo?"

He laughed heartily. "We mostly just remove stuff when it breaks. The damn thing won't stop running, no matter how hard we try."

Darren inquired, "So, they do surge through here?"

His new Pakistani friend nodded and spoke with a slight Southern Ohio accent, "They sure do. They creep up from the South Side and work through the city shoulder-to-shoulder. Most of us drive out to friendly havens in the country when they surge, but a couple dozen of us stick it out. The air traffic control tower is pretty safe. It sucks clearing this place afterward but it's worth it. You guys never got rolled on?"

Darren answered, "Not since Super Tuesday. We know they're up there in Cleveland, but we don't let them get a foothold any further, at least not West of Youngstown."

Fakhar wiped his chin. "Cleveland and Detroit have it bad. Louisville is fucked, upstate New York is fucked. As far as we know the East Coast is fucked except maybe Vermont and New Hampshire. I mean, as a rule, everyone should stay out of cities. We probably shouldn't be here either, but with this school setup it would be hard to be too far out. I mean, look at this scene we have here," and he gestured to the myriad of uniquely dressed, reasonably healthy young people walking around in the springtime sun, smiling.

"You don't get, like, bandits and stuff?"

Fakhar answered with a rhetorical question, "Do you?"

He twisted his mouth. "Not really. Why is that?"

Fakhar grinned. "You ever think about going on raids? I mean, just to survive. But for what? Stealing someone's half-brewed ethanol? Scoring a thousand rounds of some useless ammo caliber? Money is worthless, and nobody else has food or fuel either. It's basic economics. I studied Econ for a couple semesters before this got started."

Darren was about to blurt out his academic credentials but realized he had already told Fakhar about it. He looked over to see the bearded man staring infinitely into the horizon before snapping out of it and patting Darren on the shoulder with his meaty palm. "We were raided a lot early on. I've killed people, my friend. Real people. Hopefully, that's over."

He slid off the van onto his feet and said with an enthusiastic bounce. "Alright, dude, I'm going to try to get each of you a whole chicken."

Darren blushed, jumped up, made a goofy smile, and then switched the cup of cider to his other hand to bump his girlish knuckles against Fakhar's bricklike fist. Then, the man righted a vintage white road bicycle, kicked his leg over, and rode toward the barbecue pit with his cider in one hand.

Darren liked Fakhar, but he wrinkled his nose with contempt. He felt like he bearded man was simple-minded and went along with the pack without any brilliant skills or exceptional talents.

He moseyed outside the hangar where the sun was warm and the air was cool, but the heat radiating from the tarmac made it feel like summer. He saw a girl with enormous eyes, knee-length dirty blonde hair, and giant glutes stuffed into hiking shorts. Her belly bulged out ever so slightly between her tight-fitting brown tube top and shorts. She wore a blue and orange Hawaiian shirt unbuttoned over the ensemble, the silhouette of which, along with her makeup-less face and Birkenstock sandals, gave her an androgynous character despite her steep curves.

He saw a girl with long black dreadlocks laid on top of her head and winged eyeliner arrive on a beach cruiser with a rifle slung across her back. She stepped off, and the dress caught on the seat so that she had to hop on one of her canvas sneakers until she could free her skirt, but somehow she made it seem elegant.

She looked around and saw a short, stocky man with a boyish face who looked like a cartoon version of a rugby player. He wore khaki shorts and a stained button-down shirt, and his short, straight brown hair fell flat on his head. Darren thought to himself, *'I bet this guy hasn't read a book since the third grade.'*

More and more people were arriving, and he decided to leave the solace of the shaded van for a little social mingling. He wanted to make a good impression, so he took stock of his belongings and evaluated which would be the best representation of his abilities. His copy of Madame Bovary would demonstrate his intellect, but these people don't seem knowledgeable about French literature. He could take his rifle, but it didn't seem like that would make him stand out, especially with such a small caliber. Ultimately, he strapped his guitar over his shoulder and proceeded to the party.

He walked toward the barbecue pit where aromatic smoke tickled across rows of chicken carcasses on an industrial-sized metal grille and hung low across the gathering. Both of the uninjured white guys from the ambush were holding court, with freshly-trimmed beards and blue bandanas around their heads. The one who led the breech along with Will was wearing a girly apron over his camo pants and dirty pink polo, and the other one had a blue jumpsuit peeled down to his waist and tied up with the arms to reveal a clean white 'wife-beater' tank-top.

They looked like jocks to Darren, and he imagined that they probably bullied their way to the top of the pecking order while disrespecting women and intellectuals. Their broad chests and swagger gave them cheap access to status, but they didn't earn his respect.

The first guy had tongs and a fork and was tending the grill, occasionally ordering one of the other men to flip a bird, add sauce, or remove it from the heat. The second stood by the bar, affably arbitrating each person's service. When they settled, the bearded guy hugged them and directed them to the bartender, a womanly girl in high-waisted short shorts and a halter top with heavy eye shadow, big hoop earrings, and piles of auburn hair atop her head.

Another large bearded guy was chatting cross-armed with the barmaid. She suddenly cracked up, patted him on the shoulder, and put a manicured hand on his chest as she doubled over in laughter. Darren realized it was Will. The bespectacled bassist smiled but remained relatively stoic, trading quips with the blue jumpsuit guy as he negotiated the flow of booze.

As Fakhar had informed him, the distillery collective school looked at many prospective locations in the former John Glenn International Airport for the festival but this was chosen because it was right in front of the terminal where most of the group lived, and the long concrete corner created an intimate nook in the otherwise sprawling campus.

Young Nuns spent the past couple of days recuperating from the raid and getting to know their hosts, a group of two dozen people who not only produced fuel, food, and booze through their distillation acumen but taught the craft as well.

Today, this stretch of the runway had a freewheeling carnival atmosphere, as their extended network was invited. There were families with gaunt and overworked children who gazed in wide-eyed astonishment at the brightly-colored murals or chased the rambunctious dogs. There were dozens of rough-looking men who were paranoid and armed to the teeth but softened up little by little. And there was a handful of attractive women with expressive clothing and bold makeup, some nearly as heavily armed as the men.

As he neared the gathering, he saw the spritely silhouette of a lively girl emerge from behind a cluster of stoic roughnecks, and his jaw dropped when she turned around and smiled at him. She had a brown bob haircut, bright red lipstick, light makeup, and a yellow floral summer dress with a purple mini-backpack and black combat boots. She had a feminine face albeit with thin lips, and her skin was pale and blemished with cuts and bruises. She was rail thin except for her modestly sized hemispherical breasts and buttocks.

He was instantly in love with her and didn't know what to do with himself. There was a cluster of lawn chairs under the shade of a massive tarp held up by four scissor-lifts. He sat in one, set the cider at his feet, and tried to angle his Schecter for some nonchalant strumming, but the chair was low and laid back with arm rests that kept his guitar out of playing position. He shimmied around a little bit, unsure of how to sit and hold the guitar comfortably without playing it. Then heard, "Hey! Are you Davin?"

He squinted and looked up to see the girl in the yellow dress standing above him with her hands on her hip bones. He was awestruck and tried to play it cool. "Sorry, hi. Am I allowed to be here? Sorry, I just saw the chairs. Sorry."

She laughed, "You're Davin? I was just coming to say 'thanks.' Everyone's been talking about it." Her soprano voice had an immature tension, and she formed a bratty melodic intonation from the back of her throat. It was the most beautiful thing he had ever heard.

"Huh?"

"You took out those engineers, right? At Dave and Buster's?"

"Sorry, oh yeah, um. You're welcome. Sorry."

"I heard they had pistols and ARs. You don't see them with pistols much anymore. So, are you going to play soon?"

"Oh no, I'm just, uh…" He fumbled with the guitar one last time but gave up and pulled it over his head, but it caught on the arm rest and he was forced to unbutton the strap. He said, "Sorry," and slid the guitar onto an adjacent chair to stand up, desperately hoping to keep the girl's attention.

"I'm Darren."

"I'm Sara." She swung her hips hard to one side and bent one knee slightly while keeping her torso in place. "You know, I was this close to being there myself."

"You go on raids?"

"Just to Dave and Buster's. That's actually my car they're running. It's an old Mercedes, it runs on anything."

He scoffed, "I mean, it doesn't *run*, right?"

She shimmied her shoulders. "It sure does! It isn't good for much, but we drove it there and use it for other stuff sometimes. That whole scheme was my idea. Did they tell you how it works?"

"A little. They said that zombies would converge at Dave and Buster's anyway, so when you powered up the flashing lights, you would trap them by the dozen."

"Yeah! A lot of our farms are out that way, so it's better for everyone. It's crazy how many of them were there. JR said a hundred-and-thirty-eight. Nobody was expecting that. I don't like shooting, but we usually go swimming and visit a farm while we're up there. Normally, I take an AR and shoot the ones wandering around rubbing off."

"Sometimes they're the most dangerous."

"Ew, it's so pathetic. In the dopamine crisis, kids would just jerk it in the middle of class. I wish I could have shot them then. Anyway, this time we were about to do an azeotropic distillation for the advanced students so I wanted to stick around so they didn't screw it up."

"You're a student here?"

Sara sighed, her chest rising and falling gracefully. "I've been here since the beginning. I gave them my car and worked the tuition off, but we never got around to collectivizing. I also gave them two pigs and fixed up the dormitories. It's a long story. See, JR — I mean, all the guys you met..." She stopped herself and changed the subject. "This is kind of cool, isn't it? We've only done this once before. A carnival, I mean."

"I like your dress."

She beamed "Thank you!" and gave him an expressive twirl. She opened her eyes wide, "I have something for you," and reached in her shiny purple backpack to pull out a small jar and hand it to him. "It's elderberry jam. I canned it last Summer! It doesn't have any sugar, but it's really good on meat."

Darren's heart was beating out of his chest. He blurted out, "I went to college. I studied English literature."

Sara was distracted. "Oh, there's my friend. I want to go say 'hi.' When are you playing?"

He stammered, "Umm, i think, uh…"

"It doesn't matter, I'll be here."

She leaned in, put her skinny arms around his narrow waist, and gave a quick squeeze. Her aroma instantly caused him to sweat and become disoriented.

"Bye, Davin!"

Sara turned to walk away, and he shouted, "Oh, it's Darren."

She spun and backpedaled with a quizzical eyebrow.

He stammered, "My name, uh, you said 'Davin.' But it's Darren. Sorry."

Wordlessly, she pointed a finger gun at him and made a *'click click'* sound, then skipped away.

Darren plunked back in the chair, trying to calculate how he would break it to the band that he wasn't going with them; he was going to stay here with Sara. People had to trade or pay to join their distillation school, and he'd have to come up with something. His guns weren't that unique, and surely nobody cared about his guitar. He had intellect, and he had skills, but perhaps if Sara was his girlfriend and she vouched for him, they would accept him. He thought to himself, *She makes elderberry jelly and kills zombies!*

Their relationship was still in its genesis, so he felt like he needed some advice. He stood up to find Cody; not because he had a way with the ladies, but together they could think about what Tyler would have done. Their former singer got all of the attention from girls. He was the heir to his dad's beverage distribution company and went to Kent State to study business administration. He would roll home from campus with a car full of fashion design students and models, fawning over his coke bottle glasses and angelic face.

He saw a hippie-style school bus on the opposite side of the barbecue pit and powerwalked toward it with singular purpose but then spun around to retrieve the guitar, cider, and jelly he had left behind. He bundled them in his arms, walked briskly through the loose crowd, and peeked into the bus.

"Ayo, D-pain, whassup. Come on and get a lil' hitta dis."

He looked back to see the heavily bandaged DeShaun and Freddy lying on mattresses while Cody slouched on a sofa. The drummer chanted, "Dar-ren! Dar-ren!" He was now wearing a blue bandana like several others at the distillery school had been wearing.

Deshaun hollered deeply, like a quarterback hyping up his team, "Young Nuns, son!"

Cody giggled and echoed in a weak tone, "Young Nuns, son!"

"Hey, DeShaun. Hey, Freddy." He sat next to Cody on the couch, and the fragrant blunt passed from hand to hand until it reached him. The whole band smoked plenty of weed before society fell apart, but he was nervous about playing their first gig high. However, he could tell that it was ditchweed, so he puffed on it, made a single sputtering cough, and then passed it back.

Darren bobbed his head and joked, "So what is this, bloods vs. crips?" and chuckled forcedly.

Deshaun replied immediately, "Ain't no Bloods about it, cuz. We straight Crippin' out here. We about dat. Always *been* about dat. For what you guys did for us we puttin' it out there, you been jumped in, y'heard? Cradle to the casket, cuzz."

Cody responded enthusiastically, "Hell yeah, cuzz," and bumped Freddy's fist.

Freddy turned to Darren, "How you gettin' on? Homegirl ask about me?"

Cody kicked him gently in his uninjured knee, and Freddy tossed a pillow back at him. Cody caught it and then turned to Darren excitedly, "Dude, they're gonna have whores!"

Freddy added, "Belie' dat."

Darren scoffed, "What?"

Cody clarified, "Yeah, I guess there is an actual brothel out there. They sent the other bus to pick them up. Dudes said they're hot."

Freddy added, "They fire, most of 'em. Good girls, real good girls."

"Listen, man, I met someone, and we really hit it off. She's so sweet, and I think we already have a thing going."

Freddy asked, "Yeah? You runnin' game?"

Darren said dreamily, "I don't know. We have such a connection, I think I'm already in."

DeShaun jumped in, "Ay yo, you can't be all soft like that. You gotta be on point. You don't gotta be a dick to her, but you can't let on. You got to get another girl all up on you, make her sweat you."

Cody nodded. "Tyler did that all the time. He'd like, mack on some fat chick and then go home with a hottie." Then he passed Darren the blunt.

He nodded as he smoked. "Alright, yeah. I see that."

Freddy added, "Maybe take Britt-dog over wit' you. Easier to get you a girl when you got you a girl. Yo, is it true them zombies don't fuck wit' her?"

Darren passed the weed back to Cody. "It's true. They didn't even beat off around her. They just brought her snacks and left her alone."

"Das whassup. I mean, it don't matter to me that she's Brittany Spears. But to dem? All up on them phones? Seein' her videos and commercials all day e'ry day? I can see dat. Me, I got her back from now on 'cause she saved my life, no doubt. She family too."

Darren nodded, then squirmed to peek outside where more and more carnival attendees had arrived.

The guys grinned, and DeShaun sang, "Aw, he gonna get it on."

Darren replied, "Yeah guys, thanks."

Freddy said, "C-love, cuzz," and turned his hands upside-down to make a complex symmetrical shape. Darren thought about mimicking it but noticed that he had bandages covering two missing fingers, so he waved feebly and walked out with his items.

He headed over to the bar to get a refill on cider and waited in the long line while each person begged or bartered with Derek for their cup. He found himself attracted to the girl who queued up behind him, and averted his eyes so she wouldn't think he was creepy. Then he put the jelly in his hoodie pocket and strapped on his guitar to check the tuning. The girl sighed listlessly, and he realized he might be able to talk to her, maybe even strike up a conversation to make Sara jealous.

He turned toward her quickly, and the headstock of his guitar clocked her in the shoulder. She knitted her brow and rubbed it as he pleaded, "Oh my god, I'm so sorry, are you ok? I'm such an idiot."

She smiled under her flexed eyebrows and laughed, "I'm fine, I'm fine. What were you going to say?"

He shook his head under his hoodie, "It's nothing, I don't even—"

She prodded, "What?"

"I like your hair, that's all."

She touched it up and said, "Thanks! I used to do hair. haven't gotten all done up since I was queening." She had very close-cropped hair held tight with barrettes, long wisps down the side of her overly-eye-shadowed face, a hint of bangs down into her forehead, and a single bejeweled dreadlock in the back. She wore a load of gold jewelry around her neck that spilled all in and around the XXL Coal Chamber t-shirt that was altered into a narrow dress. Her fishnet stockings descended into a pair of high-heeled pumps that even an ignoramus like Darren could tell were designer.

"Is that like a looter king? I just heard about that."

"Yeah! Oh, right, you guys are from the country. Most towns have a lot of kings. They never last long. Columbus still has dozens of them, I saw a bunch here already. They won't last long."

Darren started to speak but coughed instead, then wiped his chin and uttered, "Did you like it?"

She reached her arms back to adjust the ornament on the base of her dreadlock, pumping up her boyish chest. "Yeah, I mean I was pretty good at it. I wasn't dumb, at least. Some of these guys still flaunt their loot and stake their claim. I mostly hid. Al would come and hook me up with food, and I'd get him medicine, .45 ACP, and gas. Did you meet Al?"

Darren nodded nonchalantly and spoke low in the bottom of his register, "Yeah, he delivered eggs here right after the raid. He's a nice guy, really funny. Kind of a hick, right? You're in the distillery school?" He glanced over the girl's shoulder and saw that Sara was watching. His plan was working.

"I just got in! I haven't started yet."

Darren said, "It's so cool how they put it together. You guys can learn how to distill fuel and wine in exchange for chickens, skills, or whatever."

She rolled her eyes. "We're in the process of collectivizing, and I'm actually supposed to be a member/ owner when I graduate. I paid them pretty much the best tuition anyone could offer." She stuck out her tongue irreverently.

Darren blushed and stammered, "Oh, uh. Yeah, that's… If you got it, flaunt it. Sorry, I, uh… Sorry?"

Maybe if things didn't work out with Sara, he could date this girl instead; she certainly wasn't going to be interested in any of the schlubs he had seen around thus far. She may have a checkered history, but that's all the more reason why she would need a sensitive intellectual like Darren to boost her up.

She put her hand up to her black lips and said, "Oh my god, not that." She laughed, then leaned forward and whispered, "Infinite gasoline." She raised her eyebrows, nodded her head, and then looked around to see if anyone was listening. She put an arm around Darren, pulled back his hood, and spoke softly in his ear while her small midnight eyes darted around, looking for eavesdroppers, "At first I was siphoning from cars but..."

Her odor was sweet insofar as it had notes of vinegar. It was somewhat masculine, with dark, smooth tones and bitter spice.

She backed off, "I shouldn't have said anything. Part of the deal is that I'm supposed to keep a secret. "

He was paralyzed and bewitched, slurring dreamily, "What's your name?"

"Haha, well, around here, people call me Queen, but my name is Vanessa."

"Hi, I'm Darren."

She slapped his chest flirtatiously. "I know!"

Someone tapped him on the shoulder, and he turned carefully to see Derek beckoning him to advance to the bar. "You're all good, bud. Rocky's got you."

Derek's girlfriend smiled from behind the bar, her tanned skin and athletic body harmonizing perfectly with her simple outfit and jewelry. She had more dramatic curves than Britney, but he never felt a connection with a woman like that, even though he recognized that she was attractive. Girls like that always seem to date some brain-damaged football player or unemployed alcoholic.

He handed her his cup, and she scooped it full from the vat. "You having a good time so far?"

"Oh, hell yeah. How about you?"

"Al is supposed to take over for me when you guys start playing. I'm going to eat this bag of mushrooms and freak out. But this is already awesome. I know we keep saying this, but we've literally never had a party like this. We did a pig roast once, and it was cool, but it got shot up by some dumbass kings. We were more careful about the invites this time, but the turnout is huge."

Vanessa bounded over to the bar, and Rocky reached out to hug her shoulder across the bar. "You're going to give away all your necklaces, Queenie!"

The goth girl chuckled, "That's the point!"

Darren looked back to see Derek pocketing a few of the gold pieces. He asked, "Is gold even worth anything?"

The girls shrugged, and Vanessa answered, "It isn't now, but it always has been. I think it's smart to hold on to it."

Rocky gave Darren his cup, and he raised it in the air, saluting in a forcedly deep voice, "Ladies…" He waddled away, trying his best to look cool while spilling drops from his overflowing cup onto the low-slung guitar, jelly jar-laden pocket, and tenting jeans, all bobbing together with the unwieldiness of a donkey.

He started meandering back toward Sara, but Will intercepted, "They're going to pull up the stage now. Let's rip it soon so we can relax?"

"We're playing on the loader?"

A large flat vehicle rumbled toward the congregation, honked its horn, and parked squarely to confine the festival goers around the smoky barbecue and the bustling bar.

The loader shut off with a lurch. JR jumped out, still wearing the frilly apron, and he shouted "D-pain!" and slapped Darren's bony shoulder. "I was telling Will you can play whenever you're ready, but I think you should wait a couple hours until the sun goes down. I was going to light a fire."

Another rumbling vehicle cruised slowly down the runway, shut off the engine, and continued to roll. A skinny middle-aged man with frizzy gray hair and a baggy three-piece suit tumbled out of the school bus with giant wedges to chock the wheels before the bus rolled away. JR slapped his head, "Oh my god, Alex is back. I'm going to be in so much trouble. I didn't think they'd make it there and back without brakes."

Six or seven wide-eyed barefoot women came off the bus, mostly in the filthy lingerie that one would expect from a prostitute. A few women — black and white alike— whispered to each other and waved expressively at certain partygoers. Another girl wearing only a skirt stepped off the bus with very long brown hair in a high ponytail.

A muscular blonde of perhaps forty years of age slapped the girl's bare tit, and although it sat high and tight, it swayed slowly like a pendulum. One girl was very short and wore a baggy shirt and loose jeans with a ball cap on her head to try and conceal her sharp beauty. She grabbed the hand of a blonde in a cute but conservative rodeo outfit, and they both disappeared into the crowd.

JR said ruefully, "My girlfriend is going to be so pissed." Then, he turned to Will and Darren and put his arms around them. "You know, it's a good thing we got our asses kicked at DnB. We were all going to go hit Mandy's brothel after the raid, but it turns out Al was there, and he absolutely would have ratted me out. I love him, but my girl has him wrapped around her finger."

Fakhar walked up with a big pot and set it on the edge of the stage next to a handful of plates. "I got your chickens, guys. These are primo. They're piping hot, but don't let them out of your sight."

Cody strolled up, smiling and bobbing his head excitedly, "Dude, did you see the prosti— Is that our chicken?"

Will answered, "Yeah. I say let's set up first. I already have my rig up. I'm going to find Brittany."

He had pulled the Dodge right by the stage, and Darren pulled his Mesa Boogie amp out of the back with a series of tugs. The top handle had long been broken, so he bent his knees low, scooped it up with his arm, and with great caution straightened himself up and walked it up the ramp onto the stage.

Then he did the same for his massive speaker cabinet, housing four Celestion Vintage 30 twelve-inch speakers. Fakhar kindly asked Darren if he could help as he huffed and puffed with strained shoulders, but he took pride in this routine and declined the help, choosing instead to totter on his spindly legs under the weight of the gigantic cab as a show of strength.

Finally, he brought out the case for his Schecter deluxe seven-string guitar, which had an Ibanez Tube Screamer and a couple of cables in the pocket.

In the spirit of teamwork, he made a few trips to and from the van to bring Cody his drums and hardware, and he also brought out the PA system for Brittany. He just about had it set up when the loader started up again, and he shouted frantically at JR, afraid he would drive off and they would fall off of the platform. He laid on his belly to try and lean down to where the driver could see him when he heard the man's voice behind him, "Alright, so we should have power from the inverter. I have to keep the engine on, but you guys are loud, right?"

Cody was already set up and started thumping his Axis pedals on his sunburst Yamaha Maple Custom bass drum. He smacked a few rimshots on his Ludwig Supralite and then went to town blasting across his Zildjian cymbals.

Darren was eyeballing the dials on the treaded sheet-metal face of his amplifier, and when he was satisfied, he punched the standby and stood back, hearing his rig roar to life on open strings. He muted the treble strings and played a broad open-fifth-octave on C-G-C, stood with his legs spread apart, and alternated between big expansive unmuted gongs and low chugs. He twiddled a few knobs and then stepped back to adjudicate the tone. Then he began working through scales: pentatonic, lydian, mixolydian, and octatonic, weaving them in and out of each other, always terminating them with a pinch harmonic. He heard a holler from right behind him, "Darren!"

He whipped around to see Cody, who he thought was still warming up on drums, hold up the pot and say, "Let's eat!"

Darren switched the amp to standby, leaned his guitar against the cab, and walked to the edge of the stage, where he saw Britney coming out of the terminal flanked by Vanessa and a couple of women old enough to be her mom. She was wearing the same oversized drug rug that she had found in a heap of discarded garments after her other clothes were bloodied in the raid, and this was the first time they saw her since their six-hour marathon practice the day after. It was a relief because she mostly slept and cried, and they were unsure if she would even be up for the gig.

"Hey, Brit!" Darren greeted, but she only looked at the ground in front of her with her hood hanging low over her face.

Cody pulled out a chicken from the pot and held it by the drumstick, "Chicken, motherfucker!" None of them had eaten a morsel of chicken in years. He passed the first bird to Will, who held it with two hands over his lap and savaged it.

Brittany revived a conversation with the lady next to her without glancing up. "Just like, your kids are older now, and you can't be a mom anymore."

The lady on her right's kindliness beamed through the brown

creases in her face, "It's a new chapter! We still have youth and independence—"

Britney interjected, "But why should we have to wait to be independent? Like, I think I should be able to hunt zombies AND raise my kids."

The other lady pushed her thick grayish-brown braid back over her shoulder and folded her age-spot-speckled hands, "I was lucky enough to have a partner who supported me, and I was able to thrive—"

Britney continued strenuously. "But I don't need anyone else's approval, ok? Like, and I want to fight for people who don't have someone to empower them. I want to empower, like, I don't know. The unempowered."

Vanessa seemed exhausted by the conversation and wandered away, and Darren didn't blame her. Britney could be unpleasant company when she got stuck in her head.

Fakhar returned to the stage with a Discman and a handful of adapters, "Special request of DeShaun. Can I patch into your PA?"

Will grunted, "Do it!" and Fakhar walked up the ramp trailed by their druid-like singer. Soon, the four of them were dangling their legs off the stage, elbow deep in chicken, and a cinematic voice came on the sound system.

> *Shaolin shadowboxing and the Wu Tang sword style.*
> *If what you say is true,*
> *the Shaolin and the Wu Tang could be dangerous.*
> *Do you think your Wu Tang sword can defeat me?*
> *En garde, I'll let you try my Wu Tang Style.*

And the familiar RZA beat came on.

BRING THE MOTHERFUCKING RUCKUS!

BRING THE MOTHERFUCKING RUCKUS!

Darren's chicken was rich with vinegar, fruit, and smoky flavor but the meat was hard won and it took considerable gnawing, sucking, and spitting of ligaments to get the tough little muscles out of the bird. He ate a leg and then tried to remove a wing but pulled it too hard, and the carcass flung to the ground where a scrawny old man shuffled over urgently to retrieve and devour it.

It was a feast within a feast, and the four heroes leaned back to gaze over the crowd, already bouncing and reveling to the album. The sun was low, and the colors of the vehicles, objects, and outfits began to glow evocatively.

JR, now without the apron, rolled a few foul-smelling barrels onto the ground in front of the stage, pulled a few ropes out of each one, and situated them in no discernible fashion, only to glance up, smile, and report, "It's a surprise."

> *"So what's up man?"*
> *"Coolin' man."*
> *"Chillin, chillin? "*

Will threw his head back and cackled, then sprang to his feet to fiddle with his gear. The others started to right themselves, but when the beat to *'Protect Ya Neck'* came in, it came with a visceral punch that loosed all the hips in the vicinity. Darren looked over at his bassist, who had plugged his refrigerator-sized amp into the sound system and was now pushing a nasty level of bass.

Britney looked like the ghost of a ferocious boxer, working her body within the hooded poncho. Cody did his only dance move, holding one hand high, bobbing his neck dynamically, and gyrating his torso slightly but with great effort. Will rested his hand on the PA, making up for his reluctance to dance by turning a knob here and there.

The ghost boxer flittered over and grabbed the three boys to drag them down the ramp and in front of the stage, where a hundred people were dancing with anarchistic fervor. Britney danced like a wolverine crossed with a tornado, stacking moves on top of moves until the song got to Old Dirty Bastard's verse, at which point the band knew Cody was going to hold court. They egged him on as he spit the entire verse with cartoonish expression and absolute precision, including every 'n-word.'

The jam ended, and the next song was a downtempo track, leaving the crowd squirming and itching for more energy. Will rubbed his hands with a wet rag that smelled faintly of algae and passed it around so everyone could wipe the chicken grease from their mitts. Once everyone's hands were rinsed, he smirked and suggested, "Let's do it?"

The quartet ascended the ramp to the stage, and the crowd clapped and cheered with frenzied anticipation.

Darren faced his amp and removed his crusty black hoodie, taking a moment to try and tame his shaggy red hair. He strapped his Schecter over the black, youth large size *12 Tribes* t-shirt on his chest and checked his tuning. He scanned the hopeful, encouraging faces of the crowd and heard a sugary voice scream, "Young Nuns, whoo!" and saw Sara clapping her willowy hands together for his band. He thought, *maybe she saw me chatting with Vanessa, and now she"ll try twice as hard. And she hasn't even heard me play yet!*

Britney chanted "Check, one two… testing one two," into the sound system, and Will cranked it as hard as the system would go without blowing. The mic howled with feedback and she turned back, eyes wide, to address this glaring problem. But Will was already strapped in and Cody gave four hi-hat punches to signal the intro for their first song, *Eye Gouge.*

A series of chugs cued a foreboding cymbal choke section interspersed with thrashy guitar riffs. She dropped the mic and tore off her poncho, revealing a completely unexpected custom outfit.

Darren couldn't get a good look at her, as the verse and chorus of *Eye Gouge* involved a lot of speed picking and intricate scale work, but there was no doubt that she was crushing the vocals. As Cody, Darren, and Will wailed on the heavy and complex material, Britany was pacing the stage like a caged animal for hardcore/ punk vocals, then busting assassin-grade pop dance moves while singing lustily, and striking violent defensive positions to contort her body just right to get the gutturals and shrieks just right.

During the breakdown, Darren could see her dancing in her glory, with every angle precise, every gesture popping, her makeup-less face focused and seductive. She wore cheap red knee-high boots, a black American Apparel one-piece cotton spandex jersey tank thong, and an AK-47 magazine holster strapped onto her lower thigh. She had the cut-off swallowtail tip of the Ohio flag as a sash around her waist, and a large, gaudy, Victorian-type choker necklace. Darren knew exactly what make and model of American Apparel piece it was because he used to fantasize over their advertisements with great regularity.

He put a little extra stink on his downpicks, twisting his face and bouncing off the ground. The breakdown washed into a rocksteady hardcore coda where Britney squealed away and danced on her toes with her wrists cocked in the air, and after a two-bar drum fill, the song was over.

Darren looked up to see Sara bringing a pitcher of water and four glasses, and he smiled at her dreamily. Not only did she want to secure her place as his paramour, but she also wanted to show hospitality to his friends. He thought, *maybe I should kiss her now in front of everyone so they know we're together.* He blushed and stepped toward her but felt too anxious to follow through. She saw his half-hearted move and poured him a glass of water, leaving the rest near his feet for the others to fend for themselves. Britney immediately partook, her heaving chest shining with thick sweat.

At the same time, JR approached from the rear and handed Cody a bottle of yellowish fluid. He took a drink and immediately started coughing and sputtering until his face was red and bulging with veins. Darren waited for him to put the bottle away and started the next tune with a big chunky chord followed by a meandering melodic gesture. He repeated the same chord and gesture and then played two more similar gestures over a minor chord. Then he played all four bars joined by Cody and Will on the downbeats, and Britney came crashing in on their unison rest, growling semi-unintelligibly, a cappella.

> *Ruah ba dona yaura fauna yalla rara*
> *umbrella in your ass and open it up!*

Darren and Will landed on a big, macho, bluesy, single-note riff, while Cody kept the tempo at a low and slow triple meter. Her vocals started sensually but sounded more and more like ranting. They had practiced this song the least, and it was rife with mistakes from each of the Young Nuns.

They landed together on the slow, knuckle-dragging chorus, and she oscillated her trunk with her feet planted as she regained her composure. The verse and chorus went as before, but instead of devolving into ranting, their singer strung together her aggressive dance moves until she had one knee on the ground, both knees, and then two knees and a hand. She spread her knees and rocked forward until she was lying on her belly with her heels in the air.

He stepped forward for his solo, set one foot on the PA speaker, and half-squatted. He bent a few choice high notes and then ornamented slightly lower ones before dropping to the bottom register to work some ascending scales and arpeggios. At the tip top of his guitar, he tremolo-picked a melody derived from the bluesy verse and then hit a few dive bombs. Will took over for a couple beats of an unaccompanied rolling bass line until Cody and Darren came back in to join him for the chorus, which repeated with a blast beat over it and ended abruptly.

Darren pulled his damp hair back from his face as Cody drank heavily from his bottle, wrenching and sputtering between gulps while Will stretched out his wrists. Britney turned around and said something to Darren, but he couldn't hear her over his squealing feedback. He dialed down the volume on his guitar and a different noise overwhelmed the foreground as the crowd screamed, clapped, and banged anything around them to make a din of gratitude.

"How does the next song start?" she asked, huffing and puffing.

"Jackknife? It just starts right on the verse."

She flexed her eyebrows, "How does it go?"

"It's like, *da-na-na, da-na-na, jud-jud-jud-jud-jud-jud-jud-jud*."

Her eyes darted around, and her jaw hung slack.

"I think you start it out with 'Send you up to heaven'—"

She pursed her lips and gestured knowingly with her index finger.

Darren slid further from his amp until he was close to the edge of the stage, where he could see the crowd drip with anticipation. There was a fair amount of space up front, but people were packed in the rear of the crowd so tightly that many ended up standing on one school bus or the other for a better view. The improvised shack that held the bar had a couple of women sitting on its roof, and he identified one as Derek's girlfriend and the other as Sara. He stiffened, stood tall, and waved to her with a short, rapid stroke. She didn't wave back, but he didn't have time to think about it as he heard four clicks from Cody's sticks and dropped right into the verse.

> *I'll pretend you're Kevin,*
> *and send you up to heaven!*

He now understood why there was so much space in the front of the stage as it exploded into a mass of moshing limbs and hair. Some people simply danced and got knocked around in the process, others gave each other jovial nudges. Still others were stalked menacingly, as they looked for a worthy sparring partner to grapple and slam. The fleet-footed thin riffs of the verse gave way to a deeper death metal riff for the chorus, and Britney sang a lyrical pattern on top of their uncharacteristically tonal minor chords. It was very far from anything they would have ever done with Tyler, and they probably would have mocked it years ago, but they let Britany write her own parts.

There was a short interlude where Darren kept a single-chord groove in the guitar while Cody rolled on the snare, then there was a pause for just a couple beats, and in that silence a short man with a long black beard with two rifles slung on each shoulder peeled out from the crowd and shouted, "Fuck yeah!"

Then they dropped back into the verse, sending the crowd into an even more intense frenzy which sustained through the second chorus, at which point Darren sustained a low C power chord on his open strings, puffing up his pint-sized chest and pacing the stage, striking it again with his bandmates every eight beats as Britany ranted on the mic and pounced across the stage with murderous aggression,

> *And people say that because I'm a girl*
> *I can't kill these assholes.*
> *Well, I showed them.*
> *I have a machine gun.*

The ensemble rested for a bar, and she roared to the audience with her eyes wide, one hand behind her back, and her other elbow resting on her bent knee.

> *And I'm going to blow them all away.*

Darren laid into the ensuing breakdown with a slow half-note sway, holding his guitar low and thrusting his hips. He could see out of the corner of his eye, through streaks of his hair, that Will and Britney were making the same gesture as they rocked the bulbous riff. The bridge ended with a two-bar teaser from the verse, and the song was over.

It was getting too dark to see. Cody held up a finger to indicate that he needed a moment and took another series of hits from the bottle, then gave four clicks and Darren dropped into the opening doom riff of *Whore of Babylon,* which landed oddly, causing confused glances to be cast between him and Will. Darren waved it off and trod over to confer, ultimately deciding that he had started on the wrong note.

They started it again, and this time it locked in, but before they had reached the final doom riff of the intro section, Cody switched to a driving hardcore beat unexpectedly. Once again, Darren waved it off, and Cody shook his head, "I know what I did, I know, I know."

They started the song a third time, with Brittany still looking back at her bandmates, patiently waiting for them to arrive at the verse. Before they finished the intro, a spark caught Darren's eye, and shadows danced as firelight erupted from barrels JR had placed in front of the stage. Fire leapt across the ropes he had stretched all around and hung over the stage. The intro gave way to the driving hardcore pre-verse, at which point the stage itself lurched, jostling their amplifiers and drum hardware.

The band kept playing but crouched down and secured their footing, and Darren noticed the horizon shift. Someone was operating the lift of the loader. and by the time the verse started firing away on furious blastbeats they were nearly fifty feet off the ground. The ropes continued burning with a peculiar-smelling fuel, and as the stage lifted, more rope was pulled out of the barrels.

Darren could see that the crowd was now whipped into a frenzy, with the majority of the pit fully or half-naked. Some danced with conventional dance moves, others with ecstatic spins and jumps. A particular subset of the crowd blissfully engaged in straight-up wrestling.

The Young Nuns were no less entranced, and given that their next three songs were their oldest and strongest, Darren could get up out of his head and lose himself in the music. The crowd sustained their convulsant energy to the last riff, the musicians putting the last of their effort into it.

The crowd screamed and hollered for more, and Britney shook her head gently, sending a shower of sweat onto her already heaving, soaking wet shoulders. She gasped, "We… Thank you… We don't… That's all we know… Thank you…"

JR lowered them while the crowd chanted, "Young Nuns, Young Nuns!" When the loader was all the way down, the pink-poloed muscleman handed Will a shiny burned CD. He put it in the Discman and also patched in his bass, hit a few buttons, and heard a familiar intro with strings and piano, followed by a babbling sample.

> *a milli, amilli, a milli, a milli, a mi—a mi—*
> *a milli, amilli, a milli, a milli, a mi—a mi—*

When the beat dropped, the vibe shifted instantly. Whereas the naked bodies had been in innocent revelry during their set, they were now carnal and seductive. The air still smelled of juicy smell of roasted chicken flesh, and also the spicy, acrid smell of burning alcohol-soaked ropes. And the smell of human funk was inescapable, even from above.

Cody stepped up the edge of the stage with his bottle and slurred to his guitarist, "Dude, that wash cool. I'm sho glad for your came with this, your… this here. I'm gonna… go o'er," and staggered this way and that.

JR strolled onto the stage, "Holy shit you guys, that was awesome! Woah, did you drink all of that? That was supposed to be for the whole band to share."

Cody looked at him skeptically, with one eye fluttering shut. He muttered unintelligibly but finished the sentence with "…mur *feckin'* cider?"

"That's straight moonshine, dog."

He shrugged and took another giant gulp. JR tried to coax the half-empty bottle from him but only caused the drummer to chug the moonshine while staring daggers at him. He muttered a garbled mouthful of words, several of them being the word "titties," then wandered into the crowd with his hooch. Vanessa walked up the ramp, breezed past him, and hugged Britney.

The singer balked, "Oh my god, I'm so sweaty and gross."

The black-clad girl blew it off, "You were so good! The screaming parts sounded perfect!"

"I should have let you do my makeup, I look like a total sow."

"You do not!"

Another girl joined them, the one with long hair and Birkenstocks who was now without the boxy button-down Hawaiian shirt. "Britney, you killed it! Your dancing was so fun to watch! You said you forgot how, liar."

And then his spritely princess came prancing up the ramp, her eyes squinting from the broad smile on her face. Sara's hair and breezy skirt bobbed vivaciously with every step, her skin was soft and alive, and the electricity of her youth sparked in the air. Darren's heart raced dangerously fast, and his mind spun in circles.

She stood near him and crooned lustily, "Oh my god, that was so amazing, you're so wonderful."

He cleared his throat and said, "My lady, it was all for…" but before he could finish, she leapt onto the man standing next to him, wrapped her legs around him, and drove her tongue in and out of his bearded face. JR put his massive hand around her backside and drew her in as they kissed.

She climbed down his body and waved obligingly to Darren, "Oh, hi, Davin. Good job!"

Darren backpedaled and muttered, "Thank you," as he hustled back to his amp and pretended to work the dials. He looked around for Will but didn't see him around.

His heart was broken, so he decided to woo Vanessa out of

vengeance. He leaned his guitar against his amp and hovered toward Brittany, who gossiped with her girlfriends, "Oh my god, could you imagine having a guy like JR?"

Vanessa lisped, "She's so lucky. He's such a badass."

The other girl flipped her hair and glanced enviously in the couple's direction, "I heard he cheats on her."

Vanessa replied, "Yeah, well, he's super hot and takes care of her. So who cares?"

Brittany whispered something in her ear, her eyes flickering around and briefly landing on Darren, causing her to whisper even softer.

Vanessa stood back, her eyes and mouth wide open and incredulous, then smirked and playfully slapped her shoulder, "You bitch!" then put her hands on her hips and swayed while she watched Sara and JR continue their romantic moment "Not if I get there first."

The other girl rolled her eyes, bit her lip, and played with her hair as she uttered coyly, "You're both so bad."

Darren thought, '*Tyler would walk right up to these girls and say a sleazy pickup line, and they'd lose their minds. That's what I have to do. This is my moment.*'

Before he could think of something, his legs carried him to the group. He stuck out his chin and flicked his hair with arrogance as he found a swagger in his chicken-like legs and butted into the conversation. "Excuse me ladies, I'm lost. But this must be the runway because you look like models."

They laughed and blushed, doubled over with flattery, and flapped their hands with dismissive modesty. Vanessa said, "You were so cute up there. I loved your solo."

Darren thought, '*I'm crushing it. Lean into it.*' He stepped back and took on an air guitar posture while miming a suggestive bent bluesy note with a stiff finger. "Yeah, you like that?"

The girls laughed out loud, and the unfamiliar girl played with her hair. Darren raised his eyebrows, "What's up, I'm Darren."

The girl's eyes sparkled when she said, "I'm Jackie!"

"Are you a queen too?"

She laughed, "There's only one Queenie around here. No, I'm a farmer. I live at the same kibbutz as Al."

Vanessa maintained eye contact and added softly, "He doesn't know Al. He's a *renegade.*"

Fakhar joined their group and patted Darren on the back, "Great show, Darren! Excellent performance, Britney!" He continued warmly, "Good evening! Are you having a good time?"

Jackie responded, "Yes, this is awesome!"

He asked, "You've come very far. You're from the kibbutz, right?"

"Yeah, we came down early to trade potatoes for 12 gauge shells."

Fakhar tilted his head and asked earnestly, "You rode in on horses?"

"Yeah, they're over in the other hangar."

Britney asked, "Who's Al?"

Jackie folded her hands and answered, "He was involved with the Hilel centers at The Ohio State and some other schools."

Darren thought, I'm losing them. *'I have to emphasize my intellect, my music, and my marksmanship. That's how I win them over.'*

The bearded man said to Jackie, "I would love to have horses here. Do you think anyone would like to trade? Your help with the underground Earthships has been invaluable."

Jackie put her hands behind her back and answered, "We only have a few, but we do need some equipment."

Vanessa teased, "Yeah, Fakhar, she wants your equipment."

Jackie turned beet red and covered her face, while Britney prodded at her ribs playfully.

"I studied at Baldwin Wallace!" Darren blurted out.

Everyone paused and shifted their gazes around at the interruption.

Darren ranted at a breakneck speed, "I actually got a scholarship because of my short story. It's really a novella but it was published in the student newspaper as a freshman. I was the only freshman to publish fiction in the student newspaper that year. People are always like, 'English major? So you pay to read books?' but it's so much more than that. Sure, I can read a book, and I can tell what the author was *really* trying to say. And even with people. Like, people are always trying to vie for social status even when it seems like they're talking about the weather or Earthships. And yeah, I write poems too—"

Fakhar grinned patiently and made a slow sweeping gesture with his palm, "That's very interesting. Many of us went to college. Columbus is a college town but also the state capital, so—"

Darren wrested the floor from his rival, "For instance, Rick? He's this *asshole* who we've been living with. He always says English was useless for our enclave. But Baldwin-Wallace was one of the first schools to admit women and black people. And— and brown. You're brown, right? And I look at him and he's just playing out this macho dictatorship because he peaked in high school. Whatever, it's like— I think we shouldn't just replicate what society did before."

During his monologue, Vanessa hugged Britney and Jackie, bumped Fakhar's fist, and disappeared.

Jackie interrupted and excused herself. "That's my friend over there. I'm going to go say 'Hi,'" and she bounded away.

He lingered for a moment with Britney and Fakhar, but the other man turned to her and asked, "Britney, can I ask how you came to be in Ohio?"

He left the two to chat and wandered over to the deck chairs, where he sat next to Will.

People were still dancing and partying to the mix CD, and he watched his crushes flirting their way through the crowd.

The big guy slapped his elbow. "Great show."

Darren nodded, "Probably our best ever. It was the most people, at least."

Will gazed into the distance. "I wish Tyler could be here."

"Yeah." He turned to look at the people still gathered before the stage and resolved to make something happen with Vanessa tonight.

He could see that Jackie was fawning over a shirtless, musclebound looter king. He wasn't particularly interested in her anyway, so he kept looking around for Vanessa.

He noticed the girl with dreadlocks who rode in on a bicycle, but she squatted in a defensive posture and drank with a stoic group of distillery students. He thought, '*She's good looking, but I doubt those dudes could hold a conversation.*'

Vanessa was standing toward the corner, near the bar. The firelight glittered off the gold necklaces that draped her bony shoulders. She crossed one arm across her skinny waist and gestured to a farmer couple with her long fingernails.

Darren walked toward her purposefully, thinking, '*If I introduce myself to the farmers first, I can find a way to bring them down to size. Then I can get another chance with her!*'

But when she turned to see that he was coming her way, she rolled her eyes, tapped the couple on the arms, and escaped before he got another try. Darren tried to see where she had gone, but her rejection was as overt as he could bear.

A calm, sweet voice said, "Hey! I liked your band!"

Darren turned to see the girl who had arrived by bus in Western wear. He couldn't figure out what she kept looking at, and eventually responded. "Oh, thanks. It was our first show in forever."

She said, "I used to go to shows in Louisville. My boyfriend was in a grindcore band."

He answered, "That's nice." She was considerably taller in her cowboy boots than he, and her soft, curvy body made him feel scrawny and weak.

She asked, "Can I buy you a drink?"

He looked over at the bar and responded, "Ah, uh, no thanks. I get free drinks."

She smiled at him, flung a few wisps of stray hair behind her ear, and adjusted her belt buckle.

"Where are you guys from? Do you want to go sit somewhere?"

He answered, "Ah, we're from Northeast Ohio. Middle of nowhere, really."

She pulled her tied-off pearl snap shirt a little tighter above her midriff, relaxed her hip, and shifted her weight to her other leg. "I don't know, it's kind of interesting to me! There aren't a lot of people left, you know."

Darren looked back at the girl with dreadlocks, and despite her waifish beauty, her posture and personality made her entirely unapproachable.

"Umm, do you not want to talk about it? I understand!"

He turned his head back to the cowgirl, tilting it back slightly to see her punctuate her comment with a smile. It faded and she bit her lip gently, then thrust out a hand, "I'm Whitley!"

He shook his girlish hand limply.

She continued, "You're Darren? DeShaun told me."

He nodded.

"I want you know that I'm not working tonight."

Justin played dumb. "Huh? I —"

"—Like, I'm just here to have fun. I'm not trying to—"

Darren stammered, "—Oh, you mean like… the whole —"

"—Yeah. I mean, I'm not saying we can't, but—"

"—Ah, yeah. I gotcha. Just, like, not paying—" He felt himself blush through his transparent skin.

"—I just didn't want you to feel—"

Darren pointed and smiled, "—No, I gotcha, I gotcha."

She tipped up her cowboy hat, "I mean, we don't even have to—"

He repeated, "I gotcha."

They both swayed on their ankles for a moment. Darren looked her over with her ample thighs, broad shoulders, and confident poise. He thought, *'What does she want from me?'* He scanned the cluster of guests and realized how tiny and desperate the bigger girl made him appear and felt embarrassed. He announced, "*Welp*, I better see what the band is up to."

She laughed knowingly, smirked, and dismissed him with a hospitable gesture, "Be good!"

Darren shuffled back through the party, past the stage, and beyond where Will was chatting with some new friends. He walked all the way to the van, climbed into the back seat, tucked his knees against his chest, and sulked until his angst was relieved by bitter slumber.

6.

The Hoosier

It had been thirty-six hours since he had had a drink, but Cody still felt a little hungover. He was riding shotgun, albeit with his compact rifle sitting in his lap, and he was glancing off and on at the flip phone for signs of cell tower activity. They had a solid plan for their next stop, and if Indiana was half as successful as Columbus, they would be thrilled.

They had already spun *Tha Carter III* a few times, a gift from DeShaun and their new friends, and they were listening to Britney reflect on her first gig as a metalcore vocalist.

"Like, I love that I get to be angry. Like, I don't need some guy's approval, OK? And all the girls at the distillery, like, they're so obsessed with being pretty. Like, how about you hunt zombies, god. Seriously. And why is the girl always the singer? I mean, girls can play guitar too, you know. Men want to act like we don't have what it takes. Fuck off."

Darren inquired, "You had a good time though, right?"

Brittany put her face in her hands and started to sob, "I had the best time!"

The other two passengers looked at each other wide-eyed and mouthed '*woah.*'

Darren tried to salvage the conversation. "It was great what you did for Freddy, keeping him from bleeding out."

She continued weeping noisily, "*Aanh, anh, anh, aanh,*" in a cadence reminiscent of a motorcycle changing gears.

Cody tried to deflect the tension as their new friend slid further and further off the rails, "No bars yet."

Will mentioned, "I'm gonna get under the hood here in a minute."

Cody pointed his fuzzy chin at the driver, "All good?"

"Yeah, carbs are dirty. No big deal."

Cody turned around to the others, "So what do you think? City or country?"

Darren replied, "I kind of like the vibe in the city if we can find another collective like that. But most folks think we'll be dealing with a bunch of looter kings or the dead in Indy."

Brittany wiped her tears away with her palms, blinking and stretching her chin as she slobbered, "I w-want to go to the country. I can run around and play with the kids, and maybe we can play a show at a farm or s-something."

Will reminded the group, "Remember not to talk about Columbus. We promised." He pointed to a road sign, "We're ten miles from the Indianapolis beltway, we should…" The big guy battled with the gear shift a bit and mashed the accelerator, culminating in a furious backfire.

He slowed down and pulled over at a service road that led to a bullet-riddled water tower proclaiming *Cumberland.*

The mood in the car was tense, as the fate of the entourage depended on Van Hellsing, but Darren broke the ice by gibing, "So Cody, you get those girls' numbers?"

Cody had made a series of embarrassing attempts at talking with some of the girls from the brothel, but he passed out drunk, slumped against the front wheel of a school bus very early in the night. He woke up clutching Britney's drug rug, which she used to cover him up, and the shame and regret still stung.

He jested, "Nigga' please."

Britney moaned, "You have to stop saying that!"

Darren sighed, "He won't."

"Listen, DeShaun and Freddy *literally* called me their *nigga'*, so I'm gonna keep saying it, cuzz!"

Darren mumbled, "…Dork."

The hood slammed shut with a metallic *thunk*, and Will re-entered, stating expressionlessly, "Ethanol is breaking up the varnish from the FT gas. It's clogging the jets and might get worse before it gets better, but we'll be ok."

Brittany and Darren looked to Cody for his reaction because he's the only one who understood cars.

He asked, "Did you drain the float bowls?"

Will him cast a dirty look.

Cody shrugged, "Okay, then!"

Van Hellsing was moving once again, ambling past an increasingly suburbanized landscape.

Britney hailed, while slouching in the back seat "Can I say something?"

Cody turned and shrugged.

"I just, like, don't want us to kill any of them if we don't have to."

Darren turned to her and cocked his head, "You didn't like how things went down at Dave and Buster's?"

"I just, I just don't want us to."

The van remained silent. Cody knew they disagreed, but nobody knew how to approach the proposition.

She sputtered, "Just like, my kids! A-and I think of my kids. And like, anything that could get me in trouble."

Darren asked scathingly, "Get you in trouble with who?"

Will gestured outside the windshield and uttered to Cody, "You seeing anything?"

The scruffy drummer looked at the phone, "No. Why, are you?"

"Oh yeah, there's a lot of activity."

"Why didn't you stop? We can run a flank."

"It's been like this since we got to Indiana."

They trawled to the end of the highway, where it intersected with the massive, ruined 465 beltway.

"Shit, why didn't you say something?"

Darren shouted from the back, "Let's just roll through and find some farms southwest of here. We can camp there for a couple days."

Will shifted through the gears and bounced along the city streets faster than he had on the highway, causing a lot of jostling and shaking for the passengers and their cargo.

Cody racked the slide of his gun, and Darren swapped out his ten-round mag for an extended clip.

The driver hollered, "There were people in that greenish house back there. Two men and a woman."

Brittany asked, "Do we go there?"

"No, the corpses in the lawn had been running away from the house when they got shot."

Darren shouted, "Turn around, let's camp East."

Will pivoted to head south on Emerson Avenue when the van started lurching and banging.

Cody yelled at him, "There, pull into the rail yard. We can't let anyone know we broke down."

"It's going to pull through, I just have to floor it."

Darren yelled, "Go west, we can try to make the highway."

The van was surging and sputtering, and Will put his whole body into driving the vehicle, but suddenly the engine stopped making any sound whatsoever. "Shit, fuck."

He cranked away at the starter as Cody looked around. "Darren is right; go West."

Finally the engine started turning, albeit with a crippled rhythm. The vehicle hobbled through the intersection, and a block later, Cody screamed and pointed, "Up there! Roadblock."

Will slowed down behind an upside-down car they could use for cover and commanded, "I see it. Flank."

Darren popped out of the sunroof, Will cocked his shotgun and Brittany screamed at a fever pitch, "No! No! Don't shoot them!"

Cody turned to argue with her but jumped when several hands started pounding on the window. His voice cracked with panic, "They fucking flanked us!"

They were surrounded, and the engine was turning over with less and less vitality as the battery drained. The windshield cracked as a big zombie pummeled it with his bloody knuckles again and again. Fifty fingernails scratched the cracking glass, hoping to coax it open despite the sheen of blood oozing from their fingertips. The rear doors were getting kicked and pried, and Cody could see fingers working their way inside.

A muttering girl in a blue dress and a gold necklace started humping the fender listlessly. She was shaped like a young woman, but her face was expressionless, and her thrusts were mechanical. Nevertheless, her long greasy black tresses spilled over the tattoo on her arm of a cartoon horse smoking a bong, captioned '*My Little Stony,*' and it was clear that she was beautiful once.

The humping caused the van to rock rhythmically, and the more it rocked the more of the walkers put their weight into it. The barrels of water and fuel strapped to the top caused it to totter off of its tires.

All at once, the pounding, scraping, humping, and pushing stopped and Cody turned around to see Brittany's top half sticking out of the hatch. She pulled back the hood of her poncho and shouted, "Leave us alone!" over and over. They didn't immediately oblige but shuffled around aimlessly before they started to disperse.

The van started up again, sounding worse than ever, but it had enough power to gently shove the horde aside as they moved past the flipped car and approached the barricade, which was now mostly clear. The zombies started to get restless, discontent to have missed their quarry. Brittany turned and shouted once more, "Go home! Leave us be! Go away!"

Most of them dispersed, some puttered in circles, but a few started stalking toward the van menacingly. She shouted again, "Stop!"

The aggressive vanguard hesitated and looked at each other. One of them, a young man wearing oversized jeans held up by an extension cord, checked his pockets and looked at his companions. They did the same, even the one who wore only brown briefs. They scratched themselves and rubbed their eyes, then bared their teeth with bloodlust and marched toward them even faster than before.

Will floored the accelerator, and the van popped irregularly like a cartoon jalopy until a loud bang and a cloud of black smoke erupted from under the hood.

Brittany opened the sliding door and stepped out with the Smith and Wesson revolver, and before anyone could react, she covered her face and squeezed off seven rounds in the general direction of the horde.

Cody tumbled out of the passenger seat, checked in all directions for the undead, and ran toward the attackers to take a position behind the roadblock to send thirty military-grade 5.56 rounds through head, trunk, and limb. Darren pulled Brittany into the safety of the van and then crouched alongside it to unleash his small yet lethal bullets into the vanguard at point-blank range.

Will's shotgun blasted out big hot lead bbs that moved the mob with an oceanic force, and Cody protected his retreat by flipping his mag and sending another thirty supersonic bees.

A woman wearing only a frilly pink shirt and yellow crocs fired two rounds from her subcompact pistol before it jammed. She pulled out her phone for advice, at which point she was felled by the trio in unison.

There was no more motion from the would-be bandits other than involuntary twitching, and Cody and Darren cleared the side streets of a few stragglers.

The driver handed Brittany his compact Glock and invited her to shoot some of those who had not yet expired, but she pulled a sour face, shook her head, and handed it back like a stinky dead rat. He holstered the gun, then fatalistically marched to open the hood and look inside the engine bay.

Everyone else sat on the floor of the van and caught their breath, the smell of gore, gunpowder, and burning oil thick in the air. Will returned and shared the bad news: "The carb is blown up. We need a new one."

Brittany glanced around, "We just need to find a store, right? They'll have one, right?"

Cody looked at his feet, "Not for an old one like this."

Darren suggested, "We could just steal one from another van?"

Will didn't respond. He set the van in neutral and said, "OK, everybody push."

Everybody lined up on the rear bumper except Will, who put his shoulder on the inside edge of the open driver's side door and pushed as he steered. At first, they could barely get it to move an inch, but after a hundred paces they were marching and even jogging behind it. They pushed several blocks until the street became impassable with bomb craters, then Will took a soft left. "Faster, faster, we have to hop this curb."

They rolled the van fast enough to get them up and over the curb and into a narrow triangular chain-link fenced-in area, which they immediately secured with tarps. Everyone checked their ammo and loaded their magazines. They talked through the plan as they worked.

Darren started, "I stay back on overwatch with Brittany. You two walk down the street and confront whoever meets us. If they're friendly, they can lead you to a safe house, but we hang back."

Brittany protested meekly, "I should meet them."

Cody concurred, "She's right. I mean, because she's a girl."

Will nodded, "It'll be me and Brittany. We go right to that town square and make ourselves look approachable. You stay by the van. Darren provides overwatch for both positions from that red house."

Cody asked, "Best case scenario?"

Darren looked up and answered slowly, "We meet someone from a collective. We tell them that we rolled into town silently. So as not to arouse suspicion. They don't catch on that our van is broken. We borrow bicycles and salvage a carb. Maybe we play a gig in exchange for their protection. We can trade food, ammo, water or fuel if we have to, but don't let on that we have it. You know, *'Kick ass, fuck bitches.'"*

Brittany chuckled and barked out, "Fuck ass, kick bitches!"

"Worst case scenario?"

Darren groaned, "I don't know, dude. They come in shooting, we shoot back. We steal a pickup truck, collect what we can from the van, and go back to Ohio."

Darren backpedaled toward the house, "Alright then, we good?"

Cody told them, "The password is *'Kick ass, fuck bitches.'* Anyone who tries to get in here otherwise gets blasted."

He retreated into the fenced-in area and took the opportunity to look under the hood. The carb seemed OK at first glance, but when he went to remove the air intake, he could see that a massive fragmented section of the throttle body was stuck to the hose, and other bits of the internals were jangling around loose inside.

Cody thought, *'Will surely knows that the damage could be much worse. Replacing the carb would be the first step. The engine could be totally shot. We are sitting ducks— ducks laden with a luxurious amount of fuel, water, ammo, and food.'*

He investigated the engine bay while he waited, looking for leaks underneath, coolant in the oil, fouled spark plugs and other diagnostics. He didn't see any evidence of catastrophic damage, but he didn't have a way to check engine compression, which was his main worry.

Then he removed as much gear from the roof as possible and cached it inside the van where it could be locked up. The ten gallon barrel of water was manageable, but he left the fifteen gallon drum of fuel up until he could get more helping hands. It had been about an hour and a half, and the afternoon sun was now in such a position that neither the two walls of the building nor the tarp stretched out over the chain link fence offered much shade.

He suddenly heard two noisy clangs outside the tarped-off area, and his heart scrambled to send adrenaline back through his system to prepare for combat, but the sound echoed in his mind and somehow brought him comfort even as two figures clambered up the fence. He remembered screaming '*Shoot her*!' in the rehab clinic, with Brittney's doe-eyed face pouting just in front of them.

The short barrel of the Kalashnikov remained trained on top of the fence but he held his fire and saw two bare-torsoed boys of about eleven years of age peeking over.

The first one, a white kid with his hair in a messy bowl cut blurted out "Oh snap!" and ducked back behind the fence.

The second, a skinny black kid with matted, nappy hair and an unwavering gaze, called Cody's bluff and waved politely. "Hello, sir."

Cody lowered his gun and waved back, but raised it again, "You go on, get out of here."

The other boy peeked his brown eyes over the fence and drawled, "You guys should keep going. You don't want to come here."

Cody lowered the rifle, letting it hang from the sling on his shoulder. "How come?" and he slipped a finger in his pocket to be sure he could reach his Heizer pistol if things escalated.

"People around here are real bad. They do a lot of killing and stealing."

He was unconvinced, "That's just kind of how it is everywhere, right?"

His partner now reached both of his brown elbows over the fence, crossed his arms, and set his chin on his hands as he replied earnestly, "Yes, sir."

The gesture was mundane and innocent, and in that moment he realized why the clanking sound was so endearing. "Do you guys have bicycles."

The boy replied again, "Yes, sir."

He didn't want to betray the plan but started to think of ways he could work with these kids to scout out a new carb.

"What kind of danger are we in? Walkers or people?"

"Some of the people is really nice, some of them is really bad. You should drive away."

Cody snapped his head to the side as a boy peeked under the hood and hollered, "They cain't, car's broke down."

He drew the pistol and held it in a guard position as he shooed the kid with the mop-top back over the fence.

The other boy rested in place and said soothingly, "We won't tell no one."

They climbed away, and when they landed on the ground a gang of voices whooped, "Fuck ass!" in various forms, mostly with the melodic intonation of a hearty "Yee-haw."

A tight, gruff male voice twanged, "There's before and after, there."

Cody's young visitors shied away submissively, "Hello, sir."

The gate whipped open, and a tall, clean-shaven man stepped inside wearing black sunglasses with scuffed lenses, a blue Indianapolis Colts baseball cap, and a bulletproof vest with an oversized blue unbuttoned long-sleeved Ed Hardy shirt over it. He had on purple pixel-camo pants and new balance sneakers. He had a large pistol hanging across his body from a sling on his shoulder and fingered it gently as his long, cleft chin scanned around the van, then turned to Cody and huffed, "I'm Ritter," and his gaze continued fixed on Cody with aggressive severity.

"Oh, hi, I'm Cody."

The man smiled broadly and cackled, bouncing between the balls of his feet, and when Brittany walked into view, Cody could see he was scarcely taller than her, putting him at about 5'6".

"Heckova van here. We can take it on a little trip?"

Will adjusted his glasses, "No, I'm going to try to salvage some coolant and flush it out tonight. Gonna let it cool down."

Cody thought, *'That's a pretty smart excuse for us to leave it stationary without letting on that we're stranded here.'*

"Well I'll be jiggered, haven't seen any new folks in months. I didn't think there was anything left outside Indiana. Where you say you're from? Ackton?"

Darren deepened his voice to sound more masculine and called out, "Akron. It's near Akron, Ohio."

"Well, I think you're crazy, then again people think I'm crazy. Thing is, those people didn't make it, and I did, so who's crazy now?" and he punctuated it with a noisy goose-like laugh. "And yer tryin' to play a big rock show here? Ain't it more 'n a handful."

Cody shrugged, "So what do you think, Ritter? Want to host a gig?"

He pattered like an auctioneer, "Well, I'll tell you what I'm going to do. I'm gonna go run some swaps. See, that's what I do 'round here, that's what I'm known for. That's why I'm the landlord 'round here. I keep the place clear of them zombies— mostly— and I got a guy for everything. I got ammo guys, water guys, speed guys. So then I just go 'round and make swaps, see? Maybe take a little off the top, that's just business. I take care of my people. And you guys are my people, so I'll tell everyone to come on over tonight!

"I'm all about music, everybody knows me for it. You ask anyone. I'll even let you sleep at my house. I live with my bodyguard and all my girlfriends — I got a lotta girlfriends— but I got a room where you can stay." He herded everyone along to a house around the corner, taking extremely broad steps that caused his body to sway dramatically with every pace. Cody puffed up his chest and followed, captivated by their new friend and his I-don't-give-a-damn attitude.

The two stories of the house leaned on a wooden frame clad in gray shingles. There were some sections where the exterior had given away completely, and the wall was propped up by plywood and two-by-fours.

A large, hunched man with close-cropped hair and a sweat-saturated gray t-shirt stepped out onto the sagging porch and squinted down at them with his teeth grit and his hands on his hips.

Their host twanged, "That's Prichard, he works for me."

The man continued staring without affect and nodded stiffly.

Ritter beckoned, "Come on, I'll show you to your room."

Cody looked around and saw that his two young shirtless friends had disappeared completely. Darren called out, "Why don't we sleep in the van?"

Ritter sprang out like a slingshot, made a sour face, and barked, "I don't care, sleep in the van. I don't give a fuck." He made eye contact with Darren, bulged his eyes, made a wounded face, shook his head and then ambled down the stairs. "Well, I don't got all day; I'm gonna do my swaps. I guess you don't need ol' Ritter then."

Brittany advocated for diplomacy, "Well, we could at least look at the room."

The gremlin man boomeranged back onto the porch, "Are ya or aren't ya?" He entered the building, and the group followed.

The house reeked of death and decay and was mostly stripped to the bones but was relatively clean. "That's where Prichard sleeps there." and pointed to a sloping sofa with a permanent imprint of the large man. "That's the kitchen back here. I have a propane guy, so we do a little fire now and then. Sometimes, I even run the fridge."

There was a fairly chubby young blonde girl sitting on the grimy floor hugging her knees wearing pajamas, and a gaunt lady maybe a few years older than Britany with bulging red-rimmed eyes and cobweb-thin hair just opposite her sitting against the fridge. They were grunting and wingeing, then glared at the intruding guests only to return to their commiseration without any acknowledgement from Ritter.

He walked up the stairs into the darkness and pointed to one room with a series of locks. "That's the master bedroom; ain't nobody allowed there but me and my girlfriends." He pushed open the other door, and the room had two greasy mattresses leaned against the wall.

Power tools, video games, jewelry, and other household items spilled out of the closet. Will instinctively walked over and opened the window, and the horrible smell dissipated enough to ignore.

Ritter slapped Cody on the shoulder and said, "Well I'm off to do my swaps, you coming or what?"

All eyes were on Cody, who jerked to face his bandmates "What now?"

The hoosier squawked "Well, let's go, sooner I do my swaps the more people we can tell about the gig."

Cody thought, '*It seems like the others already made this plan, and it would give Will a chance to fix up the van in private. Shit, I already kicked ass today. Maybe we'll go fuck some bitches!*'

Ritter bayed "Go on now, git!" Cody tossed the keys to Will and trotted down the stairs.

Ritter moseyed onto the front lawn and stepped into a rusted out green Ford Explorer filled with junk. Cody stood outside expecting him remove some of the stuff from the passenger seat, but his companion snapped, "What're ya waiting for?"

Cody pulled open the door and scrambled onto a small heap of DVDs. His feet searched for ground through an arsenal of kitchen utensils, and a mound of camping equipment and scrap metal in the back seat was poised to avalanche onto him at any moment.

He opened and closed the door again, as the 'door ajar' alarm buzzed nauseatingly, and Ritter fired up the machine and pulled away. He pushed in a cassette and turned up the stereo, the door alarm still audible. "I'll tell you what, nothing like rolling around in a Ford listening to AC/DC with an AK-47 on your lap, huh? American as hell, right?"

They putted back down Prospect Street and as they approached the intersection of the morning melee he growled, "What's this here? Somebody was using my ambush spot. Them zombies was using it, looks like. Hehehe."

Cody replied vaguely, "Yeah, we saw that this morning. We tried to roll in really quietly, but we saw this whole situation, yep." He couldn't think of a reason not to be candid, but he didn't want to say too much.

Ritter parked the car and went around to each carcass, checking pockets, bras, underwear, and shoes. "You guys shoot 'em?"

Cody scratched his frizzy chin quizzically, "Maybe some of them, I guess."

"Well ya didn't check 'em. Here's one, *hoo doggy*!" and he flicked a small bag of crystal meth and stuck it in his pocket. "Go on now, check 'em."

He offered instead, "How about I watch your six."

"More for me." he checked another five bodies, grunting and cursing as he did so until he got to the girl in the blue dress and tattoo and asked "You ever fuck a zombie?"

Cody froze, flabbergasted.

He guffawed, "I'm kiddin' around!"

Cody forced a chuckle, but he was too disturbed to laugh it off.

Ritter spoke low, "You have to tape up her mouth so she don't bite you, bu-hee, hee, hee…I'm just kiddin'! I'm kiddin'!"

A couple bodies later he said, "See when you're the landlord like me you get pussy all the time. All kinds of pussy my friend. These other faggots got nothing on me, I got the biggest guns, I got all the beef."

He pulled a quart-sized foil pouch from one of the corpses and stuck it in his cargo pocket. "Oh yeah, I got a beef guy. Come think of it, How 'bout in two days we do another concert? This time I'll do a barbecue. I make burgers, meat loaf, stew. I make the best stew. People come from all over. A gallon of gas you get all you can eat. These girls come up — they don't even get no beef for it — they'll suck me off cuz *I'm the man*."

Cody smiled, "Dude, you're the man!"

The last of the bodies was checked and they got back into the Explorer. As the door alarm yet buzzed, they drove a few more blocks to the green house where Will had initially seen signs of life. The car pulled right onto the lawn and ran over a putrid corpse that Cody was forced to step over in order to get to the front door.

Ritter pounded on the red door and it opened quickly. A short, round Latina lady in pajama pants and a dirty white T-shirt peeked out, expressionless.

The landlord yapped, "I'm coming around for my duties. This is Cody here, he's my backup. I warned you about him, he's the one I told you about. Me and him just mowed down forty of those fuckers at Prospect and Dunn. You got to give us a duty for that on top of the regular connect. Go see for yourself!"

A bedraggled man with only a few teeth left crept to the door, and Cody could tell that despite his geriatric appearance, he couldn't have been more than forty. He creaked slowly, "I got dieshel thish time. Lotsh of it."

Ritter scoffed, "Bullshit, you didn't get no diesel."

"I did *too* get dieshel. Them trucksh behind the Hoosier Dome, they got two tanksh. We only drilled out the one. You can shmell it." He walked away, presumably to fetch the fuel.

Drilling tanks was a common salvage technique that they used around Rick's compound, and everyone they met in Columbus used it as well. Almost everything there was to siphon was used up by 2011, but by drilling out the bottom of a fuel tank, you could access at least a few ounces from every car that appeared to be bone dry.

"Cody's in a band, you know. They're playing tonight. You guys should come, you have to carry your piece though. And not that pussy little nine millimeter. There's walkers on the streets."

The lady looked at Cody and her eyes tensed just a touch. There was a knowledge, pain and admiration in her gaze that gave Cody the uneasy feeling that he had a purpose here.

Ritter spat, "Fuck a duck, that fuel ain't no good. It's watered down!"

The sparse-toothed man contested, "No it ain't, that there'sh good enough for a grip at leasht."

"I'll give you one teener."

"Hell no, you got to give me three."

"Boy, after all them zombies we killed you should be giving *me* a grip."

"Alright, one teener."

Ritter handed the man one of the meth bags he harvested from a zombie.

"That ain't even full—" but he shook his head defeatedly. "Aw hell." He turned to Cody, "What you shay your band ish called?"

Cody sputtered, "We're Young Nuns."

"Young Nunsh, huh, I never heard a ya. Well, I'll shee you later, Ritter."

Ritter didn't respond but turned and moseyed back to the car.

The two of them navigated through the neighborhood where just hours before Will was seeing signs of danger, but Ritter had his arm out the window, leaned back, and sang as he cruised,

> *I got big balls, I got big balls*
> *They're such big balls and they dance, them big balls.*

Cody saw an imminent threat ahead but Ritter didn't seem to be paying attention.

> *BUT WE'VE GOT THE BIGGEST*
> *BALLS OF THEM ALL!*

Cody shouted, "Up, there! Stop the car!"

Ritter slowed down and squinted, "Aw yeah. There's a bunch of 'em up there." Then, he coasted closer and closer to a gang of zombies clustered around a vacant storefront.

"What are you doing?"

"I'm gettin' closer so I can shoot 'em." After he put the car in park, he reached under his seat to pull out a Mac-10.

At that moment, Cody considered this a solo operation. The ghouls were now in full sprint as the lanky man stretched the machine pistol out in one hand and unleashed three quick bursts of automatic gunfire, the recoil sending nearly all the rounds skyward.

Cody picked his targets, lined up the iron sights with the center mass of the attackers, and dropped three with just one bullet each.

A yuppie wearing a North Face jacket and adult diaper handed her phone to a posh man, who immediately started scrolling dumbly. The diapered gunner raised her rifle and popped off a feeble shot before struggling to reload the bolt action .22. Cody put a round through her chest, and then one through the phone and thus through the head of the posh fiend, splattering the posh man's brain through the hood of his gray Snuggie.

Two others grappled with Ritter, who drew his .44 magnum and let off a wild shot but then cursed over his jammed gun. Cody rushed over to him and slammed his shoulder into the first assailant, a fifty-year-old woman who looked sturdy but hit the ground like a broomstick, the excessive force causing Cody to tumble headlong. He heard another burst of machine gun fire and instinctively found cover against the wall of the storefront. Full-auto AR-15s were almost always yuppies, and this was now his first gunfight without his bandmates.

He looked over to see his partner still grappling with the undead, and he could tell by his garbled screams that soon they would scratch his face bloody and possibly eat his lips and eyelids. At the risk of friendly fire, he leveled the rifle, braced his elbow on his thigh, and turned the jolly bearded boy on top of Ritter into three hundred pounds of dead weight. He missed the lady at first, sending a round through the floral blouse that billowed over her beanpole frame, but when she squared up and rushed at him he didn't miss.

Cody shouted, "Stay there!" but it was a moot point because Ritter was trembling and babbling incoherently under the body of the young heavyweight. He moved smoothly along the wall toward the store entrance, staying as low as possible. Another peal rang out, and he could hear several rounds pepper the Explorer with a *dut, dut, dut*. He looked up in the direction of the gunfire, and a bullet hit the concrete just above his head.

He had the tunnel vision and slow-motion feeling of combat, but in that moment, he knew he was dead the next time his assailant pulled the trigger. Cody's eyes focused upon a figure on the rooftop across the street, and as effortlessly as one tosses a bottle in a trash can, he loosed a full-metal jacketed bullet into it's head.

He came to his senses and scrambled for proper cover, scanning the windows and buildings for other threats. The muffled sounds around him started to come into focus, and he became aware that his heart was racing.

There was a movement on the sidewalk, and he aimed his gun but saw that it was a brunette in a denim pantsuit grinding her pelvis into an abandoned couch cushion for sexual gratification, completely unaware that a battle had just taken place. It always felt cheap to kill them like this, but when she the masturbation ceased to satisfy her dopamine dependency, she would be thirsty for blood again. So he walked over, picked up a nearby cinder block section, and scrambled her medulla oblongata with one heave.

Ritter wriggled free, scrambled to his feet, and clambered into the SUV shouting, "Get in, let's go! Come on!"

Cody launched into the passenger seat so quickly that a casserole dish and a few mugs fell out and shattered on the pavement. Ritter started to reverse but sideswiped a rusty dumpster, then did a three-point turn with much difficulty and a few extra steps.

The Ohioan was panting, "Don't you want to check those bodies? Maybe snag that rifle?"

Ritter was pallid and clutched the wheel with bulging white knuckles, "I got the wind knocked outta me. They knocked the wind outta me, that's all." He drove a little further, wiped his face, and composed himself. He switched the cassettes, and his motorized mouth resumed twanging against a background of "Bawitaba."

"I don't need no faggot-ass 5.56. It's just a twenty-two caliber bullet, a lotta people don't know that. See my MAC-10 here, that's 45 ACP. And you know this forty-four mag drops 'em. I got an ammo guy, I can get all that shit. I can get you 7.62 for your AK there."

"Actually, this is chambered in 5.56."

"No shit? That's somethin' else, an AK in five-five-six? Dang, that's valuable. You better watch it. You're missing a few pieces, huh. Still, someone's liable to kill you for that. You could get yourself a girl for that, to keep. See, I don't need to buy a girl, they come to me."

The car slowed to a halt and he craned his back and twisted his body to get a bag of meth from his pocket, poured its contents into his hand, and tossed it into his mouth while licking his palm sloppily in one grotesque gesture. Then he stepped out of the car and took a couple of empty yellow plastic jugs with him that may have originally contained antifreeze, cooking oil, or orange juice. He dipped them into a scummy barrel aside an old garage, put the lids on, walked them to the car, and thrust them into Cody's lap, saying only, "Hold this."

He removed the .44 Magnum semi-auto pistol that he had slung around his neck and plunked it on the dashboard. Cody could see that the sling was attached to the handle via a grimy hose clamp attached to the grip. Cody's AK was beat to hell, and Darren wielded some lowbrow firearms, but he would rather go to battle with a dull screwdriver than Ritter's guns.

They drove a little further, and Cody took the blue bandana out of his pocket, soaked it in water, tied it around his neck, and felt refreshed right away.

"The skinny guy said you're going to Jew-cago. You better watch them niggers don't see them colors. I bet they'll shoot you anyway, though. Is you Jewish? No offense."

Cody's face twisted with disgust and he sighed, "No, my family is German. So what do you hear about Chicago these days?"

"You ain't gonna find nobody's aunt there, that's for sure. That's what yer skinny bandmate said. Them niggers and spics ain't benevolent like me, see them Jews are all holed up in the boats and the towers and they just watch them monkeys dance. The Jews are still running trades with Canada, smuggling in food all the way across the ocean, too. I don't know why the hell you want to go there, ain't nobody left in Chicago, unless his aunt is a nigger or a Jew."

They arrived at the next house and bounced over the curb onto the overgrown, trash-littered yard, and Ritter mumbled, "Leave the jugs," exited the car, and swaggered to the front door. A tall, young man opened the door wearing a black and white T-shirt with a symmetrical motif of vaguely religious icons and medieval weapons with the word "Affliction." He was a slight yet flabby boy, maybe just a few years younger than Cody, and his acne-riddled face appeared to sprout no facial hair whatsoever.

"What's up, Hogle? This is my friend Cody. He's a stone-cold killer, this guy. Cody, this is Hogle. And Hoge, this is your lucky day. Cody's in a band..."

He couldn't stand listening to Ritter run his mouth and zoned out while he ran his pitch of puffery and swindle. If Cody ran this town he would be running a big crew like Columbus but with him as their badass gangster don. They would kill zombies all day and party all night.

Hogle walked away, returned with an armful of objects, and whined in a nasal voice, "This is all I have. I would trade it for the water, and the syrup, and a teen." He had a couple of glass jars full of green, chunky gasoline as well as a Steve Madden shoebox.

Ritter looked through the box and pulled out a handful of blood-stained gold jewelry, "This ain't shit. For the syrup? No way. Maybe just the water."

The man's weak chin sunk deeper into his neck as he tried to poke at the collection. "There's a lot of diamonds in there. I think they're real diamonds."

Ritter slapped him upside the head and shoved the jewelry in his own pocket, "The fuck you know about diamonds? They ain't worth shit anyway. You don't get shit. This is barely the duty you owe me. Cody, get him the water. That's good drinking water, real valuable stuff. You wanna find someone else to swap, be my guest."

The man reeled and started bawling, "No! No! OK, you can have my DS too. But I need the teener and the syrup."

Ritter mumbled and pulled out the foil pouch plus a baggie of speed. Cody took the gas, fetched the water, and dropped it on the front porch without making eye contact with the blubbering kid.

"You coming to the barbecue? Two nights from now, gonna be a barnburner. Young Nuns is playing."

Hogle was still crying, "Please don't take my video game."

Ritter strode to the Explorer but turned and pointed, "Get me some real gold, and then we can talk."

They slammed the doors and rolled away with the door ajar tone still buzzing against the pompous voice of Kid Rock, but Cody spoke up, "What's the deal with the syrup?"

Ritter shot him a cockeyed glare, "They just been comin' in with it. Must have farms and factories somewhere. Tastes sweeter'n sugar, you can make hooch with it too, I reckon. I never saw one, ya know. The factories where they make them bullets and speed. They used to make phones there too, I guess."

They bounded down the street and Ritter changed the subject, "How come you only got the one gun there? See, I got two here. Plenty of guns around, ammo ain't easy to find but I got an ammo guy. You just got that there AK pistol, how come? You got a bunch of guns in that van?"

Cody boasted, "We've been doing this for awhile; me, Darren and Will. We all have a lot of guns. Brittany has my sidearm. We share it but she can't shoot very well. The other guys have a bunch of guns. I don't know, I think we're in good shape." He realized he might be saying too much so he added, "Mostly the van is full of our music stuff. Not much use to anybody else."

He couldn't help but try to compare Ritter with Rick, the man who led their enclave. Rick maintained a community for the sake of his family, an exclusive self-sustaining group that thrived on the industrial chemical business he started long before the iPhone crisis. He was a jerk, but they all respected him. Cody worked with him since he was sixteen, earning certifications in welding, commercial driving, small engine repair, and electrical work along the way.

Rick had been making gasoline from the Fischer-Tropsch process since Y2K and had plenty of time to develop his sprawling suburban neighborhood into a fortress. They achieved it, albeit through the unpaid labor of the enclave. But so far Cody had seen far more abuse from Ritter, and the community had nothing to show for it.

They drove further this time, with Ritter singing along to an entire side *Devil Without a Cause* by the time they reached their last destination, a pretty suburban house with a thick wrought-iron gate around the perimeter.

They drove just past the main gate to the corner of the property where the muttering middle-aged king found a stick attached to a metal cable and gave it three firm yanks. He hollered at the top of his lungs, "Hey, Yoder! Yoder, it's me. Open up!" He repeated this a few times until a tall, brown-haired man with a big head and small spectacles ambled down the unkempt yard with arms crossed over his solid blue button-down shirt.

"What do you want, Ritter?"

"I got swaps. Diesel. I got gold, too. And lots of really good crystal."

"How much diesel?"

"Five gallons. Now you know I gotta beef guy—"

"About that—"

"I'll swap ya for a half dozen chickens."

The enclave leader pursed his lips, "For the diesel? Two chickens. And half a bushel of zucchini."

"I don't want that shit."

"Potatoes, then."

"Them sprouted ones from your basement?"

The bespectacled man snipped, "Fine then, just one chicken."

"Now let's just hold on a minute. First things first. This here is Cody, and he's a hell of a killer, let me tell you." The man rolled his eyes and looked away. "There's zombies around here, the shoot'n type. You shoulda seen, I was just sprayin' em down like a garden hose, just sprayin' em down. And he ain't shootin.' I was thinking maybe he pussied out, but then I sees he pops 'em off one at a time, real particular. Y'all gotta watch out. Them zombies liable to come this way. I should declare a duty, you know."

The man's dour expression didn't change, and his arms remained crossed as he waited for Ritter to finish his pitch.

"So he's in a band. A rock and roll band."

The man's expression brightened, "Oh yeah? You know, I went to hear REO Speedwagon at the fair one time."

Cody responded politely, "That's a… good band."

"They got Brittany Spears singing for 'em too, you remember her?"

"No."

"Well, they're playin' up on top of the Value World today, I got 'em doing a set just for friends and family, you see. Just for my people. See? I got all kinda good people. I got people like this band Young Nuns playing here. And we're doing a barbecue in two days, so—"

"No kidding! That might—"

"So here's what I have to say, listen up. You bring twenty people on down total, bring 'em down with something to swap. You know I got good stuff, I got gold, crystal, hooch. I got water, gas, girls, beef. I got cars, ammo, guns—"

"Yeah, yeah. We can make a deal. I'll be back with three birds."

He shuffled back to the house, and Ritter kept babbling, "He's got church people he knows, lots of 'em still in the city. They got rich dads and hot daughters. They're running big farms 'n'at. I'm trying to tap into that, see what I'm saying?"

Cody deflected, "And all these people can survive the zombie waves?"

"Most of 'em are in the country. Yoder knows all kinda mormons, with the beards and the buggies."

"Amish?"

"Dumb ass horse and buggy riders."

Cody flexed his brow, "What do they want with diesel?"

Ritter bugged his eyes and puffed his cheeks at Cody as he squatted down, "I don't *fuckin'* know!"

Yoder came back down holding three limp, unplucked black hens, and gestured with his free hand as he shouted "Meet me at the gate."

Ritter got back in the Ford and drove the gate even though it was barely fifty feet away.

Yoder lacked the beard, hat, or anachronistic clothing of an Amish man but had a pious simplicity that seemed adjacent.

He said as he unlocked the gate for the visitors, "I don't think I need to tell you that Daniel has his .308 trained on you."

"Aw, Yoder, you don't gotta do that. You know me!"

The dark-haired man squared his shoulders and nodded reverently but didn't apologize. "And the diesel?"

Ritter gestured to Cody and added with a barb, "And don't go spilling any. It wasn't easy to get."

Cody obliged but eavesdropped as the men continued conversing.

Yoder warned, "They're amassing, you know. There's going to be a big one. We're going out to the country soon. They're looking for some hands."

"I ain't livin' out in the boonies with a buncha—"

"See, Daniel was out there in the Winter. They need people to do some work with small engines and AR-15s. Maybe your friend here."

Ritter responded, "People like us need the good stuff in life. He ain't interested neither."

Cody returned carrying the bucket, then the man popped off the top and spit, "There aren't but two gallons in there."

"It's nearly full, that's a five gallon bucket. A deal's a deal."

He leaned over, smelled it, and splashed it around a little. "The diesel and fifty rounds of .45 ACP for one chicken."

"I'll leave the diesel, and you can collect the ammo when you bring twenty people to my barbecue. Diesel ain't easy to come by!"

"I will bring five people."

The man sighed and handed the chicken to the huckster, "Deal."

Yoder opened the back seat, chucked the feathered chicken carcass onto the heap of scrap metal, then forced the door closed against an avalanche of rusty steel as he slid into the cockpit.

On the route home Cody found it easy to place himself in the city grid. They took one street South most of the way, with a few detours where bridges had collapsed or the street was impassable.

The Explorer pulled up to Ritter's house, and Cody was relieved to see Brittany and Darren relaxing in the grass.

He excused himself from the automobile, "Thanks, Ritter. I'm gonna check in with my band. When do you want us to play?"

"You go on at sundown, while it's still light. I have to do one more job first, I'll let ya know."

Brittany was laying on the grass in her poncho, and the little black boy wearing nothing but green denim cutoff shorts was throwing handfuls of flowers on her. She responded by throwing clumps of grass at him and then chased him around the yard. He was surprised by the physical maturity of the boy, as the years of street life outrunning zombies and fighting for survival gave him a speed and strength far beyond the woman who was almost three times his age.

When she saw him she straightened up and barked, "Darren, it's Cody."

He jogged over from his nap as she asked, "Any news? We were worried."

"Worried? How come?"

She continued, "Well, the people in the house are really loyal to Ritter but Braden and Matt say he's a bad guy."

Cody shrugged, "I think if we keep an eye on our gear we'll be fine. He's a swindler and a bully, but he likes that we're here playing a gig and thinks we're bad ass. Nobody seems to like him, but he can't be that bad if he's built up what he's got."

The boy came back over and hugged Brittany around the waist, then tilted his head up to ask, "Miss Brittany, will you cut my hair?"

"In a minute, Braden. Braden, I want you to meet my friend Cody!"

The boy straightened up and replied cordially, "Hello, mister Cody."

Cody swayed and gestured with his hands, "Whaddup!" but the boy didn't respond. Cody asked, "Where's Will?"

Darren whispered, "He borrowed Braden's bike to ride around with Alex and try and find a carb."

Cody lay in the grass and rested for a minute, then he sat up and asked Braden, who was still hugging Britney as she rocked him gently, "Hey little mans, what do you do when the zombie waves come? How do you stay safe?"

"Mr. Cody, we hide. Alex and me have a place we hide."

"And Ritter, he fights them?"

"No sir, he hide too."

"How come all these people aren't dead then?"

"Mostly they get eated, sir. Maybe some of them hide."

Brittany told Braden sweetly, "If you find some scissors, I will cut your hair."

His smile shone and he was off like a shot.

There was a clang and some cursing and Cody turned to see Ritter attaching a metal trailer to the back of the Ford.

Cody suggested, "So what do you say we set up? Maybe we can run some of the songs that didn't go so well?"

Brittany and Darren nodded, but just then Braden returned with a pair of shears.

"Oh, maybe I can join you guys after I cut his hair."

Darren grumbled and they trod toward the van, "Sure, why should the singer help set up?"

It was an inconvenient setup as they had to hoist all of the equipment on top of the van before tossing it up on the roof and carrying it to the edge overlooking the street. Afterward, they obliged themselves deservedly on water and snacks that were stashed in the van.

Prichard came over with a massive generator on a cart and Darren tried to engage him. "Wow, thanks man! That's a really nice one, it looks old. They don't make 'em like that any more, do they?"

The mammoth man didn't reply,

"Do you by chance have an extension cord we can use?"

"No."

"Hmm, because I saw one outside the kitchen door."

"No, use your own."

"Well the thing is, we don't have one."

But the oaf was already headed back to the house.

Cody leaned his head back, "Fuck, do we have to carry that thing up here?"

They pulled it onto the roof using a chain they found nearby and fired it up for soundcheck. It wasn't hard to get the levels balanced, but as they were spread out in the open air, it was nearly impossible for Cody to hear his bandmates.

When they cut the generator there were some cries of "Fuck yeah," and "Freebird!"

They looked over the edge onto the street to see people already showing up. Cody recognized Hogle and a girl who must have been his sister. There was the thin, toothless man and his Latina partner, Ritter's girlfriends from the kitchen, and a short, shirtless bald man with a ruddy complexion and a perfectly spherical gut.

They climbed down, and Cody heard the euphonious sound of two bicycles hitting the ground, and he jogged over to see if Will's pursuit was victorious. As Darren rounded the corner, Alex collided headfirst with the guitarist's red, curly noggin. Darren inhaled noisily and the shirtless boy with the bowl cut rubbed his head as his eyes welled with tears, but Britney swooped in and with one firm hug, he was ready to take a breath and wipe away his tears. Darren held out his scrawny hand for a high-five and Alex gave it a full swing but it glanced off of Darren's thumb-holed palm noiselessly.

Will announced softly, "We couldn't find one."

Darren suggested, "Will we have any luck tomorrow?"

Will looked at his young companion, "I seen 'em before. Just like yours. I seen 'em."

Cody crouched down, "Yo, yo, yo, check it. It's all good. We have two days. I bought us some time. It was his idea, Ritter. We're going to play an even bigger gig in two days."

Will patted his belly, "That's great. Everything out there is pretty busted. Walkers and people are all mixed in, and everyone is paranoid."

Brittany stroked Alex's hair, "Is it ok if you and Will ride out again tomorrow morning?"

"Yes, Miss Brittany."

Cody grinned and pointed, "Yo yo, wait. I gotta scope this. Let me see you on that bike."

The big man drew up his full size, "Don't start."

Cody smirked, "I gotta. I just gotta."

Brittany and Darren clapped along, "Do it, do it…"

Cody pressed, "Bro, me and Darren set up the whole rig. You owe me one lap."

The bassist shifted his weight and smiled knowingly. He walked over to the child-sized bike, turned his Castro cap sideways, stuck out his tongue, and crossed his eyes as he pedaled bowlegged in a zig-zag.

The band erupted in laughter and clapped when he dismounted.

Will groaned, "Do you guys want to whip up a soup or something?"

Cody pointed to Darren, "We had a handful of pemmican, how about we make a stew after we play?"

Will gestured to the others, "Want to split an apple?"

Alex roared joyfully and resumed hopping along with Braden, who snapped to his senses, grabbed his friend by the elbow, and then replied calmly, "Yes, *please.*"

Brittany put her hand on Braden's newly-trimmed head, close cropped and combed out, and added, "I'm starving to death."

Cody remembered, "Oh yeah, the gig in a couple days! It's gonna be a barbecue. There is supposed to be loads of food here. People come from all over. And they have beef! Actual beef."

Braden slipped away from her and both children paced backward toward their bikes. "No."

Alex moaned, "Nooo, don't eat the barbecue."

"It's really bad, Ritter's a bad man."

"Don't do it. Don't do it, Miss Brittany."

"Mr. Will…"

And they scurried onto their bikes and pedaled away.

She turned to Cody, "The fuck?"

"I don't know, maybe people got sick one time. It sounds like it's going to be super fresh. He knows farm people. I don't know, how bad can it be? If it tastes bad we don't eat it."

Will puffed up his chest and declared, "It isn't your call anyway. You can't just decide what we do."

Cody held up his hands, "I know. I was just improvising."

The bassist asserted, "Well, next time let *us* make the decision."

The drummer sighed and started to apologize, "I'm sorry, I was… Wait a minute, you made a bunch of decisions by yourself today."

Will scoffed, "So?" and led Brittany to the van, asking her, "You ever put salt and pepper on an apple?"

She cringed, "Ew, fucking gross!"

"Maybe you should try it."

Darren and Cody went to find shade but the drummer veered off when he saw a group of stocky, simply dressed people standing on Prospect St. He recognized one of them as Yoder and started toward the trustworthy man and his companions, but Ritter was coming at them from the house at a double-time swagger and got there first.

"Nuh-uh, nuh-uh. Get them buggy drivers outta here unless they got something to trade."

Yoder stepped forward, "I told you I'd bring five people, and they want to trade. You should hear them out. They arrived by chance right after you left. They've wanted to meet you for some time."

A chin-bearded man in suspenders who bore a resemblance to Yoder added, "It was God's will."

"Nuh-uh, these ain't real people. That one's an old-ass grandpa, that one's a kid. Shit, that one's your kid. Bet you wish you shot me today, huh? And this big'n here, and he looks like he rides the short bus. Any of you guys bring me chicken? Fresh potaters? Truck battery? Then fuck off then. And don't bring these Mormons to my barbecue neither."

The old man spoke up with a kind yet powerful voice and unusual enunciation, "Good evening to thee, Mr. Ritter. My name is John Davids. It is true, we are members of the Mennonite faith. But many of us accept modern technologies—"

"Do you wanna buy meth? Water? No? Than suck my dick and kiss my ass."

Yoder pleaded again, "Ritter, I was telling you that these people are very interested in your beef connection."

He hollered, "That's *my* beef guy. *I'm* the one with the beef guy, you see? I got a guy for everything. I don't need you retards."

The eldest man with a long white moustache-less beard, and straw hat intoned sweetly, "Now kind sir, thou have'st a great resource, and in all our community we have not seen a cow nor bull in many years. We have found that they did not survive the attacks of the New English anywhere in this land."

"The fuck's he sayin'?"

The man continued, "And so from thee we seek not the flesh but the entirety of a living cow and bull, that they may thrive in our farms. And for just the name of your man we will offer thee bountiful richness, the likes of which we are not wont to offer but feel obliged."

"You'll give me what?"

"We will offer thee a weekly stipend of goat's milk and eggs, a basket of potatoes, a live fledgeling, and a quantity of honey—"

"Well heck, I could work something like this out. But I want it all up front. I want a whole coop of chickens and I wanna have a bunch of goats over in that house. And you gotta send a girl to stay here and milk it, I ain't milking no goat. Ain't reachin' up a chicken's ass neither. I get to pick the girl, too. And I wanna do some tradin' up around your parts. You tell me where your farm is, and I'll bring my goods up to your neighbors and whatnot—"

John Davids clasped his hands and turned to his companion, "Mr. Yoder, we would like to thank you for the opportunity but this man has no such contact for livestock. I believe he is attempting to swindle us."

Ritter popped off his blue Ed Hardy shirt, dropped his .44 mag pistol, and started menacing the group, storming from side to side on the asphalt in his New Balance sneakers with his fists raised. Without his shirt Cody could see that his wrists were practically the widest part of his arms, as his forearms, biceps, and shoulders were thin, pale and puny.

Throughout this affair, the three minor children observed with such passive obedience that they were nearly invisible; one young boy in a straw hat and suspenders stood beside his grandfather, Yoder's son Dan stood next to his father, but the third boy, the one Ritter called a 'short-bus rider,' was roundabout fifteen years old, two-hundred-fifty pounds, with a back as broad as a car hood and hands the size of pumpkins.

Displaying an expression of modest annoyance, the boy grabbed the tweaker by the neck with one hand, walked him to the nearby brick wall of a library, and pinned him there while awaiting instruction.

The grandfather hissed, "*Ruhig zie*, Josiah." and rushed forward to help the man as he crumpled into a choking ball, but he stood and staggered toward the shirt and pistol he abandoned on the street, causing the Mennonites to flee.

Cody jogged back to the van before bullets started flying. He heard him shout, "Yeah, you better run, you faggots!" And pop off a couple wild shots before the gun jammed, and he stormed back into the house.

The Young Nuns were spread out in the dirt around the van. Will raised one inquisitive eyebrow but Cody blew it off, "The shooting? It's nothing. But I was thinking, maybe we get the show going soon. Ritter's losing it."

"No complaints here."

"Sounds good to me."

The band climbed onto the roof and powered up the generator, and Cody could see thirty or forty people around. Most of them were the sort of riff-raff Ritter takes advantage of, but there were more than a few who looked like they could handle themselves. Most of them sported shotguns and ill-fitting tactical gear.

He could hear Ritter bleating, "Young Nuns, fuck yeah! These are my people!" and was relieved when the amplifiers came on with whistling feedback.

He gave four slow clicks and then landed into a doom riff with crushing force. Cody imagined the Mennonite teen's massive hand and bashed his cymbals and snare with unbridled brutality. Brittany was still in her drug rug and Cody prayed she kept it on, as he didn't trust anyone below to behave themselves in the presence of a sexy female. She rocked from side to side with her back to the crowd, growling with a slow glottal fry in no particular rhythm.

Cody held a light fermata on the cymbals and then gave two generous strikes on the china cymbal and the song landed right on the march-tempo break down, with broad angular *chonks* and *wahs* in the guitar emboldened by a heavily ornamented cut time drum beat.

Hogle started jumping up and down, and then jumped into the street throwing windmill punches while he was bent over so far that his butt crack was exposed. Ritter's girlfriends raised their fists and flung their hair in the air with violent fury. A few others instinctively jumped into the pit and lost themselves to the hardcore rhythm but most people either listened motionlessly or bobbed their heads. Brittany squawked into the mic

> *ra ra raaa!*
> *ra ra raaa!*
> *breee breee breeeeee!*

They may or may not have been actual words.

Alex and Braden were jumping up and down and sprinting in circles in front of the building. Braden clearly had the beat under control but Alex was spazzing out.

It was a simple song that they knew well, and at the end he drove the double-bass pedal in a steady thirty-second note barrage. But tonight he felt badass, and decided to drop into thirty-second note triplets. His feet lost their bearing with the rest of his body, and the beat that should have been commanding and transcendental now sounded like amateur slop. When the song ended with whoops and whistles, he was ashamed.

The next song was '*Inside Job,*' and after four stick clicks, Cody locked in tightly with Darren who was throwing seagull-style dive bomb harmonics on the accents of his fills. He pushed the song faster and faster, releasing his aggression into the sound but again, at the ending he realized he pushed the song faster than he could play correctly, had to substitute a basic rock and roll beat instead of the dramatic death metal coda.

Ritter was holding court, beaming with pride and grandeur, nodding to audience members and gesturing to the band with braggadocio. He looked around for Alex and Braden, feeling somewhat protective of them but they were nowhere to be seen.

Britney started the next tune with a rhythmic chant.

> *Got fun*
>
> *shotguns*
>
> *who wants one*
>
> *a hot one?*

And the band came crashing in with a down-beat-y hip-hop-informed groove that got everyone in the crowd bouncing. The verse downshifted to jazzy chords with clean guitar and closed hi-hat, followed by the chorus with d-beat flair. He glanced around during the pre-verse to see if Ritter's giant manservant was in the crowd but dropped his stick when he saw instead the man's girlfriends; the blonde had her shirt up to her neck and was waggling a giant pink breast with each hand, and the scrawny girl was turned around with her pants at her thighs, jiggling her surprisingly supple butt.

Darren and Will turned around to admonish him for dropping the beat but he fished the stick out from under the Axis pedals and resumed drumming. He thought, *'I know I'm going to fuck some skank hoes on this tour, tonight might be one of those nights.'*

The song ended with a ripping guitar solo and galloping bass and drum thrash riff. Cody saw Brittany's face and he knew they were all on the same page, so he said, "Let's play the last song, let's just end it."

Everyone nodded matter-of-factly and Brittany mumbled into the mic, "If you want to hear more, come to the barbecue in two days! This one's called *Jackknife*."

I'll pretend you're Kevin, and send you up to heaven!

Cody came thundering in with triplet ornamentations of a slick punk groove and after a few bars he realized that everyone stopped playing. Darren walked over to him and said, "Dude, this one goes *da-na-na, da-na-na, jud-jud-jud-jud-jud-jud-jud-jud*."

Somehow he drew a blank.

"It used to be called '*Ass Blast*.'"

Cody nodded in recognition and they re-started the song. He played it straightforwardly, recognizing that he may have overdone it with his previous indulgences. He worked through the sparse verses and death metal choruses to the interlude section, where Britney's minor key singing seemed to lack gusto and sincerity. They wound down the performance with the teaser from the verse and left the crowd wanting more.

Cody wiped his brow and started to remove his cymbals.

Will suggested "Let's load into the van now."

The drummer dropped his sticks with an extended clatter as one fell off the roof, onto the van, and to the ground. "How about you and Brittany do it because Darren and I loaded in?

Darren responded, "How about we all load in and out every time? Starting now."

It was agreeable enough, but before they could do much more than wrap cables, the honking tone of Ritter's voice floated up on the evening air from where he stood next to the van, "Come on down, now! Young Nuns! *Hoo-wee*, rock and roll. I'll tell ya what, that was somethin' else." Here, let's drink to Young Nuns."

Cody tried to be diplomatic, "We're kinda tired, Ritter."

"Bull fuckin' shit, I poured this hooch for you guys, this stuff is valuable. This is mulberry and paw-paw hooch. Let's have a toast, to Young Nuns!"

Cody's neck ached slightly, remembering the daylong hangover he endured after their last gig, not to mention his grief over missing out on the brothel girls.

Darren said in a collegial tone, "Thank you, Ritter. We'll toast with you."

They all climbed down and took a glass from the man who filled each of the four scummy half-pint jelly jars from a mason jar. He then pulled a flask out of his purple camo pants pocket and held it up for himself, "To Young Nuns!"

They all echoed, "To Young Nuns." and winced as the fumes from the acrid swill hit them in the nose.

"Well go on then, drink up! Hooch ain't for sippin'. Drink that shit."

The rest of the band drained their glasses, but Cody didn't want to drink after his last experience. He intentionally jostled the glass, causing most of the contents to splash onto the dusty ground so Ritter wouldn't notice, and then he drank the rest. He couldn't tell how much had splashed out, but he ended up drinking more than he meant to.

Darren sputtered, "Thanks man, that was really good!"

"You guys saw your place, right? Hang out a couple days, have some barbecue and all that. I can get your beds all set up, come on, I'll show you."

Darren responded, "I think we're going to pack up first, and some of us might sleep in the van."

The looter king threw up his hands like a gorilla, "I don't give a fuck!" And stormed away.

Brittany chimed in, "I am sleepy though."

The rest of the band froze and exchanged glances.

She hesitated, "Oh, I'll help pack up though."

There was a collective sigh of relief, not at the reduction of labor but her respect for the effort.

They passed the gear around in an assembly-line fashion, with Darren moving the gear to the edge, Cody on the roof of the van passing it to Will on the ground, and Brittany arranging it inside the van.

As the last of the drum hardware was carefully packed away they discussed the sleeping arrangement.

Cody started, "I say we all just sleep in the van."

Brittany shook her head, "Ritter isn't going to like that."

Will muttered gruffly, "Nothing he can do to us in there that he can't do to us out here."

Darren concurred, "We rotate watch upstairs and someone sleeps in the van."

Cody ran his hand through his hair and nodded. "I'll go upstairs like we're going to sleep and then I'll sneak out. It will be safer if nobody knows I'm here."

They all nodded but Cody sensed an awkward pause.

"OK, I won't do anybody inside the van."

Brittany pulled her hood over her head to hide her disgust, "Dude that's so nasty, you're gonna get Hep C."

Darren blurted, "*Ass bitches! Fuck ass bitches!*"

And everyone taunted him in vaguely foreign accents, "*Fuck ass bitches!" Ass bitches kick ass!*"

Cody laughed and quieted them, "Ass bitches indeed, I give you that. But sometimes you need to fuck some ass bitches."

They headed toward the house where twangy voices were echoing down the street. Britney offered, "I can take the first watch."

———————————

Fuck, I fell asleep. Darren was piled on top of Cody like a corpse, but Cody lacked the strength and motivation to push him away. He was supposed to do something. He wasn't supposed to be asleep. If he would just stand up, he would remember. But laying there just felt right for his body. *Oh fuck, the girls! Damn, was it too late*? There was still hooting and hollering outside. Maybe there were girls there. That probably wasn't a great idea, he was too drunk to be social. But those girls…

———————————

"Aw no ya don't buddy, you go on ahead upstairs, go on, git. I'll tuck you in *he-he-he*, I better fix you another nice cup of water."

Cody licked his dry lips and gazed bleary-eyed at some of the figures on the porch, whose headlamps shone in his eyes so that he couldn't tell what was going on.

———————————

He came to, still wasted, piled up on the mattress with the others but had an urge. He walked to the window to get some fresh air, and was surprised to see that Brittany still had her heavy Baja hoodie on. As soon as he stood up he remembered the van. Maybe the girls were there looking for him, it couldn't be that late because there were still so many people partying in front of the house.

Ritter's muffled voice echoed in his head, and he couldn't be sure if he was imagining it or hearing it from the man himself outside the front door.

"Oh yeah man, that bitch wants me. Everyone wants to fuck the king. Even Britney fuckin' Spears. I'm gonna spear her tonight, if ya know what I mean. She told me she wants it. I'm gonna spear her, she's gonna be like 'hit me baby one more time' *he-he-he-he*, she'll be like 'hit me baby one more time,' *he-he-he-he*, and I'm gonna cum and be like 'oops, I did it again.' *He-he-he* did you hear that one? I said I'm gonna be like 'oops I did it again.'

Cody was staring at a door with a series of locks all over it, and he could hear banging and hammering on the other side. He gave it a tug but it didn't open. There was another door and he pushed but it didn't open but when he took a step back he could see that this was the back door to Ritter's house, and the one covered in locks was the door to the basement. He pushed the outside door again, and there was a percussive cracking sound as he stumbled through the broken, rotted out wooden steps and landed on the grass.

He was in a different, silent, dark house. *Where the fuck am I? What am I supposed to do here? Is this the girl's house? Fuck, I wasn't supposed to get this drunk. The van!* He thought maybe he already got some, so he reached down his pants and felt his dick, which was dry as a bone and limp as a handkerchief. He missed the feeling of his rifle on his shoulder and thought he must have left it either under the bed or in the van.

Cody could tell before he even opened his eyes he was face-down in the back of a pickup truck. The ribbed truck bed liner was full of rust flakes and broken safety glass but it wasn't moving. He slid backward out of the tailgate and leaned against the truck for a moment. He could hear the cackling of the Hoosier in the distance.

He leaned up against a tire in the fetal position, and he could tell by the smell that it was Van Hellsing. If he could just crawl inside he would be home free, he might not get laid, but he could sleep for the night and protect the gear, it was his only job. He checked his pockets, but didn't have the keys.

Cody came to in the threshold of their upstairs bedroom, and he could see that Will and Brittany were on the far side mattress. He shook the big man to get him to wake up and take watch, but while he breathed noisily, he did not stir. Brittany had snot crystals forming around her nose and had apparently pulled off her drug rug and had slid off the bed onto the floor with one of her boobs hanging out. Cody tugged on the armpit seam of her tank top to tuck her tit back into a more modest position and then turned her attention back to Will.

It was par for the course for Darren to sleep like a rock but Will was always annoyingly responsible. He shook him again and then patted down his pockets for the keys but didn't find them there, in Darren's pockets, or under the mattress. While looking around his own sleeping area, he was disappointed to find that his rifle wasn't there either, only a scummy half-pint jelly jar of ditch water. The mattress felt nice.

———————————

He found himself laying on Prichard's dented couch in the living room, with the kitchen door open and an oil lamp burning. The reek of death was stronger than ever, and Cody crawled off the sofa and followed the light down the basement steps to where dark shadows leapt across the mildewed walls.

Human arms and legs hung from hooks in the rafters, dripping blood into thick pools on the floor and casting silhouettes in the flickering firelight. One arm shone brightest, bearing a colorful 'My Little Stony' tattoo. Some of the arms hung low on the ceiling, not by hooks but by shackles on chains wrapped around the joists. Cody crawled back up and ducked behind the couch just as Prichard lumbered through the kitchen with another armload of legs.

———————————

A muffled voice and a blurred image of a person sharpened in his gathering consciousness, "Well shit, what're you doin' down here? I told you to drink that water, I warned you." The hood of the Van Hellsing was up and all doors were open while Ritter was rooting through their belongings with Cody's AK-74 slung over his shoulder. "Now listen, there was about a quart of gas in that generator, so I'm just taking what I'm owed. And I'm protecting you guys, see, so… Well shit. I'm taking all y'all's shit and that's that."

The thief's headlamp was still on and Cody was already disoriented so he shielded his eyes as he staggered, slack-jawed, and unable to protest.

He whined, "You drugged us."

"Not my fault you can't handle your liquor. Buncha lightweights, ya two-beer queers."

"You drugged us."

Ritter moseyed over to Cody and layed a full-force open-handed slap upside his head.

––––––––––––

Cody moaned from the ground in a heap, "The barbecue…"

Ritter ignored him and continued to mutter as he tried to fill a gas can from the barrel on the roof, spilling a precious quantity in the process.

He repeated, "It's not beef, it's the dead."

The man barked, "Well if you act right I might let you play my barbecue. And I might even let you have a burger. If you behave."

Cody laid his head down on his elbow, defeated.

––––––––––––

What was I doing? I'm supposed to be doing something.

––––––––––––

Ritter reached down and shook him violently by the collar of his blue Under Armor shirt, "The gas and apples, you little faggot. Was it in Dayton? Them niggers in Toledo? Answer me!" and he slapped Cody again. "I'll fucking shoot you, I don't give a fuck."

Cody reached into his pocket, unsure of what he might find.

"What, you got a knife? Well go on, stab me boy!" Ritter took a single step back, held up his hands, and thrust his face forward with defiant buffoonery.

Cody pulled out the object, which was larger than a Zippo but smaller than a flask, and before he could react he heard Ritter shout, "Oh shit, fuck." He leveled the AK and pulled the trigger, but nothing happened. Cody looked down to see the itty bitty Heizer .410 pocket shotgun pistol in his hand.

Ritter fiddled with the gun as he backpedaled until he was trapped by the van. Cody's rifle was left-handed, he never used the safety, and he rarely kept a bullet in the chamber, so it took a few seconds of flipping levers before the iconic *chk-chk* sounded and the man raised the gun to shoot the drummer while mumbling, "Gay-ass little derringer!"

Cody raised the pistol with lugubrious difficulty.

The Kalashnikov rang out with a blinding muzzle flash, and the shooter yowled in pain as the left-handed bolt cycled and pinched his hand raw while simultaneously ejecting a burning hot steel casing down his tactical vest.

The Ohioan's gun reached it's apex, he pulled the trigger, and the man's protruding jaw inverted, his face folding inside itself with a cavernous wound as a cluster of buckshot dissolved the lower half of his face and forced it out the back of his head where it tinkled off the steel panels of the van. Ritter's body hit the ground with more of a *swish* than a *thud.*

Cody felt the imperative to get up and secure the van but was still too tired. He had a euphoria welling inside of him that became soporific when combined with his high dose of downers. He lay on the lawn and gazed hypnotically at the underside of Van Hellsing, now illuminated by the lamp he had blasted from Ritter's head.

Across the lawn at the house, he heard the back door open, the thickly painted door still sticking in the swollen door frame. The door quickly slammed shut, and Cody remained still, unsure whether the beastly man had made a quick trip outside the house or had heard the shot and was coming to mete out vengeance. Even if he could get to his rifle, he doubted he could overcome a clear-headed fighter. Prichard bellowed, "Ritter!" And then again closer, at the top of his lungs, "Ritter!"

There was another sound, like a ghost on the breeze or an angel from above. Two bicycles did a lap around the block and Prichard called out, "Hey! Hey kid!"

The bicycles coasted to a stop and Alex answered, "Yes, sir?"

"Where's Ritter?"

Braden responded, "He with Miss Evans, sir. Over at the cut."

The big man grunted, "She's asposda be on her period."

Braden responded, "Y-y-you want us to go fetch him, Mr. Prichard?"

"Yeah. Yeah, go get him." And he moaned in exasperation *"Wuuagh."*

The boys pedaled away and the back door slammed once again. Cody crawled sideways to Ritter's corpse, scooting his bum along and then sliding his heels and elbow like an inchworm. He recovered his gun and checked through the dead man's pockets, finding only a spare magazine for the MAC-10, the Nintendo DS, and a few bags of meth. He dumped one bag into his hand and licked it. The revolting metallic taste zapped his brain with profound disgust and he shook the rest of it into the dirt.

Just then the boys crawled past the chain link fest. Braden asked ugently, "Mr. Cody, are you ok?"

"Yeah, I am. You saved my life."

"Mr. Ritter was a bad man. We have to go, Mr. Cody."

Cody stood up and shook his head and limbs. He felt his consciousness busting out of his head, as if his surging thoughts might spike in pressure and launch out of his eyeballs.

Cody nodded, "We have to take Ritter's car. It's the only way."

Alex shook his head, "It's out back with Mr. Prichard, sir."

"Fuck! I mean— sorry— darn."

"We have to watch out because Mr. Martens is on patrol tonight, and usually when there's a barbecue Mr. Ooley helps with the meat too."

"Mr. Ooley is bad. He'll probably be here soon."

Cody asked, "Can you boys shoot?"

They froze, and Cody answered intuitively, "Just zombies, huh? I get it. This is my first time with someone who's not a zombie."

Alex perked up, "We fixed the carb!"

Cody shook his head, "Sorry dude, that thing was blown to smithereens. It's in pieces."

"No look!" He moved a chunk of concrete in the corner of the building to pull it from its hiding place and rapped it with his knuckle to demonstrate its integrity. Cody could hear the solid *dink, dink, dink* from twelve feet away.

"Let me see." He snatched the headlamp from under the van, grabbed the component and turned it around, unable to stifle an optimistic grin.

"It's epoxy. We used epoxy. It's almost dry."

"I'll be darned." And he tossed it up and down in his hand.

Braden implored, sweetly, "Take us with you."

"Huh?"

"Take us with you, Mr. Cody. We want to go with you."

"That's not… We can't…" His eyes darted around as ideas percolated in his mind like fireworks.

He crouched down and put his arms on their shoulders like a football huddle, "OK, here's what we do. We put the carb on and get everything here set. Then you tell Prichard that Ritter needs his help and send him on a wild goose chase. If we can start the van, we load everyone into it. If not, we take the Explorer with the trailer. We'll get you out of town and then figure it out."

The boys grinned giant toothy grins and nodded, "Yes, sir!"

Cody paused. "No, uh, wait. Is it? Is that a good idea though?"

The boys cast a quizzical glance at Cody, who implored them, "What do you think we should do?"

They put a finger aside their faces and scanned their wide-open eyes across the sky with mouths agape, then Alex slowly nodded. "Let me talk to Prichard cuz I know how to *really* get him going. This is gonna be good!"

Cody nodded. "As long as he goes away and stays away, we're all set."

"What about Mr. Ooley and Mr. Martens?"

Cody rubbed his eyes, "If one of you is on lookout we should be OK. I'll need a lot of help loading the van. But let's get this going before they turn up."

Together, they made short work of the carb, bolting it to the frame and connecting it to the air intake and cylinder block with an extra set of hands for the flashlight and another to hold it steady. They returned everything to the van that had been plundered by Ritter, including Darren's Ruger and Hi Point, plus Britney's Smith and Wesson the scoundrel must have taken from the bedroom when he stole Will's keys.

The boys got back on their bikes and pedaled to the kitchen door. They yanked on it mercilessly until it slingshotted open and they scrambled inside and beat on the basement door. The boys ran outside where the big man emerged and hollered, "What? Is he coming?"

Alex spoke, "Mr. Ritter said to tell you they isn't coming."

"That little… Who is 'they'?"

"Mr. Ooley and Mr. Martens. And Mr. Fogle. They was hanging out with Miss Evans and she was doin' stuff. You know, she was doin' stuff to them. They was doin' that Chicago crank and drinking that Canada whiskey and she was doin' stuff."

He grunted, "That son of a bitch."

Alex continued, "And they said you wasn't invited cuz you wouldn't like it." He paused and tilted his head, "Mr. Prichard, what's a butt fogger?"

"That *son of a bitch*! Where are they?"

"They at the cut, at Miss Evans."

"At her old place or the new one."

Alex's voice lost all its confidence and he stammered, "Uh, I-I-I don't know, Mr. Ritter always just calls it 'The Cut.'"

"Is it got the truck in front?"

Alex stuttered, "There's… Well I seen somethin'… I didn't seen nothin.'"

"Take me there. *Hoo boy* I'm pissed off."

The boys looked at each other, unsure of what to do other than obey, and Braden said "Follow me" then pedaled slowly. As they walked past, Cody could see that he was strapped with a pistol and carried a dangerous length of 2x4.

When they were out of earshot, he tore down the blue tarps around the van, jammed the keys in the ignition, and stomped on the accelerator like a jug band fiddler while he gave the key a solid crank. At first it spun with youthful enthusiasm but quickly wound down to a dull whir and at last, a lethargic swoop.

"Fuck. Fuck."

Cody patted down Ritter's corpse for the keys to the Explorer, but his pockets were empty.

He hopped out, shook his head, then sprinted to the house and bolted up the steps. He knew everyone had a bigger dose of the knockout drug than he had, and knew that the amphetamine could be dangerous. But he wet his finger and rubbed a sprinkle of coarse powder inside everyone's gums. They came to within a minute, but nobody could manage to string more than a few words together.

"What time?"

"Where?"

"Gun…"

Cody shone the headlamp in their faces, "Everybody, we have to go now. Grab your shit. Fuck it, grab whatever you can."

Will growled, "The barbecue…"

Cody threw the drug rug at Britney and shouted, "Put it on!" Then he took a small box of jewelry, added a handheld power sprayer and cordless drill, thrust it in his guitarist's hands, and scooped him up to carry him down the stairs like a bride.

"You're on lookout, you see anyone make a noise like a crow." He set Darren on the front porch steps.

Britney was still lying down, but managed to crawl inside the poncho, and he stuck a box of ammo and a can of creamed corn in her hands before he carried her to the porch.

When he went upstairs and saw Will still lounging on the mattress, he thought better than to try to roll him down the stairs and instead poured another pinch of meth into his mouth. "Come on big guy, we gotta go."

He pulled Will to his feet, and the heavyweight hesitated. He reached below the mattress and pulled out the Glocks from where he had stashed them, and returned them to their holsters. Cody steadied him as they took the stairs one at a time and deposited him on the porch with the others.

Cody ran around the house to the Ford, opened the door, and put one foot inside to start the engine but the keys were missing. He flicked on the headlamp and looked for them inside, but with the mess and clutter it was impossible to find anything. He dashed to the back door and flung it open, but they weren't anywhere around the kitchen, front room, or bedroom. Ritter's room and the basement were locked up tight, and Cody didn't have the strength to break down the door.

He thought, '*I bet Prichard has the keys. He's going to be pissed off and paranoid when he comes back. Even if I try to hide and ambush him, people are going to die.*' He decided that the Explorer would be more of a threat than an asset, so he blasted the front tire to shreds with a single shot.

They would have to hide. They could get somewhere safe in time for the drugs to wear off. Or if they did enough speed, they could fight. Cody leveled his rifle and fixed his iron sights on a nearby stop sign. The sign was blurry and jumped around, and the barrel of his rifle bobbed around like a duck in the water. He was never going to win a gunfight in this condition.

He heard screaming in the distance, "Mayday, mayday Mr. Cody!"

"He's coming, HE'S COMING!"

The boys pedaled wildly, their faces terrified. "We just runned off. He's pissed, he shooted at us."

Cody pulled his hair back with both hands, "Boys, you better keep pedaling. You know what, there's a man around 46th and Emerson. He was here earlier. His name is Yoder."

The boys were huffing, puffing, and panicking, but Alex responded, "We never been out of Fountain Square."

"Well, you have to go there now."

The boys were crestfallen. Alex threw his bike to the pavement and sobbed while Braden tried to soothe him, "It's ok, Alex. Let's go to our hiding place."

"I don't wanna go to the hiding place. I wanna go with Miss Brittany." He wailed until his face was red and wet.

Cody looked around, trying to think of an effective strategy, but the boys would be no help, and his bandmates were a liability. Good people were going to die tonight unless they left immediately.

He sighed, uttered, "One sec," and then paced down to their van. He popped the hood, drizzled a little gas from Ritter's can into his hand, opened the air filter housing, and dribbled it in. He engaged the starter, but this time it coughed, sputtered, and smoked during the initial crank. He gave it another anemic crank and the engine started to run but died.

The third time, it barely turned over but eventually made a chaotic series of low swampy rumbles and pops, the engine leaping violently on its mounts, shuddering and banging. It revved a little faster, then still faster yet until it sneezed and lurched violently. Cody eased off the accelerator until it was just about to stall, then brought the RPMs back up. First, it surged beyond 2K, then settled at a purring idle.

The boys hollered joyfully as Cody reversed through the chain link gate and skidded the tires on the pavement. He hopped out and tossed their bikes haphazardly on the roof, then they jumped in the passenger seat, and Cody hopped back to lay tire with the doors still open.

He mounted the curb and pulled onto the lawn just in front of the house, and as gunshots rang out, Will had just enough wherewithal to hobble down the porch steps, force open the sliding door and yank his diminutive bandmates inside.

Cody stepped out of the van and emptied his magazine blindly in the direction of the gunfire in hopes it would keep their assailants at bay, but bullets kept whizzing by, piercing the windshield and body of the car. "Everybody down!"

He sped away past Prichard's mask-like face through the familiar cratered streets and crisscrossed to safety. He hesitated for a moment outside of a house as Will slurred, "Fucking drive."

Alex calmly pointed out, "That's Mr. Hogle's house."

Cody laid on the horn with annoying persistence until he saw the front door open a crack, then he chucked the DS out the window onto the grass and shouted "Fuck Ritter!"

The door opened wide and the sad, round boy crept out toward the video game while Van Hellsing peeled away.

Alex and Braden were ecstatic, riding in the front seat as if it was a roller coaster while pointing at insignificant houses and objects like they were historic monuments.

They arrived at a house with a thick wrought iron gate just before dawn when the sky was starting to turn blue. Everyone except Darren cleared out of the car and sorted themselves as Cody found the cable on the corner of the building and gave it three full yanks.

Brittany sat on the grass and looked up at Cody, "What are we going to do? We can't take them with us, and we can't leave them here."

Will said "We need to get out of Indy. We can camp with them but we can't take them to Chicago."

Brandon hugged Brittany from as she crouched and leaned his weight on her shoulder. Alex reached down to play with her hair, and Cody put his hands on the lad's bare skinny shoulders and gave a gentle squeeze, unsurprisingly finding them solid and muscular.

Yoder and the other Mennonite around his age strolled down the hill with vexed expressions, carrying shotguns and hollering, "My son has a .308 trained on you, be it known."

Cody held up his palms and stepped forward. "Ritter is dead. He was a bad guy and he tried to kill us. He was a liar. You were right."

The bearded man responded, "You have my forgiveness, son. But there is no justification for murder, except for the New English. Was he New English?"

Cody didn't answer but asked instead, "Are you still looking for a couple hands?"

The man responded, "We will not have murderers among us."

He tapped Alex and Braden on the shoulders, "Not me. These are the best boys you'll ever come across. They deserve the best. We want them to be safe. They saved our lives."

Yoder looked at them, then wrinkled his lower lip and looked at his companion. He turned to look at Yoder, then faced the boys and asked, "Do you want to come with us, lads?"

Brittany leaned back to make stern eye contact with Braden and said, "Tell the man, 'Thank you, it would be an honor.'"

"But Miss Brittany—"

"No '*buts*.' Say it."

He looked at the man, his lip quivered, and he said in as grown-up a voice as he could muster, "We want to go with you, sir. It would… um…"

Brittany whispered, "It would be an honor."

"It would be an honor, sir."

Alex echoed crudely, "It would be honored to, uh, we go with you."

There was a quick volley of hugs as Cody pulled the bikes off the roof and passed them to the boys. Brittany started to follow the kids to the gate, but Will squeezed her shoulder, "It's better if we go now." And before the boys could turn back to look at Young Nuns, they had already started the van and pulled away.

7.

Chicago Mayhem

The words spewed from Brittany's face with graceless force, every muscle from her toes to her eyebrows articulating every syllable. The band played a syncopated percussive breakdown, and she whipped the microphone cord with punishing fury. Then with her feet set wide, she crouched down and braced her hands on her knees to moan gutturally.

Rrrrrruuuuuuuuughhhh…

The strings rested and Cody terminated a two-beat tom tom fill on his cymbal bells while Darren stepped to the edge of the stage, spun his guitar over his shoulder, and caught it in time for them to cut the time again.

Rrrrrruuuuuuuuughhhh…

She swayed hypnotically like a southeast Asian dancer, with undulating hands and bewitching eye contact.
The band came in with a skank drumbeat and a tumbling guitar riff, and she stalked the stage with stiff arms as she sang,

> *I am the child and the crone!*
> *I am the mother and the daughter!*
> *I am the master and the slave!*

I am the fire and the water!

Darren soloed and she danced fantastically, improvising gyrations in reaction to the melody. She had the American Apparel tank top/ thong rocking, and tonight she felt sexier than she had in years, with her skin nice and clean, her makeup on point, and her hair professionally styled.

She shrieked the final verse and sang the last chorus while doing sharp choreography with gymnastic floor work and controlled contortions. She alternately whipped her hair and shook her bosom on the rock-and-roll riffs of the coda, and on the last note, she planted her boots and announced over the feedback from Darren's guitar, "Thank you, we're Young Nuns. We have two more."

But the whistling of the amps stopped abruptly, and a man grunted from just behind the stage, "You're done *now*! You're *done*."

Brittany turned back in annoyance without moving her legs and sneered, "We're not done. Turn it back on!" But the man raised his eyebrows and scoffed, made a 'jack-off' motion with his hand followed by a toss in their general direction. Then he placed his gloved hand back on his M-16 rifle, slung high on his chest. He sashayed back to a group of similarly puffed-up men with unkempt beards, doughy blemished skin, big flabby biceps, tactical police vests, and black baseball hats.

Her new friend Karla strode to the stage on tiptoes in her shimmering robe with a pink bob wig, clapping her hands flamboyantly and warbling, "Brittany— that was so— amazing!" She slid her hand down Darren's shin, "I love your little pants!" Then she gestured to the mercenaries, "They're such *assholes*, oh my god."

Darren inquired, "What's going on?"

The buxom lady huffed, "Oh these boys always have to be in control. They're locking us down, or something."

Will leaned his bass on his cab and hopped off the stage, "What? When?"

"I guess whenever Kumar says so."

Cody rushed over to confer, "Are we rolling out now? We're good to go, right?"

Darren scanned the room, "Where's Martin?"

Karla waved her hand and hooted, "Mar-*teen*! Mar-*teeeen*!"

A neatly-coiffed gentleman about Will's height but with a thin, toned physique behind a tailored shirt approached, speaking enthusiastically with a Spanish accent, "Yes, that was amazing! *Yoonga Noons*! It was the best!"

Darren spoke urgently, "So your guy, Enrique. We just roll up, mention your name, and he'll hook us up with parts?"

"*Si*, yes, this is my job. Mr. Kumar exports many things. There are many fine cars but they no run, they no have windows. So we have chop shop in garage here where we fix cars. Aston Martin, Bentley, Rolls Royce. Enrique can find many things, if he no have he find."

Will asked, "Is it safe?"

"Goose Island is always safe, ver, ver safe. The streets is ver safe early evening. The nations no fight much at night, the dead no come around much in day. Sunset is ver safe everywhere."

Cody flexed his brow, "Will they let us park in the garage tonight?"

"*No se*, I'm sorry but *no se*. Sometimes they allow, sometimes no. They are ver worried about something tonight, ver worried."

Karla re-emphasized, "They're such *assholes*, oh my god."

Darren turned to his singer, "You're going to be OK here? We might have to stay out overnight."

Brittany buzzed her lips, "*Pfft*, yeah."

He whispered in her ear, "Look for us downstairs every twelve hours starting now. I don't trust the security here. If we don't see you in forty-eight hours, we come in shooting."

She laughed dismissively, then saw that he meant it in earnest. She hugged him and patted his back condescendingly. "You boys have fun. Try not to give away *all* the diamonds."

They grabbed their bedrolls and sleeping bags and retreated down the steps. Brittany grit her teeth as their guns — crudely wrapped inside the blankets — were considerably more conspicuous than when they had smuggled them in from the van. But the security tacticians were too interested in each other's ribaldry to notice.

She turned around to see nearly a dozen faces poised to engage her in conversation and revelry, and she pushed past them toward the water tank to freshen up and come down alone for a moment.

———————————

The few days after Indy were rough, and it took them a lot of time and resources to get their heads right and their van operable. She didn't understand what was going on with the engine, and even though she didn't know anything about car stuff she tried to be helpful, but her companions didn't appreciate her ideas. When they would drive or change camps, they would ask her to check out the flip phone for cell phone activity, and they did get a signal at one point.

While they were investigating the signal and she was bored, she browsed the phone for games and programs. There was a game called Snake, and she was good at the first few levels but it quickly became too difficult. The black and white low-res screen was small and she lost interest.

She opened the web browser and got an "error 404" signal instead of *nokia.com*. She got the same error from *billboard.com* and *yahoo.com*, but *aol.com* displayed a logo. At the time, she thought, *If that one works, other websites probably work, too. If only I could remember any websites.*

So she went to her fan club page — britneyarmy.com — and was surprised to see it was still up, and the message board had hundreds of posts in the past year. Most posts seemed like glitches full of random letters, but a handful were coherent, reaching out from one corner of the world or another. The message board was important to her because she was often given free reign on how she interacted with fans on just this one platform, and she remembered her login credentials immediately.

On the seventh or eighth page —posted years ago— a fan was looking for other survivors in the Britney Army near Chicago. Britney responded and was thrilled that the girl wrote back, but she didn't have an opportunity to stay in contact.

They hit the road shortly thereafter, and the road was difficult. And every mile or so, the boys had to dive out of the car to run a flank on a zombie horde or go off-road to avoid a possible human threat.

They rolled into the city through Darren's aunt's neighborhood, which appeared to have been carpet-bombed to oblivion. While the guys walked around to investigate, she received a message with her new friend's address. She couldn't admit to using the internet function on the flip-phone because of how insistent they were that smartphones turn people into zombies, so she lied and said she suddenly recalled the address of her cousin's flat. They showed up, were ushered in by security, and so far it was going extremely well.

Now the sun was setting, and they had a beautiful view from the 42nd floor. There were dwelling spaces on the back half of the building — retrofitted offices — where they had already enjoyed a peaceful and restful day and a half. She had already seen the sun set over the Chicagoland area from there and now got to see the reflection of the colors in the buildings and lake from the Eastward view.

The bottom half of the building was vacant, and a series of gates on every floor allowed the security tacticians to retreat little by little while eliminating the walkers during attack waves. Upon arrival, there were five or six guards. But there were more soldiers in the building today, presumably because Kumar Gyldenhal was present. Most of the attendees work for him or another of the billionaires on offshore yachts, and it was a coincidence that he had planned this rare visit on a day that Young Nuns was available to play.

Britney poured herself a mug full of water, stepped forward to look outside, and Karla brought her a bathrobe similar to her own. It was a strange offering given that Britney felt so beautiful and was happy to sport her toned curves and detailed visage. But then she looked at the oafish soldiers who leered at her and gesticulated crudely with an air of lustful grandeur. She accepted the pink floral robe but threw it over her shoulder defiantly, instead of concealing her provocative ensemble.

Karla asked in a hushed tone, "So is everything cool with your band? Like, with the Britney Army board?"

Britney matched her tone and answered, "Yeah, thanks for not letting on. I think they do actually believe that you're my cousin. Like, I know it's bad to be on the phone—"

"It's all good girl—"

"I just wanted to look around—"

"Treat yourself, girl—"

"You didn't tell anyone, did you?"

Karla squared her body, rested her hands on Britney's shoulders, then extended one pinky and whispered, "Pinky promise."

They made an oath, and Britney inquired, "How do you get online?"

"Kumar lets me use his computer sometimes. Jarod watches me do it and points a gun to my head. A fucking gun. He's such an *asshole,* oh my god. He calls me 'Toolie Toots.' I guess now some people can turn if they use a computer long enough. That's what happened to Jonathan."

"Was he… He was the one here who turned?"

"No, that was Marina. She had a fucking iPhone. She found it on the seventh floor in a desk. Nobody had any idea she turned until she ate half the girls on the 35th."

"So they have the internet on the ships?"

"They do literally whatever they want. They're smugglers. Honestly, they're the worst. But they don't want to go zombie. Jonathan couldn't pace himself and lost his shit. He started smuggling iPhones and doing shady shit for the dead until most of his crew got eaten. The ship ended up sinking."

Britney clutched her chest, "It feels so good to hear something from the world. Anything. The guys are super paranoid about this stuff. I didn't want to ask when they were around."

"Yeah, everyone here too, especially after Jonathan and Marina. It's like the… what did they call it? The *whatever ultimatum*. I don't know, I'm not really into politics."

"So what do you hear from California? I really want to get my kids."

"It's supposed to be bad, but there are still people there. Inland at least. I guess the East Coast is pretty much gone. West Coast and Midwest are hit or miss. Canada is a little better. Mexico is supposed to be good. China is fucked as bad as we are. England too. There are supposed to be a few havens but it sounds like everyone who isn't fucked with zombies is at war with another country."

"What about the South?"

Karla cackled, "Who cares?"

Britney looked down at her shoes, "I'm from Louisiana."

"I don't know, they're probably— like— I don't know."

Britney was expecting an apology but a mature young lady in a smart black dress stood on the stage and tapped an empty wine glass with a spoon. "Excuse me everyone, excuse me!" she said in a bold but sweet voice, her designer earrings bobbing playfully below the tight braids of her ornate hairstyle.

Britney jumped with a start when a security agent with a weak chin and patchy beard turned and shouted out, "Hey! Listen up!"

The lady bit her lip and nodded, then continued affably with sophisticated decorum, "Thank you Justin. For those of you who don't know me, I'm Tara—"

Another tactician whooped, "Yeah Tara, yee-ha!"

"—And Kumar and I would like to thank you for your warm welcome! Our brave servicemen have told us what a good time they have here, not just with Karla's girls but with all the friendly people in this community. Do we have anyone from the thirty-first floor?"

There was a light applause, and she quickly moved on. "How about the thirty-sixth floor? That's right! Hello Chuck, good to see you. forty-first floor? Yay! Fortieth floor? All right! And how about the forty-second floor!"

There was the biggest applause as Karla and the sex workers she employs squealed and rocked their bodies.

"But before I invite Kumar to say a few words, I want to give a special shout out to our brave security tacticians. Brad Hinkley! Timmy Durkins! Pappy Greiner! Hunter Avery! Chris Belcher…"

The list went on and Britney noticed how with each name one of the men received a series of slaps to the butt, a few complimentary grunts, and a curt nod from the others in the group. Some of them got a special informal recognition from one of the whores in the form of exposed flesh or a blown kiss. After about fifteen names, the men huddled up, engaged in an indecipherable chant, and bounded down the steps. Britney slipped into the pink robe and felt safer and cleaner than before.

Kumar stepped to the stage, a balding Indian man with wide-set eyes, a very short football-shaped head, woefully thinning hair, and narrow sloping shoulders. He was wearing very baggy pants of fine material, and a cheap button-down shirt comprised of overlapping Playboy logos with Teva sandals. "Hey, everyone! Sup!"

There was a polite and collegial response.

"I said… WAZZZUUUUUUUUUUP!"

There was a slightly stronger response and he then ran his mouth at a dizzying speed, "So I'm not going to tell the technicians because I've already talked their ear off again, and again. And furthermore I think they are primed and ready to go especially after that — shall we say— *aggressive* performance of rather violent music. It almost makes me want to join the tactical unit, but I'm afraid that is out of the question.

"And can I just say; Miss Britney Spears, it is such an honor for you to be here as well. Your band didn't stick around? They're in the back with the girls, perhaps? No matter, we are going to have continued entertainment from my tacticians.

"You see, there is the Folk Nation, and there is the People Nation. These are the *gangs*— so to speak— that do so much essential labor in this city. And I have yet been neutral in the matter, conducting business freely as I see fit. But a business opportunity with the Folk Nation has arisen that would result in monumentally favorable market conditions. And we will be aligning ourselves with them forthwith.

"What you are about to witness is a plan born of military expertise as well as economic acumen, the likes of which represent the future and vision of the ArvoCorp initiative in the former USA which will yield you— the shareholders, the very backbone of this company— exponential growth and stability on a scale your portfolio has not seen since September eleventh."

Brittany realized he was speaking to a mini camcorder set up on a tripod on the opposite side of the room.

"Now, if you would join me, we can see the future unfold before us."

She looked around the room and took a step back, eager for the room to clear out so she could relax by herself. But Karla squeezed her skinny wrist and drew her forward. "He's worth easily fifteen bill. Like, there are richer guys out there but… *Yummmm…*" She licked her lips and shimmied her shoulders. "Come on! I'll introduce you to everyone!" and

Britney graciously accepted.

Tara pressed 'play' on a heavy boombox and carried it along with the unwieldy tripod. The sound of heavy metal mixed with rap pumped out of the speakers.

Soooouuh! Are you breathing?

Soooouuh! How you breathing?

There was a slight bottleneck at the first gate, a man-sized door within solid metal sheets braced against the floor and wall with multiple bolts, rivets, and concrete. The security agent, Justin, held it open for people to pass through one by one. Next to the door, there was a grating made of steel rebar welded into a crude grid.

She continued down the stairs past different heavy steel gates that swung wide open from a hinge at the wall. Many of them were chain-link, but others looked solid. They all appeared to be locked in a wide-open position, which was a relief because on their ascent, they had to stop at each gate to clear security and open the doors.

At a certain point, Justin rudely shoved his way back to the front of the group, and at the twenty-eighth floor, there was another man-sized door, much like the one on floor forty-two. This time, as the group cleared the gate, she noticed that Justin had to reach through the grate to click the locks back in place.

On the 17th floor, they filtered into a vacant room with a dozen chairs by the East-facing windows and binoculars slung on each one.

Kumar stood by the row of chairs with his hands folded in front of him and blessed each attendee with a nod and a plastic smile. Tara beckoned people to the viewing area as she set the camera on the tripod and faded the music out.

Kumar spoke at the same insufferably fast pace, "In some ways this is a partnership, but the truth is we are buying out the Folk Nation. Their infrastructure and brand are invaluable resources, and we consider their labor structure optimal, even utopian. We offer them the real global trade network that takes them from being a nation in name only to a multi-national power player. While ArvoCorp is a fraction of their size, our market capitalization is billions greater than theirs.

"Our first offering to them is the eradication of their, that is to say 'our,' competition, the group known as People Nation who happen to be our neighbors. They have not been particularly bothersome as this is known to be their symbolic headquarters, with their strength and business apparatus located in the South of the metropolitan area. As part of our uneasy peace, we have allowed each other to clean up zombies in the streets from time to time, employing massive shows of heavy force that would otherwise be considered a threat.

"You may have noticed an increase of walkers in the past weeks, and this is not an oversight on our part but rather an intentional strategy employed to facilitate this ruse. At this very moment, our expert security tacticians are amassing outside of our building, and at any second, they will stage an assault. Not on the walkers but on the People Nation building, swiftly neutralizing the ground floor defenses and clearing the building of our new enemy. Tara?"

Tara unpaused the music, but Kumar beckoned, "No, track three, please. Track three."

> *Uh-huh, we bring you another disturbing creation...*
> *From the mind of a sick animal who can't see the*
difference...
> *And gets stupefied.*

Britney sat at a chair and took a pair of binoculars, but the security forces were merely milling about.

Karla came over with a glass of wine for her and sassed, "It's not the good stuff, but it's not the bad stuff either. Ben makes this shit that the staff likes to drink, and it tastes like puke. You should come out to the ship sometime, *mmm*, mostly you just lay around by the pool, and he talks like he does. He likes to rub sunscreen on the girls." She giggled naughtily.

"I mean, if you touch his thing, he'll give you champagne and bacon-wrapped scallops. I knew a girl who got a fully gassed up Escalade from him, and let me tell you, that bitch earned it, the shit he did to her. Some of the other CEOs pay better, but he's a pushover."

Britney wanted to be polite and entertain her host in this conversation but looked around for any way to change the subject. She noticed one of the girls leaning over a chair, causing her flabby belly to droop noticeably. "So are there, like, different prices for different girls?"

Karla chortled, then sneered. "Uh, yeah. Like, Shalia over there? She's been here as long as me. It's like, I love her, and she's amazing. And I love her. But like, that's what four babies does to your body, you know? She only works once a week, usually for one of the security bros. I think he pays her in bullets. Like, what the fuck. Like, when she was pregnant, Kumar would rub lotion on her belly. But it's just, ew. I'm never having kids."

Britney grimaced and traced a finger down her own abs, which were well-trained but not what they used to be before her boys.

Karla went on, "Speaking of lotion, look at Martin over there. I hear that when he works on cars he wears neat little gloves and an apron." She covered her mouth and giggled, "Look at his hair! Every morning he uses a personal trimmer to do his little nose hairs and clean up his sideburns. He won't anyone else use it and sometimes leaves the little hairs in the sink. He's married to Beatrice, and they make soap on the thirty-fifth floor. It's so gay, are you serious?"

Tara shouted, "Ladies and Gentlemen!"

The group shifted forward, and Britney looked down to the street to see the security squad line up and stalk down the street in formation. Then suddenly, a pickup truck rocketed out of their building's garage and crashed into the tower across the street. The men followed it, and gunfire erupted from inside the building and continued until a rising dust cloud increasingly obscured the view.

Britney wasn't keen on watching more violence and turned to look at Beatrice and Martin. They both looked very neat and well put-together.

"They don't have kids?" she asked Karla.

"Those two? Uh, no. He's probably gay."

Having interacted with Martin a little over the past couple of days, she recognized that he was very prim and tidy but didn't seem gay. She didn't care either way, but Beatrice was just as neat and well-put-together and it bothered Britney, who spent so much time being a frazzled mom. It hurt her to see a childless woman with the privilege of skin care, manicures, and tidy hairstyles.

"What does she do here? Martin's wife."

"She's a pastry chef. Mostly for Kumar. We get leftovers here sometimes, but she never bakes for us."

Britney glared at Beatrice with contempt, knowing that the lady could have an opportunity to have children but instead makes pastries and soap. Britney thought, '*And she has the nerve to maintain a sharp appearance.*'

Karla continued, "That's '*Mom*', sitting next to her. His kid is on floor forty-two with Beth. His name is Chuck, but we call him '*Mom*' because he's just, like, a big old fluffy mom. Look at him. Like, he could totally do security and make bank, but he's always doing mom stuff. We always see him passed out on the couch with a children's book on his gut."

"What does he do instead?"

"Underwater basket weaving." She laughed heartily and touched her breast, "That's what I call it. It's underwater welding, I guess. He barely ever works, and oh my god, you should see him in a wetsuit. *Barf.*"

A voice barked, "Hey, KNOCK IT OFF!"

Karla rolled her eyes, "Fucking Justin…"

He tilted back his head and shouted, "HO!"

Britney realized the music was paused, and Tara again addressed the group, "If you look closely, the dust is starting to settle and you can see the group ascending the building."

The music faded back in, and the lady in the black dress maneuvered the camera to focus on the action.

> *Do ya feel it?*
> *Ah shit…*
> *OO-WAH-AH-AH-AH!*

The assault team moved nimbly through the 8th, 9th, 12th, and 14th floors, and now that the sun was fully set, they could see much of the action. Teams of two and three cleared rooms and cubicles from positions of cover while gangland hoods either ducked behind desks or stood and fired blindly. The mercenaries were even smoother and better organized than Cody, Darren, and Will, whose obsessive discipline was already exhausting to her. Their hand gestures alone were so bold and clear that she almost felt like she could follow them herself.

The forces appeared to hold a position by a staircase, and Britney was bored listening to Disturbed. She turned to her pretend cousin, "Beth. She's the Nanny? Does she watch all the kids?"

Karla snorted, "Just as a favor. She mostly nannies Kumar's kids. They have like, five au pairs, but she rotates in a couple times a week. Did you ever try and talk to her?"

"Not much. She was asking about Arkansas since I'm from the South, but I haven't been there. She was really nice."

"Yeah, poor people are always nice *haha*. She was homeschooled in some church, and it's like talking to a brick. I heard her talking to Martin and she kept asking him about Spain. He kept correcting her and saying

Mexico but I don't think she knows the difference."

That touched a nerve with Britney, who people often regarded as a dumb blonde even though she now had black roots showing through her blonde hair, "Oof, that's pathetic. I mean, I was technically homeschooled but I mean, I'm really smart. Like, kind of book smart a little bit, but also really people smart. And emotionally. You know, there's emotion smart, too. And Spiritual."

A regrettably familiar, insistent voice blindsided their conversation. "There she is, the diva of heavy metal. I was once described by Forbes as the '*Punk CEO*,' and while they may have meant it as a pejorative, I wholeheartedly embrace it. You and your friends have eaten your fill? Slept comfortably? Karla requested that I extend my full hospitality, but you see…" he deepened his voice and spoke somewhat slower and breathier, "I have not yet *fully extended*." He raised his eyebrows and guffawed cheekily, exposing white schmutz on the corners of his mouth.

Brittany turned her body askew of her pursuer but took advantage of his advance. "That's so great to hear! Our van is running on empty. Martin says there is a garage. Maybe we can fill up with gas?"

He scoffed and continued his high-velocity blitz. "Miss Spears, I command oil tankers from Chicago to Venezuela moving barrels by the millions. I can give you enough fuel to your heart's content. Believe me, you should see how much fuel two Deutz marine engines consume. Have you ever been on a Martin Francis vessel? Perhaps tomorrow, you would accompany me to the yacht for cocktails in the afternoon?"

Karla shot Brittany a look of giddy jealousy, but the singer responded plainly, "It could be nice to have a relaxing day. Let me check with the boys when they get back and see if they're free."

Kumar stammered, "Well you see, tomorrow I have chef Didier Villefranche in the kitchen on *stagier* from Len Blavatnik, and he is preparing a unique Greco-Tuscan luncheon using flavor profiles of my own device, and I plan to open a *Domaine d'Auvenay*. Do you enjoy a *Grand-*

Cru? Perhaps the two of us can enjoy a luncheon, and I can have your friends shuttled over on my helicopter if they so choose?"

Karla's jaw dropped, "Ooh, Kumie! You finally have the chopper running!" She slipped one nude shoulder out of her robe, puckered her lips, and winked.

"Please excuse me, Mr. Gyldenhal?" Tara tapped him on the shoulder and peeled him into a huddle with Justin.

The billionaire apologized, "Would you excuse us for a moment?"

A plain but spunky girl skipped over wearing an understated blouse with a few girly ruffles over her scrawny shoulders and a pair of oversized capri pants that exposed her cylindrical cankles. She was Chinese but didn't have an accent. "Britney? Hey, I'm Stephanie. I don't think we've officially met. Do you know where Cody is?"

The girl and Cody had connected, and Britney was happy for her bandmate. "They went to work on the van. We have a bad carburetor, and I think the radiator is bad? And there are some fluids that are also bad. It's a really old van! Sorry, I don't know car stuff."

Stephanie chirped, "That's ok, I don't know a lot of stuff!"

She swayed, and Britney broached a conversation. "What do you know? You look like you know things."

She bowed her head humbly. "I just do genetic consulting. We have a lab on the 59th floor. It's mostly Kumar's friends. They're all obsessed with their progeny, but they're dealing with a shallowing gene pool. It's weird but not that interesting."

Britney looked down at the girl, with her side ponytail and eyeglasses that bore multiple improvised repairs, "Yeah, I get it though. I wonder how you guys manage relationships already. Like, there's nobody to date."

Karla smirked aggressively at Britney, but Stephanie continued unaffected, "I mostly stay busy. In my downtime, I try to find markers in the infected. I don't think there's a genetic cure, but I think we could learn something. So I hear you guys are going across—"

Karla primped her wig and interrupted, "That's one way to do it. Then there's Justin. He's tried to put the moves on, like, so many girls."

Stephanie scrunched her face, "Oh, he's sweet, though. He brings me flowers sometimes. Not in a creepy way, but he knows when I'm sad."

"Like, if you're that desperate, just pay up. There are twenty girls here. Is he cheap or stupid?"

The scientist hooted, "Oh, I like Justin. He's my friend. I think he just needs a relationship."

"He needs some Clearasil and a Stairmaster, *ew*."

Britney had just about had enough of Karla's continued insults, but thankfully Tara again commanded the floor, "Ladies and Gentlemen, once again, Kumar Gyldenhal!" She gestured for the audience to applaud.

Stephanie raised her hands and clapped feebly, her arms thin and puffy like funnel cake. Kumar continued babbling with the white spots on the corners of his mouth still visible, but Britney was exhausted by him and instead whispered to Karla, "So do people here not ever have to fight the zombies?"

Karla waved dismissively, "Yeah, like *Professor Ching-Chang* here would stand a chance. I go to the gym twice a week. There's one on the fourth floor and one on the yacht. I usually use that one. God knows we have to be ready because if we have to depend on *Officer Pud* over there, we'd be in trouble." and she gestured to Justin, who had his hand up to his earpiece.

"Now that bitch there, I'd like to see her take on a walker. I could go either way with that matchup."

Britney scanned the room and saw the lady she was pointing at. She had a very square face, wore a mismatched track suit, and stood at attention while grabbing her wrist in front of her body. Her ball cap was low on her face, causing her to tilt her head back very far to see past it. The posture caused her massive jaw even further out, and caused her eyes to squint aggressively.

Karla elaborated, "She's so fucking bossy and —let's be honest— she's fucking ugly. And I'm sorry, but it matters. It just does. Justin is security, so it's whatever. But she's the skipper for Kumar's tall ships, and everyone has to see her when they're going out for a party."

Britney looked at the lady, and her face twisted slightly. "What's her name?"

"Oh, that's Dana. She's always—" Her turned and her voice jumped up an octave and a half, "*Blaaaaine*!"

She wrapped her arms around a scrawny, unkempt young man with erratically-braided hair on his head and short, curly hairs bursting out from every orifice of his v-neck striped t-shirt. He spoke with a bored, disaffected, yet sassy cadence just like Karla. "I did so much ketamine today, oh my god. I think I finally told Ben to like, fuck off."

Karla spoke in baby-talk, "Britney, this is my boyfriend Blaine. Isn't he adorable?"

"Hi, I'm Britney! I just got here yesterday."

He didn't reply; he only rubbed his eyes and moped to Karla. "He's like, such a nerd, but now that he's a big shot, he acts like he can't do me a solid just because I drank all his wine —a lot of times— this one time.. Like, that was a year ago, and he could totally hook me up with power on the 9th floor, but he won't do it. Like, fuck OFF."

Karla whispered to Britney, "Ben's another uggo."

Her boyfriend continued impotently as she pet his head maternally, "Like, I was a big deal. I was grooming Fergy and Nay Nay, plus Jonathan's dogs, and he was just this white trash. So like, of course I drank his wine. Like, *what*? And now he's wiring up everyone's buildings and he's got his own floor and a truck. But don't treat me like I'm trash. I don't deserve—"

Justin hollered, "Everyone shut the FUCK up!"

The room became uncomfortably still and quiet enough for Britney to hear the radio.

"Choderboy One-Nine, do you copy?"

Justin muttered into it, "Roger, go 'head."

"Choderboy One-Nine, we're going to proceed. You need to have Simba in position."

"Affirmative, Punisher Twelve. We need ten mikes to get in position and provide overwatch."

"Choderboy One-nine, that's a negative. We want to proceed with the mission."

"Negative, Punisher Twelve. The mission requires that Simba be in position."

"Knoxville Nine, are you in position?"

A different voice on the radio responded, *"Roger that."*

"Execute."

Britney could see across the way that a charge had been detonated, and security squatted and ran from wall to wall until they filtered up the staircase to the next floor, and then the floor after and the floor after until they were too high to see. They were in groups of three or four, hiding behind walls and gunning down their foes with disciplined marksmanship while gang members jumped around and fired wildly.

Kumar's men moved fluidly, seemingly undeterred by the volley of bullets launched their way. It reminded her of the expert, choreographed dance moves of her backup dancers. They rolled over the defenders with synchronized movements like a tidal wave, but Britney could see more than a few of the assault team were limping to safety or tending to others' wounds.

A window not far from Tara and Justin pinged, and Kumar ran over to it, grinning as he stuck his finger in the bullet hole. "Tara, get this, record this over here." They improvised an interview in front of the bullet hole for their shareholders, but Britney kept listening to Justin's radio.

"Knoxville Nine, Shocker Seventeen. Move, move!"

"Violence of action! Move out, Spartans!"

Justin got on his radio, "Strike force, Simba is not in position. I have a negative on visual. I repeat, I have a negative on visual. Simba is not in position. Hold positions. I repeat, hold positions."

There was a pause on the other end followed by a single emphatic word: *"Execute!"*

Tara referenced her clipboard and jawed incisively at Justin, "They're supposed to wait. What are they doing? We need to have this on camera."

Justin barked back at her, "That's the least of our problems. They don't have any overwatch. They're going in blind."

Kumar's neck twitched, and he pointed at Justin as he shouted, "Fix this!"

Justin rolled his eyes, then shouted to the audience, "Alright, LISTEN UP! We're going up to the 28th floor. Move, move, move!"

The group sloshed toward the stairwell and awkwardly lined up while the boombox blared the aggressive rap-metal of Disturbed. Britney was squeezed against a plain and clean lady, in a blue blouse and black pants, with neatly coiffed wavy grayish-brown hair. "Oh, I beg your pardon, so sorry. You must be Britney Spears! I enjoyed your performance." She had a very sophisticated voice and held her head and body high.

Britney intoned, "Thank you! I know, it's kind of loud."

The lady smiled, "I tend to favor singer-songwriters, but I also enjoy musical theater. However, I *did* see David Bowie in concert. And Prince. Twice, as a matter of fact. They were both quite loud!"

"Yeah? Here in Chicago?"

"Indeed. I used to be a surgeon at Children's, but here I am." She sighed and chuckled affably, "So tell me about yourself, are you—"

The crowd ebbed and flowed as they approached the stairwell, and they were pushed in opposite directions. The woman squeezed Britney's elbow knowingly, "We'll catch up later. I'm Doctor Eleanor Hahn."

"Nice to meet you Eleanor! Uh, Doctor Eleanor."

Karla reached back and pulled Britney abreast of herself and Blaine as they ascended the steps. "Good thing I saved you before she pissed on your head. She thinks she's god's gift to humanity. Kumar even gave her the thirtieth floor, and I hear she grows her own food and even gets water deliveries."

Justin's radio was cut off from reception in the concrete stairwell, leaving the music to echo through the passageway. This time, all the gates were wide open, held in place by the secured padlock.

The entourage was held in place for a moment, and Britney couldn't hear the conversation over the music, but she looked up to see that one of the gates was still locked, and Justin was fussing with various keys to get it open.

Look at my face, look at my soul,
I begin to STUPIFY. Huh!
Look at my face, look at my soul,
I begin to STUPIFY. Huh!

There was a bold *"clink"* as the padlock opened and the improvised steel gate swung open; then, the attendees filtered into the 28th floor. At first, it was an obligatory queue, a large cluster of people politely waiting to get through. But then Britney felt a crush, and people were shouting in the disorienting reverberance. Soon, they pushed through into the 28th floor, which looked like an informal construction site lounge with a few tables, chairs, and culinary implements.

Justin shouted desperately into his radio, "Knoxville Nine, do you copy? Shocker Seventeen do you copy? Stiffler Thirteen, do you copy? Does anybody copy?"

Britney stepped to the window to see the opposite swarmed with zombies from lobby to penthouse, and they descended rapidly.

Dana, the skipper, shouted, "Oh my god, they're all over the street!"

A panicked voice bleated through the radio, *"Knoxville Nine, Shocker Seventeen, Punisher Twelve, does anybody copy? This is Centurion Eighty-Eight. Does anybody copy?"*

Justin shouted back, "Brian! Is the gate secure? This is Justin."

"Where is everyone?"

"They're gone. I don't know what happened. Walkers everywhere. Do you have the keys?"

"What do you mean they're gone? Do they need evac?"

"Negative. You need to secure the gates."

"Justin, you faggot, we don't leave our brothers behind. Ever."

"Brian, don't open the gate!"

Stephanie tiptoed up to Britney and clutched her arm. "Where did the soldiers go? They were just right there. Do you think Cody is okay?"

Britney held her close as they kept hearing the lone soldier's voice repeating, "Brian, come in. Brian, is the gate secure? Do not, I repeat; do not open the gates!" until he abandoned the radio and pushed through the crowd to run downstairs.

Martin and Beatrice held each other's hands and consoled one another. "It's just another wave."

"But the gates. The gates are open."

"Brian and Justin have guns, we are safe."

"Only one gate can be locked. The others are stuck open."

"He will lock. You see? He just go to lock."

Kumar held the radio and shouted into it, "Send everyone, I don't care. Give them a shrimp fork and have them swim for it. We are in dire need. Dire!"

Britney looked out the window again to see that the horde had mostly left the building, save for a few small clusters of zombies devouring the dead bodies of the tactical unit.

There was a loud *clang* and Justin re-entered the flat. "Everybody get a weapon."

Britney's blood ran cold. She had never been in a fight without Darren, Cody, Will, and their studied resolve. She put her hands on her cheeks and then checked the pockets of her robe, senselessly looking for the Smith and Wesson .22 revolver. She listened for a scrappy voice to shout out '*flank*' or '*fucking drive,*' or anything familiar from her bandmates, but instead there was silent helplessness.

Outside the building she could see flashes, reminiscent of the paparazzi that would assault her with blinding lights. That wasn't the part that hurt her, though; it was the many thousands of judgmental viewers each flash represented. Each viewer would mark her with whatever shortcoming they favored: she was too muscular or too girly, lacking ambition or an inattentive mother, too sexy or too mainstream.

Karla's piercing shriek brought Britney back into her body, and she saw the madam clutching her bloody elbow with her manicured hand.

Come on, come on get down with the sickness!
Come on, come on get down with the sickness!

Dana flipped off her ball cap and barked, "Everybody down! Everybody down. They're shooters!"

Another volley ripped through the room, and Brittany watched a muscular, mustachioed personal trainer take one to the chest and crumple, then a brothel girl clutched her stomach and landed in the fetal position, writhing and screaming.

Britney pulled Karla to the ground, removed her robe belt, and wrapped it tightly around her upper arm. She tied it off, twisted it, then put Karla's other hand on the knot. "Hold this tight, don't let it go."

Then she crawled over to the gutshot girl and pleaded, "Lay on your back for me. You'll be OK, lie back."

The girl did so with great pain, and Britney looked at her. "I'm going to put pressure on the wound. It's going to hurt."

She began to protest but Britney didn't wait, pressing both palms to the hole in her belly and thrusting downward with her shoulders. The girl only whimpered.

Chuck ran in and out of view, passing people various items like lengths of rebar, knives, bricks, and fire extinguishers.

Dana hollered from the window, "They're coming into our building."

Charles shouted back, "We have to go to forty-two!"

Justin ordered, "We stay here, gather what we can, treat the wounded, and reinforce the gate until they breach. Then we go up as one."

The skipper stood on a chair and clapped her hands. "You hear that?" There was mostly silence except for Shalia wailing. "Somebody help her. We make a stand here. We need to make spears to stab through the gate. Justin is going to shoot the shit out of them but we've seen these fuckers at the gates and they'll get through it at some point. We can spear them through the grating. Get ready to move the wounded. Brit, Autumn is gone."

Britney looked down to see that the girl had bled out. There was now an absence of gunfire from the opposite building, so she walked to the window to see that the neighboring building was vacant. However, at the ground level, a mob steadily streamed into their tower.

She heard the first few pops from the stairwell and saw Justin and his rifle set at a short, long slot designed for that purpose. Beatrice was standing by with a broken broom handle, and Chuck and Dana stood right behind, wielding different angles of rebar.

Britney looked around to see Dr. Hahn inspecting a French man with a wounded shoulder. She saw that Martin had his arm around some of the brothel girls, and he was calming them down with such graceful empathy that Shalia even laughed through her tears.

Blaine was stalking around, kicking buckets and tossing concrete chips feebly at the window with his shaggy hair hanging partially over his eyes. "This is great. Fucking great."

Karla was sulking on the floor nearby, still holding her arm and blubbering, "Eleanor! Eleanor! I'm fucking shot, Eleanor!" Britney looked down, saw a stainless steel spoon, and carried it over. "Here," she said, and used it to tighten the tourniquet, then took the remaining length of the robe belt and tied it in place. "When we get upstairs, I'll loosen it for a second."

Karla cast an impudent glance and shook her head with self-pity.

"It's so you don't lose your arm. They taught me first aid in Columbus," but the pink-haired girl continued begging for the surgeon.

"Eleanor! Eleanoooor!"

Justin's gunshots were steady now, and the staircase swelled with the murmuring of voices and then crescendoed to a metallic boom as the wave hit the gate. Beatrice jammed her stick through the grating, first with a probing motion and again with violence. She continued thrusting the spear until it became wet with blood and slipped from her hands.

As Justin continued to fire into the horde, Dana took over and jabbed a thin piece of sharp rebar, but she lost control of it as a dozen hands got a hold of it and pulled it into the other side. They then reached through the grating, nearly getting a hold of her as well. Chuck stepped up and shouted,

"Move back," then swung a large piece of concrete using a protruding length of rebar as a handle. He continued bashing it against the grate, pulverizing entire limbs.

Britney walked over to a young man with short bleach-blonde hair sitting on the floor poking at the bloody sole of his foot. "My flip-flop broke, my foot's all fucked up."

"Let me see… It's not that bad, there's just some glass in there." She sat on the ground, set the foot on her lap, and picked at it for a moment.

Kumar squatted next to them, running his motorized mouth into the radio while Tara rifled through a binder. "We are at 409, how many times do I have to say it? Yes, we will meet you on the roof. Well, who the hell does have a helicopter? My helicopter seems to be inoperable at the moment. Well, it was running flawlessly when I offered to sell it to you. Ok, ok, let's be honest. Your cargo vessel was not exactly in prime condition either…

"No, you moron, of course I asked Wally. So how many units can you send? Do you still have the quick reaction force? You do know that your ships only sail to Cuba on my good graces. If you'd like to continue… Well for the love of fuck, give your janitor a gun and send him here. Anything…

"Ok, thank you. I won't forget this, Samir. Thank you so very much. We really are in a bind here. Wally is sending his Blue Brigade. If you and your staff can come and offer support— What? How can Wally be at O'Hare if he just told me they're here? Are you calling me a liar? I can see the Blue Brigade right now. Yes. So we will see you soon? Thanks a million, Samir. K-Money out."

He set the radio on the floor and buried his head in his hands. Tara squeaked, "Is the Blue Brigade really coming?"

Kumar dropped his hands to the ground and glared at his assistant, "No, they're not fucking coming. They're all leaving me, the swine. Give me another." and he stood and handed the radio back for her to find a different channel.

Britney removed the glass from the boy's foot and noticed he had a utility knife as a weapon. "Let me see the knife." She cut off a sleeve from the lad's t-shirt, doubled it up, and slipped it snugly over his foot as a bandage, then handed it back to him.

The rattling of the gate grew louder and louder, and Beatrice was again stabbing wildly through the grate. There were a couple more shots from the other side of the gate, and the defenders all piled into the flat from the stairwell. "Shooters!"

Dana rallied, "We can't stop. We have to keep fighting. It's just a .22."

There was no response but a faint murmur.

"I said we have to KEEP FIGHTING."

The gate was now making more and more clanging as the horde had broken something, and the the barrier had a bit of free play.

The skipper barked, "Everyone upstairs! Justin first, you open the gate to forty-two. Then anyone without weapons. The rest of us hold them here and fight until they break through."

Justin hollered, "Ten-four!" and tumbled up the stairs.

Britney steadied the boy to his feet with his arm around her neck and helped him limp toward the door. Kumar and Tara pushed past to ascend the steps in the first wave, and Martin shepherded the distraught behind. Britney turned back to look for stragglers and yelped, "Karla! Blaine!"

Blaine, slouched against the wall, looked up and whined, "Where are we going now?" But Britney and the wounded boy were already halfway to the stairwell.

After she had helped the injured blonde to the landing, she turned back around to get Blaine and Karla as they dilly-dallied behind. She left the boy at the landing and started to walk down the steps, but Karla now strode into the passageway. She berated her partner, "It's just always about your drama, and I'm over it. I'm just done with it. I'm done. I'm *so* over it."

He lurked through the threshold, hunched and irate "You don't even
—"

A wet, bloody hand grabbed his elbow and yanked hit. A middle-aged man wearing duct tape wrapped bath towels squeezed his head tightly and then ripped open his neck with a series of bites as if it was an ear of corn. Another set of hands from a muttering long-haired hipster grabbed his leg and tugged greedily as the other man munched upward from his ear to his wide, terrified eyeball.

"HELP ME! OH SHIT FUCK! OH SHIT FUCK! HELP!"

Karla was screaming and clutched the railing with one hand, flapping in the air with the other. She scooted backward up the stairs using her feet and butt.

The hipster gave up on tugging the body back across the gate and instead flayed open the remainder of Blaine's face with his fingernails. Beatrice gored the attacker through the kidney with her broom-spear but it didn't stop him from muttering as he devoured the young man's nose.

She speared him a few more times, but the gate was now rocking on a single hinge with a deafening *ka-chung, ka-chung.*

Chuck ran in with the fire extinguisher and flattened the hipster's skull, then swung and clocked the older man. The hipster dropped to the ground, stone dead, but the other had enough initiative to drag the still-squirming hairy young dog groomer back across the broken grating through which they arrived. The clothing and skin were torn off as soon as the body passed through the grate, and within seconds, the body was quartered, butchered, and devoured.

The underwater welder then took his concrete and rebar hammer and hurled it mightily into the hole in the grating where it knocked the army backward.

Britney reached for Karla and pulled her by her hand up to the landing, then pushed her to ascend the stairs in front of her. A shot rang out, and Beatrice fell full force into the wall, streaming gallons of blood from the bullet wound in her head.

Dana yelled, "Everybody run!"

Everyone bolted up the stairwell. Britney implored them, "You guys go first; you go ahead."

But Ben the electrician and Dr. Eleanor stayed right behind the pair, "You're doing fine." "We're here for you."

Britney helped the boy limp past floors twenty-nine, thirty, and thirty-one when a couple of young poshes and a hipster caught up to them. Chuck hit the preppy boy in the head with the extinguisher and then kicked the soccer mom down the stairs.

The hipster girl mumbled as she menaced them with covetous

fingers, "They're magically delicious. Frosted Funky Charms," and Chuck swung and hit her upside the head with the big red cylinder.

She kept muttering as her jaw hung by a thread. "Mazhicly delizhuzh, they're mazhicly delizhuzh. Frozhted—"

Dana jabbed her in the eye with her rebar, then raised it high and gave two forceful strikes on her crown resulting in a catastrophic *squish.*

They ran past floors thirty-two, thirty-three, and thirty-four when Britney stopped. "Listen!"

Chuck rested the extinguisher on the floor. "Justin still hasn't opened the forty-second floor gate."

Eleanor inquired, "What do we do?"

The skipper hollered, "Keep going!"

And they went up another floor when a noisy *boom* echoed up the stairs, and a dull roar started to crescendo.

Britney slid the hobbled young man to Eleanor. "The zombies broke down the gate."

Dana shook her head and pointed up the stairs, bellowing, "Run!"

But Britney waved everyone past, taking up the rear and following the group past floors thirty-five, thirty-six, and thirty-seven. The muffled roar sharpened and she could hear moans and hisses right at her heels.

At last, she rounded the corner of the 40th floor and saw the entirety of Kumar's entourage huddled against the gate in horror. Just then, a crusty hand reached out and grabbed her ankle, laying her flat on the steps. More hands grasped her leg, and she could feel mouths and teeth rubbing against her wriggling calf, trying to acquire an angle to take a solid mouthful of her flesh.

Britney spun around, now set upon on all sides by the walkers, and kicked until she had enough space to crab-walk up the steps and face the assailants, screaming "Stop!"

Shouts and cries echoed around the hallway, although they came not from the zombies but from her new friends. Soon, the only coherent sounds were Shalia's prayers, Justin bumbling for the right keys, and Kumar shouting at him uselessly, "Open the door! Open the door! Open the door!"

Britney could see the front line of greasy, tattered walkers, comprised of an overweight big-eyed pubescent girl with jet black hair, several square-jawed frat boys in polo shirts and Cubs jerseys, a big-nosed, barefoot Eastern European man wearing a gold chain, and a very tall hipster with a neon tank top and cyclist's hat. Behind the vanguard, a woman wearing a black turtleneck and enormous horn-rimmed glasses squinted at the pop star and then at her cell phone. She scratched her head with her pistol, put her phone between her teeth, and began to load more pill-sized cartridges directly into the gun.

The horde was still surging and moshing as the floors below still heaved lustily toward their prey, but the front lines only gazed at the pop star with empty eyes, attempting to hold their ground against the crush behind them.

The metallic click of an unlocked padlock rang out through the stairwell, and the survivors jammed through the gate. Britney backpedaled up the steps as the mob pushed closer and closer. "No. You stop! Bad!"

A scrawny teenage boy in an Abercrombie shirt circumvented Britney and strode two stairs at a time only for Chuck to bash his head against the concrete wall with the extinguisher and then kick his limp body into the Cubs fan.

The tall hipster lunged at her and touched her shoulder impudently, muttering "Ba, bau, Hit me baby, *babybaby*. Nothing but the hits, neh. Hits and acquits. *babybaby*... If the glove don't fits…" He lunged again and laid a scratch across her cheek, and she slapped his hand, reiterating, "No. No! Stoooop-*puh*!"

The bro in the pink polo shirt imitated the hipster and managed to poke crudely at her face, one of his fingers penetrating her lips and scratching her gums.

She admonished him, "Staapit-*tuh*!"

A small girl set upon Britney with clawed hands spinning like windmills, but Britney kneed her in the head, causing her to disappear under the horde's advancing feet.

"Britney! Hurry!" She looked back to see Justin preparing to secure the door.

She reached down to the leather holster strapped to her thigh and withdrew the metal AK-47 magazine loaded with thirty steel-cased full-metal jacket rounds, bashed the hipster and the big-nosed man on the side of the head, then turned and sprinted through the gate.

It slammed shut, brutalizing a dozen zombie fingers in the process.

Justin and the other fighters collapsed in the entryway while Shalia and Chuck rushed to the back to see their kids. Beth came out to meet them, wide-eyed and innocent, pleading, "What's going on? What happened? Are we in trouble?"

Martin walked toward the gate, "Beatrice?"

Justin wheezed, "She's dead."

Chuck added, "We lost Autumn, Peters, and Amanda downstairs. And Blaine is gone."

Stephanie escorted Martin away to console him in private, but she turned and asked, "Where is Eleanor?"

Chuck looked around. "I don't see Ben either. I could have sworn I saw them on the stairs. They must have got him."

Karla snapped, "No. They left us, the assholes. Are you *serious?!*"

Britney walked over to the nanny, who was still fixed in a doe-eyed stare. "Hey Beth, I'm Britney. Kumar's security went on a raid, but something went wrong, and a whole wave of these things stormed in. We need weapons. Anything. Are there any guns here?"

The southerner wrinkled her nose, "Guns? Umm, I have a hair dryer."

Britney paused and scanned the girl's blank expression.

The girl tilted her head, "Does that help?"

She winced, "Why don't you go check on the kids."

Beth nodded and returned to the back room.

Stephanie yelled out, "Hey! We need to get to work." Her voice didn't project like Dana's, and her words sounded like the beeping of a small car. "Barricade the door! Use whatever you can find!"

Darren and Will's speaker cabinets went first, and the amalgamation of the Young Nuns gear practically sealed the door. They then lifted an island from the kitchen area to bolster it and stacked chairs for reinforcement. People began to pile whatever they could find; cinder blocks, mattresses, and broken dehumidifiers.

Justin stood up, unslung his AR-15, and dropped his backpack to the ground. He tore through it and tossed some items around. He yelled "Martin!" and tossed the grieving young man a tactical knife. "Chuck!"

Britney yelled, "He's with the kids!"

"Well, we need him. Shalia and Beth can watch the kids."

Shalia came out to join the group along with Chuck and said "Unh-Uh, no way. I got them kids. Ain't nothing gonna happen to them, I swear. I swear to *god*. Chuck, you good. And yo, homegirl can scrap too. Beth gonna whoop ass. Belie' dat."

Chuck stepped forward and took a blood-streaked bulletproof plate carrier from Justin.

"Justin, you're wounded."

Justin uttered, "Fuck, fuck." and dumped the remainder of his backpack on the ground.

Shalia picked up a big flashlight, swung it to feel its heft, and then rapped it into her palm a few times.

Dana picked up a spool of paracord and began lashing the barricade together, while Stephanie handed out kitchen knives, saucepans, fire extinguishers, and broom handles to the twenty-odd whores, domestic staff, artisans, and luxury purveyors who had not yet joined the fight. Some of them held the items limply by their side, others rocked back and forth and prepared their muscles for combat, and a few, Karla included, immediately set the items on the floor and wept.

There was another series of shots from the gate, and the clanging intensified.

Everyone looked to Justin for leadership, but he sat cross-legged and buried his face in his hands. "There's no more ammo. Knoxville company took it all."

Stephanie crouched down and put her hand on his shoulder, "Justin, are there any guns on this floor?"

He shook his head, "No. Only security has guns. We cleared it before Kumar came."

Karla moaned from the other side of the room, "We can't afford guns anyway, not on what they pay us."

The gate outside rattled noisily, and a large metal piece clattered to the ground.

Shalia clicked her tongue, raised a finger and chimed, "I gotchu."

The gate started to shake rhythmically with an abrasive grating sound.

Britney pulled out the magazine from her thigh holster and offered it to the gunman, "Cody said these won't work with your gun."

Justin crawled forward in anticipation but then sank back on his knees. "Wrong caliber."

Shalia returned with a big stack of boxes balanced on her hands, "I got nine milli, fi-fi-sik, bu'shot, foty-five…"

She was startled and dropped the boxes, running to the back room as the gate crashed down and the screaming, moaning zombies were right outside the room, pounding at the barricade with closed fists and scrabbling at the wood with their fingertips.

Justin reached into his chest rig, pulled out three empty magazines, and tossed them to Stephanie. "Reload!"

She shook her hands with anxiety "I- I don't know…"

"Figure it out!"

She knelt down and rocked back and forth to soothe herself as she tore open the boxes until one seemed like it would fit, then started jamming rounds in.

Shalia briefly re-emerged as she forcefully shoved Tara and Kumar from the sanctuary of the kids' room into the fray.

The first few attackers peeked through the barricade and Justin ran right up to doorway to blast them with headshots, but they were quickly replaced by one if not two more.

Justin's gun went *'click',* and he shouted, "Mag!"

Stephanie stood and yelled, "It's not full, but here it comes!" She bravely stood, squared her shoulders, wound up, and threw the magazine, which flubbed at the ground two feet in front of her.

Justin retrieved the fresh mag as Stephanie called to some of the onlookers, "Kumar! Tara! Come help me load!" Kumar and Tara escaped to the far side of the room by the windows and kept fiddling with the radio, but a couple of cooks named Sasha and Doug timidly obliged.

Justin's AR sang once more, this time claiming bodies that had already climbed over the barricade. The assemblage itself started to shift, and the entire mass of it budged toward the center of the room like a football sled. Justin strafed and sent rounds through the doorway, and the instant the rifle clicked Stephanie was by his side to swap the empty clip for a full one.

Chuck ran to the right flank of intruders and bashed in skull after skull with the fire extinguisher. A black-haired financier in a ripped white dress shirt, a curly-haired realtor in a wool skirt, a masturbating hipster in sunglasses, and a cardigan all fell with a bell-like tone.

Dana ran up to his six o'clock and swung the rusty rebar viciously, sometimes catching a zombie in the head or knee, sometimes thrusting to push them off the underwater welding father.

But by the time Justin was done with his magazine, they were overrun, grappling with zombies in hand-to-mouth combat. Martin strode forth and buried his blade in a teenage girl wearing booty shorts emblazoned with *Juicy* and then jammed it three times in the neck of a fat man in sweat pants.

He continued his offensive forward, reluctantly followed by a few working girls with kitchen implements who put the wounded zombies out of their misery, but a burst of machine-gun fire pealed into the room, paralyzing everyone with fear. Britney turned to see that Tara's head was now partly splattered across window and partly splashed across Kumar's horrified face.

Britney stepped forward and shouted, "Stop!"

The entire procession halted like a herd of cattle and looked at Britney.

Three yuppies entered the room, each with an AR15 in one hand and a phone in the other. They scowled into their phones, and the rest of the horde crowded around them, desperate for the dopamine rush they got from each glance at the unintelligible glowing rectangle. The first one, a dead-eyed lady with grayish-brown hair and a khaki skirt. Another gunner wore an *Umphrey's McGee* shirt with a big wooden beaded necklace and long curly hair. The third gunman was a large, white, three-hundred-pound bald man wearing a tattered gray suit. Behind them, fifty walkers filed in, lusting to view the phones and consume the inhabitants, then fifty more.

The yuppies curled their lips and scowled at their phones while the others shifted their eyes listlessly. A doctor wearing OR scrubs staggered around aimlessly with his eyes rolled back in his head, smacking his hard hooked penis with disrespectful vigor.

A zombie girl in red pants and a bomber jacket ignorantly floated over to the injured curly-haired boy and scratched at his legs violently as he defended himself with open-handed slaps.

"Hey!" she yelled. "Hey! No!"

The girl backed off for a moment and then resumed scratching, but the boy yanked her to the ground, rolled over her, and slashed her across her throat with a utility knife until she stopped clawing.

The blonde pop star screamed, "I said NOOO-*wah*!"

The group scrambled to find refuge behind Britney, but the horde kept advancing, albeit slowly. Justin reached down to get a fresh mag, but two boys in high school basketball jerseys galloped out from the pack and slammed him to the ground, bracing their feet on the ground to get better leverage as they attacked his head and neck with their jaws. Stephanie and another man tried to get a hold of them but they both suffered bites and scratches.

Louder gunshots sent shockwaves through the air, and the stairwell lit up like the fourth of July. The *boom, boom, boom* came closer and closer, and soon innards and outards were flying out of the horde like mardi gras. Ben and Eleanor let loose sixteen shotgun rounds from semi-automatic cannons and burst through the vanguard before the yuppies could level their guns. But before they could neutralize the gunmen, they exhausted their shotgun ammo and rolled to the corners of the room to reload.

Chuck tackled the jam band fan, and Dana blindsided the armed lady with a spear thrust that went through her eyeball and out the back of her skull.

Justin kicked the first boy off him with both feet, reloaded his mag, and shot him as he pounced again. He then aimed his rifle and put seven rounds into the bald gunman, yet the man kept creeping forward.

Britney took out her steel magazine and hammered Justin's other attacker over the head until he quit moving.

Justin picked targets from the crush of walkers still flooding into the room. Britney looked over to see that the bald zombie was now steadying his rifle to take a shot at Justin, but his head and torso disintegrated into a pulp. Bethany stood a couple feet away holding a smoking gun she retrieved from the hippie and asked with deadpan seriousness, "Is he dead?"

The zombies fanned out on all sides like an oozing liquid as Justin and Bethany's rifles mowed down the threats at the middle of the room. Some attackers crept in from the flanks, and Dana, Martin, and Chuck set about stabbing, thrusting, clubbing and grappling the invaders.

Britney's charm was no match for the sheer volume of bloodthirsty waddling drones, but one-on-one, her face would still cause an individual zombie to stand still and allow her to bludgeon it with her Kalashnikov hammer. She stood guard, defending the reloading effort, which was now bolstered by a couple of bags of rifle ammo plundered from the dead yuppies.

She heard a pathetic plea squeak, "No, no no, NO NO NO!"

Britney turned back to see Karla huddled against the glass, pulling her robe tight against herself as she closed her eyes and turned away from the lurking feeders. The zombies laid into her unceremoniously, kneeling around her to graze on her flesh like sheep. At first, her cries were hysterical, then they became anxious, resigned, and ultimately a wet gurgle.

Ben and Eleanor's shotguns roared once more, cutting off the flank from the unit and pushing the advancing dead back behind the barricade while the encircled survivors fought for their lives.

The doctor in OR scrubs floated past, still masturbating vigorously while also lazily gnawing the bloody flesh from the bottom of Kumar's severed head.

The gunshots ceased, the group's four guns and waning stash of ammo being insufficient to keep up with the zombies still pouring in from the stairwell. The group consolidated at the velvet-curtained corridor to the back rooms, swatting and slicing at the mindless attackers. A broomstick-wielding young man got pulled into the horde and devoured, then a scrappy girl with a brick in each hand. A golf pro was shot by the turtlenecked yuppie, and a muscular, green-haired whore was killed after trying to retrieve another rifle.

Ben fired off two shots and then beat at the vanguard with the butt of the shotgun. Eleanor was already empty and swung her 12 gauge like a bat, but a bloody hand grabbed it and it was lost in the sea of moaning bodies. Beth stood back, waiting for Doug to shake free the last few rounds from the final ammo bag.

Justin aimed steadily and took out five of the biggest threats until his gun clicked. Doug shrugged and held up a magazine. "Last three rounds."

A streak of negligent automatic rifle shots flew from the ceiling to the floor. A few zombies were killed, but none of the survivors. Britney stood on an empty bucket and saw that a tall, floppy-haired yuppie with busted spectacles and a rifle shoved through the mob. She also saw that the zombies had stopped streaming in from the stairwell, so this was likely the last of the horde.

Justin fired, and the shot went wide, going through a garbage bag-clad hipster's pierced nose. He fired once more and punctured the shooter's chest, but he nevertheless leveled the gun and squeezed the trigger, recklessly spraying hot lead in their direction until Justin's bullet painted a blossoming crimson flower in his forehead, leaking down his face and onto his tailored shirt as he sank to the ground.

The zombies pushed past the downed gunman, but Stephanie dove in to recover his body and was instantly set upon by the bloodthirsty. Dana yelled out, "Help her, push them back! Get the ammo!"

Britney pushed at the group with all of her strength but felt no reaction, not even the slightest response or budge as her comrade was trampled. She pulled back and saw that her entire arm was bitten up and bleeding.

More shots rang out, and it sounded like a whole yuppie army had entered to reinforce the sixty or seventy poshes and hipsters, who were just moments away from eating the last of the building's inhabitants. The mob stirred and shifted, then broke into two confused factions; one ran toward the exit while the other still lunged at the survivors.

Britney and her new friends pushed once more, and this time were able to pull Stephanie from underneath the pile. She was gasping for air and covered in blood, but Stephanie dumped her hard-won bag of ammo on the pile of empty magazines and started loading.

The crowd was now thin enough for her to see that it was not an army of yuppies that had entered the room, it was the remaining Young Nuns. They swung into position, standing abreast with Justin, and turned body after body into piles of fleshy debris.

Will emptied his shotgun and threw it back to Britney with a bandolier of 12-gauge shells, then he drew his Glock 19 and popped off 9mm rounds into hunched bodies. Eleanor and Ben moved to help her load Will's gun, and then Ben loaded his from the bandolier.

Cody's AK was empty, so Will tossed him the Glock 17 from his shoulder holster. Darren's rifle had already exhausted his ammo, and he, too, was down to his pistol.

But with Ben now blasting basketball-sized holes in their foes and Justin racking a full magazine into his rifle, the remaining dozens of assailants fell like flies.

Will ran over to Britney, "What the hell happened?"

She sobbed, "I don't know! There was a raid and it all got fucked."

Stephanie ran over and kissed Cody's cheek as he clutched her waist and said to his singer, "The whole island was locked tight. You could tell something was about to go down." He turned, aimed the Glock, and blasted an injured posh lady in pajama pants and a sports bra before she could rise up again. "Babe, you're hurt!" He said, gesturing to Stephanie's wounds.

Dana came over, gave Darren an earnest, brotherly hug, and then stepped back and put her hands on her hips. "It was a setup. I don't know who or what for, but someone played Kumar. We have to get out of here."

Beth asked, "Where is Kumar?"

The blonde boy with an injured foot answered, "He tried to hide in the bathroom, but they got him."

Beth continued, flummoxed, "So where do we go?"

Chuck stormed out of the back bedroom with his little boy. "We can't stay here."

Martin announced, "Attention everyone, there are five cars in the basement that I can give. They all run, and there is some barrel of gas."

Chuck eaned into Martin's face aggressively, "Listen, I'm taking Shalia's family and Beth. We're taking the Escalade, and you're going to give us enough gas to get to Canada.

Martin clasped his hands, "I think is good, but I cannot promise."

Will barked, "We need at least twenty-five gallons."

Martin gestured broadly, "I think everyone want you have anything."

Eleanor called out in a small but confident voice, "We're going to the ship. Ben, Dana and I. Stephanie, you too? We don't have a plan as of yet, but we will call a council in ten minutes."

Darren stepped up abreast with the rest of the band, looked around at the piles of dead bodies and huffed, "Load-out is going to suck."

8.

Pay to Play

"Are we out of gas? Are we in trouble?" Britney whipped back the hood of her drug rug and braced her bandaged arms tightly as her voice escalated from desperation to panic.

Will kept his eyes on the road and responded coolly, "I just shut off the engine to save gas. We're going to coast into this town."

Cody and Darren charged their rifles as Will wrestled with the van until it coasted to the shoulder of a small town street. They quickly vacated the vehicle, split into two divisions, and held their positions. Will and Britney were crouched one car ahead of Van Hellsing and waited to see if anyone would come to investigate.

The highways were bombed out and rife with zombies, so they took the country roads. They encountered many traps and shooters, and found the worst thing they could do was to try and speed through. So instead, they set their own ambush as soon as they reached the outskirts of each town, hoping that friends or foe would come to them.

Zombies were easy to recognize, and the band could usually muscle their way through. Hostile humans were overly eager and eventually left their roadblocks and sniper nests to hunt them, at which point they could use a combination of gunplay and fancy driving to push past. They didn't know what an encounter with friendly people would look like, but they needed to find out in a bad way. Cody and Darren were down to about fifty rounds each, and they had no shotgun shells, gas, water, or food.

Will thought about Maddy and what she might be doing at this moment. Perhaps she would be lying on the couch, re-reading *The Da Vinci*

177

Code, then Rick would storm in to guzzle a jelly jar of water and cast a fistful of cherry tomatoes into the fruit bowl. He would reach down to kiss her cheek and croon, 'My little muffin…' before going outside to yell at Crystal and Dan Parker.

He looked up and thought, *"Where the hell am I?"* His thoughts moved slowly, and his vision faded until he remembered that he was with Young Nuns and they had driven West from Chicago.

They wasted a couple of days around Rockford trying to find a replacement carburetor and radiator, even though the carb the Indianapolis boys rebuilt was working fine and the radiator patch job only leaked a cup a day.

A looter king in Iowa tried to stick them up at gunpoint after offering to barter. As a result, Will killed a man for the first time, but he was too hungry and stressed to have feelings about it.

They made it to Kansas City, MO, found it to be full of zombies, and it took them the rest of the day to scavenge some gas and get across the Missouri River.

Will scanned the perimeter, but he only saw burned-out cars and dilapidated houses. The biggest problem with their counter-ambush technique was that it took a very long time. They might wait for an hour or two before proceeding to the next town. Will knew it had only been twenty minutes, but he was bored and exhausted. He attempted to make the sound of a cawing crow, but the words just came out in a low, disaffected *"Ca-ca,"* and he abandoned his discretion and trudged over to where Darren and Cody were crouched behind a dumpster.

He cleared his throat, "Let's do me and Darren with you and Britney. We'll go down to that gas station. You guys check these houses for food."

Cody nodded wordlessly, and they all retrieved tools for their tasks. Will put a cordless drill in an empty backpack, along with a long funnel, a thin rubber tube, and a couple of empty plastic jugs. Britney asked, "How long until we leave?"

Darren sighed, "We don't have anywhere to go. It's barely what, nine?"

Britney flipped open the phone and corrected him, "10:13. Fuck, there's a bar."

There was a collective groan, and Cody asked, "Just one?" She nodded and he spit, "Fuck it, let's just get supplies and then roll out of here."

Cody tapped Britney on the shoulder and led her toward a row of houses, turning around to say, "Shoot anything edible."

Will chortled and started striding away toward a ransacked gas station clustered with busted cars and debris. A small town gas station like this would surely have been repeatedly looted, but if the car's tanks hadn't been drilled out, there might be enough backwash in each to add up to a gallon.

He thought about how far he would go to eat something.

When he worked at *Fa-Heat-O's* restaurant, he would close out his shift and make two burritos, usually something experimental for himself, and a 'Chicken 'n Rice Cheese-a-Rito' with extra lettuce and sour cream (hold the jalapeños) for Maddy. On his way home, he'd stop at Hollywood Video and rent a movie, maybe *40 Year Old Virgin* or *Wedding Crashers*. But if he wanted to get some 'under the shirt,' he'd rent *Garden State*. One time, he rented *The Notebook* and got to third base but had to withdraw because, like clockwork, Rick came down to lock up at 11:25 PM and would have undoubtedly murdered Will if he caught him fingering his daughter on the living room sofa.

Any good burrito filling needs to be marinated and slow-cooked. Venison wouldn't be fatty enough, but maybe something like duck or goose could work. They had never hunted a rabbit or groundhog, but it seemed like it could make for a decent burrito. He wondered about rat meat, as it would probably be greasy and strong, but if they had enough hot peppers to cut the gaminess, it could make for a good filling.

He imagined himself sitting on the sofa with Maddy, peeling back the foil of the burrito to reveal a whole barbecued rat, then cuddling up and chowing down while watching Lindsay Lohan walk through the doors of North Shore High School in *Mean Girls*.

Darren interrupted, "Dude, I can't see Britney."

Will slowed down and looked around to see he had walked a solid block past the gas station. His chest deflated, "Dude, I can't think straight."

"I know, me too. I'm so fucking hungry."

"I was thinking about—"

"I kept thinking of this girl in Columbus.

"I know, man, you keep telling us about the girl from Columbus. And the other one you're in love with, and the other one."

"The Queen, Vanessa."

Darren kept whining as they walked back to the gas station, "She said she found out how to get infinite gas."

"Yeah, well, it was probably distillation or Fischer-Tropsch—"

"No, because she figured it out before she went to the distillation school."

Will didn't care to indulge the fantasy, but his partner continued, "Do you think there's a black market?"

Darren kept yammering, "Well, that doesn't really make sense because that wouldn't be infinite. I mean, nothing's infinite but..."

Will walked up to a Dodge Neon, pulled out the thin tube, stuck it into the open fuel door, and put the other end to his ear. Darren bounced the car up and down, then side to side, and Will shook his head and proceeded to a nearby GMC SUV.

"Do you think anyone is running a refinery? Zombies do shit like that, I hear."

"I can't hear if you keep talking..." Will sneered.

Once again, he inserted the tube and Darren bounced the car. Will furrowed his brow, "Do it again," and he bounced it once more.

Will rubbed his eyes and shrugged, then laid down, slid under the SUV, and drilled out the corner of the gas tank while Darren got on his hands and knees and held the funnel and jug under the drill bit. Eight or nine ounces drizzled out, half of it trickling down the drill and soaking Will's hand.

Darren mused, "Or she could have found a tanker truck somewhere."

He mumbled patronizingly as he tried to let the gas dribble backwards from the drill into the bottle, "Yeah, that's probably it."

Darren paced over to an exposed manhole cover, "I guess this is where the tankers dump the gas. So tell me again, what all is going on here?"

Will mumbled, monotone, "That's the pump. Someone jumped the solenoid and pumped the tank dry. They're all like that."

"But did they get it all?"

Will dribbled the last few drops of gas from his hand into the bottle and then wiped it on his leg, "You think they left some just in case a metalcore band rolled through town?"

The skinny guitarist shouted defensively, "I don't know, maybe there's a reserve tank or something! I'm just thinking."

Will mouthed the words *'reserve'*, glanced at the drilled-out gas tank, and then looked at the array of metal covers in the concrete.

He found the one pipe cover labeled *'fill'* and drilled out the bolt heads, then pulled a screwdriver from his bag and popped off the top. The hole was deep, so he turned to Darren and said, "Find something really long."

They poked around the debris, and Darren shouted, "Hey Will," then held up a coat hanger."

"No way, we need like fifty feet."

Darren kept rooting through a trash pile while Will looked

alongside the gas station and saw a half-empty spool of coaxial cable. He considered going back to the van to get wire cutters, but he was too exhausted. So he unraveled a length and eyeballed it, then pulled it tight over his pistol and split it with a 9mm parabellum round.

His partner came running over, "What the fuck, what the fuck?"

Will held up the wire and shrugged.

Darren turned to wave to Britney, who was on the front porch of a distant house. He hollered "It's all good, false alarm."

Will walked back over to the hole and poked the cable in but it got caught after just a foot. "Oh yeah, there's probably a valve there." He sighed deeply and rubbed the bridge of his nose.

They spent about fifteen precious minutes looking for the perfect length of steel rebar to stick down the fill pipe, then Will took a chunk of concrete and bashed it until it busted the valve wide open.

Once again, Will took the coaxial cable and snaked it down the tube, twisting and turning a little but ultimately getting it through. He continued pushing, one hand over the other, until most of it was jammed into the hole. Then he pulled it out until the tip emerged, glistening and dripping with gasoline in the sunshine.

Darren sang slowly, "Ho-ly shit!"

Will cursed, "Fuck yeah!"

"Ho-ly shit!"

"Fuck yeah!"

Darren gestured toward the drill. "It's like drilling out a gas tank. But with a giant tank!"

"The last little bit of a ten thousand gallon tank ain't bad."

"We'll have to pump it out somehow."

Will smirked and wiped the sweat off his glasses, "Cody's stupid fucking pressure washer."

Darren's eyebrows leapt up to his curly hair, "That would absolutely work. He's going to give us so much shit. We busted his balls about that."

Will laughed, "He was tweaked out and stole it for no reason. He's still an idiot."

A familiar sound trumpeted on the air, and Will replaced his glasses to see their van running with a maroon Chevy Cavalier idling right beside it. His Dodge lurched backward, then forwards, then stalled out. Will strode toward the van, wondering why Cody or Britney started it up, but he froze for a second when he put his hands on his jacket pocket and felt the keys inside. He drew his Glock and loosed three shots at the driver of the car.

The van fired up again and went back into gear with the pedal to the metal, causing it to pop and weave as it sped away with the Cavalier right behind. Will ran after it for three blocks but doubled over and caught his breath, watching all of their equipment drive down the flat expanse of Lincoln Avenue and turn left on Highway 24 in the distance.

He tried his best to sprint back but his body was so depleted and in such pain that he could hardly convince his limbs to move at all.

The crisis had already set in with his bandmates, and Cody and Darren were popping hoods and checking for operable cars to steal.

Darren called over from a RAV-4, "This one has a battery."

Cody was looking at a Geo Metro, "This one's stick."

"Get a wrench."

"Screwdriver?"

"That'll work."

Will tried to explain that even if they got it started, it would be impossible for them to get enough gasoline to run a car, but he couldn't form a single intelligible word.

Cody pulled out a white bottle of Sea Foam engine treatment, wedged it between the battery housing and the fender, and taped it with five strips of brittle electrical tape. The drummer turned to Will, "Britney scored all this from under that porch."

Then he sliced open the hose that led to the fuel pump and stuck it deep into the bottle, pumping it gently to get the bubbles out. Darren plunked the oversized battery on top of the engine block and then tightened up the terminals, tying the hood down with the coaxial cable.

Darren opened the driver's side door and stuck the screwdriver into the ignition, jimmying and wrenching as he shoved it, but Cody came in through the passenger side door, shooed away the guitarist's lithe hands, and with a mighty kick drove the tool deep into the ignition. He recoiled his leg again and kicked the steering wheel with sufficient force to break the column lock.

They both immediately started pushing, and the coupe began to roll down Lincoln Avenue. Will braced his hands on the bumper and pushed along with Britney. Every so often, Darren would hop in the driver's seat and manipulate the controls, and each time he let off the clutch, they listened for a whisper of life from the engine but instead lurched to a halt and had to build up momentum again. Will felt weaker and weaker to the point that he could barely walk along, let alone push.

Britney huffed, "We're almost to the highway. Maybe we should just run after them?"

Darren let off the clutch, and it failed to pop-start, but the engine made a low, faint gurgling sound.

Britney shouted, "I think it's working!" and somehow Will found his footing, gritting his teeth and twisting his face maniacally as he pushed faster and faster until he was practically jogging. The engine coughed and sputtered, launching black, white, and blue smoke out the exhaust pipe and into his face.

Cody pulled the front seat forward and shouted, "Get in!" and Will piled into the back seat with Britney.

Darren worked the engine, and it ran like a cartoon jalopy, coughing and lurching but building more speed than they could achieve on foot. They puttered down the highway as Darren said, "The van was nearly empty, right? They couldn't have gone far."

Darren brought the compact car to an unsteady 35 MPH, then shouted, "Do we exit here?"

Cody pointed at the town, "Look! It's walled in."

Will grunted, "That's where they're going."

"What do we do? Stage an assault? Sneak in?"

Darren suggested, "Look, we're in range already, and they're not shooting."

Will wheezed, "We trade."

Britney scowled, "Trade what?"

He tapped his bandmate on the shoulder. "We trade like Vanessa traded."

Darren turned, tilted his head from side to side, and then nodded and told the others, "We found the secret to free gas. Lots of it everywhere."

Britney said, "You told me about her. Wait, is this real?"

Cody spat, "You're shitting me."

Darren answered, "Let's just hold off on that for now."

The driver blushed and coasted down the exit where he parked the car at the gates of the small walled town. The wall extended around the village as an improvised hodgepodge of building debris, refrigerators, wrecked cars, and tree branches. Military men guarded various posts, and a trio of them played cards beneath the tower, their machine guns and rocket launchers leaned against the rickety folding table.

A voice hailed them, but it looked like the men continued their game. The voice harkened again, and Will realized it was coming from the tower. He couldn't make out the words but the tone was non-threatening.

Darren popped open the door, and Britney said, "We should leave the guns in the car," but Will, Darren, and Cody stepped out with their weapons hanging from their bodies.

The tower guard shouted out in an androgynous voice, "We give and we take, but we take no lives. Do you mean to take lives?"

Will bellowed, "No! We don't!"

A young man of about nineteen years of age came down from the guard tower with an AR15 and swung open the gate. Darren got in the car and puttered through, and the others followed on foot.

Will asked the barefoot kid, "What do you guys do here?"

He answered, "We give and we take," and then ambled back to the guard tower.

Will asked as the boy climbed, "Did you see a van roll in? Just a few minutes ago?"

"Yeah, Higler had one. He took it to Mark."

"Where is Mark?"

He pointed awkwardly, "9th and Kearney. Go this way and turn left on 9th."

"Will he give it back to us?"

"I don't know. We give and we take, but we take no lives."

Will furrowed his brow, "What about zombies?"

He scoffed, "Eh, that's fine," and the boy kicked up his feet and reclined in the tower.

The band piled back into the car, and Will took the more spacious front passenger seat. They drove for a few blocks before the engine died, so Will grabbed the backpack with his tools and they continued on foot.

Manhattan, Kansas, was a calm college town, albeit much smaller than Columbus. Although there was the typical evidence of looting, rioting, and cannibalism, there was a tranquility in the air that put Will at ease. He asked the group, "Do you think this is a trap?"

Cody spoke first in a warbley voice, "I don't know what the fuck this shit is."

Britney added, "That guy seemed really nice."

Darren said soberly, "It's our only choice. They kept saying they don't kill people." He thought for a moment and said, "Then again…" and finished the thought in his head, *'That's what murderers would say.'*

Will looked around and noticed that every block had one or two houses cleared of wreckage and overgrowth. He thought, *'It feels like a neighborhood. The streets are safe. It feels like hope. It feels like the long, warm, dulcet tones of a trombone…'*

He walked with dreamy lucidity, *'I'm imagining a trombone playing ska riffs while a young couple relaxes on the ledge of a porch and slurps on peaches.'*

The boy pointed at them, and the girl turned and waved. "Hey!"

To Will's surprise, Britney squealed, "Hello!" and Will realized it was not a hallucination.

The girl wiped the juice from her dark, plain face and said through a mouthful of fruit, "I'll give you a peach?" and the next thing he knew he was he was face deep in sweet, fuzzy fruit, only for her to ask "I'll give you an egg?"

Cody answered, "Yeah, we're starving."

The red-haired boy chucked his peach pit into the street and asked, "Where are you all from?"

Darren responded, "A little town in Ohio. We're headed West to California."

"How about that. We used to see more travelers, but not so much anymore."

Darren continued, "Do you always just let anybody in?"

"Not the biters. But yeah, it's all give and take."

"What's with that? Everyone keeps saying it."

"Mark taught it to us. *Give and Take.* It's brought us together and kept us alive. Things were really bad after Super Tuesday, you remember?"

"Oh boy, yeah."

"Everyone was looting or shooting, being all paranoid and stuff. Mark taught us not to focus on what people *take*, but to focus on what you can *give*. We put our efforts into giving. Of course, we all take. But it's tolerated. Sydney is taking eggs from the coop down the street right now. They keep trying to lock it, but she goes in through the window."

Will mused, "And she won't get shot because that's the rule."

"They can kick your ass to prevent you from taking something, and they can take it back, but they can't retaliate. There's no point. Most of us enjoy when things are taken. It's another form of giving."

Will piped up, "Who is this 'Mark'? He has our van."

"Mark's the main guy. He used to run a community art space and a microbrewery before stuff went crazy. And since then, he just gives, and gives, and gives. Him and Angelique."

The trombonist inside the house started playing a familiar hook at fortissimo, *BAA-BAA BU-BU-BAA, BAA, BU-BU-BU-BU-BAA, BAA-BAA-BAA-BAA-BAA. BAA.*

Cody laughed, "Dude, that's *Play-Do*."

Darren nodded, "Such a good song," and he chanted,

When I was a boy I used to live in corduroy, OP shirts and checkered vans.

My life was very simple, I had not one pimple, my every day had these same plans.

Will asked the townies, "You guys like The Aquabats? I'm Will, by the way."

"Oh, I'm Ted."

"Hey Ted, I'm Cody."

"Darren."

"Oh yeah, I'm Britney."

Ted waved, "Hey, everyone! Yeah, this house is loaded with instruments. Tubas, harps, cellos, everything."

The bassist proposed, "We'll see, we're actually a band on tour. We're playing shows. Maybe that's something we can give you."

Ted jumped up, almost knocking an acoustic guitar from where it perched on the ledge. "Holy crap, really?" He screamed, "Mike! Hey

Mike!"

The trombone riffs ceased, and a rapid series of stomps crescendoed down the stairs until the front door whipped open, and a thin, scrappy, smooth-faced boy with floppy black hair burst outside. He was in a tattered Operation Ivy shirt and wore cut-off blue jean shorts with a chain wallet.

"Woah, who are these guys?"

Darren answered, "We're in a band called Young Nuns. We were thinking about playing a gig."

He pointed at Britney, "Woah, I think I used to have one of your CDs!"

She grinned and shimmied her shoulders, "Yeah, I'm Britney."

Sydney skipped to the porch holding a half dozen eggs in her shirt. "Eggs, eggs, eggs!"

Ted crept inside, and Will continued, "Mike, I'm Will. See, the thing is that Mark has all of our gear because he took our van."

"Woah, well, we don't have a lot of amps and stuff, but we have guitars and drums."

"Yeah, but we need the van back."

Sydney scrunched her face and made a pessimistic intonation, "Mmm, I don't know. We don't usually give stuff back, that's all. Once it's taken, that's done."

Will pressed, "I thought Mark was all about giving?"

"Yeah, but like, that stuff isn't yours anymore. You may as well ask for his house or his motorcycle. It's none of your business anymore. I'm just saying…"

Ted returned with six glasses and cracked an egg in each one while Mike suggested, "How about I'll take you to see Mark, and you can tell him you want to do a gig. I mean, you'd need your gear, right? Maybe he'd let you use it, and then who knows? Was it a nice van?"

Will sighed, "It's kind of a classic. It's a pretty rare 4x4 shorty with very big engine."

Ted replied, "I don't know. It doesn't sound like something he'd steal."

Darren answered, "He didn't steal it, I don't think. The kid at the gate said it was the giggler."

A pall went over the house residents, "Oh shit, Higler."

"Who's that?"

There was a pause, and then Ted continued, "He's just a guy who gives a lot. He gives a lot to Mark, but he also likes to hang around the college kids. And he tries to give a lot—"

Mike interrupted, "We don't like him."

Sydney put a dash of salt in each glass, passed out an egg to each person, and smiled. "Drink up!"

Britney asked, "You're not having one?"

She smiled, "It's my pleasure to give!"

Will downed his and licked his lips. "Can you take us to see Mark?"

Mike answered, "Yurp! Yeah, he's the main guy. He'll like you guys." He cracked open the front door, grabbed a pair of combat boots with no laces, and slipped his feet inside.

He led the group down the wide small-town streets, singing the same trombone hook to *Play-Do* as he strutted and waved his hands along with the melody.

Cody asked, "Do you have a band?"

"I wish, man. Woah. I'd love to have a band. We don't get a lot of electricity here unless it's a festival. We do a beer festival, an apple festival, pumpkin festival, pig festival. It's a lot of work for everyone, but there's always a generator going. You guys should play a festival! Dude, we could make it a music festival. Woah."

Britney suggested, "We should! You should play, too!"

"I don't know. I have some songs I wrote on guitar, but mostly I've been practicing piano. You guys like Bach?"

Darren answered, "I like the *Goldberg Variations.*"

"Dude, woah! Yeah, you should hear the *French Suites.* You have the Glenn Gould recordings? The old one or the new one?"

Darren hesitated, "I'm— I'm not sure. So what do you usually do during the festival?"

"Oh, I'm inventory. I do all kinds of inventory. For the festivals I usually make sure there's enough food. Stuff like that."

Will grunted, "Must be hard to do inventory with all the giving and taking."

Mike held up his hands, "Yeah, but like, woah. What I work with people, don't fuck with."

The statement was so ominously cryptic that Will didn't care to pry.

"Yeah, it's just down this street here. I like to give a little shout, "HEY, MARK!'"

They walked halfway down the block and then turned into a modest driveway. Mike walked up to the door and knocked, and a stunning woman opened the door. She was light-skinned black with tight shiny curls that spilled over her shoulder-less peasant blouse, framing her muscular, shapely body, angelic face, and kind eyes. She had a baby on one hip and a big clunky pair of boots in the other. She had the presence of a valkyrie, but her voice was sugary sweet like a teenager, and she spoke with a fairly flat yet affable facial expression, "Hey Mike."

"Hey Angelique, Is Mark around?"

She set the boots on the floor, then flung a few stray curls over her shoulder. "No, he's at the yard with Higler."

Mike said, "These are my new friends. They're in a band."

She hiked the baby up higher on her hip with a little bounce. "Cool, you guys live here now?"

Will answered, "We're on our way west."

Angelique fluttered her lengthy eyelashes, "OK. Do you know

anything about cobbling boots?"

Darren responded, "I'm sure that we don't."

Angelique glanced around, held up a finger, and floated away for a moment, quickly returning with a jug of water, "Givey give!"

Darren opened his eyes wide and smiled, "Oh my god! Thank you so much."

Britney added, "You're amazing!"

She winked and shot them each a finger gun.

Mike smiled and bobbed his head as he shifted his feet. "You guys wanna check out the yard? It's not far."

Angelique smiled and waved, "Byeee!" and gently closed the door.

"Wow, she's amazing, " Britney repeated.

"Yeah, wait til you meet Mark."

They continued down the street and made a couple of turns until they reached a rectangular building with a reinforced gate and multiple rows of barbed razor wire. Again, Mike hollered, "HEY MARK!"

And a voice from above replied, "What's up, Mike?"

They looked up to see a guard tower partly obscured within a grove of trees. Their new friend shouted, "Evan, what's up? We're coming to see Mark."

"Cool, yeah, he's in the office with Higler and Jay."

Mike tugged on his chain wallet, and a big ring of keys came out of his front pocket. He leafed through them, thrust one in the latch, and pulled open the steel man door that led inside the yard. There, parked in front of the building, was the maroon Chevy Cavalier and Van Hellsing.

Will decided not to make a big deal, but Britney squealed, "There it is! There's our van!"

Mike knocked on the heavy wooden exterior door and then found a separate key for the deadbolt and knob. He swung open the door and yelled, "Hey Mark!"

There was a cheerful call from around the corner, "Mikey!"

The trombonist strode down the hall and made the first left into an office with windows overlooking the yard. The others followed and looked in from the hallway.

Mark had curly dark brown hair that hung just past his ears, and was very tall with an elvish face, big eyes, and a slightly upturned nose. He walked and spoke soft and slow as he moved into the hallway. "You brought some new friends, huh?" He smiled genuinely with his mouth and eyes, "Hey, I'm Mark."

"Will."

"I'm Cody!"

"Darren, nice to meet you."

"I'm Britney."

Mikey blurted out, "They're in a band! I was thinking they should play a festival. What about a music festival?"

Mark continued beaming as he folded his hands and nodded, "Well, I think once they're settled in, that could be a nice idea."

A man of about forty years of age with a completely bald head, unbuttoned pinstriped dress shirt, and camouflage pants squatted low and stomped toward them while pointing and shouting.

"That's them! They shot at me! They tried to kill me for taking! These IDIOTS. It wasn't their van anymore but they tried to shoot me!"

Mark tilted his head. "Oh yeah? You guys used to have the van?"

Will sighed, "Yeah, that's my van. It has our music gear too."

The main guy turned to his friend, "Higler, they weren't in Manhattan yet. They didn't know about the *Give and Take*. Let's let it go." Then he turned back to Will, "You won't take lives, will you?"

Will's memory briefly flashed images of the Iowa looter he killed, and he felt a desire to murder Higler right now. Nevertheless, he answered, "No."

Mark held up his palms, "I mean, you're free to move along, and you're free to stay."

The bald man sneered, "Hey Mark, they were trying to siphon from cars at the gas station, *hu-hu-hu. Hu-hu* Why do you think they're at the gas station? Cuz they're out of gas, you IDIOTS, *hu-hu-hu.*"

Darren and Will exchanged glances and feigned ignorance, but Will was relieved that Higler hadn't observed their experiment.

Mark spoke, "Well, me and Hig were about to check on the vats, and then hopefully get one last crop of corn in the ground over at the University. Then Angelique and I are going to make a big fish stew with potato pancakes at the elementary school. Does any of you want to come?"

Will piped up, "I'll go."

Cody added reluctantly, "I guess we'll all go?"

Mike offered, "You can come back and chill at the house, if you want. We can jam, or you can relax. We have a guest room. We can meet them for stew later. Sydney is going to make a peach and basil relish for the pancakes."

Cody pursed his lips and nodded.

Will suggested, "You don't have to come. I just want to check out their town."

The drummer cocked his head, "Maybe we'll do that."

Mark gestured to the outside door, and the whole group shuffled through the exit. Next to the main gate, a very short red-haired boy was dumping a small bucket onto a patch of cultivated dirt.

"Evan, buddy. Is that from your latrine bucket?"

"Oh, hi Mark. Yeah, for the sunflowers."

"Evan, Evan, Evan. It has to be composted first. You know this."

"Huh?"

"Yeah, your waste has to get turned over in the compost. The longer, the better."

"Oh man, I messed it up again, Mark."

Mark shook his head and sighed, then reached behind the small of his back and drew a shiny chrome 1911 pistol. Will took a step backward and braced himself for the shot, but the man then pulled out the holster from his jeans and tucked the pistol back inside, then handed the prized weapon to the redhead.

The tall man crooned, "It's a give, man."

Evan took a step back and dropped the bucket. "Oh no, you can't—
"

"*Tut-tut-tut*. It's a give. You have to take my pistol."

Evan took the gun with two hands as tears welled in his eyes. "I'm not… I can't. It's your Colt, Mark."

"It's nothing, bud. Go ahead back to the tower, and I'll see you for stew. Maybe we can hit targets with it afterward." Mark patted his big hand on Evan's narrow shoulder.

The redhead blubbered so profusely that his words slurred and gushed, "Mark, you're just so good to everyone. Why are you so nice to me?"

Mark kept his warm expression and cool demeanor as he opened the main gate and looked out on the wide open streets. "Giving is the gift, my friend."

———————————

Young Nuns had been crashing out at the Music House for a week. The guest room was full of cozy mattresses, their hosts were gentle and hospitable, and they ate at least two meals a day. Britney and Darren tagged along with Sydney and Ted, Cody did maintenance work at the house, and Will spent most of his time with Mark. And throughout the day, the residents and guests alike would pick up an instrument and play together; either on the porch or in the sagging front room of the old wooden house.

This afternoon, Will was trembling with joy as he sauntered down the street, re-playing his lunchtime conversation in his head:

Higler grunted, "We should do a festival this weekend. The staff needs to shape up before CornStock."

Mark pursed his lips, "Hunh. Well, Xavier and the kids from Brew House have all those gruits we made. The fruity beers? It could be fun to get everyone together and try them."

Higler nodded, "Yeah, that girl Courtney is in Brew House, isn't she?"

"Hm? Yeah, Courtney. She made a dandelion jalapeño gruit."

Higler asked, "Young Nuns could play? The Music House people could play too. I love me some flute, hu-hu-huh."

"I don't know, Hig. What do you think, Will?"

"Oh gosh, yeah, we'd love to play."

Mark scratched his stubbled chin, mused, then said, "I want to tell you something. What you guys are doing is absolutely 'give and take.' The way you are crossing the country, and just giving and giving. And only taking what you need. I think it's the ultimate 'give and take.'"

"Aw, thanks Mark. I like to think that's true."

"And I want everyone to see that. I want you guys performing the way you said you could, running the inverter with Britney and Darren on top of the van. The full statement."

Will felt choked up, "Just for like... You mean..."

"I want to give. I want you to have your van back."

The bald man scoffed, "The van was my give! You have to accept a give!"

Mark shook his head, "It is my van, Higler. But I want them out there, sharing the 'give and the take' with others."

Will sobbed gently as Mark went further, "How you trained to be a head chef, taking care of your van, how you want to take care of your girlfriend, confronting her father. You're the main guy like I'm the main guy. You give the most and take the least. That's all anybody needs. So Saturday, I'll pull the van up to the University Theater, and you're free to take it from there."

Will came back to the Music House beaming. "We got it! We're going to play a festival!"

His bandmates were chilling on the porch with the house residents, and their reactions were enthusiastic.

"Hell yeah!"

"Sweet!"

"No way!"

"Awesome!"

"It's going to be a collaboration with Brew House, and that's not the best part—"

Ted rolled his eyes, "Brew House is selfish and conceited."

Sydney added, "I bet they think it's a beer festival. With music."

Mikey sat up and rested a mandolin on his knee, "How'd you talk him into it?"

"I didn't, it was actually Higler."

There was a short pause and Sydney asked, "Higler?"

"Yeah, I know he's kind of an asshole but he said he wants to have a festival before CornStock because his crew needs training."

Ted drawled, "Well, we're his crew."

Mikey added, "Anyone is his crew if he decides."

Sydney set her flute on the ledge, crossed her arms, and stated point blank, "Well, not me. I'm not going and he can fuck off."

Will thought, *'This was supposed to be good news. Everyone seems upset, for some reason. I didn't get to tell them the best part, but if they're going to act like this, I'd rather wait to tell them we're getting the van back.'*

Sydney's voice eased up, and she cooed, "Well, I don't know. If you guys are playing, I guess I'll go."

Will said "He's talking about doing it at the university theater."

Mikey said, "Woah, that would be sweet. We ran the sound system there once, and it still works."

Will continued, "I told Higler about Eva, Leah, Bekah, and Juan jamming out with us the other day, and he wanted us to do something like that."

This time, the silence was leaden, but Mikey broke it to announce, "Welp, I gotta go inventory a whole load of welding gear that the west side boys brought in from Junction City. I wanna finish before we get stew."

Will chimed in, eager to escape the unpleasant atmosphere. "I'll go with you!"

Mike hopped onto his feet. "Oh, you weren't just at the yard?"

"No, we were at the elementary school setting up a mash for the ale."

"OK, yeah come with!" Then he turned to the rest and said, "See you at dinner!"

Everyone bid them adieu, and Will jogged along as Mike ambled his spindly legs rapidly.

The ska kid asked, "So Higler and Mark are still at the school?"

"Uh, yeah. They already started peeling potatoes."

"Hmph."

They walked silently with the sound of locusts buzzing in the background. For fear of theft, Will wore his only possessions: his guns and tool bag. He noticed that very few people carried a weapon, so he asked, "So you and all the other young people, you don't fight?"

"Oh, well, we have clubs and knives and stuff. But mostly it's the older dudes who work the wall."

"And that's enough? I know you have machine guns and mortars, but everywhere we've been, most people are armed."

"Well, we do have a pistol at Music House. There's a revolver in the junk drawer, just in case. There's a house a few blocks away that has a few rifles, but they're the new kind that the zombies make."

"Zombies make them?"

"Yeah, it's a new thing and they're supposed to suck. There's a guy who can swap parts between them to make one decent rifle, but usually it takes three to make one that works right."

Will nodded, "Most gunners I meet take the gas tube out of the AR and run it as a single-shot bolt action rifle. It's less firepower but a hundred percent more reliable. Nobody has shotguns?"

"They have all kinds of stuff on the wall. But the townies only have 10 gauges. Problem is, nobody has 10 gauge ammo."

"Yeah, we dealt with that back in Ohio."

"Lots of us have .22s. For awhile, Higler didn't even consider them to be firearms, but now he's trying to grab them up. Make sure Darren doesn't let his leave his sight."

"I'm sure he won't. So who does the raids around here?"

Mike wrinkled his nose, "Raids? Well, almost all of us. We'll get a posse together and go out to grab stuff. Like your van, I guess. A few times a year, we'll go into Topeka to loot what we can."

Will shook his head, "I mean like zombies, you know. Cell towers."

Mike shrugged.

"Do you get waves here? They attack the walls, right?"

"Oh yeah, by the hundreds. I'm usually running ammo to the machine gunners. It's pretty stressful and a bunch of people have been killed but we blast the shit out of them."

"And you don't go on raids? Nobody does?"

Mike shrugged.

They arrived at the yard and unlocked the door, then walked into the office to recover a couple of binders. They then walked outside and opened a bay door to reveal an assortment of tanks, welding boxes, gloves, helmets, grinders, hoses, and torches.

Mike stuck out his tongue, "Blah, this sucks. Here, check this out."

They walked to the next bay and opened the door to reveal a

warehouse large enough to house a couple of tractor trailers. Six or seven military crates were stacked in the back corner, and Mike lifted their lids to show their contents.

"Check it out. This was all from Fort Riley. 50 cal, 5.56, 7.62, .45, hand grenades, mortars, .30-06. This place was stacked from floor to ceiling when we first built the wall."

"Where did it all…" Will's heart sank, realizing that it was all a lie. "Wh-When the ammo's gone, then what?"

Mike inhaled but said nothing. He exhaled noisily and shook his head.

Will stepped out of the garage and clutched his temples. Manhattan, Kansas, would be wiped out any day now, and he felt a mild panic that the zombies could already be on their way.

"Mike, Mike, Mike… You need to start doing raids. You guys just blast ammo when they surge at night? It's a waste of ammo and lives. If you assault their outposts, you can take out a hundred bodies with just a few people. I'll show you how."

"I mean, maybe take Higler and them—"

"No. This is a give. I'm going to take you all on a raid. You need this for your own survival."

"Woah. OK, OK. Woah."

"Right after the festival. The next day?"

"Alright, if you say so!"

Mike closed up the ammo depot, and they walked over to the welding equipment. They spent an hour sorting everything, assessing its condition, and documenting it in the binder. There was very little welding wire or gas, so most of the gear was useless, rendering their endeavor a grim bureaucratic absurdity.

Mike scribbled in the binder and imitated Mark, saying slowly and softly with a fatherly intonation, "Well, unh, the zombies are coming over the wire, but all we have is three broken welding guns. I'll tell ya what, little buddy. Why don't you inventory them as machine guns? Now ya have more machine guns. That's a give. Givey give!"

Will laughed deeply at his gallows humor.

Mike held up the binder, "Uh, maybe you can read them the inventory and bore them to death, my friend."

Will put on a big, dark welding helmet and said, "See no evil," and added a pair of protective earmuffs, "Hear no evil."

Mike laughed and slammed the binder shut. "That's all she wrote. Let's eat."

They closed up the bay, and Mike pointed to the smaller garages across the way. "Your van is in one of those. I don't have a key."

"That's OK, we'll just do the gig. It should be fun anyway."

They walked to the elementary school, cracking jokes along the way. They lined up for stew, got a bowl of greenish broth with a spoon, and took a morsel of cornbread. They sat and started to wolf down the thin briney mixture. This one was allegedly split pea with bacon, but Will had to stretch his imagination to catch a note of either ingredient. Nevertheless, he cleaned out his bowl with the crumbly bread and licked his fingers with satisfaction.

He stood, walked over to the washing station, and saw Britney coming his way. She leaned into him and spoke softly but forcefully. "We're not going to play that festival."

"Huh? No, we have to play it. We're going to get the van back!"

She blinked, "The van? OK, but… Find another way."

"I don't know. Look, we have it all set up! We can get back on the road!"

She spat, "That Higler guy? He's a raper."

"Higler? He raped someone?"

"Well, not like, *rape* rape. Like, creepy stuff."

He scoffed, "Yeah, he's pretty creepy but that doesn't make him a rapist."

Britney grunted, "I mean, he does rapey stuff but it isn't rape."

Will was exasperated. "What are you talking about?"

She gestured with an outstretched palm, "Sydney told me that he does *gives* that are like, *molest-y*. And you know how the *gives* are. You have to accept it. He does it to all the girls. Do you know what I'm saying?"

Will scoffed and walked toward the exit, setting the bowl on the 'clean' pile and shaking the dish soap from his hands. He frowned and uttered, "That's fucked up. Do you think Mark knows?"

She snorted, "Are you going to tell him?"

"Well no, but… I mean somebody must have…."

Britney held her arms akimbo, "What difference does it make? He's either a dick or an idiot. Like, nobody is going to go to the festival. I don't want to be involved anyway."

"I get that, but we could get the van back. So let's just do it and move on."

She crossed her arms, "No way. I won't do it."

"Come on!"

Britney sneered, "Uh, ok, how about let's not and say we did."

Will thought for a second, "Or… We could say we will, and we won't."

Evan came down and opened the door for Will to enter Mark's building. The little redhead asked, "Does Mark know you're coming?"

Will muttered, "Probably not."

"Okay, just a second." He disappeared into the office and came out with the tall dark-haired man.

"Hey Will, unh, how's it going, bud?"

"Oh, we're great. We were thinking about having a practice this morning."

Mark pursed his lips, "I thought we were going to meet at the University around five o'clock. I'll have the van all set up for ya."

"Yeah, but well, you see, Britney still doesn't know all the songs that well. So we were going to try and practice."

"Hunh. Well, yeah. You dudes can practice here! I can, unh, open up an empty bay for you."

"Aha, um, everyone is already at Music House."

Mark tilted his head, "Are you sure you don't just want to do all of that at the university? That was the plan."

"I know, but I wanted to check on the van."

"I don't know if Higler told you, but he jacked it with a blank key. So there wasn't even any damage."

"Please? I'm just— we're just so excited to play the festival."

"OK, hunh. I'll open up the garage. Hig put a couple of gallons in already. It's mostly ethanol, so I might need to help you start it."

Mark opened the garage door and Will jumped into the driver's seat. The main guy slapped the hood, and Will popped it open. He pulled out a can of WD-40 and shouted, "OK, crank it!"

Will turned the key and cranked the engine while his new friend shot a burst of spray into the air intake. He cranked again, and the engine fired up, running rough but steady enough.

Mark let out a whoop and slammed the hood, then took a few steps back and smiled at the traveler, beckoning him forward. He popped the van into gear and started to crawl out, and Mark jogged to the main gate. He swung it wide open and waved to Will, "I'll still see you at five, right?"

Will nodded wordlessly and his friend's voice faded into the distance, "I'll bring a few bottles of my own beer. We can celebrate!"

Will drove past the gate, and tears sputtered out of his eyes and down his face as he prepared to betray his friend. He wiped them away and cleared his sinuses with a snort, then spit a hocker out the window and set his mind to the raid they would conduct instead of showing up to Mark's festival.

He chugged down the street and parked outside of Music House next to their stolen Geo Metro, a baby blue Ford Ranger, and an Oldsmobile station wagon, all packed to the gills with people. Young Nuns were standing on the porch along with eight other kids, and they all piled into Van Hellsing. Ted and Sydney shared the front seat with Darren, and the rest double-stacked in the back seat or climbed in the back with the amps.

Will protested, "No, no, no… We don't have room. Young Nuns only."

Cody's voice droned from beneath a couple bodies, "We got a different thing now, dude."

Britney shouted from underneath a tiny brunette, "We don't even need the phone. Eva knows where they are."

A pair of big dark eyes were barely visible from beneath a dirty blue ball cap flanked by immaculately clean and straight brown hair, and Eva commanded, "Go West on Anderson out of town."

So he trucked out of town with a motley crew of former university students, food service workers, tattoo artists, survivors from the military, and grown-up military brats in tow. Over the past few days he came to learn that all of these groups were fragmented and factionalized, and none of them got along.

They were barely five miles out of town when Eva instructed Will to slow down and hold up. It was a former airport with the control tower already visible in the flat expanse of the prairie, with massive plumes of steam and smoke rising skyward. Midwesterner though he was, Will had a hard time imagining how to approach the installation tactically in such an exposed setting.

"How many are there?" He asked Eva.

She pushed the brim of her ball cap higher, "I don't know, but I saw a bunch of them there last week."

Will took the binoculars from where they hung behind his seat and climbed the ladder on the back of the van to get a better view. At first sight, he could see over a hundred zombies lurking on the periphery of the compound, with a steady stream of them walking between the three or four large buildings on site. But there could be hundreds more, maybe even a thousand.

"Cody! Darren! Britney!" He gave each of them a chance to view the installation before he weighed in, and each groaned and cursed.

Darren complained, "There's just no cover. We'll have to do a frontal assault. But we won't have anywhere to retreat."

Cody said optimistically, "We have cars, though."

Britney shook her head, "What good will that do us?"

Will looked at the unreliable vehicles, jam-packed with bodies, and signaled for them to shut off their engines.

He removed his hat and ran his fingers through his hair. "OK, everybody out." he glanced around and scratched his jaw, "Rifles, stand by the Metro. Shotguns, over here. Pistols by the Ranger. OK, hand weapons, go to the station wagon." There were about six in each gun group and twenty-five with knives and clubs.

He addressed the armed groups, "Do any of you have a sidearm? A second gun?" A couple rifleman and a shotgunner raised their hands. "OK, now how many with the hand weapons know how to use a pistol?" About ten hands went up. "Alright, pass them out." Then he pointed back to Young Nuns and said, "You guys too." And he took out his own Glock 17 from his shoulder holster and gave it to a middle-aged long-haired man with wire-rimmed glasses.

Britney handed the .22 revolver to a waifish teenager, "There ya go, Courtney."

Darren turned to her as he passed his Hi-Point 9mm to a wide-hipped, broad-chested lady with a tight ponytail. "You should keep your gun, Brit."

She shook her head, "No, I have an AFAK. I'm gonna do first aid."

"Take a club, though."

"Duh."

Will turned to the rifles, "Ammo check. What do you have?"

Cody called out, "I have maybe forty rounds."

A well-built black man with a mustache stood next to two wobbly white teenage boys and said, "We have fifteen rounds each, but their two rifles ain't worth a goddamn."

A quiet, doughy man, 30 something but with a baby face, mumbled from underneath a curtain of shaggy brown hair, "I got this AK, but I only have four rounds of 7.62."

Britney perked up, "Oh shit!" She took off her poncho and pulled out the magazine she had been using as a club. "This?"

He grinned and nodded, and in one motion swapped magazines and whooped out, "Hooo-WEE!"

The other riflemen had hunting rifles or single shot .22s with limited ammo, and the people who held them didn't appear to have much shooting experience.

None of the shotgunners had more than a few shells, and several had none whatsoever. The pistols were mostly 9mm or .45, and once they divvied up the ammo everyone had about six rounds.

Will stepped in the middle of the four groups when Sydney's voice squawked at the top of her lungs, "Alright, everyone, Will is in charge now. You all made the choice. What he says goes."

He shook his head, "No, no. No. I'm not in charge of anything. Nobody's in charge. Nobody needs to be in charge. Let's think this through together."

Cody piped up, "Well, we could go back and get more supplies. Maybe reinforcements?"

Will shifted his eyes to Mike and raised his eyebrows.

He tugged at his t-shirt and swayed as he spoke, "We're never going to get the army dudes in on this, no way. They'd— woah.. They'd try to stop us."

Britney raised her hand, and Will did a double-take. "Just say it. You don't have to raise your hand."

She enunciated, "I've been all across the country. Wherever we go, people are fighting, and yes, some people die. We have to get real. We can't live in fantasy land anymore."

There was a murmur of approval.

Will emphasized, "There are more than enough zombies here to annihilate Manhattan whenever they want. I say now is the time."

Darren probed, "Well, we don't know what guns they have. That's the main issue."

Cody added, "There are usually a few gunners mixed in with the horde, but usually they're hidden with the specialty equipment."

Darren responded, "So they're probably all inside."

Mike threw out an idea, "Let's draw them out. Cruise by in the Ranger and hit them with the pistols until they chase us. Then, when the guns come out, we can pick them off from the side."

Will uttered, "That's not a bad idea."

Mike asked, "Then we can beat back the remainder with hand weapons and maybe score more ammo?"

Darren responded, "I like the idea of drawing them out, but it's the same problem. Ammo and surprise."

Eva asked, "What's the worst-case scenario if we try to draw them out?"

Cody snorted, "There are a thousand zombies in there, mostly armed. They either don't charge at all or worse yet come after us in mass."

She responded, "So maybe we hit them from both sides?"

Britney pointed out, "They're mostly fenced in. We can shoot and stab them through the fence, and they won't be able to get at us."

He nodded and swayed, "I'm down. The second unit can stand by and roll up on their flank when they commit. Or better yet, we draw them out and ambush them just at the berm where it's safe."

Ted suggested, "How about Music House crew and Young Nuns on one side, with Brew House and Maple Street on the other?"

A short lady with close-cropped curly brown hair croaked, "What about Johnson Avenue?"

Will called out, "We could use the hand weapons. Come on over here."

Mike crept up to Will and asked, "Would you be mad if we ditch the Geo you gave me?"

Will shook his head.

"You won't be mad? We'll charge them with it, but I was thinking, woah, after I run over a few bodies and it takes a few bullets, it might be cashed."

"Pfft, that car isn't worth the battery inside it."

Eva came over to Will and announced, "Maple Street wants to switch with Johnson Avenue."

Will wrinkled his brow, "What?"

"They're pissed off at Brew House because their house captain cheated on his girlfriend, but her new boyfriend is this asshole—"

He pulled off his glasses and rubbed his reddened face, "I don't fucking care! We need their hand weapons. That's that." and she sulked away.

There was a series of side conversations about strategy and communication, and then the groups separated with the understanding that Brew House would signal the attack.

Will loaded up into the Metro with the other pistoleers, except they added Cody to engage any yuppies. The sound of the Ranger's rusted out exhaust carried faintly on the open prairie, and through his binoculars, Will could see the sluggish poshes shift slightly to the East, toward the threat. As soon as the first gunshot popped off, Mike floored the accelerator of the compact car.

The bassist kept watching through his binoculars and shouted out, "Here. That's close enough."

But the shaggy little trombonist drove right up to the rusty, blown-out chain link fence before he hopped out and drew his revolver. He aimed carefully and took out the first five zombies he saw before anyone else even stepped out of the car.

The fence was disintegrated with rust and had been cut or ripped open at so many points that the zombies flowed right through. Will wielded a tire iron and started bashing, mostly going for the skull but sometimes immobilizing them with a strike to the knee.

At first, the team advanced up to the fence, slicing through them like a weed whacker. But their opponents flooded out and nearly surrounded them

Shots rang out from Darren's gun, and then a barrage of machine gun fire came from somewhere in the compound. Will saw two dead yuppies just beyond the front line with AR15s lying next to them, and a third right by the fence slumped over a shotgun.

Cody called out, "Retreat!" and Will looked around to see that the had been overrun and would have to retreat on foot.

Will shouted, "Run! I'll cover you!" so Mike and the others started sprinting back to where Britney waited in Van Hellsing, three hundred yards away.

He aimed his Glock and fired at the zombies that pursued his friends and swung the tire iron like a tornado. Zombies hung on all sides of his body, and he felt their teeth sink into his arms. He shook them off like a dog, punted each one in the face, and beat their heads like railroad spikes.

He then turned toward the compound, leaned forward like a running back, and rammed clean through the front lines while their fingernails clawed at his head and shoulders. The door to the Metro was still open, and he popped inside, slamming the door before the walkers could get to him.

He turned the screwdriver handle and the starter made a pathetic sound of *wub, wub, wub,* but then all three cylinders started with the gusto of a drunken Lawn Boy mower and he hit the gas. He drove forward through the chain link fence and collided with zombies until the windshield and windows were busted to hell.

Will leaned forward so he could see through a tiny section that was not rendered opaque with spiderweb cracks and bounded straight toward the bloodied rifles of the dead defenders. He exited the vehicle, grabbed the guns, and pulled out a plastic bag of loose rifle ammo from the gray tweed pants pocket of the bald yuppie's suit.

Will hustled over to the fence and pulled back a corpse to see he had a Saiga AK-pattern semi-automatic shotgun on his lap, then he rolled the tracksuit-wearing gunner over and discovered he was sitting on a damp cardboard box loaded with shotgun shells.

He threw the guns and ammo into the passenger seat and then froze for a moment as the doors to the nearby air terminal building flew open and bullets whizzed past his head. A new line of zombies poured out of the building as Will dove in the car, put the pedal to the metal, and advanced with the stampeding pack of zombies back toward his comrades.

The compact car nipped at one of the runner's heels and then tripped her to the ground, only to bump and slide over the body. Ahead on his left was a stationary fifty-year-old man wearing nothing but a LiveStrong bracelet, resting one hand on his knee and steadily cranking his dong with the other. Will specifically veered toward him, launching him up and over the car where he lay on his back with crumpled legs, still fondling his unit.

Will thought, '*This wasn't part of the plan. I don't want to drive into the ambush zone while they're mowing them down. This looks like the edge of the line of fire. I'll park the car here and use it as a secondary firing position.*' Then he flopped out of the car with the shotgun. He faced the airfield and started to pick off targets as they ran toward him, but most of the second wave stayed around the fence.

He checked behind him just in time to see that not all the zombies continued running to the ambush zone, and they were upon him. He gave a few jabs with the butt of his rifle to knock two of them on their behinds. A third man wore a polo shirt and black shorts with a scarf around his neck and got a hold of the Saiga in one hand and Will's left wrist with the other, then leaned in to bite the top of his skull.

Will dropped the gun and plopped on the dusty ground onto the seat of his pants, then turned sideways and donkey-kicked the man's knee with a sickening snap. Then he grabbed the man's hand, pulled himself up while rocketing to his feet, and laid such a nasty uppercut that his head ricocheted between his back and chest several times.

There were four more assailants ready to jump on him, so he spun the 12 gauge around and put holes in two of their torsos, but the next trigger pull resulted in a *'click'*. He steeled himself for a hand-to-hand combat but saw a dozen greasy walkers closing in from all directions.

Gunshots rang out in the distance, and Will knew the horde had reached the ambush zone, but at his distance, even their sharpest shooter would be inaccurate by a matter of feet. He slid into the driver's seat and punched the gas to get out of danger, but the engine stalled as soon as he touched the pedal.

He looked at the box of cartridges and may have had time to grab a few shells, but the scabby hands were already reaching inside the windows, clawing at him and clambering inside. He knew he couldn't possibly save himself, and there was only one way he would be able to get help.

He honked the horn urgently, then reclined the driver's seat until he was nearly flat. He covered his face with his hands, and crusty nails scratched his flesh open while the rest of them beat on the pulverized windshield. He kicked at the horn again, sounding out SOS in morse code.

A hipster shouted, "They're coming to take you away, hee hee, they're coming to take you away hee hee!" and then barked, "Laserdisc!

Laserdisc!"

Bullets ripped through the glass and body of the Metro, and Will could only imagine how many bullets were passing through his own body. The barrage lasted ten seconds, and then he reached over, grabbed a fistful of shells, cracked open the passenger side door, and launched it open so wide with a mighty kick that it sent a lingering attacker into the air fully inverted. He rocked back the Saiga mag, rammed five shells into it, and stepped outside spraying buckshot and fury.

His comrades' gunfire had killed about half of his assailants, and Will engaged the remainder with the utmost brutality, swinging left then right, high then low with the tire iron until they were all down for the count.

The ambush party advanced, and Will felt his adrenaline ebb. As he saw that he and his companions were safe, he became aware of his wounds and exhaustion.

He sat flat on the grass and looked at the compound through his binoculars. The horde looked even bigger than before, with more guns, more bodies, and more preparation. He scanned over to the other team, and they had retreated into a similar lull, walking through the killing fields and braining walkers that were still twitching. He loaded a dozen rounds into his magazine and put it back in the gun.

He felt a slight chill and turned with a start to see that Van Hellsing had pulled up alongside the metro with the entire crew either on top or inside. Britney jumped out with the first aid kit. "Let me help."

Will protested, "No, no. Help the others."

She flexed her brow. "Nobody else is hurt."

"Seriously? No casualties?"

"Yep. This is going to sting."

"Sheeeyow!"

Darren set his rifle on the roof of the Geo and looked through the scope. "Dammit, there's just too many of them."

Cody asked, "Can you pick off the gunners? What if we get

closer?"

"They're moving around too much."

"It would be worth it to thin out the shooters before we charge."

Will moaned, "We need to call it. Maybe we come back another day."

Ted played devil's advocate, "What if more zombies come to reinforce them?"

Cody responded soberly, "Oh, they will."

Will huffed, "OK, let's think out loud here. We tried the raid, and it didn't seem to have an effect. There could be hundreds more in there."

Darren looked through his scope again. "No, these ones are different."

"What do you mean?"

"They're hipsters. You know how yuppies are always supervising where the action is? Hipsters usually do the work to set stuff up or keep it going. Poshes are too stupid. Like, that's how the towers work. This is the same but bigger. Whatever they're doing in there, they pulled these guys off the line."

Will coughed, "Oh hey, we did get some more ammo. Everybody load up, just in case. There might be some 9mm in the plastic bag along with the 5.56. There are a couple rifles, too."

The gang passed around the ammo and quickly distributed it among everyone.

Will lamented, "If only we had some firepower. This could be an easy job. One of those freakin' M2s."

Cody pursed his lips, "I feel like with these numbers at this distance, it won't have any effect."

Mike scratched the back of his neck. "Um, Will, don't be mad at me."

Will rolled his eyes, disinterested in any more banter about the car.

"I have some stuff in the trunk that I didn't show you."

Will picked up his binoculars, tuning out the apologetic wingeing.

The skinny inventory clerk tapped him on the shoulder with a stiff finger, "You should look at this."

He sighed, hulked his body upright, felt Britney's bandages flex against his joints, and strode to the driver's side to pop the trunk. Mike's trombone was inside, bearing a checkered flag tied to the slide that read *"Long Live Ska Nation"* in red letters.

But there was something under the trombone, and Mike picked up his horn to reveal a modern miniature bazooka. Will reeled back and crooned, "Woah."

"It's called an M72 LAW. I've seen them use it before. I took this one at the last wave. I didn't want to say anything because I didn't know if we'd need it, and I didn't want everyone to know I stole it."

Ted stepped up, put an affirming hand on Mike's shoulder, and said empathetically, "It's OK, Mike. We give and we take—"

Mike stuck out his tongue and blew a raspberry. Then he held his trombone over his crotch with the slide sticking backwards through his legs like a tail and started thrusting his pelvis in a phallic fashion while continuing to blow flatulent raspberries. Then he stuck out his butt and blew the melody of 'Stars and Stripes, Forever' with his flapping tongue and worked the slide along with the tune, while waggling his hips defiantly and shooting a dirty look at his housemate.

Will lost total control of his body, nearly blacking out from laughing so hard. After a solid minute of cathartic laughter, he wiped the tears from his eyes and stood up. "So what do we do?"

The combined forces of the Kansans and the Young Nuns had settled on a plan they were about to execute. The shotgunners loaded onto the Ranger and rolled over the grass slowly. Will watched intently as Van

Hellsing made a frontal assault at a hundred fifty yards and closing. The horizon lit up with muzzle flashes, as a couple dozen yuppies sent bullets in their general direction.

Back in Ohio, Young Nuns had fitted the van with bulletproof kevlar and ceramic panels made with bright yellow packing tape, and this plan involved Van Hellsing taking heavy fire. Will winced, as the panels could only take a couple of shots before they were no good, and the glass and engine components were unprotected. The grayish-green van parked about seventy-five yards away, and then Cody, Darren, and the AK gunner Greg took positions to return fire.

The driver of the Ranger was a curvy lady with bright eyes. Will shouted, "Let's go, Alecia!" and she pushed it past first gear into second and even hit third for a moment before braking smoothly and dropping it back into first on the far left flank of the horde. Everyone in the Ranger was shirtless, and their shotguns sang in all directions. A military brat named Devante stuffed their oil-soaked shirts into three spare tires and lit them with a Zippo. The toxic hiss and sizzle of the spare tires was audible up close, and the smell was acrid and dizzying. Devante and Will tossed the tires out of the back, rolling some further than others to get maximum smoke coverage. Alecia peeled out and flew through the gears as they bounded back over the plains to the rally point.

There, they loaded the Ford with every last fighter as Will watched the action between the van and the compound intently, which was increasingly obscured with smoke as the tires started to burn. He noticed that most of the gunfire ceased, except for an occasional crack of Darren's .22. Mike crawled out of the van, looking like he just woke up from a nap. He turned around and tugged the bazooka out from under the back seat.

The shooting escalated on both sides, and Will could see that most of the zombie shooters had ambled away from the burning tires to the far right flank, where they were pressed against the brick wall of the terminal since their sightline was the least obscured by the thick black smoke. There were about twenty of them in a cluster. All around the shooters, poshes and hipsters rocked on their heels and gathered strength, preparing to mount an overwhelming charge through the ruined fence.

Mike shouldered the M72 LAW and swayed to and fro for a moment, then shuffled to the front of the van, knelt, steadied himself, and fired. The rocket took off with a blast that shook the van. There was a massive flash and thunderous concussion followed by smoky debris, and with Will could see about a hundred feet of destruction between the terminal and the smoke screen where the shooters had previously been standing.

He signaled to the drivers, "Let's go!"

The Ranger and the station wagon rolled out and caught up with Van Hellsing, the three vehicles advancing as a squadron. Mike popped out of the hatch and pulled his trombone through. He played the hook for '*Two Tone Army*' by The Toasters with the checkered flag flapping as they charged. Will swore, "Fucking brutal," as their commando unit pumped their fists and cheered.

They drove deep into the enemy formation and stormed out of the vehicles, fighting from the inside out. Will and the other veteran gunners stayed on the lookout for yuppies as the rest of the units fought in pairs to dispatch the staggering defenders. The bassist kept his tire iron in his left hand and rested the Saiga on top of it as he took aim and dispatched the armed threats.

One yuppie had a leg blown off by the bazooka and raised his rifle to his tank-topped shoulder, but Will squeezed his finger and removed his head. A young lady with a Victoria's Secret bathrobe cinched with layers of duct tape whipped out from behind the building and held up her gun, but Will sent a wad of .00 buckshot and removed the entire upper right quarter of her torso. A couple of unarmed yuppies followed right behind her, and he gave the rotund lady a smack on the head and the teenage boy a mighty kick to the solar plexus, followed by a brain-splattering tire iron blow.

The vanguard advanced, but he trained his gun on the door to the terminal and held his position. Another armed yuppie stalked out of the building, and Will immediately laid him belly-first in the dirt with his scattergun.

AK Greg lumbered next to Will with Cody and Darren in tow and said, "Follow me. Cody, go along the opposite wall and shoot anything that moves. Will, on me. Darren, on Cody. You two don't shoot unless we get overwhelmed. Everyone got ammo?"

The Young Nuns boys nodded, and Cody said, "Plenty."

Greg roared, "Execute."

They stormed the building, and Greg took out zombies by the dozen from nooks and crannies in each room. When Greg was empty, Will instinctively handed him the Saiga and drew his pistol. They reached the opposite side of the building and exited, but Greg jogged over to a downed yuppie, took his AR and an extra mag, and bolted directly into the next hangar, where he continued blasting. His rifle barked as he zigzagged around the giant structure from one defensive position to another. They finally exited into the open air, with Will's brain so high on adrenaline that his eyeballs shook.

Cody doubled over and huffed, "I jus… I jus… a minute…" Devante waved at them from up in the air traffic control tower and made a beckoning gesture. Darren said, "I think I should go do overwatch up there. I'm the only one with a scope."

At the front, guns and joyful voices were in the air. Fresh reinforcements had arrived and made short work of the remaining walkers.

Britney skipped over through a layer of corpses, "Is Darren OK?"

Will said, "Yeah, he's in the tower."

She beamed, "People are saying we got them all. Johnson Avenue is doing some first aid, but it looks like mostly bites and scratches."

Mike sounded his trombone like a bugle and commanded, "Music House! Assemble!"

The familiar crew of Eva, Ted, Sydney, Devante, Darren, Cody, convened around Mike.

Members from each house likewise assembled, and representatives between the groups reported no casualties except a few bites and scratches.

Sydney asked Will, "What were they doing here?"

He froze for a moment, mouth agape, and was able to finally piece together snatches of what he saw in the buildings. There were disgusting piles of food products in various stages of production and crude assembly lines involving stamping machines and grinders.

He scratched his head, "They're making corn syrup, mostly. Some other stuff, too. Gun parts, maybe."

Britney flipped open her phone, "Signal's gone."

Devante nodded, "I saw something crazy rigged up there and cut the wires."

Eva rolled out a wheelbarrow of corn and started passing it out. It was limp and bland, but everyone peeled back the husk and bit into it raw.

Greg was pacing restlessly along the Johnson Avenue crowd, his white-knuckled hands still clutching the Saiga. Britney walked over to him, put her arm around his waist, and brought him back to the van to sit and decompress. She cooed, "Everybody made it Greg. You did a great job. Have some corn?"

The air was cleared of some smoke as people kicked the burning tires into a barrel and rolled it away, and in its place, the sound of WuTang filled the air:

> *The game of chess is like a sword fight.*
> *You must think first —huh ha!—*
> *before you move.*
>
> *Toad style is immensely strong,*
> *and immune to nearly any defense.*
> *When used properly, it is almost invincible.*

'Da Mystery of Chessboxin' beat dropped and bumped through Van Hellsing's sound system, and everyone's hips immediately started swinging.

Courtney came over with a bucket full of aromatic, foamy liquid and handed it to Mikey, "Yo, Brew House brought the booze. This one's a dandelion jalapeño gruit. It's like a beer without hops. There's more over at the 'dragon wagon.' You guys should come party! Sorry, we don't have cups."

Ted and Sydney held the bucket as each person got a huge gulp, and Will was excited to get his turn. The beer sent him back into his body and put a huge smile on his face. His arms stung from the bites and his legs and back were exhausted from combat, but everywhere he looked, people were dancing on cars, toasting the victory, and taking a moment to be with a loved one or a new friend.

He suddenly had an idea and thought, 'We should rip a Young Nuns set, right here right now. It's going to be hard to talk the band into it, but this could be an ideal send-off westward.

He looked around but didn't see any of his bandmates until he turned back toward Van Hellsing, where Cody and Darren already had their instruments set up, and Britney was dancing low and nasty on the roof with mic in hand.

<h1 align="center">9.</h1>

<h1 align="center">The Tramps</h1>

Britney loafed in a birdshot-ridden deck chair around the smoky coals of the fire, with the hot daylight streaming through her frayed blonde tresses into her bleary eyes. The air was clean and free from the smell of musty urine that she had emanated for so long. She still had the smell of armpit, clove, and a tinge of ivory bar soap, and her funk blended uneasily with the savory, tangy smell of venison roasting on the fire. "*Uggh*, I want water, but I'm too comfy-*yuh*."

Cody moaned in sympathy and picked his teeth as he kept his eyes glued to his novel, "Can you get more sticks while you're up?"

Darren added, "Get that cup of blackberries, too."

But rather than rise, she groaned again, "*Uggh*." The four of them remained at a stalemate, with deer bones and gristle piled unceremoniously all around them.

Will added uselessly, "I should probably smoke those hams…"

Britney blinked slowly and uttered again, "*Ugghhh,*" and thought to herself, '*Dude, this is like, the eighth time you brought this up.*'

Will finished his own thought, "But I don't know how."

Their venture to this Wyoming camp off state highway 30 was smooth. They left Kansas with a modest amount of ammo and a fair amount of corn and corn syrup. The guys figured out how to rig the power washer up to a hose to fill their tank from virtually every gas station. Towns were few and far between. so they cruised one or two hundred miles, or until they had to stop and turn wrenches.

Britney was driving the van regularly now, and although she

sometimes stalled out in first gear, she could take an hour-long driving shift in the flat country without issue. They had scarcely seen any indications of other people, alive or somnabulating, and they didn't care to be in civilization at all except that Will wanted to replace the carburetor before they went over the Rockies.

The day before, they pulled over by a stream to refill their water barrel. Cody saw a deer across the meadow and, with split-second reflexes, put a bullet through its heart. They tossed it on top of the van and fortuitously discovered this campsite nearby. It had four small rustic lean-to cabins, empty and fairly clean except for a chest of drawers and a steel-spring cot. One cabin had a queen-sized mattress and fireplace, and Britney claimed it for herself.

Each of them luxuriated in their own space, and the van was now bare as they took stock of their precious few belongings. Britney's laundry was hanging on a clothesline behind the cabin, and she was wearing a curtain from the cabin as a skirt and a purple sports bra that was a size or two too big.

She thought, *I would love to take off this stupid curtain and bra. I feel safe around the guys, I wouldn't care. Maybe I should say something. God, I wish they would get naked and take a bath. They stink, and their clothes stink worse.*

———————————

A peculiar sound undulated across the shimmering bonfire and caused Cody's heart to flutter and his hands to grip the deck chair. He looked at the others, who mirrored his expression of curiosity as they attempted to sit up, intrigued but readied for action in the deeply laid-back deck chairs.

A quartet stepped out of the tree line and onto the driveway a hundred feet away. A beautiful tattooed girl with fair brown hair — short up front with long dreadlocks in the back — played a miniature banjo while two gorgeous, chiseled, bare-chested men in embroidered pants juggled four colorful beanbags each. The girl's chord progression shuffled comfortably between the *one* and the *four* chords for about sixteen bars, and the next part sat on the minor *six* for a few bars but ran through several unfamiliar chords before abruptly restarting the riff on the *one*.

She revved up the tempo and vamped in a Texas Swing style, her frayed pink dress hanging in bits around her skinny body, naked underneath except for a pair of striped shorts. A pear-shaped woman — almost as tall as the men and likely just as heavy — with a red clown nose and dark hair sang along in a gruff contra alto while slapping a small tambourine on the bodacious tattooed flesh that hung out of her bikini-cut daisy dukes.

> *Everybody chill — hey — everybody chill.*
> *Tranquillo! Yeah, we know,*
> *These fuckers like to kill!*

Then, each man threw an extra beanbag at the other and continued cycling one bag between them with higher and higher tosses as the elven-faced girl joined in harmony.

> *We're just passing through, not gonna bother you.*
> *Don't need us? Don't bleed us.*
> *We'll gladly all just shoo!*

Cody scanned the performers paranoiacally but felt no sense of alarm. The singer's voice was a lyric baritone, the banjoist had a breezy demeanor, and the jugglers were now tossing the same beanbags between them except now entirely behind their backs.

> *If you have a snack, we can swap you something back.*

Or give handouts to this band of scouts.
We've earned it with this act.

The two jugglers faced each other and created an intricate pattern of tosses between them, and it became more intense the closer they got. One of them crouched down until he was sitting and then lay down flat on the ground while continuing to juggle.

Cody was mesmerized, dazzled by the skill of these men, and he held his breath as the man on his back extended his legs and his partner strolled forward only to be caught by his feet and suspend himself in a swanlike superman, while his partner juggled all ten beanbags, still lying on his back. Then the flyer, balanced on his partner's feet, joined in the juggling, and they performed more cycles of the bags between them, all while changing positions with gravity-defying grace. He swung and rested in a split, juggling forward and backward.

He rested his shoulders on his partner's arches and pointed his toes at the sky. Then he sat on the soles of his feet and lay flat, all while still cycling the objects. Finally, he crouched on his partner's inverted legs and rose to his feet, taking the ten beanbags for himself. The ensemble sang,

We don't expect to stay. If you like, we'll go away.
We offer you a pick-up, but don't you try a stick-up!

Then they caught the beanbags, and all four of them sang very slowly in tight jazz harmony,

Cuz we got you with the AK...

With the last line, they gestured behind the group where an androgynous green-eyed boy held a grotesque looking SKS with a steel banana magazine jammed into it in a low-ready position.

Cody clutched the armrests and looked on either side of his deck chair for his gun, but the bandits had the jump on him. He resigned himself to enjoy the a cappella sound of their dense five-part harmony singing,

Ever-y-bo-dy chill… yo… ever-y-bo-dy

And then, with a lush, jazzy thirteenth chord,

Chiiiiiill!!!

The juggler who was previously on his back sang a low, descending bass cadenza landing to an almost flatulent pitch.

Please enjoy the — shoooow.

On the last pitch, the banjo entered on a tremolo until the other juggler reached through the bass's legs and tossed beanbags into the air and into his partner's hands. Their limbs wove in and out of each other like virtuoso arachnids. All the while, the banjo played a lush instrumental ballad while the gunman blew a cowpoke melody on a harmonica, peering over it with his green eyes and keeping his rifle at the ready.

There were gymnastics, partner acrobatics, pantomimed mirror acts, and slapstick comedy while the jugglers performed their virtuoso work over a background of breezy instrumental music.

Cody thought, '*I can't believe how smooth and gentle these dudes are. This might be the coolest thing I've ever seen, but they're so chill about it, so graceful. They're like gods!*'

A sudden apparition skittered across the ground, and a black dachshund with a gold chest leapt onto one man's back. The bass put one foot on his partner's shoulders, and as they both rose and stood like a living totem pole, the dog clambered up and onto the top of the top man's head. Both men made a tandem gesture of gratitude with their hands, and the instrumentalists played a coda reminiscent of '*shave and a haircut.*'

The Young Nuns applauded recklessly, with Cody whistling and whooping while wiping tears from his eyes. They kept it up until the acrobats tossed the dog to the singer and dismounted. They took just a moment to decompress while the Ohioans and pop star exchanged anxious glances, Cody felt happy for this unexpected encounter but was still rattled by the fact that they could have just been ambushed.

The singer rasped, "You guys, is that a Kylesa sticker on your van?"

The green-eyed gunman laughed sweetly, "Are you kidding?"

The flyer flicked sweat from his torso with his hands and guffawed as he caught his breath, "I saw that sticker, and I was like, 'This bitch is gonna pop before we finish the act.'"

The banjoist grinned and said with a fixed jaw, "I almost just stopped because when I saw it, I thought there was no way." For a moment, she turned to look at the van. Cody realized that she held her profile to the left side throughout the performance because when she turned to the left, he could see that the left side of her face had a mass of scar tissue over her decimated cheekbone and jaw.

The other juggler chided, "She talks about that band non-fucking-stop."

Will responded, "Yeah, that's Van Hellsing. We're in a band too."

The girl nodded, "Nice. I'm from New Orleans. I was in a band there for a while. I'm Roni, by the way."

Britney clapped her hands, "Oh, I grew up in Kentwood, Louisiana! Did you sing in contests?"

She shook her head, "Well, I didn't grow up there; I grew up in Little Rock."

Darren blurted, "We could listen to *Middle Course* right now."

Roni shouted, "Shut. Up."

"Yeah, we listened to it yesterday." Will stood to start the van and run the engine with Roni in pursuit.

"I just wanted to say, I'm sorry for sneaking up behind you with the gun, but maybe you understand." The harmonica player bowed his head to the others and pursed his lips earnestly.

There was a murmur of forgiveness.

Cody said, "Well, we do have some food, so…"

Britney and Darren shot him a look of disapproval, so he rescinded his offer, "I mean we have an antelope for ourselves, so, you know, we don't need any of your food. I'm Cody, by the way."

The harmonica player slung his rifle over the shoulder of his *Grave Digger* long-sleeved monster truck t-shirt, reached out his lanky hand, and said sweetly, "I'm Little Bear."

The guitar intro for *In Memory* by Kylesa sounded out, and the riff dropped in an asymmetrical compound meter. The girl set her feet wide, held her hands in an air-guitar position, and flung her shoulder-length undercut hair with fury.

Little Bear said, "She's so happy right now."

"Hi, I'm Britney! That's Will over with Roni. Oh my GOD! YOU PERFECT ANGEL!"

The dog pattered up to her and started licking her hand, and she slid off the chair to get as close as possible.

The acrobats came over, drinking from a gallon jug of water, and the deep-voiced one said. "I see you've met Trouser! Does anybody want some water?"

Darren nodded and extended his hand.

"I'm Jory, and this is Travis." He passed the water to Darren, who took a gulp and handed off the jug.

Cody stood, "You guys were amazing! Holy shit! How do you even do that?"

Travis spoke cheerfully but with a bratty voice, "We drop more than we catch."

Jory added, "In the long run."

Will and Roni came back over while Kylesa's Sabbath-y sludge still ripped through the glen, and she said excitedly, "They're in a band too! They're actually on tour. Like, they have instruments and everything."

Jory put a hand on his hip and slowly turned to the group with an expression that suggested '*not too shabby.*'

Cody shook his head, "I mean, we're not like you guys. We're not like, anything special."

The rest of the Young Nuns shot him an admonishing glare, and he shrugged, "Just sayin'…"

Jory gently patted him on the shoulder and smiled with his square jaw and clean-shaven chin, "You're very kind."

The banjoist reclined lavishly in her ripped-up dress on the arm of a deck chair with her good side facing the group, "Where are you headed?"

Britney looked away from the dog but rested her hand on his head. "We're going to the Hollywood Hills to find my kids."

Jory extended a hand and introduced their fifth companion, "This is Opera, she also does all of our costuming."

Roni twisted her face, "You know all of L.A. is pretty busted."

Will nodded, "We've heard of some compounds in the hills, and we might find a clue at her estate."

Travis scrunched his face and flung his fingers outward, lisping "Fuck the West coast."

Opera shrugged, "I liked Big Sur."

Travis shook his head and held up his palms, "It's just, *no*. The West Coast is *no*. For me? It's *no*."

Jory turned to Britney, "We used to do a run there every Summer, but it's getting worse. We're going back to Pittsburgh instead."

Darren perked up, "You're going through Ohio? That's where we're from!"

Will inquired, "We never went to Pittsburgh. We heard the East

Coast is toast."

Roni roared with a laughter that shook her chest under her threadbare black tank top.

Travis smirked, "Pittsburgh is the safest place in the country."

Will, Darren, and Cody dropped their jaws, "What?"

Jory answered, "It's true. You absolutely cannot go East from there, but the North and South sides of the city are well-defended. Plus a little bit in between. You didn't know that? You were so close by."

Darren moaned, "We barely ever saw anyone."

Opera chimed, "That's for the best."

Britney smiled, "I like your banjo!"

She smiled, and her tongue darted out for a moment, "Thanks, it's a banjolele. It's smaller than a banjo."

Jory cleared his throat and then spoke up, "There is rain coming. I have a good sense for this."

Roni bayed, "It's fucking freaky, he's so good."

Jory continued, "So I'd like to start by asking about the parts of the antelope that you may have discarded. Those hams look fresh, yes?"

Will answered, "Yeah, we cut it up yesterday morning."

"I see, and what might you have done with the scraps?"

"Well, the head and hide are back in the woods. We buried the guts nearby."

"Hmm, what guts?"

Will and Cody looked at each other dumbfounded, "Just like, the insides."

Jory stroked his chin, "Did you bury them right away, or did they cool off first?"

Cody answered, "They sat for a few hours while we figured out how to skin it and cut off the legs."

Jory held up his hand to make a proposition. "So how about you take us there? Maybe you can show Little Bear where you buried it, and we can take a few of the goodies, if they're still fresh. Call it a freebee?"

Will paced to the van and faded down the music before turning off the ignition, then gestured for Little Bear to follow him into the woods. Cody looked up at the splotchy blue sky, thinking about how there were four cabins for nine people.

Little Bear stepped delicately through the deadfall with his Chuck Taylors as Will led him to the tree they used for butchering the antelope. Will's lithe companion didn't say much, but his steadfast gaze offered constant affirmation.

Will pointed to the head and the hide, "Well, there's that."

The newcomer grinned and rubbed his crew cut hair, "That's a whitetail deer."

Will stomped over to get a better look. "No, see that there? It has antelope horns."

"It's a yearling. A two-point. It's pretty big, though."

The bassist nodded but didn't want to admit he was wrong. He quietly kicked around the dead leaves until he said, "Here. It's buried in here."

They carved up the earth with the butts of their guns at first, and then with their hands. While they worked, Will huffed and puffed, but his lanky new friend took calm, measured breaths.

Will asked, "So how are you guys getting around?"

"Bikes. We rode up to Billings on three diesel KLRs and then picked up mine there. It got doohickeyed on our last run. This is only my second time out with them."

"You're…The bikes… Diesel?"

Little Bear looked up at Will from his squatted position and smiled, "Jory was at Fort Lewis, and when things got bad, he took a whole pallet of them. I think he got six bikes and a dozen diesel engines."

"Here it is; be careful."

They picked through the guts by hand, and while it smelled strong, it wasn't rancid.

Will interrupted the sickly sound by asking, "You guys do a lot of gigs like this, Little Bear?"

The blonde gingerly removed the stomach and set it off to the side "You can call me L.B. Not that much. There aren't a lot of people around. And it's been getting worse with the second wavers."

"What's that?"

Little Bear plucked out a kidney, dug around for another, set them on a long, rounded rock, then returned to the pile. "It's a frog!"

Will chuckled under his breath as the kidneys really did look like eyes on a frog, then he looked down. pulled out a gleaming chunk of gore, and asked, "Is this good?"

"I mostly want the liver, but we can give the heart and lungs to Trouser. Those are the lungs."

They dug around for a moment more, found the oblong organ, and cut it from the connective tissue. L.B. removed his monster truck shirt, wrapped up the giblets, and said, "They're the ones who just started to turn."

Will cocked his brow in confusion.

"The second wavers. There are all kinds of people trying to turn."

Will gasped, "Seriously? On purpose?"

"Yeah, out West. They grab up phones and tweak out on them. That's why we left Billings."

"Why?"

L.B. trod gingerly through the undergrowth and thought a moment before answering, "Some people are bored or hungry. I think a lot of them think it's a lost cause for humans."

"How long does it take?"

"It sets in within a week, and by two or three months, they're one of them. Did you notice that the zombies look less and less like the original iPhone users?"

Will sighed, "I guess." He walked along the still woods with his shirtless friend for another minute and then asked, "Would you have really shot me during the juggling routine?"

Little Bear looked at Will with the timid grin still adorning his face, "I don't think so."

"Like, if I reached for my gun or whatever."

"I don't think I would shoot you."

They kept walking, and the cabins came into sight through the brush. Again, Will prodded, "Have you ever had to shoot someone like that?"

The harmonicist moaned weakly, gulped, and then answered, "One time. We don't see a lot of people."

"So if I would have pointed my gun at you…"

"I don't think I would have shot you."

Will grappled with his unsatisfactory response as he stepped toward the clearing, and then Little Bear asked, "Are we talking about me shooting you, or you shooting me?"

Will wrinkled his nose, "Huh?"

Little Bear rested his arm tenderly on Will's shoulder, and his voice wavered ever so slightly behind his cool grin, "Will, I've killed a lot of people. A lot. I was in New Orleans for a year. They don't have any zombies, just bad, bad people. I got by, and I got out, and it's just something that happened."

Will nodded, took one step over a downed tree, stepped back, covered his face, and started to cry. "I killed a guy in Iowa. He was going to stick up my friends."

L.B. gave him a brief hug. "It's just a thing that happened. It's ok."

There was a rustle behind a tree, and Trouser came bounding

toward him. Will crouched down, and the dog jumped in his arms. Will picked him up and smiled at the peppy dog, which fanatically licked the deer blood from his hands. "Good puppy!"

"You like my dog?"

Will carried the dog back toward the camp and walked broadly next to Little Bear. He thought, *'I've never met anyone like L.B. Everyone in his group is cool, but I'd love to find more time with just the two of us. Nobody in Young Nuns ever cares about my feelings. As a matter of fact, even my girlfriend never cared about my feelings.*

'I'll invite him to sleep in my cabin. He can take the bed, I'll take the floor. We can just talk about this crazy new world, my girlfriend, our dads, anything. It just feels good to have someone to listen and understand. And we could play with Trouser!'

There was a series of cackles and bleats from the campfire, with Travis' voice squawking sibilantly in the air. Will asked, "Not that it matters, but Jory and Travis. They're gay right?"

Little Bear repositioned the bag of organ meat over his shoulder, "Oh, they say everyone's a little queer. I feel like I'm pretty straight." He chuckled, "I like girls a lot. Opera and Roni are maybe a little bit into girls, but I've never seen it. And yeah, Jory and Travis are long-term boyfriends."

Will scratched his head, "Yeah, I have a girlfriend back in Ohio. But I know for a fact that Britney's going to want to curl up with those guys tonight. She loves gay dudes. I don't know what everyone else is going to do, though. For sleeping."

L.B. agreed, "Yeah, I don't know how we'll divide up the cabins."

Britney bowed low at the waist and shouted, "Yeah, I bet you know how to smoke a ham! I bet you know how to smoke two hams at once!"

Travis dropped his jaw and cocked his hand on his waist, "Bitch, please!"

She sashayed toward him and pointed her finger, "Say my name."

He flipped up his palm and looked away, "Talk to the hand, cuz the face don't wanna hear it."

She jumped up and down and growled, "Say my fucking name!"

Jory leaned over and tickled Travis' ribs causing him to jump this way and that, and he fell backwards into his boyfriend's arms, "IT'S BRITNEY, BITCH!" Then he turned around and started swatting at his lover.

Britney wished she was wearing anything other than the rags she had on. She grabbed Jory's waistline and pulled him in close. "I love these pants!"

Jory pointed one toe, then the other, "Aren't they chic? Opera embroiders them."

Britney turned to look at the sylvan girl, who was rolling a joint on the body of her banjo.

He added, "She does Roni's tattoos, as well."

Travis turned and put his arms around both of them.

Roni rolled up on a strange motorcycle, and Will went right over to her to check it out. Britney couldn't hear much until the girl shut off the engine, then she heard, "It'll run on any oil in Summertime."

Travis groaned and shifted his weight to Jory, "Is she going to make us move the bikes right now? Why's she so bossy-*yuh*."

Jory pinched his cheek and kissed him quickly, "We should move them anyway. I want to get these hams in the chimney asap."

Travis whined, "I don't want to eat liver-*ruh*!"

Jory slapped his ass, "Well you should have some but—" and he slapped it again harder, "you don't have to because—" and harder yet again "We're going to barbecue these ribs." and the last slap echoed around the camp site.

"Owww-*wah*!"

Travis slunk back in the direction they came and Jory walked abreast, with a gentlemanly gait.

Britney flittered toward Opera but felt such a dark, complex, subdued energy that she diverted. She looked over to see Cody sitting on the arm of a deck chair, unusually quiet and focused on something further down the street. She thought, *'Cody's acting weird, like he has a crush. Oooh! I wonder who it is!'*

Opera tapped her on the shoulder and passed her the lit joint. Britney held it to her mouth and pretended to inhale, then tried to pass it to Cody but had to first shake him out of his trance. "Code. Hey Code. Cody!" and then he stepped over to grab the joint.

Britney turned to the girl and gestured to Will and Roni, "I guess the two of them can be a little bossy?"

Opera's angular doe eyes oscillated to face Britney with dispassionate effortlessness. "Roni? She can be a tour de force. She's such a Capricorn."

"I bet the two of them get a cabin together and talk about logistics all night."

Opera smirked on her good side, then pulled her smile so wide that the scarred side of her face flexed. "When I tattoo her, she spends the whole time explaining how to fix guns and bikes, and I neither shoot nor ride! She likes to yak about stuff she knows."

Britney smiled and laughed, elated to have candor with this delicate creature. She replied, "I thought I had to be a shooter at first. Like, the boys in Louisiana shot guns all the time. Just last week, I decided it's not for me. But I'm a driver now, and I'm a medic."

Opera nodded, then Darren walked over, handed her the joint, and asked, "Do you guys sell this stuff?"

She said cooly, "I'm sure we can trade. Talk to Roni," and she gestured to where the tattooed lady was talking shop with Will.

Britney noticed that while Opera's tattoos on her slender limbs were scribbles and scrawls that seemed to have no theme or unifying features, Roni's tracts of skin were covered in bubbly black images of flying intestines, blown out heart valves, disembodied toes, and other familiar carnage. She said, "I love your tattoos! And your embroidery, oh my god!"

"Thanks! I like your skirt, too."

Britney blushed, "Oh my god, this isn't even a thing."

The last three bikes rumbled up to the campfire, piled with guns, camping gear, and other sundries.

Darren turned to Opera and asked, "I can set up my guitar at the van. Do you want to jam?"

"Oh, I'm not a real musician."

He shrugged. "Sounded like music to me. Just play some of that stuff, and I'll comp changes?"

She stood up and stretched from side to side, then answered, "I want to have a little moonshine first."

Britney smelled her smoky girlishness, and she realized that she had to get to know Opera better. She thought, *'We can share a cabin and hunker down during the rainstorm. We can try to give each other crazy hairstyles, and I can tell her about Fakhar. Maybe she'll give me a tattoo! We could even get matching tattoos.*

'But of course, Darren is going to be trying to get with her. Him and his whole damsel-in-distress thing. He'll probably get rejected, and then we'll have to hear him whine about it...'

Darren pulled his amp and speaker cabinet out of the back of the van, set them against the broad side, and plugged the power cable into the inverter. It took him a moment to plug in the cables and dial in a decent tone, and then he set up a microphone for Opera's banjo.

Will had gone off with Jory to rig up the hams in the only cabin with a chimney, which Britney had claimed already. Travis and Britney were rubbing the deer ribs with corn syrup and pepper so they could be roasted over the fire, but they were goofing around so much that this one-minute job had been going on for ten minutes.

Opera walked over to sit on Darren's amp and recline against the van like a cat, and Darren set the mic in front of her and smiled. She started noodling around, Darren threw in some little ornaments and responses, she started cooking on a set of *one-four-five* changes, and he started thumb picking along in an olde-tymey style.

They vamped for a few repetitions, and then Roni joined them to add a backbeat with her tambourine while reclined on her motorcycle. She bobbed her head rhythmically, but her hardened, commanding expression contrasted with the swing in her rhythm.

Hazy streaks of smoke from the cooking ribs played against the grotesque, dark tattoos on her skin. Darren changed up his strumming pattern to put a syncopation on the third beat, and Roni turned to flex her brow approvingly.

He looked back at Opera, who pushed the tempo faster and faster until she cut the time and added a nasty percussive chop to her strum. She bobbed her head deeply, flashed her heavy-lidded eyes at Darren, then flicked her tongue through her crooked smile.

He sensed an opening for a solo so he wiped his left hand on his jeans, but before he started, he thought, *'A speed metal solo doesn't make sense in this music. I know that. Am I just tyring to impress Opera? There aren't any other dudes here who I need to compete with. I don't need to be cooler, or smarter, or more badass anyway.'* He relaxed, listened to the music around him, and noticed that the tambourine was absent.

He looked over to see that Roni was watching him with her face relaxed yet attentive. Her lips were red and slack, looking like they might drip down from her face. Her eyes were soft and sweet yet reflected a lifetime of pain in their darkness and gravity. Even the shape of her body changed; her shoulders were broader and her chest more buoyant.

She held his gaze for a beat, then deflated, wrinkled her brow, scowled, and tapped her tambourine again.

Darren brought the original riff back in but couldn't stop thinking about Roni's face in that one brief instant. *'I want that for her. I want her to feel how she felt in that moment. I don't know what it will take, but I want to try. I'm not going to try to get with her, but I want to listen to her, act like goofy kids, or talk about old times. We could share my cabin!*

I'm usually into girls who need me for my abilities, intellect, or status. She's got herself together but she has emotional needs. Like a woman. Vulnerability— that's what it is.

I'll see if I can get Britney to ask for me. I bet she would. I'll do her a solid and make sure she gets to have her little slumber party with Jory and Travis.'

———————————

Cody was sitting on the ground, listening to the duet and leaning against the deck chair where Travis sat on Jory's lap, and the two of them held court. Jory continued his oratory in a prim and proper deep voice, "Travis and I saw this coming back in Washington. I went AWOL just before Super Tuesday, and we went out to my cabin on the Tye river."

Travis pointed his hands to the sky and squawked, "R.I.P. the Brat Cave."

"Yes, we had a nice little collective there. Seattle expats, military queens, a bunch of straights, too. We lost a lot of friends to zombies and preppers, and when the second wavers came, we had to split. I still have some bikes hidden there, though."

Cody looked up and asked, "So where did you go?"

"We mostly ran and starved. We started trying out the juggling routine so that we would be more disarming—"

The frizzy drummer interrupted, "But you've been juggling before that, right?"

Travis looked down and cocked an eyebrow, "Honey…"

Jory briefly rubbed Cody's shoulder as he answered, "We were in San Fran for ten years and had a little circus in the Haight. After the Brat Cave, we followed the railroads and loafed around in the forest. That's where we found Opera, just wandering around eating berries."

"Oh, ok. I figured you'd been juggling for a while."

Britney swooned with her hand under her chin as she watched the banjoist, "Yeah, she's wonderful."

"And then we had a stint in New Orleans where we met Roni."

Travis chimed in, "Roni is a *real* badass bitch."

Cody picked up one of the juggling beanbags to squeeze it and felt that it was full of .22lr ammo.

Jory laughed, "I don't know if I've ever seen anyone so pissed off as when she met us."

"Girl was like, '*Giiiirl*… how you gonna tell me you got all this bike and you ain't doing shit?"

His partner nodded, "It's true; she was so upset that we had no direction. She got us set up on a little route, and it's been hard, but it worked well. We get weed and auto parts from the West Coast and traded it for food across the Rockies. We'd go south to get guns and ammo, and in between, we help to plant and harvest at our ranch in Billings, Montana."

Travis flicked his wrist, "Fucking second wavers. They're all dopamine sick now."

Roni waddled over and grunted, "Fuckin' truckers."

Jory nudged Cody's shoulder, looked down, and asked, "Have you seen them yet? The truckers?"

Cody slid upward from the ground and half sat/ half leaned onto the arm of Jory's deck chair, "What's that?"

The juggler grasped Cody's wrist gently and sighed, "Oh, you guys aren't going to like this."

He released Cody's hand and leaned forward to hug Travis like a teddy bear. "The ones you call *yuppies* started to put rail wheels on F-250 pickup trucks. We saw it six months ago. Hipsters drive them on the tracks with big loads of corn or meth or whatever. At first, it was awesome because they were easy to jack."

Travis moaned, "Baby misses candy…"

"It was even easier than taking candy from a baby at first. We always traveled the railroad tracks on our KLRs. But now there are so many of them. They can get big masses around the country quickly, and before you know it, there's a horde and a factory in an empty town."

Roni whined, "Did you guys flip those ribs yet?"

Little Bear answered, "Yeah, I think they need another twenty minutes on this side."

The lady groaned, and Jory chastised her, "You can still have a liver kebab."

She feigned a gag and retorted, "I'll give you a kebab."

Jory quipped, repugnantly, "You wish."

Cody felt a magnetism to Jory and Travis that he couldn't articulate. He thought, *'I like watching them love on each other, and yeah, the way they looked all sweaty and juggling was badass. Jory is a classy, sturdy dude, and Travis is like a little wolverine.*

When I used to live at my Mom's place, I would dial up to AOL and look up all kinds of porn. What my friends don't know, is that some of it was dudes with other dudes. I don't know, I'll try anything. I mean, we could share a cabin with the three of us. They could tell me about their circus, about the scene in San Francisco, military life, and maybe some workout tips.

Darren's chill, I don't think he would rag me about wanting to share a room with them. Maybe he'll help me to ask them about it.'

———————————

Will gnawed on the scant, unpleasant meat of a venison rib, which did not taste like the ribs he was used to and stuck in his teeth.

An aromatic wind started to gust in the setting sun, and now the storm that Jory forecast was imminent, so Will was going to ask Little Bear about joining him for the night.

Jory walked over and asked, "Shall we check on the smoker?"

Will agreed, and they walked into Britney's cabin. Jory felt the heat from the coals with his hand and then licked a finger to feel the air rising in the chimney. "It's good, the fire is strong. It's ready for the chips now. This part is important. You have to keep the smoke and temperature consistent. Go ahead, just a little."

The bassist put a little handful of wet bark into the fire, and it immediately started to sputter and smoke.

Jory patted his shoulder and said, "Perfect."

He turned and raised a finger. "Jory?"

"Yes?"

"I believe that Britney is going to want to share a cabin with you, and this is her cabin. So maybe you can keep an eye on it?"

"Oh, well, that is interesting. Yeah, we'd have a super fun sleepover. The thing is, I already pushed my bike into cabin two because the front door is flush with the ground."

Will scratched his chin, "Cabin two, that's Cody's cabin. Did you talk to him yet?"

"Well, not exactly but…"

"Well, yeah we can swap or whatever. She can stay there and I can stay in here with… Well, I should maybe ask first."

"Oh. Well, we thought about checking in with Cody about sharing the cabin with him. The three of us."

Will snorted, "Cody? No way. Definitely you and Britney."

Jory laughed and stretched, "Britney told me who you'd be staying with."

Will chuckled, heartened by his bandmate's insight that he wanted to stay with L.B. "Well, that's very keen of her."

The biker added, "She said you Capricorns would be gabbing about logistics."

"Haha, that's funny. How did you know I was a Capricorn?" Will wasn't into astrology but made a mental note about asking Little Bear about his birthday.

Jory shot him an expression that said, *'Honey, get serious'* and looked him over from head to toe and said, "You're a Capricorn, alright."

Cody paced anxiously, turning away from the group as he tore into his ribs. He was upset with himself for taking so many, as the storm would set in by the time he finished them, and Jory and Travis would surely find the sticky grease on his chin beard to be repulsive.

Opera slinked past him with a small book, bedroll, and a candle, and he turned and spoke, looking like a raving fiend with ribs stuck all in his teeth, "*nn*-Oh *ff*-hey, *nn*-Opera." A chunk flung out of his mouth, and he prayed it didn't land on her skin.

She smiled obligingly.

"Oh, *nahm*, I didn't know if you were *num* headed off to bed or *ff*-what."

Opera said in a melodic tone, "I'm going to write in my diary."

"Ah, well hey… *Num*, so I think my *nnuff* friend was going to *ff*-ask you to stay in *numm* a cabin together."

She put her hand to her chest, blushed, and bent her knees slightly, "Yeah? Is it who I think it is?"

"Oh, I'm sure, *nnaum* because he—" He was interrupted when a lump of cartilage lodged in his windpipe, and he coughed and gagged violently as it worked itself out.

He strained to finish his sentence as his beet red face drooled, "I think… He's just—" and his hacking resumed. "…He… He looked…"

She nodded with a curt "*Hm.*" and walked away stiffly. Her body language didn't seem to match what he expected, but he knew he had just done something good for his bro. It had been a while since he got to play wingman, and he felt like he had done his job, so now maybe Darren would pay him back.

Britney surrendered Trouser to his owner as the wind from the gathering storm caused him to shiver in fear. She patted his head, "Aw, he wants to go in for the night.

L.B. kissed his dog and smiled a blank yet genuine smile to the pop star. "I'm glad I got to meet you, Britney."

She giggled, "Yeah, this has been fun, right? We're two groups of the closest friends, but it feels good to meet new people."

Little Bear smiled, and the firelight flickered in his eyes. She thought about how just a few months earlier, she was a complete stranger. Now she was part of the band and had a chance to come in clutch for her friends.

She suggested, "You know, you're such a good listener. I know who you should camp with tonight."

He tilted his head inquiringly.

"I bet Cody would love to camp with you. He loves to talk, and sometimes we just can't cope. He talks and talks. And you like to listen! I think you would get along great."

Little Bear nodded silently, then asked, "What about Will? He seems like he's got a lot to say."

Britney laughed, "Yeah, right. He barely ever says what's on his mind. He's going to talk Roni's ear off, though. They can talk all night about miles per gallon and carburetors, interstate highways and mountain passes, or how to make your own shotgun shells. *Booo-riiiing*."

L.B. excused himself, "Well, I'm going to check in with Roni because I think we're about ready to turn in."

Darren closed up the van and turned to walk up to the fire, but Cody met him there, rinsing his face as he asked, "Have you seen Jory and Travis?"

Will was a few paces behind, having similarly washed and groomed his visage behind the van, and said, "Oh, they're in your cabin with Britney."

Britney stood and hollered from the other side of the fire, "What?"

The big guy continued, "Oh, there you are. I told them you were going to stay with them. That was almost an hour ago."

Cody asked Will, "So they're staying with Britney, or what?"

She shook her head, "No, no, no. I'm staying with Opera. She went for a walk, I think."

Cody winced, "She went into a cabin to write in her diary. Darren, I thought you had that in the bag!"

He threw up his hands, "What?"

Britney turned to Will, "Where have you been? I thought you were already in your cabin talking shop with Roni."

Darren interjected, "Roni? I thought she was working on her bike. Where is she?"

Cody shrugged, "Probably in Will's cabin with Opera or Darren's with L.B."

Britney stormed to her cabin, "I'm going to bed."

Cody turned to Darren and egged him on, "Dude, you could probably still hook it up with Opera."

"What are you talking about? I don't even like her. Hey, Brit!" and he chased after her.

Will and Cody shrugged at each other, and the drummer said, "Yo, everybody thought you and Roni were going to have an executive council."

"A what?"

Cody broadened his shrug, "I don't know, they said you were both Capricorns or something!"

Will folded his arms over his chest, "What the fuck? Where are we supposed to sleep?"

Cody cocked his head, "There might still be some space in one of those cabins."

"Dude, we're not going to go knocking on their doors after dark while they're asleep. We don't know them well enough. That's how people get shot. Come on, we'll have to just pile in." And they both chased after Darren to get inside the cabin before the rain came.

The deluge was in it's tenth hour, and the four Young Nuns slept restlessly, all piled onto the damp mattress in the smoke-filled cabin while the smell of rank pants, putrid body odor, and venison farts added a fetid complexity to the acrid air.

10.

The New Driver

Britney gestured broadly with her hand between twists and jerks of the gear shifter while her red boots alternated left and right to work the clutch and gas. She had just taken over driving duties and felt fresh and chipper. Her pink robe from Chicago was laundered but still blood-stained, and aside from the boots, it was the only thing she had on her body. A breeze wafted in through the rusty floor, and she felt the fresh air between her thighs.

"Listen, we do the passenger side of the van with *Y, O, empty space, N, G.* And then right below it, *N, empty space, N, S* with a giant *U* that goes from top to bottom of both words."

Darren scoffed, "That's kind of weak. It's like a fast food restaurant logo or something."

Will rode shotgun and had been persistently backseat-driving, "Downshift before you get to this hill. Also, that design won't work. That's not how it's spelled."

Cody shouted out, "Y, U, N, G!"

Darren chuckled and shoved him forcefully, "You're so dumb."

The drummer laughed, "N, U, N, Z, Z, Z baby!"

Britney turned, "Are you serious?"

Will and Darren shouted, "NO!" while simultaneously Cody shouted, "YES!" and added, "In rotating caps!"

Will sighed, "Whenever we perform with the van, we have the door open anyway. So your logo would be obscured."

Cody clapped his hands, "Yo, that's even sicker. It could say, Y-N-G, N-N-S!"

Britney asked, "How do you usually spell it?"

Will turned to Darren, and the guitarist said in a calm and sober voice, "*Lowercase x, capital X, lowercase x Y, O, U, N, G, lowercase x, N, U, N, S, lowercase X, capital X, lowercase x.*"

Britney muttered, "That's so stupid."

Cody poked at Darren's ribs, "First show ever, '*Yung Nunzzz*'! I still have the flyer."

Will turned back, "That's because you made the stupid flyer!" Then he turned to the driver and said apologetically, "Some guy in Denmark had a MySpace with the regular spelling of '*Young Nuns,*' so we made it with all the *X*s."

Britney laughed mockingly, and Will chuckled along.

They were crossing a wasteland between Idaho and Oregon, and the vacant, overgrown farmland was depressing but felt far safer than the twists and valleys of the mountains, where there could be an ambush or breakdown at any moment. Nevertheless, the mile markers whizzed by.

Then Darren cleared his throat, "I know we've talked through this a few times, but I just want to clarify…"

Britney closed her eyes and felt tension enter her shoulders. She swung her left leg wide and braced it against the door to summon more strength.

He went on, "So we are all in agreement that we want to find a friendly enclave before we attempt to enter L.A. County.

Will shook his head, "I'm not going over the grapevine until we get some intel."

Darren pointed a finger, "OK, so we won't go anywhere near the Southern California coast until we rendezvous with some survivors?"

He paused to invite dissent, but nobody protested, so he went on,

"Now, we discussed Will's theory that highway 101 would be clear. I favor that theory but—"

Cody interjected, "That's a plan without an escape—"

The guitarist calmly escalated his voice, "Let me finish." He continued with measured words, "I am willing to admit that I am biased toward that plan because I want to see the Pacific Ocean."

Will muttered, "We could stroll right down the shore. Right down the shore."

Darren reclaimed his platform, "Now. We know for a fact that Jory has friends just north of Bend, and also at Pyramid Lake. And we can mention his name and get a comfortable campsite. We could regroup for a day, gather fuel reserves, and gather intel before we go further."

Britney sneered, "My cousins have all of that stuff—"

Darren held his ground. "Ope! Ope! *Insofar* as I have communicated *my* bias regarding Will's plan, I would like for *you* to acknowledge that you are biased in that *A*, you *want to believe* your cousins are still alive, and *B*, you want to get to the Hollywood Hills as soon as possible."

Britney snapped her legs shut and shouted, "Fuck you! I know what I'm doing."

"Woah, woah!"

"Easy now,"

"Hey!"

She twisted her face into a frown and jerked the van unnecessarily into low gear, sending the engine screaming as her bandmates took offense.

Cody interjected, "I'm not opposed to stopping by Ashland. It makes more sense to visit Bend this morning and then go to Ashland in a day or two."

Will nodded, "Brit, are you willing to admit that your cousins might be dead? I mean, we've lived through this shit a lot longer than you. You know *everyone you know might be dead*, right? I mean, I know you *know* that, but do you *realize* that?"

She spat, "Yeah, Kevin is probably dead, and maybe my kids are dead, and hopefully Jamie is dead. But I know my cousins are alive, and that's where we're going. Period. End of story. *Let me drive.*"

The group bounded along in stony silence, and she thought, *'They're clearly on to me. I shouldn't have snapped at them. Now they think I'm a bitch. But I'd rather they think I'm a crazy bitch than for them to find out I've been on the web.'*

She took a breath and tried to reconcile. "OK, fine, yeah. My cousins might be dead. Sure. But they're, like, *survivalers*. You know what I mean? They have a bomb shelter and a radio. And horses, and they know all kinds of people out there. They know a guy who does Dodge Rams and he probably has all the stuff to fix this thing. And we can play a gig."

Britney could hear the whispering behind her, "Dude, just let her go to this stupid town if it makes her happy."

"Then we backtrack and go to Bend."

"She's being totally crazy."

"She's better than she was, though. Back then…"

"That's for sure."

Britney relaxed her face into a sassy pout, and her again leg swung out against the door with such a thud that it startled Will.

They had ambled through the Rocky Mountains and were now ripping through long stretches of desert plains that felt to Britney a lot like California. Darren wasn't wrong; she had a feverish desire to be home with her kids, and she did recognize that she yearned for a home that would never exist again.

But the reason why she wanted to rush to Ashland was because a new friend on britneyarmy.com was organizing a gig for them, and they were already a day late.

A sign indicated *Brothers, 2 mi.,* and Will popped open the glove compartment. Britney's shoulders tensed once again, she slammed her knees together and began to itch all over as she thought, '*Oh fuck, oh fuck! Did I remember to X out of the browser?*'

He pulled out the phone, and she reached over. "Here, give it to me. I'll check."

Will stayed her hand and cast her a dirty look. "No, it's ok. You can just drive."

She strenuously reached for it, but he scowled and held the phone out of her reach.

Will casually flipped it open and murmured, "Yeah, there is a bar. What am I… hmm…"

Darren added, "We're on a hilltop so it's probably really far away."

Then he slammed it shut, held it like a club, and shouted louder than Britney had ever heard, "WHAT THE FUCK IS THIS!?"

He held up the phone for his bandmates to see. "She's on the *goddamn* internet."

Cody asked, "Is she dopamine sick?"

Darren shook his head. "Clearly not."

Will passed the phone back, "She's all over the web browser."

Britney squealed, "No, I'm not!"

Cody asked, "That's a smartphone?"

Will replied, "No, but it has the internet."

Cody scratched his beard, "It does?"

Darren nodded, "Yeah, I mean most phones always did but we never used it."

They had been talking as though she wasn't present, but now Will turned toward her and shouted, "Stop the van."

Britney fixed her gaze on the horizon and uttered, "No."

Her face swelled with blood, and her reddened eyes dripped with tears. He shouted again, "Stop the van!"

She cried, "No!"

Darren opened the phone and then closed it. "What the fuck is

BritneyArmy?"

She wept, "It's my fan club. I just wanted to see if it was still there."

Will yelled, "How long have you been using it?"

She blubbered noisily but didn't answer.

"Stop the van!"

She whimpered, "Let me drive!"

"Stop the van!"

Darren called out, "You've posted a lot on here."

Britney choked, "Only since Indianapolis."

Will hollered, "That was weeks ago!"

Darren continued inquiring. "What is this? Who is Debra18?"

She sputtered, "She's my friend in Ashland!"

Will snatched the phone back. "Oh, your cousin, huh?"

Britney's wiped the tears from her eyes. "She got us a gig!"

Cody snarled, "And your cousin in Chicago?"

She choked, "I found Karla on BritneyArmy."

Cody asked, "What is this. Is she on MySpace?"

Darren shook his head, "No, it's like an old 1990s message board. It's all HTML. No file hosting or anything. Old school shit."

Will's voice sounded forcefully calm but agitated. "Stop the van, please. Now."

Britney sobbed, "Let me drive." She started banging her knee against the outside door with violent fervor.

He raised his voice, "God dammit, stop the van."

She banged her knee louder and burst out yelling. "You motherfuckers don't know your *asshole* from your *elbow*. You were just sitting around in Ohio with your *thumbs* up your *asses*, eating the *corn* out of *Rick's shit* for breakfast and saying '*thank you*' until *I* got you to realize what you've got.

"And even then we just did things your way — running the flank and checking out random towns — but you're *still* not doing shit compared with what we should be doing. Chicago wasn't the best gig, but what the fuck were you guys going to do? Cody wanted to drive around with blue bandanas hanging out of the van like a *goddamn retard.*"

She punched the steering wheel for emphasis. "And you don't even know what I have lined up in Ashland. Car parts, ammo, food — fucking — slutty chicks and news from all over the place. And there's another rock and roll band. What else do you want? Debra knows all kinds of people. You want to ride a fucking horse? How about coffee? When was the last time you had coffee? She's got coffee. What do you want?"

The rest of the band rode along dumbstruck, and she realized that her knee was still thumping against the door. She added, *"Let me fucking drive."*

They rode silently past Brothers, OR as well as Millican, and then Will mumbled, "Columbus Sucks."

Cody asked confusedly, "Columbus was cool, wasn't it?"

Will replied softly, "No, *Columbus Sucks Because You Suck.*"

Darren asked, "Isn't that the—"

Will nodded, "Yeah, that's their music scene message board. HTML, like Britney's fan page." He entered the URL into the browser and uttered, *"Hmph.* It's still online."

Cody exclaimed, "OPIUM!"

Darren furrowed his brow and narrowed his eyes.

Cody recited, *"Olympia Punk, Indie, and Independent Music.* That was their scene board."

Will turned around, "Was it?"

"I'm pretty sure. Look it up! No, *Indie and Underground Music.* OPIUM."

Will typed the website into the browser and nodded. "Yeah, it's online too. Shit, lost the reception."

Britney cooed, "Debra says they have a signal near their place."

Darren laughed, "*Never Tell Me the Odds*."

Cody pointed at him, "Oh yeah! Is that… Cleveland?"

"Buffalo, I think."

Will reclined in his seat somewhat. "Do you remember our password for all these? I think it was the same for all of them. *Password? Young Nuns?*"

Cody slapped his forehead, "*Ballsack*."

Darren laughed, "Oh my god, it is. *Ballsack* in rotating caps."

Will turned his head, "Aren't we banned from some of them?"

The drummer leaned back in his seat, "We're banned from *PC-PDX* for sure. I don't know, we trolled the shit out of all of them when we were trying to book our tour."

Britney rolled her shoulders, straightened her posture, and shimmied her hips. Her body felt relaxed, and she kept cruising. Bend, OR was fifteen miles away, and she was confident that they would make the gig.

The rear seat from Van Hellsing had been removed from the vehicle, and Darren, Britney, and Cody reclined on it under the branches of a maple tree.

They each had a sausage in one hand and a beer in the other. Nate, the pig farmer, was skinny as a twig, with long black hair and a beard peppered with grays. He passed a joint as he yammered, "I tell ya, I got myself a nice little homestead in the holler just upstream from here. Just a couple miles, as the crow flies. I only travel by the crick. You don't see a lot of 'em in the water."

Will pursed his lips and glared at his bandmates. "Pacific Coast, I'm telling you."

Weed smoke dumped out of Britney's mouth and nose as she croaked, "You guys get waves ever?"

Nate's eyes narrowed. "The biters? Oh yeah. Had one a couple years ago. All San Francisco county let loose. Portland, too. Wouldn'ta been that bad, but they picked up all the stragglers on the way. We didn't have a lot of phones 'round these parts, and the few that had 'em and turned, we had 'em on the run. But they hit the towns first, and since then, anyone with any sense is in the country."

Britney nodded, bleary-eyed, and gnawed at the sausage, "'S-rlly gwd!" She heard an unusual noise and turned to see a beautiful brown horse.

She said, "Oh wow," and a chunk of pork dropped out of her mouth and down her robe, resting in the faint crease of her belly.

The horse trotted forward, and a bold-faced woman in her late thirties with a muscular physique smiled broadly. "Hey, Brit, welcome to Oregon!"

She nodded for fear of spitting more meat chunks.

Two clean-shaven cowboys cruised past them on horses. The cowgirl reached into her saddle bag. "I have something for you!" and pulled out a square jewel case.

Nate took it from the horsewoman and handed it off to Britney, who looked to see that it was a CD labeled '*Brittany's Best*' in multicolored markers, decorated with dozens of hearts.

Britney covered her mouth and laughed, washed the sausage down with the beer, and held it up to show the others. "Don't you dare play this in the van!"

Cody hit the joint defiantly and grunted, "I'm gonna."

Britney leaned forward and swatted at him playfully.

The horse lady beamed, "I made it when I started nursing school. I thought you might like it."

Britney sat up and situated her robe for modesty. "So this is my band; this is Cody, Darren, and Will.

The cowgirl waved, "I'm Leah. Me and the fellas have a ranch over near Klamath."

Will stepped away from the tree. "Isn't that far?"

"It's a ways. We like the opportunity to make a trip, check in on the kin."

Britney cocked her head, "So you're the ones she talks to on the radio?"

Leah nodded, "Yep, we keep in touch. We often come out this way around the fourth of July, just after we plant our last fields of corn and alfalfa. When it turned out you might be passing through, we decided it was high time we got all our neighbors together for a festival. We never imagined it would be like this!"

Brit asked, "Debra says that you surf the web on a Nokia too."

Leach chuckled, "I've done it before. There's a community board on the Ellensburg Gazette that still runs. Some of us post there when it's important. It's a lifesaver."

Britney thought about gloating over the effectiveness of flip-phone internet communication, but chose to feel her vindication privately.

The warmth spread over her as she looked out the festival, where a gray-haired couple and a youth were setting up folk instruments on an improvised stage in front of Van Hellsing. Just behind, a family of five was splashing naked in the creek while an elderly hippie couple was fishing in the buff.

A large contingent of black families rested under a large oak on the opposite side of the clearing, with potatoes and hunting rifles on display for barter. A dozen young boys perpetually chased a soccer ball, with no discernible rules whatsoever. The biggest and meanest guys, the only ones other than Cody who wore rifles, had been tending to a pig on a spit for an extremely long time, and Britney thought, *'Those guys don't look like they have any clue how to cook an egg, let alone a pig.'*

A young teenage boy wearing only cutoff sweatpants, and a young teenage girl in an oversized white dress — both of whose hair was long, matted, and disheveled — flitted around and intermittently made out with furious passion. A large group of scowling androgynous people kept to themselves, some lone farmers hawked their produce, and some wild-eyed ascetics ranted conspiracy theories.

All told, about a hundred people milled about the hillside, with another hundred in the camping area on the other side of the hill.

Leah bid her adieu, saying, "Well, we're gonna pasture these horses and listen to a little fiddling here. I'll see ya later."

She spun her horse around and raised herself out of her saddle ever so slightly so that her ass bore the definition of each glute and thigh muscle through her blue jeans. She turned to Cody, narrowed her eyes lustily, and twanged, "I love a man with an AK."

Britney dropped her jaw and bugged her eyes at Cody, and Darren goosed his ribs until he fell off the bench. Will laughed, reached down, and gave him a hand, slapping him jovially on the shoulder as he re-situated himself.

Will took off his black Levis jacket and chucked it on the ground.

A thirteen-year-old boy with very tan skin and curly blonde hair stalked over —mid-tantrum — and clambered up the tree that Will was leaning against. A short woman with a round, youthful face and long blonde hair, wearing a plain homemade canvas dress, followed him laboriously.

The boy shouted down, "I hate that kid! I wish he was dead!"

She called up sweetly but with palpable annoyance, "Layton, honey, I understand that, but you know that you can't hit him."

"I don't care! He was *puppy-guarding*, and he wouldn't stop."

"That sounds frustrating, sweet pea, but when you're playing in a group, you have to compromise."

He sassed, "Fuck him, and fuck you!"

She stepped back, became livid, stared daggers, balled her fists, and roared, "LAYTON PRESTON!"

He immediately recanted, whining, "No, no, *I didn't mean it*. I'm sorry. *I didn't mean it*."

She took a breath and wiped the sweat from her brow. "Now you stay up there and calm down, but you *will* apologize." She looked up at Will and attempted to smile cheerfully, although her face was still aghast.

He wordlessly handed her his half-empty bottle of beer, and she took a gulp. She held it out for him to retrieve, but when he refused, she downed the bottle with a smirk.

Britney felt a touch of envy and sympathy as she watched this display of maternity.

The mother asked, her voice sweet once more. "Do you have kids?"

Will laughed, "No, but Britney does. That's where we're headed. That's our van; we're coming from Ohio."

The lady chuckled, "Sometimes I want to pack up my kids and send them in a van across the country. I have four of them."

He asked, "Are you part of one of these communities?"

"No, it's just me and the kids. I was in Portland for a while after Super Tuesday, but we made our way to the country. We have a little homestead where we fish and forage."

"I'm Will, by the way."

"Hi *Will by the way*, I'm Meadow."

She stepped back and looked at his body, breathing in slightly with her hand on her chest. The smirk returned to her face, and she asked, "What's on your shirt?"

He looked down, "Oh this? It's a band called *See You Next Tuesday*."

"Have you ever heard of *Dystopia*?"

"Yeah, they're like the original powerviolence band."

"I used to go to all of their shows in Arcata. Layton used to wear my *Dystopia* t-shirt BUT HE LOST IT."

A defiant adolescent voice shouted from above, "I didn't lose it!"

She rolled her eyes skyward, "Then where is it?"

"It's somewhere!"

She sighed, fixed her heavy eyes on Will, and cooed, "Here, breathe with me."

She embraced him, set her forehead against his sternum, and reached up to place two fingers along each shoulder blade. Britney thought, *'Oh-kaayeee, they're having a moment,'* then turned away to give them some privacy.

The string band down by the van started stomping, and with a gleeful glissando, they started jangling a delightful tune at a fast yet conservative tempo. The gray-haired lady was dancing on clogs, revealing a formidable set of legs while the fiddler, mandolin, and two guitars picked over the thumping electric bass, which Will had loaned to the washtub bassist.

Britney glanced back at Will and saw Meadow was methodically sliding her hands up Will's back.

"Britney! You guys are having a good time?" Britney turned and saw Debra, a wiry lady roundabout forty with long black hair, dark features, and masculine hands.

Darren spoke first, "Oh shit, this is Debra?"

Britney answered, "Ah, yeah, you were out hiking when we linked up. This is Darren."

He reached out, shook her hand, and commented, "This is so much fun. Your friends are amazing!"

Debra shook her head, "I don't hardly know any of these people. Most of us only know one or two others. People got real excited about the show, and they still just keep coming from god-knows-where."

Britney winced, "Yeah, sorry about that. I thought we were going straight to the coast, but we took a couple extra days to camp."

"Oh no, that's fine. The first day, we all just got blind drunk, and the second day, we raided the zombie tower by the tracks. That's why I couldn't send any more messages, by the way. No more service. And after that the boys got so excited that we went and raided the Nazi pig farm in

Medford. They were scared shitless! I felt kinda bad so I gave them the zombie meth we got from the raid. You guys don't do that stuff, do you?"

Britney stated emphatically, "No way!"

But after a pause, Cody intoned, "*Weeeelll*, maybe in an emergency…"

Debra dismissed his confession with her hand, "We all have a little emergency speed, hon. So this is Jenny's band here. She's the clogger. Actually it's just her and the fiddler. These other folks are just here by happenstance. But I was thinking you guys should go next. Butch's band is liable to play for hours. We'll put them on last. Did you meet Butch?"

Britney shook her head.

"That's him down there with the pig now. God damn, he's in rare form. He just killed twenty zombies and a Nazi yesterday. And it's the first time his daughter's been out of their enclave since she was nine years old. And here she is, running around with Jenny's boy. If Butch and Cassie weren't tending to that pig I think that boy might lose a nut or two."

Britney laughed.

Darren turned and said, "I'm going to wash and get warmed up before we play," and then ambled away.

Debra sat in his place, and Britney listened to the band, feeling more freedom than she could remember in her whole life.

In between songs, Debra pointed out, "That fella with the mando. That's Harris. He's the one with all the Dodge Rams. I think he mostly does trucks, but he should have what you want."

Britney smiled but was still reluctant to interrupt Will.

Debra went on, "And that lady there selling the fresh linens—"

Britney interrupted, "Oh my god, I have to buy some. I was down there earlier. They smell so clean!"

"Well, she's the one whose husband has all the chemicals. I don't know if she has what you're looking for, but I'm sure she'd be happy to clear out that warehouse. She's trying to raise cows."

They listened to the rest of the song, and then Britney heard a soft voice speaking behind her. "You're a Capricorn." She turned to see Meadow still meditating over Will's body and realized that they had been there all along, albeit silently.

Will replied, "How did you know?"

Britney thought, *'He usually carries himself like a mound of shit. Now his posture is broad, healthy…'*

The boy dropped out of the tree and started to jog away, but his mother yelled, "Layton, I'm not done with you yet!"

"Come on, Mom!"

"Layton, if you're going to play with the other kids, we have to have an agreement."

"It isn't fair! Come on, Mom!"

Will reached down and popped the lid off an empty five-gallon bucket that was placed there as a seat.

"Hey bud, do you know how to play ultimate frisbee?"

"Huh?"

"Here, catch," and he spun the lid toward the boy.

Layton reached out but knocked the flying disc to the ground with a thud, and he held up his finger in pain. "Ow!"

"You're good, dude. Here, try to throw it back."

Layton looked like he was going to burst into tears and throw a tantrum, but he picked up the lid, wound up, and rocketed the disc to the ground.

Cody tucked his rifle under the seat and jogged past them, "Here, Will. I'm open!"

Will retrieved the lid and showed the little man the technique in slow motion. "It's like this. You flick it at the end." He floated the disc into the air, where Cody plucked it with a flourish.

Cody handed it off to the boy. "Ready?"

Layton practiced the motion, then whipped a laser beam pass that

Will clapped between his hands. "Woah, nice toss!"

The singer looked at Meadow, who rested her hands on the small of her back and watched with humble satisfaction, experiencing what Britney recognized as the joy and loss of her child growing up.

'*I wonder what Braden and Alex are up to. I bet they're working hard, and also getting into a little mischief out on the farm. I hope they still have the hairstyles I gave them. Maybe Meadow would let me give her kids' hair a trim. Meadow is a supermom, and Leah is a badass. But I don't have to compare herself to them. My three best friends think I'm enough, and it's time for me to believe it too. I want to do something spiritual. Something for myself. Something with my hair...*'

Britney was pouring sweat and blood from her shimmering bald head. She cut off her locks in the stream, and Debra gave her a close shave with her bowie knife. She only nicked one tiny spot, and although it didn't hurt, it wouldn't stop bleeding.

Debra's F-150 provided stage lighting with its headlights and deer spotter, and the pervasive rollicking dancers, leaping children, and rowdy drunks cast flickering silhouettes as Young Nuns closed out the spectacle of sunset and carried on into the night.

Fucking paparazzi, go get fucked.
Shove an umbrella in your ass and then open it up!

The band hit a riff with a lewd, bluesy feel, and she barked out new words to the verse,

If you don't have my back,
go on back and whack it.

> *I'm always kind of small*
> *But I got black magic.*

> *Better back me on habit*
> *'cuz the stars say I have it.*
> *I don't know where we'll go*
> *But you'll fuck like a rabbit.*

The chorus was very downbeat heavy, with a kind of *oom-pah* feel in the instruments, and she sang a broad, sultry melody in contrast.

> *Mmm, you've got to feel me too.*
> *Let me shake the costume off the real you.*

> *Mmm, you've got to feel me too.*
> *Let me shake the costume off the real you.*

Darren and Will walked down in triplets to cue the next bluesy verse,

> *One time I knew a girl,*
> *I think her name was Pearl.*
> *She couldn't rest til she was the best*
> *at everything in the world.*

> *All day her toes would curl.*
> *All day she'd have to hurl.*
> *Her friends let her know, she could let it go*
> *She'd perfect just as Pearl.*

She walked up to Will, spun around, strutted to Darren, then whipped back to face front and sing the chorus,

Mmm, you've got to feel me too.
Let me shake the costume off the real you.

Mmm, you've got to feel me too.
Let me shake the costume off the real you.

Two colossal figures blacked out the headlights of the F150, and she saw Debra and Savannah supported by two stocky fellows, chicken fighting in the mosh pit. Another cowboy swooped behind the singer, crouched down, and picked her up on his shoulders.

The three Gargantua came up together, and the ladies on top slapped each other about the chest and shoulders playfully with some fake punches thrown in for theatrical effect. Britney was thrown backwards, and a sea of hands carried her over dozens of festival-goers. She could feel some of the hands supporting her naked scalp while she crowd surfed, and it was a strange but provocative feeling.

After about sixteen bars in, she realized that Darren was near the end of his solo, so she hopped to the ground and grabbed the mic to scream the chorus over a more intense drum beat.

Mmm, you've got to feel me too.
Let me shake the costume off the real you.

Ironically, she felt relaxed and positive yet yelled with nihilistic fury,

Mmm, you've got to feel me too.
Let me shake the costume off the real you.

She ended the song in a dramatic pose as the instruments cut off into howling feedback and raging applause. She loosened up, bounced, and smiled with coy appreciation. She turned to her band to see that Will tune his base, Cody remove his shirt to wipe his face, and Darren was beckon Jenny the clogger for a cup of water.

Britney spoke softly into the mic, "How's everyone doing tonight?"

The crowd pulsed with sonic and visceral appreciation.

"Listen, you guys, I just want to tell you all. No matter what anyone ever told you, no matter what you feel. You are enough. You don't have to be everything in the world. Just love what you do and find people to support you. And fuck Nazis!"

The crowd cheered and whooped, and Darren chugged the intro riff with steady downpicks as Britney hopped with giddiness. She spoke, "This song is called *Enough.* It is one of the first Young Nuns songs I learned, but we're going to play it a little differently."

Cody and Will terminated the intro riff with a fill, the band rested for a beat of silence, and Britney reeled back and punched the sky with a gutsy "*Hunh*!" The band came in on a skank beat, and she dropped the mic and dove back into the crowd, where she jostled around with the other bodies.

She ran to the mic and sang,

> *I am the child!*
> *I am the mother!*
> *I am the master!*
> *I am fire!*

The guitar and drums kicked back into full force with a slightly more serpentine riff that moved through a few tasty chords.

> *I am the enough!*
> *I am the enough!*

I am the enough!
I am the… enough!

In the second verse, the guitar and drums played full force, and she shouted the same lyrics. She repeated the same chorus, now red in the face as well as red in the scalp.

Will and Cody played a harmonious, chorale-like progression over a pounding eighth-note bass drum beat for the bridge, and she realized that blood was still streaming down her cheek, neck and chest. She started to play with it, streaking war paint over her face and limbs.

There was a final cymbal choke, a single ride bell from the drums, and she bent forward, turning her eyes aggressively toward the audience and squatting with vulgarity, growling,

I am the enoooough!

The breakdown was savage, with bodies cascading over each other in an eruption of bruised limbs and pints of sweat exchanged between people who had scarcely seen another human in years.

Britney threw the mic over the van and shoved a stocky man who rebounded just a little too close to her. She jazz-ran to the back of the van, dashed up the stairs, retrieved the mic and moaned,

Rrrrrruuuuuuuuughhhh…

Cody played a quick fill on his cymbal bells, and Darren cut the time into the breakdown with scythe-like swings of his headstock.

Rrrrrruuuuuuuuughhhh…

She opened her eyes wide and puffed her shoulders, throwing in just a couple of hard-working hip and shoulder pops to prove her mettle while stalking around with bravado.

The band launched back into the final verse, and she yelled,

I am the child!
I am the mother!
I am the master!
I am fire!

The band terminated the song into raging applause, and Britney tried to stifle a giggle with an '*aw shucks*' gesture.

"I think I'm going to sing the last song from up here!"

There was a groan of protest from the crowd but she held up her hand, "It's all we know. Those are all of our songs. Let me introduce the band! On drums, we have the studly and debonaire Cody Wiecharski! This is our van dad but he's a sensitive man and a killer bassist, Will Jenkson! And all the girls love Sir Darren Kerome. I'm Britney Spears and this song is called *Ass Blast*."

Will shouted up to her with annoyance, "It's called *Jackknife*."

Britney asked the crowd through the mic, "What do you think the name should be? *Jackknife* or *Ass Blast*. Let's hear it for *Jackknife*."

There was a smattering of applause and a few bleating voices.

"Let's hear it for *Ass Blast*!"

The valley echoed with shouts of adulation for the latter, and the band shook their head and rolled their eyes at their singer, who shrugged and then crouched down and yelled, "This song is called Ass Blast!"

I'll pretend you're Kevin, and send you up to heaven!

The band came thundering in on a raucous beat that made Britney jump up and down on top of the van with such intensity that it bounced on the shocks.

They hit the verse, with its noodley, spastic riffs, and she yakked over top of it with acrobatic sass,

> *Alone, we're herded to the slaughter.*
> *With whip marks that we set on our own backs.*
> *The whips were handed down from father to daughter.*
> *But it's our own hand that cracks.*

The lyrics were based on the previous singer's words, but over the past few weeks, she spun them to suit herself. The band then crashed into the chorus like a flurry, and she arched her back, twisted her throat, and croaked with inhuman euphony,

> *Save your fury*
> *For the real foes.*
> *My baby's father.*
> *This hungry posh.*

The instruments stuck to a single note while Cody laid down a drum roll, and she gyrated her body ominously, quickly jerking into a closed fetal position before switching personas and exploding her energy in all directions for the verse, yammering recklessly,

> *Mostly, I ain't gonna shoot 'ya.*
> *I'll fill the clips and pass them down.*
> *Soon, you'll smell worse than my kombucha*
> *You shouldn't step to me, clown.*

Darren snapped into the melody, jumping so hard on the flimsy plywood stage that his amplifier looked like it was inches from tipping over completely. He stepped up onto Cody's bass drum to face the drummer and held the long open chords while pinning his arms tight at his sides and turning his head side to side with gusto. Cody reached up and thwhacked his strings with his drumstick, and Darren hopped off the drum with a silly-goose grin.

She sang a bluesy solo on '*Oohs*' over the bridge, ascending higher and higher until reaching a fever pitch, and then pointed a finger and commanded with demonic insistence,

I'm just a girl. Worship me!

The band hit the breakdown, and she put her hands on her knees to headbang before tumbling into the audience. She half-danced, half-fought, half-swam through the maelstrom until she reached the back of the crowd, where a cluster of little girls was standing outside the violence, bopping around to the beat.

When they saw Britney, they screamed in terror and hopped up and down, their terror melting into joy as they clutched her limbs and cheered,

"Young Nuns!"

"AAHHH!"

"Britneeeeey!"

"EEEE! Young Nuns!"

"Oh my gosh!"

"WHOOO!"

Britney blew them a kiss with a flourish and then jazz-ran around the mosh pit to get to the mic just in time for the verse teaser.

I'll pretend you're Kevin, and send you up to heaven!

They ended the song with a strong downbeat, and the crowd screamed and cheered, clapping rhythmically and cheering "Young Nuns, Young Nuns!"

Will shook his head and removed his bass, stalking over to Debra's truck to kill the headlights and signal the end of their set. While this quieted the rhythmic clapping, it caused the crowd to rush toward the stage in adulation.

Britney announced through the PA, "Folks, please. Young Nuns will offer a brief meet-and-greet, but we need you to form a single file line. Ladies and gentlemen!"

Darren snickered and rolled his eyes at Britney, and as a receiving line formed for each of them, she realized he'd never experienced fandom before.

A plain-faced, slightly paunchy, bespectacled lady about the same age as Britney was first in line and prepared to gush, but Britney's periphery blacked out, and she realized she was exhausted. She smiled, held up a finger, and then sat flat on the floor, panting.

The lady looked at her concernedly then said, "I'm going to find you some water, ok?"

Britney nodded and rested in front of Darren's amp. He was still fiddling around with his gear, perhaps too shy to meet the public. The big, mean hog roaster stepped onto the stage with his guitar and gruffly asserted, "Debra says I'm to use this amp. It better not sound like a dang Jap chopper when I play it. I want a clean tone. I'm a Harley man."

Darren turned to face him, then pointed at the guitar and said, "Is that a Les Paul?"

Butch spat, "Sixty-nine custom."

Darren prepared to remove his guitar and then hesitated, "Do you want to use my Tube Screamer?"

The big guy snorted and rotated the cabinet with one hand. "A fella with your build oughtta have wheels on his furniture."

Darren reset a few dials, then flipped the amp off *standby*. A warm, dynamic sound flowed from the speakers like crimson oil paint as he worked his way in and out of a few blues licks. Then he stomped on the box and continued riffing, but held onto some bends, juicing them for all they're worth. He looked back at the man whose blue eyes blinked above his stuttering mouth.

"Th-th-that… Hey, that's pretty good. Yeah." Then he smiled broadly over his bucket of a chin and nodded, pulling his eyebrows high. "Yeah, man!"

Darren smiled back, "Do you want to try it?"

Butch shook his head, "Do another one!"

Darren walked up a few staccato pitches and landed with cursive blue notes that scampered back down to the bottom of the register. He imitated the lick in the lower register but lingered at the end of the phrase, terminating it with some easy-swinging blues chords. Butch laughed like a biker Santa and turned to Darren's receiving line who shared his enthusiasm.

Britney thought, *'Debra thought this guy was going to kill someone. I mean, he killed someone yesterday. Now he's breaking out of his shell. And it looks like Darren is doing it on purpose. Like, he's not even trying to romance the sullen young women here. He's not even judgemental or condescending at all. He's actually trying to build this guy up!*

Will shook hands and greeted the audience, but Meadow and a couple of her kids stood fixed by his side.

She thought, *'I always call him the 'van dad,' but he hasn't really been all that bossy lately. And now he's acting like an actual dad, but in the best way.'*

'And Cody still seems like he wants to party, but he's respectful. There's something different in him. I could swear that he had a twinkle in his eye when he was hanging out with Jory and Travis.

'Did I do that? Am I vain to think that I changed them?'

She took some pride in herself for getting them out of their shell but was interrupted by seven or eight munchkin girls who surrounded her and screamed fanatically, practically jumping on top of her red boots.

11.

The Yuba Concert

Britney knelt on the passenger seat and looked behind her at Cody and Darren while Will gripped the steering wheel with white knuckles and trawled down the country highway in second gear.

She scratched her bald scalp and mused, "Would you rather..." Her eyes darted around until she held up her index finger and grinned, "Eat Ritter's barbecue in Indianapolis or drink dog pee?"

Cody wreched, "Aw man. Pee."

Darren wrinkled his face, "Pee, for sure."

Britney leaned further over the seat. "Really?"

Darren asked, "Do I have to know that it's people when I eat the barbecue?"

Britney shrugged, "You can pretend it's whatever you want."

He repeated, "Dog pee, for sure."

She laughed, "*Haha*! Okay, next one. Would you rather... *hmm*... Would you rather fuck the pig from the festival, or roast Butch and eat him?"

Darren waved his hands, "No, aw, come on. He's a nice guy. He put casters on my speaker cab. Next one. Next. Do another."

Will quipped from the driver's seat, "Darren, you're like an orc whisperer."

Cody cracked up, "Haha, *orc whisperer*."

Britney teased, "You weren't with him all night, though. I saw you with that little freckle-face!"

Cody gasped, "Yo, did you get with Red? She was cute."

Darren protested, "We're going to change the subject. I'll do one. Would you rather…"

Britney mouthed, *'He did.'*

Darren cleared his throat. "Would you rather with Meadow or Savannah?"

Cody's lip curled ever so slightly, and his cheeks blushed. Britney pointed and shouted, "You did, didn't you!"

He covered his face, "Yo, we were just chilling in the yurt."

She persisted, "And her boyfriends were in there too! What were you guys doing in there?"

He tried to bury his face in his new Western pearl-snap shirt, but she read him like a book.

Brit opened her eyes wide. "You all did it together, didn't you! I knew it. With which one? Brent was so hot."

He wiped his face and peeked around. "I didn't like, *do it* with any of them. Just like, we were all kind of doing stuff together."

Will held up a finger and demanded, "But you did Savannah though, right?"

Cody chortled, "Yeah man, I did her good."

Everyone in the van hollered, and he tried to regain his footing in the conversation, "But she's a very special woman, and it's not like that."

Britney turned to Will, "What about you? Did you hook up with Meadow?"

He glared back at her and said mockingly, "*What about you? Did you hook up with Alan?*"

She craned her neck toward him and said in a juvenile voice, "Nooooo-*wah*! I didn't. Did you hook up with Meadow?"

He imitated her. "Noooo-*wah*."

She was lying, but he was telling the truth, although she could tell they had a romantic connection.

Will drove for a moment longer and added, "I won't cheat on

Maddy."

Britney flipped around and sat properly in the seat, glancing back at Will to see that despite the brief levity, he was still vexed with consternation, and the tension was welling in the van again as they ambled down the road in the dark.

After their gig, they were blessed with a bounty of food, ammo, van parts, a deer spotter, replacement speakers, bass strings, handmade drum sticks, and — course — intimate human contact. But additionally, Sandy — who gave Britney clean linens, fresh-smelling dance pants, and a cute crop top with a graphic of a peach with the word 'Fuzzy' — had shown them her late husband's chemical warehouse. Will went nuts for it and overloaded the van with over a hundred gallons.

Darren uttered, "Savannah."

Britney cocked her head and he added, "Who I'd rather. Just saying."

Cody gave him a fist bump, then smelled his own finger and guffawed.

Britney rolled her eyes and faced forward again. "I liked Meadow better. I don't know if I'd do her, but maybe. Yeah, I'd pick Meadow."

They drove in silence for mile after mile, trekking through the darkness until Britney popped open the phone and mumbled audibly, "Ten forty-four. *Doot-da-doo-doo-doo…*"

Nobody commented until a road sign came into view, and Cody read it aloud as though nobody else could see it: "Yuba City, fifteen miles."

Darren squirmed around in his seat and stretched his neck to look at the dashboard.

Will grunted, "Twenty. We're going twenty miles an hour, okay? The springs are completely compressed, and if we go faster, a pothole could split the chassis. We'll get there before midnight, okay?"

Nobody said a peep, but then Britney rolled her window up and down, sighing and huffing until at last she pleaded, "Okay, maybe — I'm just saying — when we get to Yuba City, we can switch the barrels so the cat pee one is on top? I'm just saying."

Will's retort was curmudgeonly, "Listen, if even a little trace of those chemicals mix, we're going to have bigger problems. So just drop it."

Darren twisted the knife unapologetically, "How in the fuck are we going to cross the country with three barrels of industrial chemicals—"

The driver shot back, "I wasn't going to leave premium-grade product rotting in that garage—

Darren leaned in, "What's the point?"

Will grunted, "We can cache it, or we can trade."

Britney was diplomatic, "Do you think maybe it's because of Maddy? Like, you're rushing into your deal with Rick—"

The guitarist persisted, "Can we cache it here? Like, right here, right now?"

He grunted, "We're almost there."

Darren muttered, "Not at this rate."

Britney's lashed out, "Why the fuck does anyone in this day and age need fifty-five gallons of bleach?"

Will spat, "I didn't say it was bleach, I said it was *like* bleach. If you don't know—"

Cody joined the dogpile, "Rick didn't even ask for half of this shit. He certainly didn't ask for fifty-five gallons of hydrochloric strapped to the front bumper."

Will turned around, his face beet red, "Shut up, Cody!"

Cody continued, "Yo, I'm just saying—"

"I said, shut up!"

"What would Rick say—"

"Shut up, Cody."

"What would Rick say about your safety prep?"

"Shut the *fuck* up."

The mile markers crept by, one after the other, while an anemic breeze wafted through Britney's window.

Eventually, Will drawled in Rick's Northeast Ohio accent, *"What the hell are you numbskulls doing with the sodium hypochlorite on the roof? And fifty-five gosh-dang gallons of concentrated ammonia hanging out the ass of your darn stupid van? Don't you know you should have each one in a separate van?"*

Cody scoffed, good-naturedly and play-acted along, "Oh, sorry Rick. We have a clean-up kit."

'Rick' continued, *"Well, dangit son, I don't want those chems in the same zip code. You turkeys have hazmat suits and an OSHA spill kit?"*

Cody added the punch line, "Uh, no. But we have a brand new mop head and a box of baking soda."

Everyone laughed, and then Will apologized, "Look, I'm sorry. Maybe this was too stressful, but almost everything we've done has been stressful. I just thought it was worth the struggle."

Britney asked, "Do you still think it's worth it?"

"I don't know. I guess. Maybe. Who knows. I mean, Cody's stupid fucking power washer turned out to be clutch. Who would have guessed?"

Cody pushed his palms up to the sky, "Whoop, whoop!"

Darren proposed, "How about we get where we're going first, and then figure out how to skinny down. I don't like the looks of this town so far. I don't want to stop on the outskirts here."

Will nodded, "Yeah, this looks really bad. But Yuba City sounds awesome. What's your friend's name?"

Britney chirped, "Denise!"

Darren inquired, "They're expecting us, right? Like, they're not going to shoot us, are they?"

Britney scoffed, "No, she said we can drive right in."

Cody scratched his chin, "I wonder why Jory and them don't know about this place. I mean, it's a pretty big city to be totally liberated. It's not exactly Manhattan, Kansas."

Will added, "It's so close to San Francisco, too. Maybe they defend it like Mark and Higler. They just wall it off and run machine guns?"

Britney waved her hand, "No, it's like a real city. Everyone works their asses off. No *give and take* bullshit."

Will nodded, "Sounds alright to me. But they're cool? They're down with us doing a gig?"

Britney nodded, "Yeah, she's super excited. She had a million ideas."

Darren asked again, "And they know we're coming tonight?"

She nodded laboriously. "Yes, I told them sometime today."

Darren pressed, "But it's very late at night."

She shrugged, "Denise is up all night most of the time. She told me she can hook us up with her friend Patrick who does assembly at the shop. He could show us a good place to perform. She said that Patrick is always writing to her about things he sees. She rambles on and on about it. Every time I look at the message board, she has a whole bunch of posts and DMs about it, just one after the other."

The car was silent for another mile. Will took a breath, hesitated, and then exhaled noisily.

Cody asked, "Brit, are you checking the phone for bars?"

"Oh yeah." she mumbled, and looked at the screen. "Three bars."

Will choked, "Three bars?"

Britney shrugged, "There were three bars in Manhattan."

Will corrected her, "There were *two* bars in Manhattan, *three* when we got to the tower."

Darren suggested, "Maybe we should just stash the ammonia and acid. We can undo those straps real quick and come back later. We won't be able to maneuver much with all this weight."

Will nodded, but he slammed it into third, practically redlining the engine and causing massive traumatic bumps with every pothole and crater.

Britney thought, *'Something is up. I know they trust me, and we know the BritneyArmy board works. But Will wouldn't be driving like this unless he sees something bad.'*

Cody leaned forward to Britney, "Britney, do you mind if I look at Denise's messages?"

She rolled her eyes and passed the phone back.

He gasped, "Dude, she messages you all day long."

Britney spat back, "Well, maybe she's bored."

"These last few messages don't even make any sense."

"It's probably just a computer thing."

Darren asked, "She's using a computer?"

Brit said, "I don't know. I guess a computer, or something."

Darren peeked at the screen and asked, "When did she start talking to you?"

Britney sighed, "Kansas, okay?"

Cody and Darren looked at each other, and Darren whispered, "Two weeks."

Britney sank back in her seat and crossed her arms, frowning as she watched Van Hellsing roll past the burned-out, shot-up wreckage. "Okay, it seems bad now, but it will all be worth it when we get to Yuba City, and Debra makes us her signature bagel pizzas."

A couple of miles later, she saw the city lights glowing in the distance and slapped her thighs. "Ha! I told you!"

Will continued down the highway, and a distant light appeared in the rearview mirror. He suddenly took in the clutch, dropped it back into second, rocked it into four-wheel drive, and blazed a trail through deserted farmland.

Britney held onto the grip as the van jostled wildly, the extra weight causing them to slam and bang concussively. She fumbled with her seat belt and screamed at Will, "Wha-at are yo-ou do-oing?"

Will shook his head and hunched over the steering wheel, attempting to see past the weeds, dust, and cracked windshield as his head whipped this way and that. "No w-ay in *hell* I wa-as staying on tha-at hi-ighway. No-o way in *he-ell*."

Britney whined as she shook like a rag doll, "De-enise said we-e can just dri-ive right in. The-ey're expecting u-us."

Darren clicked his seat belt and then clicked up his rifle. "Bri-itney, li-isten to Wi-ill."

Cody didn't say anything but racked his AK.

They reached the end of the cornfield where a mini-mall seemed to mark the limits of Yuba City. Darren swiveled his head around to get a better view, and he asked, "Isn't there a wall?"

Britney sassed, "I never said there was a wall."

Will drove forward and descended the curb onto Main Street, then killed his headlights and rolled down the road, all the while looking for active threats. He pulled a quick maneuver and with a rapid left and right turn ended up on a parallel street headed into town.

He asked Britney, "How many bars?"

She sneered and prepared to comment, but he reiterated, "How many *bars*?"

She stuck out her tongue and curled her lip in contempt but then looked at the phone and meekly confessed. "Four."

Will pushed the accellerator as hard as he could to get it back up into third gear.

Britney said, "If we can just get to the lights, we'll be safe."

Cody tapped her on the shoulder, "Brit."

She snapped, "WHAT?"

Darren turned to her and said, "Denise. She might be a zombie."

"She's not a fucking *zombie*, zombies can't talk."

Will called out, "Zombies, three o'clock."

Cody whispered, "What the fuck?"

Will grabbed his shotgun and chambered a shell. "They set up an ambush on main street. Was Denise going to tell us about that? Right there.

They would have got us."

She started to cry, "Stop saying that. She's a regular person."

Darren clutched her forearm with firm compassion. "She's a second waver, Britney. She's dopamine sick. She's done for."

Britney curled into a ball and started to weep. She felt so stupid. They were clearly right, but she didn't want to admit it.

Will executed another series of turns and ran the van through an alleyway at a very slow speed before getting back onto the side street, and hightailed in a Northerly direction out of town.

Just after he got into second gear he called out, "What the fuck is that?" and Britney saw two headlights in the distance coming straight for them.

"Fuck, Fuck." Will had no option other than to turn left and dime the engine.

Britney wiped her tears, "Maybe that's Denise's friends. It could be! It could be, right?"

Cody crooned, "It could be anything. We don't know what it is."

The vehicles were now on their tail and bumped them ever so slightly. Darren yelled out, "Lose the barrel! We're overloaded!"

Cody reached over the amps but shouted back, "I can't get to it from here."

Darren cursed, "It's already half hanging out of the back. The fuck do you…" but he turned, looked at the mountain of music gear and conceded.

Britney looked into the rearview mirror and saw that they were pursued by Ford pickup trucks, one red and one tan, both beat to hell. The driver and passenger were immersed in their smartphones and paid no attention to the road.

The red truck advanced and bumped them again, but with all the weight on their van, it didn't respond much. Darren popped out of the roof hatch and pulled his entire body through it in order to brace his rifle on the barrel of sodium hypochlorite and send rounds toward the truck. He loosed his ten-round rotary magazine but then dropped the gun into the van, calling out, "Cody, I need the AK."

Cody slapped the safety on and held it up by the barrel so Darren could reach down with his pale hand and grab the pistol grip. A rifleman standing in the truck bed leaned over the cab and pumped twenty machine gun rounds in their direction, but Darren doled out ten clean shots through the windshield, and the truck swerved off the road and into a building. Britney could see more clearly that the trucks had an extra set of wheels dangling below the frame, perhaps so they could ride on railroad tracks like Jory mentioned.

Darren popped off more rounds, but gunfire started pouring into the van from all directions, so Darren dropped inside. Bullets hailed from all sides, but there was no refuge as the side streets were now clogged with bustling zombies.

The Young Nuns lurched forward toward the windshield and squinted their eyes in disbelief. They had arrived at the city center, and the only bridge out of town had collapsed. She could see all the different classes of zombies in rank and file, almost like humans at work in a factory, albeit with significantly more people distractedly pleasuring themselves in plain sight.

The presence of the van brought bloodlust and violence to their faces: yuppie, hipster, and posh alike. They abandoned their assembly line work and stalked toward them from all sides.

Britney caught her breath and climbed over the armrest into the back seat. She gripped the edge of the hatch and prepared to hoist herself up, but Darren grabbed her other hand, "No, don't."

Britney looked down. "It's the only thing that works."

Cody was loading more bullets into his magazine. "Let her go. We need to reload."

Will put the van in park and removed his seat belt. "Do it. She can hold them off, and maybe we can blast our way out."

Britney peeked out of the hatch and then dropped back in. "There's too many of them!"

Will spat, "This was your idea!"

Darren concurred, "There's no other way."

She pulled herself onto the roof, noticing a noxious granulated powder all over the van, and shouted, "Stop!" Then she faced each direction. "Stop! Hey! Hey you, STAAAHP-*pah!*"

The horde hesitated, milled about for a moment, but kept lurking toward them slowly in the heavy, still night air. Darren yelled, "Her hair! Will, give me your hat!"

He passed up the hat and the mop head. She looked at it and shouted down. "What am I supposed to do with this?"

Cody yelled, "It's a wig!"

She put the mop head on her scalp along with Will's big Castro hat and repeated, "STAAAHP-*pah!*"

The zombies froze, swaying ever so slightly. Will called out, "On my mark, jump out and blast. Try to clear the road behind us. Be sure to take out that truck. Ready? Three, two—"

Britney crouched down and stuck her head inside the van. "Britney's Best! Play Britney's Best!"

Will bellowed back, "What?"

She called down, "The CD. It's in the booklet. Play it loud!"

Will hollered, "Why?"

She yelled, "I have an idea!"

The old burned CD started with a *bang-bang-bang* on an electric piano, and she sang,

> *Oh baby, baby.*

The volume swelled to max, and she sang another

Oh baby, baby.

She worked all of her moves, just like the old days. The choreography felt natural and smooth, and she felt more at peace than she had in years. A bright light blinded her, and she saw that someone had rigged up the deer spotter as a spotlight.

Oh baby, baby,
How was I supposed to know
That something wasn't right there.
Oh baby, baby,
I shouldn't be letting go
And now you're too far away.

The horde was transfixed, rapt with attention to her every move. She sang the song: taunting them, teasing them, bewitching them. Every thrust and pop underscored the assertion that she was *Britney Spears*, and they drank it up.

The song ended, and she was startled by a rattling sound behind her. She whipped around to see Darren tapping the microphone on the roof. "Here, use this."

She picked up the mic, and in her best showbiz voice said, "Hey Yuba City, how are you feeling?!"

There was silence from the crowd except for a noisy shuffling of feet, and she saw that the crowd, already twenty thousand strong, was gaining hundreds and hundreds more by the minute.

"I'm just so happy to be here in beautiful Yuba City! Now, I want everyone to step out of the street! That's right! Step back. Just step back! Yeah!"

The walkers stepped stiffly backward like penguins, not quite clearing the street but thinning it out.

Will yelled, "More! We need them to push back more!"

Brit hissed, "Play another fucking song!"

He grunted back, "Hold on."

She could see thousands of the somnambulists holding up their phones, recording, streaming, or doing whatever it is that they do. Others, lacking a device of their own, craned their necks to see her image on their neighbor's glowing rectangles.

A song started with a treble-heavy string track and repeated the iconic *wee-woo-wee-dee-woo.* Britney was in the zone, popping under her crop top and throwing her legs around in her loose, flow-y pants.

> *Oh baby can you see me calling?*
> *A man like you should wear a warning.*
> *It's dangerous and I'm falling.*

Her wig almost slipped off, but she caught it in time. She worked her hips extra hard and improvised alternative words.

> *Everybody, off the street!*
> *Britney says to get off the street!*
> *Make room, everyone step back!*

It was working little by little, and as she worked her way through the song with jiggles and pleas, she heard a flurry of frantic activity from her bandmates below.

She sang the last chorus with a little extra funk and sugar.

> *Intoxicate me now, give me your lovin' now*
> *I'm really ready now, I think I'm ready now.*
> *Intoxicate me now, give me your lovin' now*

I think I'm ready now.

Darren yelled up, "One more! Do one more!"

She shouted, "The streets are getting thinner, but the sidewalks just keep filling up."

He barked back, "One last song!"

She smiled and swiveled her hips, ending in a diva-esque pose while the next song came on, but she couldn't place it. There was some murmuring in the recording, then a melismatic *ooooh* line.

The recorded voice sang,

> *I feel like I was locked up tight*
> *for a century of lonely nights.*

Britney looked down into the van and yelled, "Next song!" but she couldn't get anyone's attention. "Guys. GUYS!"

Cody stuck his neck into the van and looked up at her dumbly.

She yelled, "NEXT SONG!"

He scrunched his nose and shrugged dumbly as the recorded voice sang.

> *If you want to get with me,*
> *Honey, there's a price to pay.*
> *There's a genie in your bottle,*
> *Baby, rub me the right way.*

"CODY, THIS ISN'T ME!"

Will's confused face appeared next to Cody's and she shouted, "THIS IS FUCKING CHRISTINA!"

Cody bugged his eyes and said, "Oh, shit!"

The song abruptly switched to ensemble stabs, and she started to wiggle along with it, adding sultry *ooh yeahs* until the beat came in and she laid in.

Yeah, yeah, yeah, yeah, yeah, yeah, yeah.

Will climbed up the ladder quietly and stabbed the big plastic barrel they had obtained from the laundry lady. He filled two sleeping bags with the white granules that spilled out, and by then she was at the chorus.

Oops, I did it again.
I messed with your heart.
I'm up in the game.
Ooh baby, baby.

When she sang the second half of the chorus, her beats got an extra boost; first when Will's bass cab came to life supporting the PA system, and again when Cody joined on drum set.

After the chorus, she took the opportunity to command once more,

I need all of you! Yes you! Move off the street.

She moaned and caressed her neck with maximum sexuality.

Britney baby wants you to move off the street, papa!

And then she switched to a spry, bossy persona.

Let's see some girl power out there. Move off the street, ladies!

They were still looking at packed sidewalks and hundreds of bodies in the streets as far as the eye could see, and Britney thought, *'There's still no way. We don't have enough bullets, and the van isn't powerful enough.'*

Will revved the engine, and Cody shouted, "Get in!"

Britney pencil-dove into the van, and Will laid tire as he spun the automobile around. Cody jumped out of the sliding door with a chemical-laden sleeping bag over his shoulder and heaved it ten or twenty feet behind the van. Then he pulled out the Smith and Wesson revolver and popped four shots into the barrel that was hanging out of the back. He jumped back in and Will sped away down the street as the zombies snapped out of their stupor and closed in on Van Hellsing.

They made it two or three blocks, streaming liquid out the back and plowing over a dozen bystanders. Darren looked over Britney and asked, "You don't have any of that white stuff on you, do you?"

Britney couldn't believe they were asking her for meth at a time like this, but Darren clarified, "The powder that was on the roof."

She shook her head wordlessly.

He told her, "The ammonia leaking out of that barrel in the back is reacting with it to make a poison gas. There's a little bit scattered all along the road from where that truck shot at us." Then he said to Cody, "Let's go to the roof. You dump more sodium hypochlorite. I'll cover you."

Britney's hypnosis had allowed them to truck down loosely occupied streets, but now they were surrounded, and the engine couldn't push through. Darren climbed out the sunroof and dumped two magazines on the crowd ahead of them while Cody followed him up and used Will's hat to scoop loads of sodium hypochlorite into the pooling puddles of ammonia on the street.

Will trawled forward, jamming the van into four-wheel drive to get over the bodies. Cody's rifle was now barking, and clusters of magazines dropped through the sunroof.

"Reload! Reload!"

"I'm empty!"

Britney grabbed them and tore open her bandmate's packs to find packages of 5.56 and .22lr ammo. She got one of each mag filled in time to hear them both empty their pistols, and she exchanged the reloaded mags for their sidearms.

She left the pistols on the seat as she refilled the other mags but couldn't fill them as fast as they were shooting. Enemy rifles started shooting back, and the boys dropped back inside, giving her a chance to catch up.

Will shouted, "Keep shooting! Fuck! Give me a path!"

But the second they put their heads up, gunfire tickled the body of the van, dangerously close to them.

Britney screamed, "Just drive over them!"

Will gunned it and drove full force into the mob. The first wave went flying, but the weight of the bodies was too great, and he was struggling to get out of first gear.

Cody shouted, "You have to drive! The gas is rolling in!"

Britney looked outside the partially-ajar back door for the first time and saw that most of the bodies behind them were dead or dying.

Will pressed forward but started to spin all four tires. The zombies swatted at the van and spit, their faces becoming more twisted and grotesque. Many of them stared with unblinking skeletal eyes, their lipless teeth bared and their nostrils wide open like pigs.

She shielded her eyes, "What the fuck?"

The zombies clawed at the windshield with smaller and smaller fingers that wore away to nubs.

Will yelled, "It's the hydrochloric acid! It's drizzling out from the cracks in the barrel!" and pushed forward again.

The vanguard of zombies lost their footing as they lost their feet, giving Will enough space to stick the clutch, build up some inertia, and begin plowing through more bodies, their torsos, limbs, and faces coated in burning acid.

Darren and Cody methodically peeked through the hatch and swept the roofline, picking off a couple of gunners each before posting up and raining lead on the masses in their path.

The strap that held the back door closed gave way, and the whole barrel of ammonia tumbled out. Britney could hear a loud sound that rolled across the roof as Cody unstrapped the plastic barrel of powder and let it roll off and crash onto the pavement. The chemicals immediately started reacting with each other to generate a yellow plume of deadly poison gas. Will looked back and punched the steering wheel in anger, accidentally honking the feeble horn.

A dozen attackers piled in the back of the van through the open doors, causing the rear end to sink downward. Darren's massive speaker cabinet rolled down the cargo area on its newly-installed wheels and it gathered enough inertia to push the infiltrators out and smash them outside on the ground. Britney chased after it to close one rear door and grasp a swinging ratchet strap to pull the other door shut before more zombies could breach.

Cody and Darren were shooting their rifles faster than Britney could reload, and she was scraping the bottoms of their backpacks to get any ammo whatsoever. Will passed his Mossberg back, and she extended the shoulder stock and handed it up. When she counted eight blasts, she handed up a box of shells and focused on the empty mags.

Two young zombie boys in rapidly decaying Hollister shirts climbed up the front bumper and reached through a broken section of the driver's side window. Will drew his Glock 19 and peppered the acid-burned zombies with 9mm bullets, then emptied his Glock 17 into the next round of walkers that were trying to climb over the bumper. He threw the pistols to Britney, who refilled the clips with the plentiful 9mm ammo and then reloaded Darren's Hi-Point pistol.

The sliding door rocketed open, and a sea of hands reached for her. For a moment, she imagined the paparazzi crowding around her car while she tried to buckle her kids in. She took a Glock in each hand and dumped lead into the intruders, then dual-wielded the Hi-Point and the revolver. After all four pistols were empty, she kicked the limp bodies out of the door and secured it properly.

She filled two AK magazines with the last of the 5.56 and handed them up in exchange for the Mossberg, which she loaded as fast as she could. Zombie gunfire was still taunting them, with little bits of steel spall and kevlar-wrapped ceramic dusting her face.

She looked up to see how much further they had to go and started to choke in the acrid, poisonous air. She could hardly see through the windshield as it was coated in a reddish-brown slime, but Will turned on the windshield wipers and she could see that they were a matter of blocks from open road.

The zombies were packed in, and Van Hellsing had lost inertia, so they were spinning all four tires again. The fleshy humanoid roadblocks were slowly melting from the spray of acid, but the van moved too slowly to outrun the gas.

There was another commotion on the roof, and a smaller barrel rolled down the front. It landed on their adversaries and squashed them flat. It didn't clear enough space for them to gain momentum, but she recognized it as a barrel they'd had with them all along as their auxiliary fuel supply.

Britney put the last round in the Mossberg and handed it up through the hatch. Cody grabbed it and quipped in a British accent, "*Roit!*"

He pointed it at the small barrel and pulled the trigger, and the explosion engulfed their opponents in devastating fire.

Will redlined the engine and dropped it into second, laying tire and leveling a solid city block of zombies when she heard the most beautiful music she had heard all day: the sound of Van Hellsing accelerating through second, third, and fourth gears. They were moving fast enough to catch a breeze and the streets were clear except for the odd and end aimless masturbator.

About a mile out of town, he parked the van, and the guys went about slicing the acid barrel straps and removing the corrosive container, spreading baking soda in strategic places to save the most vulnerable parts of Van Hellsing. However, the hood had been eaten clean through in several places, and their fenders and bumper would not be salvageable.

Britney could breathe again. She still felt anxious, so she reloaded all the guns while the guys talked van stuff.

Cody sauntered over to her and smirked, "We want to get the PA."

Britney flexed her brow. "What"

"Yeah, and my drums."

Will added, "There's a lot of good shit back there."

She blinked, "You're joking."

Darren held up his palms, "Most of them are dead already. We're going to round up ammo and fuel. We'll give it twenty minutes for the gas to clear."

Britney smiled and balled her fists. "You guys are crazy."

Cody howled, "Fuck Denise!"

She joined, "Fuck you Deniiiiiise!"

An exceptionally raucous album came on the van's sound system, with spastic crooked meters that culminated in a snare roll that dragged slower and slower until the band pivoted into a nasty verse. Cody hopped around with four warm beers cradled in his cowboy shirt. He put one in everyone's hand, and then popped the tops with a screwdriver.

It sounded like the first song had ended, but she could scarcely believe it because of how short it was, however last note sustained through the feedback into a sample from a sci-fi movie.

> *Twenty-eight days, six hours,*
> *forty-two minutes, twelve seconds.*
> *That is when the world will end.*

The second song came in with more violent verses and choruses, although the form was so choppy that she couldn't tell what was a verse and what was a chorus. She couldn't even feel a steady beat with how unexpectedly they jumped from riff to riff. She asked, "What is this?"

Darren bobbed his head and wrinkled his brow, "We didn't play this ever? I guess not. They're called 'Ed Gien.' It's grindcore. Hold on!" And he gripped her wrist tightly.

She could feel the beat for the first time as the guitar repeated a four-note pattern and the other instruments built up around it. Will threw his jacket to the ground, and Cody set his beer down to quickly touch his toes and stretch his shoulders. Darren bobbed up and down and started jumping on the beat so high that Britney felt compelled to jump with him.

At the climax the band dropped into a seven-beat breakdown and the Young Nuns lost their shit. Cody cartwheeled and donkey-kicked in the desert dust while Will switched between windmill punches and shadow-boxing, adding some impressively high side kicks. Darren handed Britney his beer and threw a series of spinkicks, capping it off with a legit backflip that threw his hood off his head to reveal a devilish grin.

Britney set the beers in the van and did a combination of handsprings and round-offs, ending with a front tuck half-twist. Her landing was dirty, but she slid down into a split and held up her middle fingers.

Darren was bouncing recklessly against his bandmates, and Cody staggered backward, tripping and falling over Britney. Britney covered her head, then popped up and tackled her drummer as he tried to stand upright again. Darren moshed over to give them a shove, but she yanked him forward, and he went tumbling. Will did a somersault attack, reaching out and pulling Cody's leg out from under him and landing him on his ass.

Britney grabbed him around his neck, but he easily picked her up and righted himself. Cody held up his arms in a *V,* "Give her the stunner!" Will shook his head and spun her around so her head dangled just above his knees. Darren clapped his hand and hooted, "Suuu-pleeex!"

Britney swatted and protested playfully, "No! No!"

Cody and Darren cheered, and Will bellowed, "Suuuu-pleeex!"

He slammed to his knees where Britney harmlessly felt a jolt of inertia and freed herself, adding a few slaps about Will's face as the breakdown faded out.

She staggered back to the van and retrieved a beer. Simply being in the California night air gave her an uncanny feeling of accomplishment.

She thought, *'There's got to be a note in my mansion with some clue as to where Kevin took the kids. I bet one of his wingnut friends has them safe and sound in a mountain compound. I know that's a slim chance, but I had to do everything I could for them. I did do everything. We did.'*

Britney climbed onto the roof and danced easy while drinking her beer. She swayed in the desert moonlight, feeling her own skin and being comfortable in her body. She felt awesome, she felt loved, she felt powerful as her roar echoed across the expanse,

"IT'S BRITNEY, BITCH!"

12.

Dear Opera,

Hey, girl! Sup! Darren's been going to Pittsburgh a lot, and he said Liz knows you guys really well. So if you're reading this I'm assuming you made it to Pittsburgh!

It was nice to cross paths with you, it's too bad we couldn't get to know each other better. We had a really cool time in Ashland (you should meet my friend Debra) and then crazy stuff happened in California. We raided a whole zombie factory!

LA county was a nightmare, oh man. It was the hardest part of the trip, but we got to my mansion and I found a lot of clues. I think my assistant Felicia took my kids to my dad's place, so I'm going to head South after all. I could have just gone with you guys!

We met your friend Havoc in Slab City. They said they were all going to Yuba to take over the factory we raided. That would be awesome for everyone! We can get more ammo and gasoline for real people.

We had some cool gigs on the way back, like Tulsa and Carbondale. We also stopped and saw some old friends, and got them set up with radios. I don't know why we weren't doing that all along. It's called SSB, they were using it out West, and now all these different cities can talk to each other.

The rest of the band is doing great. Will and Cody keep talking about going West, but I don't think Cody will go. Will is definitely in love with this girl he met there. His girlfriend is kind of awful and it isn't working out. It's funny because that was, like, the main reason we left!

The guys got really good at robbing trains on the way home. They spread out and pick off the trucks from the back. It takes a lot of waiting, but we get more chemicals and supplies than we need.

We played Columbus again, and I stuck around to hang out with this guy Fakhar. He's cute and nice. He's a partner at the distillery. I kinda like him a lot. OK, I love him!!!! But promise not to tell! Aaahh!!! It's so crazy!!!!!!! I'm in love!!!!!

He's talking about driving me down South in his Volvo. He wants to camp, but I have a couple new songs I've been doing with a drum machine called an 404. Right now, I just have a little speaker I use, but I want to get a bigger speaker and play shows like we did with Young Nuns. All by myself!

So a lot of good stuff is happening because we've been using these websites. We are NOT using iPhones, I repeat, WE ARE NOT USING IPHONES. A lot of people don't realize that you can get online with old phones too. We use old message boards that music fans used to use, and we can plan big things. You guys should try it.

I mean, not to sound stuck up, but the word has been spreading super fast, and BritneyArmy.com has a hundred thousand new members, and no second wavers anymore. People have used the boards to organize attacks on zombie cities or fix up an oil refinery. I've heard people call any of these kinds of sites a 'Britney Board.'

I just wanted to let you know that I've been thinking about you! We'd love to see you! Come visit our place in Ohio. Or maybe you want to come with me and Fakhar! It would be fun! Anyway, I wrote the addresses and drew some maps on the other sheet of paper. I hope to see you around!

Love, your friend,
Britney

P.S. I hope ur not mad that we were online! It's safe, I promise!

Epilogue

Dear Diary,

*There's not much more to write. Today was another damp and rainy Appalachian day. Winter is just about here, and I can't motivate myself to finish my cabin or forage. If I had gone straight to Pittsburgh, I would have been there by now. But nooo, I **had to find that pack of cigarettes in Chattanooga and think it was a sign from the universe.** Stupid Opera. Silly Opera.*

I'm going to get on my bicycle and ride south soon. The tube patch I made with pine sap is holding up OK. If I can get past Atlanta and find a spot to noodle catfish, I'll be alright. Chattanooga was kind of nice, but I don't think I'll survive the Winter, not the way the dead have been surging lately.

I spend a lot of time wishing I learned to ride one of those diesel motorcycles, but in the end, I'm going to be alone, and I don't think I'd be able to do all the fuel processing and mechanical work. So the bicycle is better. That's what I'll tell myself when I'm trying to pedal up one of these hills.

I see the ghosts of Jory, Travis, and Roni everywhere. I worry about L.B. and Trouser a lot, and I miss Roni. I'm so mad at Jory and Travis, but I just don't know who to blame.

That week in New Orleans was one of the best weeks of my life. It *was so calm, and at the time nobody was talking about why. I keep thinking of everyone's faces when Little Bear murdered that girl who was scrolling an iPhone. It used to be, **that's just what you did**. And instead, they acted like he was a monster.*

*It felt like me, Roni and L.B. were the only people in NOLA that held to the old rules about phones. Maybe it's because Jory and Travis were a little older. They used to call them '**Britney Boards**' but I don't think she knew was involved. I hope not. I think about her so much. I hope she found her kids.*

*When they killed Roni, it broke my heart. I had to leave Little Bear, and I hope he understands. It still hurts so bad. I don't **want** to be alone, but now more than ever, you can't trust anyone. Fucking Toolies.*

The third wave is worse than the second. People think they can stop with flip phone browsing, and then they move on to a little iPhone browsing on the weekends, and before you know it they're stabbing the shit out of your best friend.

Some people say the problem is that the technology itself is taking over. Other people say that humans are wicked, and the phone is just a tool. I think the problem is that people are weak. We're too weak to put down the phone, too weak to face the emptiness of life, too weak to accept our weakness.

That's rich coming from a gal who can't get out from under her tarp to pick a few berries and light a fire. I wish I could be strong like Britney. When I imagine her strength, it makes me want to do better. Actually, fuck this. Fuck you diary, I'm going to get up and make a fire.
J/K I love you,

Sincerely,
Opera Buffa

ABOUT THE AUTHOR

Joey Molinaro is a working, creative, and touring musician. He writes black metal/ grindcore concept albums for acoustic violin, plays trumpet in heavy metal marching bands, DJs industrial motorcycle music, teaches 90s alternative to junior jazz combos, and plays pop music for money.

He has lived in Pittsburgh, Indiana, and New York City and has a music degree from the IU Jacobs School of Music. His experience is colored with farming, activism, and vehicles that are equally cool and sketchy.

Joey has logged thousands of gigs touring across dozens of countries in spectacular fashion. Storytelling has always been a part of his craft, culminating in the podcast, *Tightrope*, and the novels *Heart of Gold*, *Young Nuns*, and *YearZer0*.

He now lives in Pittsburgh with his wife, kids, dog, and cat. He continues to organize concerts, play in bands, ride motorcycles, and teach.